Michael Farris's *Anonymous Tip* is fictitious, but you will be swept away as if the events are happening to you. This enthralling story reveals that reliance on God is the only way to stand up for righteousness; something that this attorney knows all too well from his own battles in the courtroom. With parental rights issues, big government, and Supreme Court authority at the forefront of today's controversies, Michael Farris has created a novel that is hugely relevant to our time.

Beverly LaHaye
Chairman, Concerned Women for America

Mike Farris has written a gripping novel that is as up-to-date as today's headlines. The book deals with serious social problems and contrasts treachery and intrigue with kindness and compassion. Set against a background of religious conflict, the story's imaginative twists and continuing suspense will capture your attention and engage your mind.

Edwin Meese, III
Former United States Attorney General

Children are our most precious asset. They deserve our love and protection.

Michael Farris has written a lively and entertaining novel underscoring how the self-serving interests and ethical pragmatism of the child abuse industry are damaging innocent parents, innocent children, and society itself. Even the law is being increasingly abused through the perceived interests of those who would manipulate it to their own ends.

I would like to recommend this book as one that is not only highly entertaining, but simultaneously educates us to a growing problem, one that must be addressed for the welfare of our children and our families.

John Ankerberg
President, The John Ankerberg Show,
Ankerberg Theological Research Institute

Anonymous Tip is a novel, yes, but is also lifts the curtain to reveal the real-life intrigue, tragedy, and heroism occurring every day in the war being fought on a basic question: Who gets the children?

Marlin Maddoux
Host of "Point of View"
USA Radio Network

Compelling, provocative, and all too real. Enjoy the reading for entertainment, but act on the implications of a system gone awry.

Kay James
Former Secretary of Health and Human
Resources for the Commonwealth of Virginia

anonymous tip

anonymous
tip

A NOVEL

MICHAEL
FARRIS

BROADMAN
&HOLMAN
PUBLISHERS

Nashville, Tennessee

Published by Broadman & Holman Publishers, Nashville, Tennessee
Acquisitions & Development Editor: Matt Jacobson
Interior Design: Desktop Miracles, Inc., Addison, Texas
Printed in the United States of America

4262-93
0-8054-6293-7

Dewey Decimal Classification: F
Subject Heading: FICTION / SINGLE FAMILY / FAMILY—FICTION
Library of Congress Card Catalog Number: 96-18723

Library of Congress Cataloging-in-Publication Data
Farris, Michael
    Anonymous tip / Michael Farris
        p.   cm.
    ISBN 0-8054-6293-7
    I. Title.
PS3556.A7774A83   1996
813'.54—dc20

96-18723
CIP

96 97 98 99 00 5 4 3 2 1

To my mom, who believed I could do anything

1

He knew it was wrong. But it wasn't a big deal. Just a little hassle. And she certainly deserved it. Without further thought, he punched in the number on the touch-tone phone.

"Hello. Child Abuse Hotline."

"Uh . . . uh . . . Hi," he stammered.

"This is the Child Abuse Hotline," the female voice answered warmly. "May I help you?"

"Yeah, is this call anonymous?"

"It is if that's what you want. We just want to protect children."

"Yeah. Me too. There's this little girl whose mom is really mean. She beats her and stuff."

"Do you know the identity of this girl?" The intake operator asked with practiced sympathy in her professional phone voice.

"Yeah. Her name is Casey Landis. She's four."

"And do you know the name of Casey's mother or father?

"Her mother's name is Gwen. Gwen Landis. She doesn't have a father. Er, uh, I mean she doesn't live with her father. They're divorced. This is just about the way her mother treats her."

"Okay, okay. Gwen L-a-n-d-i-s, right?"

"Right."

"And do you know Mrs. Landis's address?"

"Yeah. It's South 2717 Janelle Court."

"Is that in Spokane?"

"Yeah, on the South Hill—about six blocks from Comstock Park."

1

"Phone number?"

"Nice try. I thought this was anonymous."

"Oh, no sir, I'm very sorry. I meant, do you know Mrs. Landis's number?"

"Yeah. It's 555-4837."

"Fine. What is the nature of the problem with Casey?"

"Her mom beats her . . . with a stick."

"What kind of stick? Do you know?"

"Like a ruler or something. She hits her real hard."

"Are there any bruises?"

"How would I know?"

"When was the last time you saw Casey?"

"You've got enough. I'm tired of these questions. Just go protect this little girl."

Gordon Landis, Gwen's ex and Casey's father, slammed down the receiver as a burst of air forced its way out of his lungs. He glared at the phone in a moment of silent revenge before walking back to the refrigerator for another Bud.

～

The intake operator sniffed at the rudeness of the caller, then dutifully finished her entries in the computer data base. Date of Complaint: Thursday, May 5, 1994. Time: 9:43 P.M. Name of complainant: Unknown.

Upon completion of the data entry, the operator looked at her duty roster to see which Child Protective Services investigator was up next. Donna Corliss was at the top of the list.

The report was e-mailed to Donna Corliss, MSW, CPS Investigator II, while an electronic copy went automatically to Gerald Blackburn, her division supervisor.

The operator marked it Priority 2—"Possible Physical Abuse, Unknown Injuries." She rolled her eyes and wished for more information, but the caller didn't indicate a knowledge of bruises. She couldn't enter the report as a Priority 1—"Bodily Injuries Reported."

Well, at least it's a 2. Corliss will get to it tomorrow, she said to herself with a disgusted sigh while reaching for her Danielle Steele novel.

~

The late morning sun crept slowly across the bedroom floor. The first ray of light crawled up the bed, touched her eyes and stabbed deep into her skull like a flash of lightning. Donna Corliss would be getting into nothing that Friday, except the bicarbonate of soda.

"Ugh!" she moaned as she sat up in bed and clutched the hair at her temples with tight fists.

"Why do I do this? . . . oh, my stomach," she groaned.

Just then a grunt emanated from beneath the sheets next to her. Donna pulled them back and said sarcastically, "Well, well, Stephen J. Stockton in all his glory. I thought that someone two days away from his Juris Doctorate could have found a loophole for a hangover. But you're hung over worse than me—and you should be. You drank like a fish last night."

He lifted his head for a moment and then collapsed back into oblivion.

As she looked down at him she thought, *You're good-looking even when you're passed out. I love living with you.*

Stephen had finished his last final at Gonzaga University School of Law the previous afternoon. The pressure of acing it and finishing number one in his class was drowned in kegs of beer that night at the Bull Dog Pub with a number of other prospective lawyers, judges, legislators, and civic leaders.

Happy as they were with finishing law school, there was an edge of pent-up anticipation that was universal among the throng of partyers. Inside their clouded minds, the nagging reality of the three day Washington State Bar Examination, coming in ten weeks, prevented Stockton and his classmates from a true emotional release.

Donna pulled herself out of bed and stumbled to the coffee maker. As she reached for the filter she smiled and then shook her head at how miserable she felt.

"Stephen, get up. We've got to get going to Priest Lake. Your folks will be waiting." *This'll help him wake up*, she thought as she depressed the "ON" switch on the coffee grinder.

"Enough already!" Stephen yelled as he tried to cover his head with the pillows.

Donna laughed and said, "C'mon, get up. Your folks are going to be sitting in that new summer home on the lake wondering what happened to us."

Stephen, the only son of Connor Stockton, Esq., sat up in bed and looked blankly out the window for a moment before speaking.

His father was the second "name" partner of the 40-man firm of Wilson, Stockton & Bodecker which occupied the top two floors of the Washington Trust Bank Building.

"My dad doesn't wonder about anything. Too successful to stop and wonder even at the lake. He has it all."

"Well, not everything." Donna said with a smile. "He only graduated fifth from Gonzaga, not first. He is so proud of you."

"Maybe a little. Perhaps a bit jealous, too," Stephen answered with a wry grin. The conversation had sapped all his strength. He collapsed back on the bed moaning, "Oh, I feel terrible."

Donna reached for the phone and hit the auto-dial button for her office.

"Hello, Mr. Blackburn, this is Donna. I don't think I can come in today. I'm not feeling well."

"What's wrong? Anything serious?"

"Oh, I'll be OK. Just a bad headache and some stomach upset," she answered truthfully enough. "I'm sure I'll be fine on Monday."

Blackburn suspected the "illness" was alcohol related but he said nothing since Donna had a near perfect work record and was as tough as nails—one of his stars.

"Well, now I know you're human. You take care of yourself. I can't have my ace investigator out for long. How will we maintain the number one rating in the state?"

"I know . . . I know Mr. Blackburn. Most successful investigations. Most prosecutions. Most convictions. I know all that. But you can still win that Top Child Advocate award again even if I'm sick a day or two."

"Simmer down, Donna. Just get better. No pressure from me, OK?"

"Yeah, right, no pressure."

"Hey, I'm joking. Anything pressing on your agenda?" Blackburn asked.

You're only half-joking and we both know it, Donna thought.

"No . . . there is nothing pressing unless I got something assigned by e-mail overnight."

"Let me log in and check." . . . "Well, you did get a Priority 2 complaint, but no Priority 1's. I guess it can wait till Monday."

In her relief, Donna forgot that on Monday she would be leading an "in service" training session for the bulk of the day, teaching new social workers the proper techniques for physical abuse investigations. "See ya," was all she could say, happy to get off the phone. She dropped the receiver roughly on the cradle, weaved slowly across the room, and collapsed back on the bed.

～

Monday morning, Donna made a left turn off Mission Avenue into the parking lot of the two-story office building that housed the Spokane office of the Child Protective Services division of the Department of Social and Health Services of the State of Washington—and a few other Eastern Washington branch offices of various state agencies.

Donna had come to work for CPS five years earlier straight from graduate school at Washington State University in Pullman, some sixty miles to the south of Spokane. Her undergraduate degree in sociology was from the "wet side" of the state—Western Washington University in Bellingham. Western had a beautiful campus but was equally well known as a great party school. When she graduated, Donna had left the university's reputation well intact. WWU was located ninety miles north of Seattle and just fifty miles south of Vancouver, British Columbia.

After graduation, Donna's childhood roots proved to be strong. Having been born and raised in Connell, a small town south of Spokane, she preferred the drier and warmer climate of Eastern Washington.

After five years on the job, Donna had seen it all. Sexually molested children. Mostly step-fathers and live-in boyfriends. Broken arms. Broken skulls. Scalds. Cigarette burns. And more than a handful of uptight religious nuts who insisted on spanking their children.

She strode briskly down the corridor, popped her head into Mr. Blackburn's office to show him that she was indeed well and back on the job—fifteen minutes early, as usual. She logged into her computer to check for new referrals and any updates on her e-mail. The only message of any consequence was the report of the suspected abuse of Casey Landis. She read it and muttered a few foul words under her breath about mothers who beat their kids. After reviewing her schedule she said to herself, *No evidence of a real emergency. It'll keep 'til Wednesday.*

Today would be spent at the downtown Sheraton teaching her in-service training session and then Stephen would be waiting at The Black Angus for lunch. Tuesday was taken up with hearings in juvenile court. A look into the life of Casey Landis would have to wait until Wednesday.

～

Gwen Landis was in her backyard pushing a giggling Casey on the swing.

"Higher, Mom. Push me higher." Casey laughed.

The doorbell rang at 9:32.

"I'll be right back, honey. Just keep pumping your legs. You can keep it going."

Gwen opened the door to find an unknown, professionally dressed woman standing on her porch. *Doesn't look like a sales pitch*, was her first thought. *I wonder what's up.* "Good morning," Gwen said quizzically.

Thrusting a business card forward, the woman said, "Mrs. Landis. I'm Donna Corliss from Child Protective Services. I'd like to talk with you about Casey. May I come in?"

The lines were practiced and smoothly delivered with the voice of a friendly second grade teacher. Her lines had gained her entry, consensual entry, into over 90% of the homes she approached. She could hear herself giving the seminar on this technique to the new recruits.

"I'm not sure," Gwen stammered in reply. "Why do you want to talk about Casey? Is something wrong?"

"That's what I am here to find out. It would be much more convenient and potentially less embarrassing if we could have this discussion in the privacy of your living room rather than out here in front of the neighbors."

It was her next best line. She had taught both of them on Monday to the new investigators. Getting in the door with consent was the key to successful, quick investigations. If the first line failed, the second rarely did.

Something in Gwen's spirit warned, *Hang on. Not yet.*

"Before I let you into my home," Gwen said, "I want to know at least something of the nature of your reason for coming here. Are you accusing me of abusing Casey?"

"We are investigating an allegation generally to that effect, but I am sorry I cannot reveal the details of the allegations. It may compromise our investigation. Let me say just two things. I must come into your home and I must talk with Casey alone, this morning."

"No way. I am not going to let some total stranger come into my house to grill my child. I have no idea who you are. Don't you people make appointments?"

"Mrs. Landis, we are simply trying to protect children. And it is our policy to investigate all abuse complaints in person. Once we got the complaint about Casey last Thursday, we have a duty under state law to come into Casey's home, examine her living environment and talk personally to Casey as we do each child. It is simply standard policy and I do hope you will be cooperative. It's really in your best interest in the long run."

Gwen heard little footsteps running from the back of the house toward the front door. Her heart froze. The last thing she wanted right now was to have this aggressive bureaucrat putting her four year old sweetheart through the third degree about who knows what.

"Mrs. Cur . . ." Gwen hesitated, not remembering the name.

"Ms. Corliss," Donna sharply corrected.

"Ms. Corliss, I really have no intention of letting you in my home unless you are willing to tell me what this is all about. Since you are not, I'm busy. Good-bye."

Gwen stepped inside, quickly closing the door just before Casey bounded up and hugged her leg. Casey's green eyes were full of curiosity.

"Who was that, Mommy?"

Gwen leaned against the door breathing hard, trying desperately to collect her thoughts.

"Some lady, I really don't know who she is."

"What did she want?"

"Honey, I don't know that either."

Instinctively Gwen bent down, took Casey in her arms and patted and rubbed her back as she did whenever Casey had a bad dream at night. It was a comforting, gentle touch. Gwen didn't real- ize it was she who was seeking comfort from her own fears that had arrived in broad daylight.

～

Stan Mansfield, Gwen's father, responded to her phone call for help almost immediately by showing up to offer advice, comfort, and protection. He was on her front porch in ten minutes. When the bell rang Gwen's heart leapt in fear that it might not be her father, but Donna Corliss.

Gwen opened the door and tightly hugged her father who said, "Honey, don't worry about it. She won't be back today. I'm sure she has to go back to talk to her supervisor before she does anything else. You know bureaucrats—they have to get permission to sneeze."

"Dad, I am so scared. She acted like she might take Casey from me. She threatened that if I didn't cooperate there might be trouble. You know how I felt after Gordon filed for divorce . . . about the possibility that he would get custody?"

"Yeah, but that never happened, did it? He just gave up and you never even needed a lawyer."

"But, I might need one now. And I don't have a clue. Where do you start? I certainly don't want to hire that jerk who advertises on TV—John B. Garrett, attorney at law and your friend at all hours," she said, mimicking the advertisement.

"Apparently it's effective advertising since you remember his slogan."

"It effectively makes me eliminate him from consideration. There would be at least a random chance I'd pick him out of the phone book if it weren't for his goofy ads."

"I don't think you will even need a lawyer. But if you do, I met a lawyer playing golf over at Downriver last Saturday, Bill Walinski. He seemed like a good guy. We can at least ask. And if he doesn't do this kind of work he can probably tell us who is actually good for this kind of case."

"I can't believe we're having this conversation. Thirty minutes ago I was pushing Casey on the swing in peace and sunshine. Now this."

"Did she give any clue as to why she had come?" Stan asked.

"No. She wouldn't tell me anything except that there had been some allegations. That's why I wasn't about to let her in. She gave me the creeps."

"Well, you're probably overreacting. Let's just take a step at a time. I'm sure everything will be fine tomorrow."

On Thursday morning at 9:30 two cars came to a stop in front of Gwen Landis's home. The first was the office car assigned to Investigator Corliss. Today she was accompanied by Rita Coballo, another investigator of equivalent rank. The second car was a Spokane Police Department cruiser with Corporal Mark Donahue in command, accompanied by his partner, officer Ken Dailey.

"Geez, Dailey, I hate these assignments," Donahue said in frustration. "I don't know why they can't call ahead and try to work things out. Half the time they never even know if there is anything wrong."

"Yeah, I know," Dailey answered.

"When they've got strong evidence of an emergency I'm all for it. But fuzzy deals like this one are something else," Donahue said.

"Well, the City Attorney's office always tells us that child abuse cases are an exception. Warrants for everything else, but in child abuse investigations it's unnecessary," Officer Dailey answered.

"Thanks for the information, Wonder Boy. Next time tell me something I don't know," Donahue said sarcastically. "I'm just saying I don't like it. But, you do your job and keep your mouth shut, right? You wait in the car. Hopefully this won't take long."

Corliss took the lead when the trio assembled on Gwen's front porch and rang the bell.

Gwen opened the door and for an instant was paralyzed with fear. *What is this, the gestapo?* she thought to herself.

Seeing the fear in Gwen's eyes, Corliss lifted one eyebrow in triumph and began, "Mrs. Landis, you can see I am back. Let me ask you once again to cooperate. I just need to come in for a few minutes. A few questions for you. A few minutes with Casey. That's all. If you don't cooperate, you can see for yourself that I have the legal authorities here to assist me in carrying out my statutory responsibilities."

"I suppose you have a warrant, Ms. Corliss?" Gwen challenged, doing her best to mask the terror that was racing through her soul.

"You've been watching too much television, Mrs. Landis. A warrant is simply not necessary in these kinds of situations."

"What kind of situation?" Gwen questioned raising her voice in growing anger. "Well, . . . I am not volunteering. It just doesn't seem right that you can come barging into my house, frightening my daughter and me, without so much as telling me what is supposed to be wrong. If you would tell me I would probably let you in. But. . . ." fear took over and she simply couldn't go on.

"I am sorry you feel this way, but we are just following policy. And the law. Mrs. Landis, this police officer will now let me in your house and I will talk with your daughter. You haven't hidden her, have you?"

"Of course not."

"Fine, please step aside."

"Officer, can they do this?" Gwen pleaded, tears welling up in her eyes.

In that instant, Officer Donahue looked deep into Gwen's imploring green eyes. Suddenly she felt a glimmer of hope—maybe he would indeed protect her from the intruders. His eyes had betrayed him. He really did want to help.

She seemed so nice and was certainly easy to look at. He then looked to the ground and said, "I'm very sorry, ma'am. These ladies are right. I am here to make sure they get in and talk to your child."

Rita Coballo bristled at the sexist term "ladies." She glared at Officer Donahue but said nothing.

Gwen bit her lower lip. Her sense of powerlessness etched a blank expression on her face. Quietly, slowly, she stepped aside as the two investigators walked into her living room with stern deliberation.

"Casey, are you here?" Corliss called.

Casey came slowly through her bedroom door, unsure of the strange voice calling her name.

"Casey, I'm Donna," Corliss said with practiced sweetness. "Will you come with me and Rita, back to your room? We just want to talk for a minute."

Casey's fear-filled eyes turned to see her mother's face, but the CPS workers had already nudged her down the hall.

Impulsively, Gwen lunged for Casey. Office Donahue gently but decisively grabbed her elbow. "I'm sorry. They have to do their job."

Rita Coballo quietly closed the bedroom door.

"Casey," Corliss began. "Rita and I help little children. We want to help you. If you need any help we'll be right here for you."

Casey ran to her bed and scooped up her rag-doll, hugging it tightly. She began to rock back and forth against the edge of her bed as she looked at the two strange ladies.

"Casey, are you afraid of anyone?"

"Uh . . . sometimes."

"Who are you afraid of?"

"Taz."

"Who's Taz, honey?"

"He chases Daffy."

"Daffy?"

"You know, Daffy Duck. Taz chases him. He makes mean noises."

"On TV?"

"Yeah."

"Are there any people who you are afraid of? Any people you see a lot that do bad things to you?"

Casey stared and a moment later shrugged her shoulders.

"Are you ever afraid of your mommy?"

"Sometimes."

"Tell me what happens when you are afraid of your mommy."

"If I do something bad sometimes she yells, 'Don't do that.'"

"Does your Mommy yell at you a lot?"

"Uh . . . I dunno."

"Casey, this is very important. Does your Mommy ever hit you?"

"I don't think so."

"Are you sure?"

Casey shrugged.

"Does your Mommy ever spank you?"

"Uh-huh," she nodded, her lips pressed together in a faint smile, glad that she could finally answer a question in a way this lady seemed to like.

"Does she spank you with her hand or something else?"

"Her hand sometimes."

"And something else other times?"

"Uh-huh."

"What does she hit, er, spank you with other times?"

"The spoon."

"Is it wooden or metal?"

Casey just shrugged.

"What color is it, honey?"

"Brown."

"Does it hurt you a lot?"

Again Casey shrugged.

"Casey, Rita and I need to look at you to see if you are OK. Don't be afraid."

Casey felt strange up until this point. But when Corliss told her not to be afraid, it reminded her of what the doctor said just before he gave her a shot.

"Casey, I need you to take off your clothes like you do when you go to the doctor so I can see if you are all right."

The mounting strangeness of the whole episode finally broke through Casey's four year old emotional barrier, and she began to cry. "My mommy is with me at the doctors'. I want my mommy. I want my mommy."

"We need to see if you are OK right now, your mommy is just in the living room."

"I want her here."

"I'm sorry, Casey, the rules say she can't come in right now."

Casey just cried louder.

Up to this point, Gwen had been straining to hear what was being said. Now she had no difficulty in discerning the escalating levels of Casey's crying. She started for the door. Officer Donahue laid his hand on his holster and simply said, "Don't."

"I'm supposed to just stand here while those witches are molesting my daughter?" she thundered. "This is not right. This is just not right."

"I'm sorry," was all Donahue could say.

Gwen had never been more stricken with panic and despair in her entire life. Her little girl was afraid. Never, never had she failed to come and comfort her when Casey cried out needing help. Gwen put her hands over her face and began to sob convulsively.

"Casey, Rita and I just need to look for a minute. Here, let me take your shirt off first."

Casey backed away and leaned as hard as possible against her bed trying to disappear.

"Mommy, Mommy!" Casey cried as Corliss gripped her arm tightly.

"Come on, Casey, this won't hurt."

Corliss was tiring of going slowly. She moved with firm deliberation. She quickly grabbed Casey's other arm and held her down on the bed. "Rita, quick, take off her shirt and jeans and pull her panties down. Quickly."

Casey writhed in terror. Her cries turned to screams as the two social workers stripped all her clothes off.

"Nooooo!" Gwen yelled from the living room.

There was nothing but perfectly unblemished skin. No bruises. No scrapes. Hardly even any freckles. The investigators' eyes met expressing grim disappointment. They wanted to get back at this woman for bucking their authority. Finding no bruises, they were out of business.

"OK, Casey. It's OK. We can put your clothes on now."

Casey sobbed helplessly.

"I'm sorry, Casey. If you would have just cooperated, it wouldn't have been so bad."

～

Corliss led the investigative duo back into the living room. Gwen darted toward Casey's room and bumped heavily into Coballo. Casey ran out into the hall, desperate to find her mother. Gwen swept up her terrified daughter in her own violently shaking arms.

Corliss turned toward the huddled mother and child who were in the hallway just steps from the living room.

"Mrs. Landis, now that we have talked to Casey and examined her we can tell you a bit about the nature of our investigation."

Gwen clung to Casey, refusing to acknowledge her.

"If you like we can have Casey go sit with the officer in the kitchen so we can talk a bit more privately."

Gwen bitterly choked out the words, "No way."

"Have it your way," Corless answered dispassionately. "We received a complaint night before last that you spank Casey in an excessive manner. Would you mind explaining to us your spanking practices?"

"I mind very much indeed. How dare you strip my little girl and then start asking me questions!"

"Mrs. Landis, we can probably close this investigation if you will just answer a few questions."

Gwen wanted Corliss out of her house more than she had ever wanted anything. She would do almost anything to get her out right then.

"OK. Anything to stop this. Sometimes I spank her but never excessively. She has never been hurt in her life by spanking."

"The great weight of psychological opinion concludes that hitting children only teaches them aggressiveness—especially if you employ a device other than your hand. Casey told us you hit her with a spoon. Is that correct?"

"Yes. But I have never, ever bruised her. Are you saying it's illegal for me to spank my daughter with a spoon?"

"Let's just say it's legally unwise and you wouldn't be in this situation if you would use other means of discipline. We have some wonderful parenting courses and counselors we could make available to you."

"The only thing I want from you is to get out of my house and leave me and my daughter alone. Go! Now!"

"We will be leaving shortly," Corliss said, emphasizing her control, "but your attitude is just prolonging everything."

The CPS workers walked to the front door. Corliss paused and turned back toward the mother and daughter, still clinging tightly to each other. "Mrs. Landis, we will be writing a report shortly. You will get a copy in a few days. Good-bye."

"Just leave. You . . . you . . . witches . . . Nazis . . . just leave! Get out! Now!" Gwen screamed.

They opened the door and were half way out when Gwen's anguished voice cried out again. "So help me, I'm going to sue you for this!"

For fifteen minutes Casey sobbed in her mother's arms while Gwen rocked her back and forth and softly said, over and over, "I love you. You are safe. No one will ever hurt you." As the minutes passed, Gwen was able to compose herself enough to carry Casey to the kitchen and call her father for help.

"Grandpa's coming, Casey doll. He'll protect us. Grandpa'll protect us."

She sank to her knees on the kitchen floor and began rocking Casey back and forth again. They both cried softly for the eight-and-a-half minutes it took for Grandpa Mansfield to arrive.

2

~

Donna Corliss marched angrily down the corridor of the CPS office. *Nazi . . . witch . . .* She rolled the words over again in her mind. *I'm just trying to help kids and instead I get this kind of vilification. We'll just see.*

She stopped abruptly at Blackburn's door and rapped three times. "Come in," the supervisor's voice intoned.

She swung open the door and slapped her file folder on the edge of Blackburn's desk. With dripping sarcasm, Corliss said, "I'm back to report on my latest efforts to protect the lives and health of innocent children."

"Sounds like you had fun. What was the name of the family again?"

"Landis. Gwen Landis. An uncooperative cheerleader type who hits her kid with a stick. She admitted it!"

"Any bruises? You did examine the kid didn't you?"

"Of course I did, the little rat. She, like her mother, refused to cooperate with the physical examination. I had to hold her while Rita took off her clothes. But no bruises. Nothing. A perfect little angel."

"What did this lady do to make you so upset?"

"Well, on top of her total non-cooperation from beginning to end, she called me a Nazi and a witch and threatened to sue me."

"Well, you'll be pleased to know that I've heard a lot worse, and besides, we hear threats to sue all the time."

"Yeah, I know, but I think she's the type who will probably do it."

"You really think so?"

17

"Absolutely. This woman is very intelligent. She speaks with perfect grammar and is very precise. She is also very emotional and is furious with us—me in particular. I haven't heard as many threats as you, but I've heard my share. I think she is serious."

Blackburn despised anyone who challenged the authority of CPS.

"Well, we could always implement Code B for this file."

"That is exactly what I was going to ask you," Donna said, leaning forward in her chair. "If we don't, I'm going to have to unfound this report and close our investigation, giving this blond-child-beating-chick a clean bill of health."

"We have to use Code B very infrequently," Blackburn said with great earnestness. "If we use it too much—it might blow up in our faces someday."

"I know, I know. But we've been careful. We use it only when we must and the judges here totally trust our credibility. When it's our word against the word of a child abuser, the judge is always going to side with us."

"What's your strategy?"

"I'm going to wait a few days. Then I'll file a report that says I found fading bruises that looked seven to ten days old. By the time Mrs. Landis gets the report, and her lawyer—I'm sure she'll get one—advises her to take the child to her pediatrician for an examination, the bruises will have had time to fade away completely and he will find nothing, yet our report will be perfectly believable."

"Not bad. But what if she gets a lawyer today and he tells her to get the kid examined pronto?"

"I don't think she will. I told her that I probably was going to close the case. Plus, if she was thinking strategically, she would have gotten a lawyer after my visit yesterday, and she would have handed me a pediatrician's report when I stepped on her porch."

"You amaze me. You are almost as good as me."

"I'll get even better," Corliss laughed. "Just give me time."

～

Gail Willet joined the office of the Spokane County Prosecuting Attorney on the first of May. Her marriage to a Seattle architect had been on the rocks for two years. A cute young secretary proved to be just too alluring. The divorce was final in March.

She had been a top child abuse prosecutor in the King County Prosecutor's office for most of the six years since she graduated from the University of Washington law school. Willet wanted to be away from Seattle, and Spokane was as far as she could get without having to go through the hassle of another bar examination.

The chief prosecutor, Charles Sexton, was only too glad to have an experienced attorney joining his staff for a change. The normal routine was for attorneys to join his office for a few years straight out of law school, amass substantial trial experience, and then move into private practice.

Sexton was glad for Willet's experience, but he was a bit concerned about her tendency to display a harder edge than was the norm among Spokane legal practitioners. Seattle was definitely a more cutthroat environment with little camaraderie between members of the bar. Gail Willet was competent, tough, and would take no prisoners in the court room.

Twelve-hour days were the norm. If she got busy, she would do more. Work was more than a career for Willet at the moment. It was the salve she chose to place on her inner hurts.

"Ms. Corliss is here to see you," the intercom announced, at 10:30 A.M., Wednesday, May 18.

"Send her in," Willet said, standing up to clear a stack of files off one of her side chairs.

"Come in, Ms. Corliss."

"Donna, please."

"Fine, I'm Gail."

"So you've got a possible case for me?" Willet said, purposefully avoiding chit-chat. She was sick of having to answer the painful question, "So, why did you decide to move here from Seattle?"

"Yes, thanks for seeing me right away. We have such a workload and I just finished the report on this case late yesterday. I hope you can review it and take some quick action . . . if you think it's appropriate, of course."

"Why don't you just tell me the most salient facts? Pretend I'm the judge. Tell me why I should order immediate action against these people." She instinctively began taking notes on her yellow pad.

"Last Tuesday after normal hours, May 10th, we received a hotline tip that Gwen Landis regularly hits her four-year old daughter, Casey, with a stick, perhaps a ruler. Mrs. Landis is divorced and lives alone with the child. The caller was uncertain about bruises or the extent of injuries. I went out the next morning. The mother refused to allow me to interview the child, examine the child, answer any of my questions, or even allow me to come into the home, even for a moment."

Donna paused, expecting Gail Willet to say something, which she did not. After a moment, Willet looked up from her yellow pad, raised her left eyebrow and cocked her head as if to ask, *Why have you stopped?* Sensing an awkward moment, Donna continued.

"This course of action heightened my concern for the child because experience has shown that real abusers are often uncooperative. I was required to return the following day, with another CPS investigator and a police officer. After an initial refusal, Mrs. Landis allowed us in. The other CPS worker, who is also a female for obvious reasons, assisted me in interviewing the child and conducting a routine search for bruises. We found evidence of seven-to-ten day old bruises, 'fading bruises' I believe I call them on page three of the report," Corliss said, flipping to the correct page. "We then questioned Mrs. Landis who admitted hitting the girl with a wooden object on a regular basis, but denied any bruising. We obviously observed otherwise."

"Mrs. Landis appeared irrational throughout the process, and I believe that the child needs to be taken into protective custody for a seven day period to allow a full physical and psychological evaluation. We don't have enough information to make final conclusions, but we do have clear facts to raise questions about the safety of this child and the stability of Mrs. Landis. She's been through a divorce recently, perhaps she's coming a bit apart at the seams."

Willet sat back in her chair and appraised Donna carefully. There was little the new prosecutor hadn't heard and Donna's last remark cost her some points. Willet quickly let it pass and said, "OK. Not bad. You obviously don't have enough to get permanent custody, but I think I can get the judge to sign a temporary Shelter Care Order. I think it'll sound reasonable and appropriate. Obviously we will want to conduct a thorough physical and psychological examination while we have her in temporary custody."

"Absolutely."

"Do you have an examination team in mind?"

"Randall McGuire is the best child psychologist in town. I've checked, he's available. Dr. Stratton is a pediatrician I've worked with in several prior cases of abuse. He's good and testifies quite convincingly."

"OK. And foster parents? Do you have some real seasoned people who can observe her on a regular basis and testify appropriately? Some of these foster parents love kids, but they just can't talk to a judge."

"I've got the perfect couple. The wife was a social worker for Methodist Family Services for several years before they had twins and she decided to stay home."

"Sounds good. You seem to have thought of everything."

"Well, it's all there in my report."

"OK. I'll dictate the affidavit and petition for you to sign, and if this infernal word processing pool can pump out the paperwork, I should be able to present the Show Cause Order this afternoon. We can have a hearing next Monday or Tuesday."

"I have a conflict on Monday. Another hearing," Corliss said.

"OK, Tuesday it is—if the judge will schedule it."

"I'll be in my office all afternoon. I'll stay by the phone waiting for word to come sign the papers."

"Great. Please shut the door on the way out, Some of these other prosecutors shoot the breeze so loudly in the hall, I can't get any work done."

~

Five hours later, Superior Court Judge Philip Romer, who was assigned to Juvenile Court for the months of April, May, and June signed the order requested by Prosecutor Willet and supported by the affidavit of Investigator Corliss.

The order required Gwen Landis to appear in court Tuesday, May 24, 1994, at 10:00 A.M. and, in typical legalese, "to produce then and there the child known as Casey Landis and to show cause, if any you have, why a Shelter Care Order should not be issued for a seven day period; and further, why the court should not order an examination to ascertain the physical and psychological condition of the child; and further, why the court should not order a psychological and parenting assessment of said named Respondent."

It meant that Gwen had to bring Casey to court next Tuesday and tell the judge her reasons why Casey should not be taken away for seven days to be examined. Gwen would face the prospect of being interrogated herself by a psychologist and perhaps a social worker or two.

The judge thought the papers were in order, presented professionally by this new member of the Prosecutor's staff, and was particularly moved by the affidavit signed under oath by Investigator Corliss.

~

Sheriff's Deputy Wally Elrod had eight court orders to serve that Thursday. Two on the South Hill, one in Mead just north of Spokane, one over by Shadle Park High School, one twelve miles west of town in Medical Lake at the State Psychiatric Hospital, and three out in the rapidly growing Spokane valley which lay to the east of the center city and stretched for almost twenty miles out toward the Idaho border. Beautiful Coeur d'Alene Lake lay just a few minutes over the border. He would really rack up the miles today. And he doubted he would catch everyone at home.

He decided to go just north of the Courthouse toward Shadle Park, hit the Mead location, head out to the Valley, then do the South Hill, and finish with serving the crazy dude out at Medical Lake. They might be irrational at Medical Lake, but at least they were always there to receive their papers. Gwen Landis was sixth in line on his mental schedule.

It was relatively rare to see a sheriff's brown cruiser on the near South Hill. All police work for this area was done in the blue and silver cars of the Spokane City Police Department. The Spokane County Sheriff's Department had criminal and traffic jurisdiction in all areas of the county outside the city limits. But all court orders for the entire county were served by the Sheriff's Department.

At 1:45 P.M., Deputy Elrod turned left off of 29th street onto Janelle Court. It was an older neighborhood of modest homes. The South Hill as a whole was considered the richest part of the city. But there were many well-kept modest little neighborhoods woven here and there amongst the substantial, sprawling homes that gave the South Hill its reputation.

He parked just in front of the home of Gwen and Casey Landis, deliberately blocking Gwen's '89 Taurus which was parked in the driveway. "Her car's home, that's a good sign," Elrod muttered to himself.

Gwen was not expecting any visitors that afternoon. When the bell rang, her heart froze thinking it might be Donna Corliss once again. But when she glanced out the window and saw the brown cruiser, her fear became full blown.

"May I help you?" Gwen asked with a barely concealed tremor as she held the door half way open for the gray-haired officer clad in a brown uniform.

"Just need to give you some papers, ma'am. Your name Gwen Landis?"

She nodded.

"Well, these papers are for you," the deputy said, stretching out his left arm with a thin stack of legal papers.

"I don't think I should sign anything until I read them."

"Don't have to sign anything. Just take the papers and I'm out of your hair."

"OK, I guess. Do you know what these are all about?"

"No, ma'am. I just deliver 'em. Don't read 'em, and I sure as shoot'n don't explain 'em. Just call your lawyer. He gets paid to explain these things."

"But I don't have a lawyer."

"Might want to look into it. It's up to you, ma'am. I don't give advice and I don't recommend any particular lawyers. My job's just to hand out the papers. See you later, ma'am."

As the officer walked back to his cruiser, Gwen didn't respond. She stood frozen in concentration, staring at the top sheet on the stack of papers. NOTICE OF HEARING, it read, Tuesday, May 24, 10:00 A.M., Spokane County Superior Court, Juvenile Division.

She tried to read the attached "Complaint, Affidavit, and Order to Show Cause" through her tears while sitting on the front porch. She didn't understand much of the mumbo-jumbo, but she could clearly understand she had been accused of spanking Casey and leaving bruises. *That vicious liar,* Gwen thought, picturing Donna Corliss's stern face in her mind's eye.

She was glad to have already taken Casey to her parents' house so she could get ready for work at Sacred Heart Hospital. Even though the trauma of the last several days was still fresh, she had been doing her best to make life as normal as possible for Casey. During the day, Casey seemed fine. But whenever it was time for bed, Casey refused to go into her room alone. She was terrified "the mean ladies" were hiding under her bed. When Gwen finally got Casey to sleep, the early morning hours were often pierced by Casey's bloodcurdling screams. Nearly every night since the incident, Gwen would sit on Casey's bed and comfort her from the fear of terrifying nightmares.

Gwen's parents watched Casey at their home until shortly after dinner when they would alternate taking Casey to Gwen's, putting her to bed and waiting for Gwen to return from her shift at the hospital. This became increasingly difficult for all concerned. And so for the last few days, Casey was put to bed at her grandparents. Gwen would go there from work, sleep fitfully on the couch in their family room, and wait for the inevitable screams.

~

Gwen reached for the phone and touched the speed-dial button for her parents phone.

"Dad, a sheriff was just here and served me with some legal papers. There is some kind of hearing next Tuesday." At first Gwen managed to control her emotions, but then she broke down. "Dad, I am so scared. They want to take Casey away from me."

"They what?" Stan Mansfield gasped, angry that someone had made his daughter cry again.

"I don't know if I am reading this thing correctly or not, but from what I can tell, they are trying to take Casey away—maybe for seven days or something, I don't know. Daddy, please, help me."

"Those idiots. Those stupid idiots!"

"Dad, I've got to get a lawyer now. Who was that guy you mentioned?"

"Bill Walinski. His office is on Northwest Boulevard."

"Can we go see him today? I'm going to call in and tell my supervisor I can't go to work."

"Honey, don't you think you should go to work? You're going to need all the money you can get for the lawyer. Mom and I just aren't in a position to help you with more than four or five hundred dollars. I wish I was rich, but my pension and social security barely cover our bills."

"Maybe I should go to Legal Services."

"No, let's go to a real lawyer first."

"Daddy, I really want to go today. Can you call him while I call the hospital?"

"OK. I'll do it. I'll call you back and let you know if we can get in."

3

~

"Sorry, what was the last name?"

"Stan Mansfield. We played golf together a few days ago."

"Oh yes, of course. I think I let you win, didn't I?" Bill Walinski said, laughing into the receiver. "What's up?"

"Well, my daughter is having some legal hassles and I was wondering if you could take a look at some papers she's been served regarding her daughter."

"Absolutely. I've handled a number of juvenile court cases. Now, I'm a general practitioner, not a specialist. But that won't matter."

"We're kind of anxious. When is the earliest you could see us?"

"Ooooh, let's see. I wouldn't be available until Thursday, next week."

"Next week!? We can't wait that long. We have to see somebody now."

"Well, listen. I wouldn't do this for everybody but, since it's so urgent, I'll clear my schedule for today. Can you come in at three-thirty this afternoon?"

"Great. We'll be there." Stan exhaled a sigh of relief and placed the phone back on the cradle.

Gwen and her father arrived at the single-story stucco building at 3:15. When Stan saw the office, he frowned and hoped Gwen didn't see his disapproval. It was an office duplex, in the moderate-to-low-rent business district which blanketed both sides of Northwest Boulevard for about twenty blocks. There was a small print shop in the other half of the complex.

Gwen and Stan stepped through the door and passed a blue vinyl couch and two black plastic chairs. On the two side tables sat disheveled stacks of old *People* magazines. Gwen frowned at the condition of the room while Stan nodded in the direction of the middle-aged secretary sitting behind an obsolete computer monitor. As she typed furiously the long cigarette which hung precariously from her lips bobbed wildly up and down.

"Can I help you?" she asked flatly without looking up.

"Uh . . . Gwen Landis here to see Mr. Walinski," Stan Mansfield said. "I'm her father. I met Mr. Walinski on the golf course."

"Big surprise," she answered sarcastically. "I'll let him know you're here. He's on the phone right now. Why don't you have a seat over there," she offered, pointing to the vinyl couch.

The secretary opened Walinski's door, mouthed the words "They're here" then sat back at her desk.

"Tee time at 5:30 this afternoon. Sounds great. I'll see you there. Loser buys drinks."

Walinski threw open his office door and walked briskly to his secretary's desk.

"Oh, hi Stan. I'll be with you in a minute." Then turning to his secretary he continued, "Here's the Dombrowski file. Tell them we've got the check from the insurance company. Every penny of it. They can come in at five and get their money."

Every time, the Dombrowski file. Doesn't he ever get tired of this little act? she thought. *If he put as much time into his practice as he does into golf and acting he'd be the most successful lawyer in town.*

When Walinski did practice law it was usually in the dregs of legal work; divorce cases between those of modest means; drunk driving defense; petty criminal cases; a few real estate disputes.

Occasionally a big case would land in his lap by chance, but he rarely managed to hold on to it. Most clients of such cases soon realized that he was swimming in the wrong pond when the big downtown firms sent three immaculately dressed and coifed sharks.

He turned from his secretary, looked up with what he called his "money smile," and said, "Stan, come on in. This must be your daughter." Walinski did a double-take as he focused on Gwen Landis. *What a babe,* he thought. *I think I could work with her real well.* He flashed a glance down at her left hand to see if there was a ring, and kept smiling.

"Well, well. Gwen, glad to meet you! I'm sure you've figured out I'm Bill Walinski. Please come in."

Gwen felt a little unsettling pang. She was indeed an exceptionally beautiful woman and was no stranger to lingering stares and comments. She knew how to give such men an icy stare of disinterest, but this man was supposed to help her protect the most precious thing in her life, and the looks confused her. She focused her mind on protecting Casey and assured herself that she was misinterpreting his glances and words.

Once in Walinski's office, Gwen was glad to discover that it was a bit more upscale than the waiting area. Walinski motioned for them to sit in the older green leather chairs while he moved behind his desk and sat comfortably in a burgundy leather high-back.

Gwen sat on the edge of her chair and looked at the large stack of files that apparently contained current cases. Stan and the lawyer engaged in small talk while Gwen appraised the room in which they sat. A few pieces of generic art covered three walls, but on the wall behind his head hung four framed legal certificates. Gwen noted his law school diploma from Gonzaga, his Supreme Court of Washington bar admission, and his federal court admission for the Eastern District of Washington. Gwen was very impressed to discover the fourth certificate revealed that Bill Walinski had been admitted to practice before the Supreme Court of the United States.

Walinski had been keeping one eye on Gwen and took note when she paused over the Supreme Court certificate.

"I think we should get started. Gwen, why don't you tell me what's going on," Walinski began.

"Well, some child abuse investigator is trying to get me. She's trying to take Casey away from me."

Walinski was enough of a lawyer to know he would have to go about this with a bit more precision if he was going to get the whole story without listening to an hour or so of rambling from a frightened mother.

"Your father told me you were served with some legal papers today. Did you bring them with you?"

"Yeah, they're here in my purse." Gwen dug deep in her oversized satchel, drawing out twelve sheets of paper.

Walinski quickly glanced at the notice of hearing, immediately ascertaining its meaning. "It'll take me just a couple of minutes to read these papers and then I can ask you more intelligent questions."

He read the Petition, the supporting Affidavit by Donna Corliss, and the Show Cause Order which had been prepared by Gail Willet and signed by Judge Romer.

"Well, that's quite a story. I hope at least some of it's not true," Walinski said, placing the papers squarely in front of him.

"I have never bruised Casey in my life," Gwen said defensively. "I had hoped you would believe me."

"Oh, I believe you. You're my client. I just want to know what parts you agree with and what charges you dispute. Okay? I'm on your side completely."

Gwen was not completely reassured. *I want to be believed, not merely represented,* she thought, looking straight at Walinski.

"Well, let me explain the meaning of these papers. There are four separate documents. This is the Notice of Hearing. All it says is that there is going to be a hearing at ten next Tuesday in front of Judge Romer. No big deal. This second document is the petition. This is the formal complaint against you written by the prosecutor, a new woman called Gail Willet. It gives the charges and some of the facts according to them. This is an affidavit by the CPS investigator, Donna Corliss," Walinski said, showing the document to them. "I've seen her around a little but have only dealt directly with her once or twice."

In reality Walinski's "dealings" with Corliss had consisted of greeting her in the hallway outside the juvenile courtroom.

"The judge will pay a lot of attention to this affidavit because it contains the real factual meat of their case. And finally, this document is called a Show Cause Order. It doesn't mean that the judge has decided to take Casey away from you or has decided against you. What it means is that the judge wants you to come to court to answer the charges. By signing this order the judge has said that if these facts turn out to be true, then he believes there are probable grounds for some kind of action against you. Maybe he will take Casey away, maybe something else *if* these facts are true."

Walinski's explanation made both Gwen and Stan feel better about him. He explained the papers in terms they could really understand.

"The real problem is the bruises. If it wasn't for the allegation that you bruised Casey they wouldn't have a case at all. Are you sure she wasn't bruised from something else? Does she ride a bike? Roller skate? Anything like that?"

"She does ride a bike with training wheels, but I am positive she was not bruised at all when they did their strip-search, looking for bruises. Her screams broke my heart while they were doing this and the police officer in the living room made sure I couldn't get to her and help her."

"Do you have a regular family doctor or pediatrician for Casey?"

"I'm a nurse at Sacred Heart. I know lots of doctors. But normally I take Casey to Dr. Davenport."

"Have you taken Casey to see him since they did the strip search?"

"No, should I?"

"It would have been a good idea. It's been seven days since the search was done. That's more than enough time for bruises to fade. If you would have called me right then I would have advised you to get to the doctor that day for his inspection and report."

Gwen felt sick. Stan felt guilty for discouraging his daughter from seeking a lawyer back then.

"Well, it may not help, but at least we can try to do our best. I want Casey to be seen by a doctor, any doctor—today. And I want a medical release from you so that I can get Dr. Davenport to sign an affidavit that he has never observed any bruises on Casey. That's what he'll say, isn't it?"

"Of course. And doesn't it help that I'm a nurse and I say there were no bruises at the time they invaded my home?"

"You being a nurse will help some. If you were signing an affidavit about somebody else's child your word about the existence of bruises would be almost the same as an affidavit from your doctor. But you're the one being accused here. The judge will discount your credibility because you have a compelling reason to lie."

Walinksi's advice seemed good to both Gwen and her father. Gwen wondered why he didn't ask any questions about why the social worker was there in the first place. Before she could ask Walinski said, "Well, we need to talk for just a minute about fees. I normally charge $150 an hour . . . but I charge my golfing buddies $125 an hour," flashing a smile, he continued, "I'm going to need $500 up front and then we can reassess after this first hearing."

Stan spoke up. "I can write you a check for $500. But I need you to hold it until tomorrow so I can go and transfer that much from my savings. You also need to know that my wife and I are not wealthy people. Gwen has no money to speak of and $500 is the absolute limit we can pay. You've just got to win this first hearing or we are really up against it financially."

Gwen appreciated her father's generosity and even more his willingness to explain the realities of their financial life to this lawyer.

"Can't we sue and get the money back and make them pay you?" Gwen asked.

"That's real tough to do and for now neither you nor I should count on that as a source of funds for this case. Your dad's right," Walinski said, standing to indicate that the conference was over. "Let's just win this first hearing and money won't become an issue. I'll prepare an affidavit for you to sign, and then I'll call Dr. Davenport to sign an affidavit after you've taken Casey in to see him. We'll do battle at ten on Tuesday. My secretary will call you,

Gwen, when your affidavit is ready. You'll need to drop by at your convenience tomorrow to sign it. Thanks for coming. I think we should do well."

Walinski hoped that his efforts would help Gwen, if only to put him in good stead with a gorgeous woman. But time is money and there was only $500 to be made in this case. He'd do what he could for $500.

Sometime after his fourth Canadian Club that evening, Bill Walinski sat at home imagining Gwen Landis's beautiful green eyes and her other womanly attractions. The alcohol and the dancing flames in the fireplace combined to produce powerful intentions in his clouding mind.

Yes! he exclaimed to himself.

Bill Walinski had found a way to continue his relationship with Gwen Landis—even if the hearing didn't end in her favor.

～

Gwen went to work again on Friday. She was pleased that her rounds in the surgery ward were busier than usual. The added pressure kept her mind off the hearing. *I've never enjoyed my paperwork so much,* she thought, smiling to herself.

Gwen's parents left for Walla Walla first thing Saturday morning. Placing flowers on the grave of Grandfather Mansfield was an annual affair on Memorial Day weekend. Under the circumstances of the past few days, Gwen decided it would be better if Casey didn't have to spend the night in an unfamiliar place and decided not to go this year. On their way out of town, Stan thought he would stop by Gwen's house and try one more time.

"She'll be all right in a motel," Stan offered, vying for tradition.

"Well, maybe you're right," Gwen answered. "But Gordon is going to exercise visitation rights tomorrow. I've been trying to cooperate with him . . . for Casey's sake."

"Which means you'll be sitting around waiting for him to show up. I wish he'd get a real job and stop bumming around trying to get rich in a day."

Gwen just shrugged without expression. It was still a sore point.

Her father continued, "When was the last time he paid his child support? You know I've tried to talk to him, but work for wages? Not Gordon. No sir. He is going to win the lottery. And you know the thing that amazes me? How is it that he walked out on you? There were no women. No alcohol, at least not before he walked out—just because you wanted him to get a job. I still can't believe it . . . accusing you of sabotaging his dreams of success. What a joke."

Stan then looked at Gwen and realized he was venting and being inconsiderate of her.

"Oh, honey, I'm sorry. I've been running off at the mouth."

"I know Gordon has problems, Dad, but Casey has fun feeding the ducks in Manito Park with him. Last time he took her to the carousel in Riverfront Park. And, to his credit, he has never asked prying questions."

"Of course, I guess it's best if you stay here this time," Stan acquiesced. "We'd better get going."

Stan gave Gwen a long hug before he walked to his car. Both her parents waved as their car pulled away.

~

It was true that Gordon didn't usually pry into Gwen's life through Casey, but this Sunday would be different. Sitting on a park bench eating a strawberry ice cream cone, Casey tried her best to please her daddy and answer the questions he asked.

Gordon discovered some ladies and a policeman had been to the home and that Gwen was crying when they left. *Good,* he thought, *a little hassle. Nothing too dramatic.* Gordon hated Gwen for refusing to take him back even though he had been the one who filed for divorce. Although he had never changed his career ideas and work habits that led to their difficulties in the first place, maybe this little scare would make Gwen think it would be good to have a man around for protection.

Gwen had made plans for her free time during Gordon's visitation; a walk, pick up a couple of items at the grocery store, and a nap. Casey's nightmares were taking a toll on her stamina.

She walked up to 29th, a beautiful tree-lined thoroughfare that carries east-west traffic across the South Hill, and started out toward Manito Center, a small shopping area with a Safeway, a clothing store, and a drug store. The upcoming events of Tuesday crowded everything else out of her mind. She didn't feel like shopping and continued walking.

Two blocks past the Safeway, Gwen heard organ music coming from a small church on the corner of 29th & Arthur. South Hill Bible Church the sign read. She had never noticed the name before. To her it had simply been the pink church, a color she always thought a very odd choice for a church.

She paused for a moment on the sidewalk. The hymn sounded vaguely familiar. Her parents had taken her to church three or four times a year during childhood, but she could not remember the last time she had been in church other than for a wedding.

Gwen had attended a youth camp sponsored by Fourth Memorial Church when she was thirteen. *Maybe we sang that song at camp,* she thought. Gwen had walked an aisle and prayed a prayer of commitment. She had been really interested in God at that moment, but when she came back to town she never went back to any church and whatever was in her heart was lost in the sea of daily living during her teen years.

Maybe I should go inside and pray about the trial. The very thought led to a surge of anxiety.

Gwen scrutinized how she was dressed. She wondered if a cotton skirt, sleeveless white blouse, and sandals were appropriate. A couple walked in from the back parking lot. Gwen noticed that the woman was dressed pretty much as she.

It can't hurt, she thought. *I'll just sneak in the back. Pray a little and slip back out. I sure don't want to talk with anyone.*

Gwen slipped quietly into the last pew. Momentary self-consciousness soon left and Gwen's mind once again focused on the upcoming hearing.

God, please help me win on Tuesday. Please help. I haven't done anything wrong and I don't know how this happened. Please keep Casey safe from these people.

There was something pleasingly familiar about the bits of the service she heard in the twenty minutes she was inside. The singing and especially the first ten minutes of the sermon, reminded her of the week at church camp fifteen years earlier. It was a happy time then and the memory brought a warm feeling.

∽

Monday's overcast sky only added to the bleakness growing in Gwen's soul. She had the holiday off and spent it obsessively cleaning her already spotless house. Bursts of energy were punctuated by furtive glances at the Vienna wall clock Gwen's grandfather had left her in his will—a constant reminder of the coming hearing.

The thought of telling Casey about the impending court appearance added further layers of anxiety to her already laden soul. But she knew putting it off further was not fair to Casey. After all, the court order specifically directed her to bring her daughter to court. Walinski advised Casey sit with her grandmother in a waiting room and not listen to the bulk of the hearing. But she had to be in the building. The judge wanted her to be available and would hold Gwen in contempt if she failed to produce Casey at the time and place directed in the order.

Gwen bit her lower lip as she walked down the hall to Casey's bedroom. As she pushed open the door and saw the uncluttered room, Gwen beamed, "Well, look at you. You've picked up all your toys. I'm *so* proud of you, Casey!"

Casey giggled with delight at her mom's approval and then said, "We are cleaning aren't we, Mom?"

"We sure are, little princess," Gwen said as she pulled Casey close for a tight hug. Gwen then took a deep breath, held Casey by the shoulders so she could look into her eyes, and began, "Casey doll, tomorrow we're going to have to do something that might not be real fun. We are going to go downtown to the court house. There is going to be a lot of talking between grown-ups called a trial. You have to go to the building, but you don't have to listen to the talking. You and Grandma will be able to sit outside the room where mommy will be talking to some people. Everything will be fine. OK?"

"Why, Mommy? What are we going to talk about?" Casey asked inquisitively.

"Remember those ladies who came here and frightened you?"

Casey's brow darkened at the mention of the "bad ladies" as she called them. Gwen saw the change in her countenance and quickly said, "Don't worry about them, Honey. They can't hurt you any more. They just want me to answer some more questions. They won't try to talk with you. But I have to bring you with me. Grandma will stay right by your side the whole time."

Casey's lip began to quiver as she reached for her rag doll and clutched it close to her chest. "Mommy, I don't like those bad ladies. They scared me and tried to hurt me. Please don't take me. I don't want them to see me. They're mean."

"Casey doll, Grandma or I will be right with you the whole time and this time we won't let those ladies take you no matter what. Grandpa will be with me and we have another man to help us, Mr. Walinski. He's a lawyer, and he will protect you, too. Nobody is going to take you from me, Casey. Nobody. Now, come here so I can give you another hug."

Casey took her rag doll, held her up to Gwen and said, "Here Mommy, Annie needs a kiss. She's scared too."

The trio kissed and hugged on the floor of Casey's bedroom.

It was a fitful night. Gwen wouldn't have slept much even if Casey hadn't awakened twice with nightmares. After the second episode, Gwen lay awake on her bed, staring up at the ceiling.

God, please make this work. I'm begging.

4

Stan and June Mansfield pulled in the driveway of Gwen's house at 8:45 Tuesday morning. Walinski had called and asked them to be at the courthouse at 9:30. It was a fifteen minute drive to the courthouse.

There were a dozen padded chairs in the comfortable waiting area for the Juvenile Court. Casey, clinging tightly to Gwen, sat quietly in her lap, while the foursome waited for Walinski. Between deep breaths and constant checking of watches, the conversation was stilted.

At 9:35, Walinski walked through the front door looking every bit a poor man's lawyer—blue blazer, gray slacks, red striped tie, unshined wingtips. He smiled broadly and went right up to Casey.

"So this must be our little girl," he said in a loud voice.

Casey cringed and clung more tightly to Gwen.

"How ya doin', Sweetheart," Walinski said winking in a friendly way at Casey.

Casey emitted a slight whimper.

"Well, folks, why don't we go into the conference room and talk for a couple minutes?"

"Should we bring Casey with us?" Gwen queried.

"Uh . . . maybe not. Can she stay here with Grandma?"

Casey wasn't thrilled about being separated from her mother and Grandpa, but she wasn't panicked because being Grandma was OK. At least that's the way she felt until Donna Corliss entered the room at a quarter till ten.

"The ladies, the mean ladies! Grandma, help!" Casey screamed.

Corliss was embarrassed but said nothing. A twenty-something clerk who sat behind the counter, turned to observe the commotion—somewhat unusual even for the emotional-laden-setting of the Juvenile Court.

Gwen heard Casey's screams from forty feet down the hall and through a closed door. She immediately burst out of the room and scooped Casey up in her arms, glared at the CPS investigator, and marched quickly back to the conference room. June Mansfield quietly, and with a bit of embarrassment, gathered up their things, and went to join the rest of her family in the conference room.

At five to ten, Walinski left them alone in the conference room, saying, "Wait here. I'll go see if the judge is ready for us and then will come get you."

Ten anxious minutes past before he returned, saying simply, "Gwen and Stan, let's go."

The Juvenile Courtroom was very informal compared to the regular courtrooms in the main building. The judge's chair back rose up behind a modern, light oak paneled bench that was elevated only a few inches off the floor. A clerk sat behind a small table on the right. A place for a court reporter was on the left. They used a tape recorder unless counsel demanded a live court reporter. Walinski had not done so.

～

Judge Philip Romer had been appointed to the bench six years earlier when Democrat Booth Gardner was Governor. He was in his early fifties, balding, and slightly overweight.

He had been a Deputy Prosecutor for his first fifteen years in practice, then had tried private practice for about a half-dozen years. While he was quite competent as a litigator, he was unable to break into the real money associated with private practice because he had chosen to go solo and simply didn't have the client base. But he had been involved in Democrat Party activities, and this, plus his fifteen years as a Deputy Prosecutor, led to his appointment to the Superior Court bench to fill a vacancy created by retirement.

As required by law, judges appointed to fill a vacancy must stand for election at the next general election. Judge Romer had been a fair-minded, workman-like, non-controversial judge and had been unopposed in his election. He was now in his fourth year of his first six-year elected term. He hoped to be elected a few more times until he could retire with an adequate judicial pension.

Judge Romer walked in from a door just behind the bench without the benefit of a bailiff crying, "All rise," as would have been the case in the main courthouse. Juvenile Court was intended to be informal and non-threatening.

Both Walinski and Deputy Prosecutor Willet jumped to their feet upon seeing the judge out of years of habit.

"Please sit down," Romer said warmly, smiling at everyone in the room.

Romer was genuinely a nice man. Afraid to take legal risks, he liked to play everything down the middle. Some of the eleven Superior Court judges hated the three month rotation in juvenile court they all were required to take every three years. Romer had been on this duty twice before and enjoyed it. It gave him a chance to be nice, but stern with juvenile offenders who were the usual fare in this branch of the court. About a third of the cases in juvenile court involved parents accused of a civil form of child abuse or neglect. The hard core abusers, those who molested their children, beat them severely, or worse, were normally first tried in the main courthouse in a full-blown criminal trial. Any civil issues concerning custody and treatment were easier to handle in Juvenile Court after the criminal charges were out of the way.

"Good morning."

"Good morning, Your Honor," the lawyers replied in unison.

"Well, let's see what we have here today. In the Matter of Casey Landis. You must be Gwen Landis, the respondent," he said with a slight smile. I see you are represented by Mr. Walinski. And who may I ask is that distinguished gentleman sitting right behind you?"

Walinski stood. "That's Stan Mansfield, Your Honor, Mrs. Landis's father and, of course, Casey's grandfather. Just here for moral support."

"That's fine," the judge said. "Mr. Mansfield, welcome. I just had to ask because juvenile court proceedings are closed to the public. But I allow immediate family members in to observe."

"Ms. Willet, I don't believe we've had the pleasure of meeting before."

"No, Your Honor. I'm new to the Prosecutor's Office."

"Yes, I've heard that Mr. Sexton had landed an experienced advocate from King County. Welcome to Spokane."

"Thank you, Your Honor."

"Ms. Willet, I've read the complaint and sworn affidavits from your witnesses. I see no point in calling Ms. Corliss to testify unless either you or Mr. Walinski think it's necessary."

Walinski spoke first. "Your Honor, I do have a couple of questions I would like to ask Investigator Corliss."

"All right, Ms. Willet, do you have any questions on direct examination or would you like her affidavit to stand as her direct testimony?"

"We'll stand for now on the affidavit, Your Honor, and reserve any questions for redirect."

"Fine. Ms. Corliss, please come over here and my clerk will swear you in."

Corliss raised her hand and swore before God and man that she would tell the whole truth.

"Ms. Corliss, let me get right to the point," Walinski began. "What did you observe after you and your partner ripped the clothes off this terrified four-year old girl?"

"Objection, Your Honor, the question is argumentative."

"Sustained. Mr. Walinski," Judge Romer said, "this is Juvenile Court, we try to be more informal here. Why don't you just ask her what she saw?"

Walinski was only slightly embarrassed. "OK, Ms. Corliss, what did you see after you strip searched Casey Landis?"

"There were bruises. Although they were fading, I would have judged them to be seven to ten days old."

"And do you have a medical background to judge how old bruises are?"

"No, sir. But I have been trained as a Child Protective Services investigator and we are given much training on the nature of bruises. I have had the sad duty to observe dozens of bruises on abused little children in the last six years."

"Can you please describe the bruises for me?"

"They were fading, kind of green and discolored a bit. They didn't look like they had been terribly severe when they were fresh, but I believe that any bruising caused by a parental spanking is child abuse."

"Where were they located?"

"On her buttocks."

"Can you be more specific?"

"On the lower half of the buttocks with a prominence of greater bruising on the left hand side."

"Are you sure you are not mixing this up with some other case?"

"I am absolutely certain of what I have told you."

Her lies were all the more convincing to the judge because Gwen's own lawyer had given Corliss a chance to invent some new details. Corliss lied with conviction and humane concern emoting from her voice.

"Any redirect?" the judge asked Willet after Walinski signaled he was finished by sitting down.

"No, Your Honor. I don't believe I have anything to add after that fine examination by counsel."

Both Walinski and the judge recognized her statement as a cheap shot typical for a Seattle lawyer. Neither of them appreciated it. But both of them knew that her sarcasm was well justified.

"Ms. Willet, do you have anything else?"

"No, Your Honor, the state will rest."

"All right, Mr. Walinski. I have read the affidavits from your client and from the pediatrician. Do you wish to add anything or call any witnesses for clarification?"

Walinski paused a moment. "Your Honor, I think I'll call Gwen Landis to testify."

"All right Mrs. Landis, you may come over here and raise your hand and be sworn."

Walinski began. "Mrs. Landis, please tell Judge Romer your occupation and where you work."

"I am a registered nurse working in the surgical department at Sacred Heart."

"How long have you been a registered nurse?"

"For seven years."

"Are nurses trained to recognize bruises?"

"Yes, we are. All kinds of things cause bruises, and we must be able to recognize bruises from both the severity of the injury and the likely nature of the bruise or contusion as we more often call them in the medical profession."

"In other words, you know a bruise when you see one?"

"Objection," Willet barked. "Leading question."

"It is leading, but its a harmless question. Mr. Walinski, I understand that as a nurse this lady is well-qualified to recognize a bruise. You may go on."

"Thank you, Your Honor. Mrs. Landis, were there any bruises on your daughter's buttocks on Thursday, May 12th, the date Ms. Corliss conducted her little inspection?"

"None whatsoever."

"How do you know?"

"I gave her a bath that morning, and I checked her again after this woman and her partner had finished terrifying my little girl."

"Any fading bruises?"

"No. There were no bruises whatsoever."

"You may inquire," Walinski said looking at Willet.

"Mrs. Landis, you spank your child with a wooden spoon, don't you?"

"Sometimes."

"How often is sometimes?"

"Once or twice a week."

"And how many strokes do you administer each time when you strike her with this implement?"

"It's just a wooden spoon. And I barely tap her."

"Just answer my question. How many strokes do you usually administer?"

"Usually just one. Sometimes two swats. If Casey has done something very bad, I will give her three little swats."

"When was the last time you had spanked Casey with this wooden implement prior to the date in question?"

"About three or four days earlier."

"Three or four days?"

"Yes."

"And how many times did you strike your child on that occasion?"

"Just once and it was light."

"What had Casey done to deserve this spanking?"

"Objection," Walinski said jumping to his feet, nearly upsetting his chair. "It is legal to reasonably spank one's children in the State of Washington—even in Seattle. A parent cannot be put on trial for choosing to spank her daughter. If she injures her that's different. But a parent has the prerogative to use spanking to punish misbehavior without having to justify that decision to the government here."

"I'll let her answer this one question," the judge replied. "But Ms. Willet, I don't want to go too far down this road. Both for the reasons as stated by Mr. Walinski and because I have five other cases to hear after this one. Please get on with it."

"All right, Your Honor. Mrs. Landis, my question is this: What had Casey done to deserve this particular spanking?" Willet continued unfazed.

"She refused to pick up her crayons and coloring book after I told her to do it twice. I always warn her to correct her behavior, and I use spanking only when it appears to me that she is choosing to deliberately disobey. It's the same way my parents raised me and I think I turned out okay."

"Has Casey ever been bruised in any manner whatsoever?"

"Of course, she's a kid. But I have never bruised her by spanking her—ever!"

"That's what I understand your story to be," Willet shot back sitting down.

"Nothing more, Your Honor."

"All right. Mr. Walinski, do you have any more witnesses?"

"No, Your Honor. Unless you want to hear from Mr. Mansfield."

"Mr. Mansfield, I assume that you would testify that your daughter is a good parent and you have never observed bruises on Casey. Is that about right?"

"Yes, that's true, judge."

"Well, in the interest of time, let's just let that stand as Mr. Mansfield's testimony. Is that all right with you, Ms. Willet?"

Willet was going to object to this very informal interchange being considered as formal testimony. However, she wisely decided that the judge was not going to base his decision on the fact that a father would stick up for his daughter and simply said, "That's fine, Your Honor. We don't have anything else, except a few points in argument."

"All right, I'll hear from you now, but please be brief."

"Your Honor, we have a classic case of the word of an officer of the State, Donna Corliss, against the word of the accused mother. Corliss says there were bruises on this little girl. Her mother, of course, denies it. The affidavit from the pediatrician is simply not particularly helpful. The doctor states he examined the girl five days after the CPS worker had conducted her examination. This is more than enough time for the fading bruises to have completely healed from the injury and blows which produced them.

"Keep in mind, Your Honor, we are not asking for permanent custody in this hearing. Just a Shelter Care Order to place this child in an environment we know is safe for seven days. During that time, we can have Casey examined by an independent pediatrician, a psychologist, and I think it would be appropriate to have a psychological and parenting assessment done of Mrs. Landis as well. Ms. Corliss's affidavit details some very strange and uncooperative behavior on Mrs. Landis's part.

"Again, we are simply asking for a seven-day custodial Shelter Care Order to protect this little girl while we check things out."

She sat down and Walinski stood up, knowing he had just been clobbered with an effective summation.

"Well, Your Honor, Ms. Willet correctly framed the key issue: This *is* a case of the CPS worker's word against the word of Gwen Landis. Gwen's a registered nurse and she should know bruises. She has testified there were no bruises. The pediatrician testified there were no bruises. I recognize it was several days later, but if the bruises were as severe as CPS makes them out to be, there should have been something visible for the doctor to see.

"We have to remember, Your Honor, that the state carries the burden of proof here. And I don't think they have done an adequate job of that when the whole case is just one person's word against another. They should have had more. Some other kind of corroborating evidence. This just hasn't been enough."

"Any rebuttal?" the judge asked the prosecutor. She just shook her head.

"Well counsel, this is a close case. And if it were a permanent order or even for a longer period of time than seven days, I would fully agree with Mr. Walinski that this is not enough evidence to remove this girl from her mother."

Gwen's heart began to explode as she correctly discerned what was coming next. Tears filled her eyes.

"But, this is only for seven days. And in case of doubt, I try to resolve these things in favor of the children. It will give us an opportunity to check things out."

The judge observed Gwen's tears which were flowing freely down both cheeks.

"Mrs. Landis, you are probably a good parent. And in all likelihood, this little seven day experience will prove to exonerate you in the end. I'm just trying to think of what's best for Casey. You did bring her today, didn't you?"

Gwen nodded, but Walinski spoke up. "She's in the conference room with her grandmother, Your Honor."

"OK. Fine. Take Casey home, pack her some things, and bring her to the CPS office over on Mission by two this afternoon. We'll schedule a follow-up hearing for a week from today. Ten o'clock. Mrs. Landis, you'll do a lot better with this court if you comply fully with my orders. If you fail to have Casey delivered by two, I will direct the Sheriff to be at your home by two-thirty. Do you understand me?"

"We understand, Your Honor. She'll be there on time," Walinski said protecting Gwen from having to speak while crying.

"I'm sure she will. Thank you. We'll see you here next Tuesday."

The judge left the courtroom and Gwen collapsed in sobs in her father's arms.

5

Gwen could not bring herself to tell Casey what had happened. She just sat in the conference room quietly crying, holding her daughter firmly in her arms. Her father undertook the difficult task of telling Casey she was going to have to live somewhere else for seven days.

"Casey, honey," her Grandpa began, crouching by Casey's side holding her right hand, "I have to tell you something."

Casey looked anxiously about the room, sensing trouble but being too young to guess at its meaning.

"A judge just decided that he wants some special doctors to look at you for a few days. Those ladies who came to your home said some bad things and he wants the doctors to see if it is true."

So far Casey didn't see anything all that terrible from what she was able to comprehend.

"While you are being checked out by these special doctors, you are going to have to stay with a different family."

"Are you going to go with me, too, Grandpa, or just Mommy?" Casey asked with wide-eyed innocence.

"Honey," her grandfather said softly, "none of us get to come with you to this other family's house."

Stan Mansfield kept his grip of reassurance on Casey's hand, but turned his head toward their lawyer. "Mr. Walinski, will you go in and ask the judge if we can give Casey to this family at the prosecutor's office or here at the court—anywhere except the CPS office. Casey is legitimately fearful of those women."

"Sure. I'll have to move fast to see if I can get the prosecutor to come in with me. Technically, I am not supposed to talk with the judge alone about anything of substance." He departed quickly.

Casey's grandmother was on the verge of tears, but maintained her composure. Gwen continued to cry but was more in control than she had been in the courtroom. Her fear that this might happen was somehow worse than the actual event. Perhaps it was the numbness of the moment, perhaps it was her refusal to believe that this would last longer than seven days. Whatever the reason, she was shaken, but clearly not hysterical.

The adults quietly talked over the logistics of gathering Casey's things in words designed to prevent her from understanding if possible. They were reasonably successful in keeping Casey from understanding the full implications of their statements.

About five minutes later, Walinski returned. "It's all set. The foster family will meet us in this room at 2:00 P.M. No CPS workers."

"Thanks," Stan replied with a hint of sharpness in his voice which implied "at least you were able to accomplish *that*."

Gwen finally mustered the composure to speak. "What do we do differently so that we can beat this thing in seven days?"

"Well, we certainly have our work cut out for us," Walinski began. "But the first thing we need to do is get this transfer accomplished. If we don't do that in a timely fashion, this judge will never rule our way next Tuesday. I'll tell you what. Gwen, why don't you and I stay here and let me see if we can figure out what other evidence we can pull together? Mr. and Mrs. Mansfield, you take Casey and get her things and meet us back here at 1:30. OK?"

Gwen was torn. Her mind rebelled at the thought of leaving Casey even for a second, but the idea of going home and packing her things was more than she could bear.

Sensing her indecision, Walinski said, "Gwen, I know you probably want to be with Casey right now, but my schedule is so busy this week I'm going to have a hard time meeting with you to plan strategy any time except right now. I have about an hour or just a bit more."

Gwen reluctantly nodded in approval. "I guess winning is more important than the next couple of hours," she said with a deep sigh.

"All right," Stan replied. "Casey, Grandma and I are going to take you home, pack a few things, and then we will go to Wendy's, and meet your Mommy back here in a few hours."

Casey was used to going and staying with her grandparents and this was perfectly comfortable to her. Judge Romer would have undoubtedly allowed Casey to stay in their custody during the seven day period, if Walinski had thought to suggest it at the time.

Just before the door closed, Gwen gave Casey an impassioned hug and said, "See you soon, Casey doll."

Walinski pulled out his file and yellow legal pad and positioned himself directly across from Gwen as if he were really going to talk legal strategy with her.

"Gwen, I am sorry we lost that hearing, but we can do more next week. Frankly, it was the financial limitations that I was working under which hampered my ability to do everything possible today."

Gwen looked bewildered but waited for him to conclude his thought.

"I had an idea about how we might be able to work out an arrangement on this case that doesn't involve money, and in effect would allow me to do this case for free."

Gwen pushed her long, blond hair behind her left ear. It was a move meant to calm her nerves, but he thought she looked even more alluring and was emboldened to continue.

"Gwen, my marriage is a failure. And I am in real need of female companionship."

She began to understand but was frozen speechless in disbelief.

"And if you could see your way clear to be my special friend for a while, and help me with my need for cozy companionship . . . ."

As he said the word cozy, he reached across the table and placed his left hand firmly on top of her right hand and started to rub her hand with his thumb.

Her temper erupted in undisguised anger. "You pig! You incompetent, immoral pig! You are the most disgusting . . . ."

She had much more to say, but suddenly wanted out more than she wanted to yell at this philandering lawyer.

She ran out the door toward the parking lot behind the court-house complex. After running, panting and crying, she turned the corner of the Public Safety building just to see her father's car half a block away pulling steadily away from her.

Gwen steadied herself on a white Ford Explorer that was parked in the first row of the lot, her panting gradually waning, while her sobs were gaining by the moment.

Suddenly, she felt a presence behind her. She started and whipped around in momentary fright, thinking Walinski had followed her. It was a lawyer, she thought, but, thank God, it wasn't Walinski. He was tall, had black hair that fell slightly over his ears, and had piercing blue eyes.

"Ma'am, is something wrong?" he queried after ten seconds of being stared at by a distraught, beautiful woman.

She tried to speak, but could only shake her head.

"Are you sure there is nothing wrong?" he repeated.

"Yes, but it's not your problem," Gwen said, finally able to gain enough composure to talk.

"Well, in a way it kind of is my problem, I guess."

Gwen gave him a look and said, "What do you mean?"

"You're leaning on my car and unless I am able to help you, it seems that I'll be unable to go back to my law office," he said with a friendly laugh.

Gwen smiled. "Oh, I'm sorry. Let me get out of your way. I hope I didn't get your car dirty or anything."

"Hey, don't worry about it. Listen, I am serious. Can I help you in any way? I can make an educated guess that a woman who is crying in the courthouse parking lot just might need the help of a competent lawyer."

"A competent lawyer? An honest lawyer? Ha! You should have heard what *my* lawyer just said to me."

"Who's your lawyer anyway?"

"Bill Walinski."

"What did he say that upset you so much?"

"You wouldn't believe me if I told you."

"Walinski? He has a reputation. . . ." The lawyer stopped himself, thinking better of telling a stranger of Walinski's scurrilous reputation. "Let's say I'd believe just about anything you might tell me."

"It's kind of embarrassing."

Suddenly he was aware that people were walking by and this woman might need some privacy.

"Listen," he said. "Let me be a bit more professional. My name is Peter Barron. I'm an attorney as you may have guessed. My office is just five minutes away over in the Paulsen Building, across the street from the Old National Bank Building. If you would like, why don't I meet you in my office in ten minutes and let me see if I can help you. Lawyers have an ethical obligation to take cases for free from time to time. I won't charge you to just come talk. OK?"

Gwen was torn. She would be needing another lawyer. He seemed forthright. But another lawyer offering free services?

"Well, that's impossible for me right now," Gwen replied. "My father just left here with my daughter. We were supposed to meet back here at 1:30, but that's a long story involving your friend Mr. Walinski."

"I can't wait to hear the rest of this story. Why don't we just walk over to the Flour Mill, get a table at a restaurant away from other people, and let you tell me your story and see if I can help. What do you say?"

Gwen sighed heavily and relented. With little choice, and a sense of relief, yet mixed lingering apprehension, she said, "OK. That sounds fine."

Peter unlocked his Explorer. "Just let me call my secretary to tell her I won't be back to the office right away." He reached in, pulled the phone out while still standing in the parking lot and punched in the speed dial code for his office.

"Sally, something's come up. I'll be back around one-thirty or a bit after. . . . Oh, that's right. Well, put them in the conference room and have them read all the papers and tell them I'll be there as soon as I can."

He threw in his briefcase after taking out a clean yellow pad, and relocked his car explaining, "Some people coming in at 1:30 to sign some wills. This'll work fine. Come on, let's go find some place to talk."

～

Two disparate couples discussed the same lawsuit over lunch in the Flour Mill that day. The ancient grinding mill, perched on the banks of the Spokane River, had been turned into an upscale mini-mall of gift shops and restaurants.

Down on a lower level of the mill, sitting by the windows facing southwest, was the victor—Donna Corliss, with her boyfriend, Stephen Stockton, catching a quick lunch at Pizza Haven.

Stockton was well into his nine weeks of intensive study for the bar exam. Every evening a two-and-a-half hour session of bar review instruction capped an eight hour day of review, memorization, and practice questions. His dad was adamant about Stephen's schedule even though, one might surmise that having finished at the very top of his class, the younger Stockton would have no difficulty with the bar. His father would never let him forget the story of Raymond Wolff who graduated number one in his class, two years behind the elder Stockton. Wolff flunked the bar exam—twice! It was a story that had been told so many times Stephen wasn't sure whether he wanted to pass the bar to be licensed as a lawyer, or so he would stop hearing the sad tale of Raymond Wolff.

But this luncheon discussion of the law was not of hypothetical exam questions and legal theory. Donna had just been in a real court and Stephen wanted to know all about it.

"So how was the new prosecutor, Gail what's-her-name?" Stockton asked.

"Willet," Corliss answered. "She's fine, and seems to know what she is doing. I like her style—tough."

"But, of course, she had the best investigator in the business digging up facts for her. How could she lose?" Stockton said with an endearing stare.

Smiling with a trace of embarrassment, Corliss lowered her eyes. "Stephen, can I tell you something in absolute confidence?"

"Of course. What is it?"

"I mean really in confidence. You won't get in any legal ethics problems or anything if I tell you something strictly off the record?" Corliss asked.

"Hey, if it makes you feel better, give me a quarter."

"What?"

"Give me a quarter and you have just paid the retainer of the law firm of Wilson, Stockton & Bodecker. I am still officially a legal intern there and now we have an official attorney-client privilege and I cannot say a word. Of course," he continued, "if you would accept my proposal of marriage then you could tell me anything you want and it would all be within the husband-wife privilege. I could never testify against you."

"Stephen, we've been through that before. When you get back from D.C., in two years, I will be thrilled to accept your proposal. I love my work and I just don't want to leave Spokane and try to find social services work in some D.C. bureaucracy."

Grasping her glass with both hands, she continued, "And why did you have to joke about marriage right now? I have something very serious to talk about and I want your promise of confidentiality."

"OK, OK, you've got it."

"Stephen, the reason we won that case today is not because of the facts I dug up in the investigation."

Stephen raised an eyebrow, as if to say, "Excuse me?"

"We won it because of facts I made up in my affidavit."

The soon-to-be lawyer sat absolutely still for more than a moment. Finally he said, "You're kidding, of course."

"No, I am serious. I signed an affidavit that said I saw bruises, fading bruises on this girl, but really I didn't."

Stockton stared in open disbelief.

"You don't understand. You haven't seen all the beaten children I have. Sometimes you have to embellish the facts to advance the cause you believe in," Corliss said.

"What cause were you advancing this way?" Stockton quietly demanded, becoming increasingly nervous that someone might overhear what was being said.

"This woman admitted what her child told us, that she regularly beats her child with a wooden spoon. We didn't find any bruises that day, but there is a 100% likelihood, in my opinion, that when you have a child abuser, sooner or later you are going to have bruises. I did it to protect this little girl. I may not have seen actual bruises, but I know in my heart there are bruises there sometimes, and so the morality of it is just the same."

"Well, I can certainly understand your motivation, but you could get in big trouble for perjury if you were ever caught lying in an affidavit."

"If I only have to face lawyers like the one in there today, I have nothing to worry about," Corliss said. "He was simply not up to it."

"But you might run into a legal buzz saw someday."

"Don't worry, we're very careful," Corliss said rocking slightly in her chair because of her increasing nervousness that her boyfriend seemed truly offended at her behavior.

"Who is this 'we'?" Stephen said, beginning his own cross-examination.

"I think I have probably said enough. Stephen, don't you believe in doing whatever it takes to advance a good cause?"

"Well, sometimes. But this is a little scary. Maybe I've just read a few too many cases about legal ethics and criminal law."

"Didn't you tell me about some famous constitutional case you studied where the woman made up some facts to advance her cause and then years later revealed that the facts had been fictitious?"

"Yes, that was *Roe v. Wade*. But in that case all she said is that she needed an abortion because she had been raped. And it turned out that years later she revealed she had just been involved with her boyfriend."

"Yeah, see," Corliss said with a voice declaring triumph in the argument.

"But that was different, she didn't lie about the central fact in the case. The existence of bruises are the essential facts of your case against this lady. Roe didn't lie about what the modern courts call 'essential facts'." It was a perfect recitation of a law school lecture which he remembered from a class in Constitutional law.

"I don't see the difference. Roe stretched the facts to advance women's rights. I stretched these facts to protect children's rights. It sounds the same to me."

"You've got a good point," Stockton conceded. "But Geez Louise, don't you dare say a word about this to anyone else. You could easily run into someone who had a legal duty to turn this in to the authorities."

"All right, honey I won't. And I'll always have my Washington, D.C., sweetheart to defend me if I am ever falsely accused," she laughed. "I am sure going to miss you when you're in Washington. Don't you want to just stay here and work for your father's firm? Surely he will pay you enough."

"Money's not the issue. My job in Washington is the chance of a lifetime. And it will go quickly. It'll be over before you know it and I'll see you at least three or four times a year. You can come stay with me in my apartment during your vacation."

"Oh, I will miss you so," Corliss said with an affectionate sigh.

"Me too, love," Stockton replied, smiling behind his glass of Coke. But her revelation of perjury cast a shadow on his feelings for her that was cold and dark.

～

In the upper level of the Flour Mill, Peter Barron was anxiously awaiting the chance to hear the story of Gwen Landis. They got outside seats on the deck of Clinckerdagger's Restaurant, an upscale establishment with an Old English motif. Although the day was sunny and bright, the northwest air was still not warm. Even so, Peter chose the outside deck for greater privacy.

Their view of Spokane was quite different from that enjoyed by Corliss and Stockton, although they were only separated by a few hundred feet. They faced the southeast, with a magnificent view of the middle section of Spokane Falls and the maze of second-story skywalks downtown which enable both shoppers and business people to walk throughout the major portion of the downtown area and never go outside. It was a superfluous system on a day like this one. But during the winter, when snow and frozen temperatures prevailed more often than not, it turned the entire downtown into a climate controlled indoor mall.

After the waitress took their order for soft drinks, Peter said, "Well, Gwen, where do you want to start?" During their two-block walk from the courthouse to the Flour Mill, he had uncovered the basic facts of her name, that the case concerned alleged abuse of her daughter Casey, that she was divorced, and worked as a nurse at Sacred Heart Hospital.

"Oh, there's so much to tell. I'm really not sure where I should begin," she said.

"Well, I guess since I'm the lawyer and have my yellow pad, let me walk you through some logical progressions. OK?"

"Sure," she said, glad to have the burden of organizing the presentation off her shoulders.

"The first thing, and this may seem out of order to you, but since you officially have another lawyer, I need to ask you about that to see if it is appropriate for me to undertake your case."

Gwen nodded grimly.

"What happened with good ole Bill Walinski this morning? He really shook you up, didn't he?"

"I still can't believe what happened. And I am more than a little embarrassed to tell you what he said."

"Go ahead. Like I said before, I won't be surprised about anything you say about Walinski."

"To try to put it delicately, he offered to do my case for free from this point forward—my dad already paid him $500—if I would become his 'cozy friend.' I think that's how he put it."

Peter blushed and stared at his napkin on the table for a moment. "Wow. That's unbelievable. Even for Walinski. Are you sure that's what he meant?"

"I have no doubt whatsoever."

"Boy. Well, like I said, with him I would believe almost anything, and while this is shocking, he is one of the few lawyers in town crass enough to make such a proposition. When we get this all behind you, we need to look into a complaint with the state bar association. But you have more important matters at the moment. In any event," he continued, "you have more than enough reason to switch lawyers." He paused and looked her straight in the eyes. "Are you okay? I'm sure that his behavior would shake anyone up pretty good. Are you going to be all right?"

"I really don't have any choice. I've got the custody of my little girl on my mind. And, frankly, I already feel a bit better because of your willingness to at least listen to me. Let's go on."

"OK. Why don't you start from the very first thing that happened?"

The waitress approached with their drinks, and they paused to place their orders for lunch. Gwen's stomach was still unsettled from the events of the morning but she felt she should try to eat something and settled on a chicken caesar salad. Peter ordered the London broil luncheon selection. He knew it would take longer to prepare.

"Well, the very first thing I knew about this was when this child abuse investigator showed up at my house."

"When?"

"Let's see, it was the Wednesday before last," Gwen replied.

"That would be the 11th," Peter noted on his yellow pad. "What time of day?"

"About 9:30 in the morning."

"What did she say she wanted?"

"She wanted to come into the house and talk with Casey. She didn't say anything about strip searching her—"

"Strip searching?" Peter interjected.

"That's what she and a partner did the next day."

"Whoa," Peter said. "This is going to be good. Sorry to interrupt. Let's go back to the first day."

When the waitress brought their food, Peter interrupted his questions to pause and say, "Gwen, is it okay if I give thanks?"

She was surprised but pleased. *A praying lawyer,* she thought. *That's different.*

In twenty-five minutes of careful interviewing, Peter Barron, Esq., learned more about the underlying facts than Bill Walinski knew after several days on the case and, more importantly, after having already conducted a hearing that had cost Gwen the custody of her child.

Gwen could sense the difference in competence in the two lawyers, just by the way she had been interviewed. Peter was thorough and sympathetic. Walinski had been superficial.

"Do I have any chance? What could you have done differently? Can I get Casey back next week?" Gwen pleaded.

"Yes, you have a chance. But I would be a fool to tell you that I can guarantee you victory next Tuesday, especially after you, or should I say your lawyer, lost the first round. And since we don't have a lot of time, let's not focus on exactly what could have been done differently this morning. Let me just tell you some of the things I want to do differently next Tuesday."

Gwen liked his response.

"Let me ask you about one other area first. It's a bit risky, but really offers our very best legal argument for overturning today's ruling."

"What's that?"

"Gwen, tell me about your relationship with your ex-husband."

Gwen was taken aback. Because of the recent incident with Walinski, this was beginning to sound all too familiar. Her radar went on red alert.

"Why? What's that got to do with this?"

Sensing her discomfort, Peter quickly replied, "Don't worry, it's not what you may think. There is a strong legal reason for me bringing this up. Your ex-husband was entitled to formal notice of today's hearing. In the helter-skelter of CPS's effort to take Casey from you, they missed an obvious legal requirement."

Gwen was completely relieved. "Oh, that's why you need to know. That's fine."

"But, before we discuss your relationship," Peter interjected, "let me tell you why I said that this area is risky."

"Sure."

"If we notify your ex-husband—Gordon, isn't it?" Gwen nodded. "Then he has the right to appear at the court hearings and even argue that the court should award custody to him. What I want to know from you is if you think he would want custody, or if he might actually come to court and testify on your behalf? He's absolutely entitled to be notified, and I have a hunch that if we approach him, we are more likely to get him on your side than if the judge suddenly remembers to ask about a father and sends CPS out to find him. What do you think?"

"Oh, boy, I don't know," Gwen said with a rush of air pushing the last word out of her lungs. "When we got divorced, he did not contest custody at all. He has told me lots of times that he thinks I'm a great mother. But he is still really irritated with me, so I'm not sure."

"Why is he so irritated with you?" Peter asked.

"He keeps dropping hints that he wants us to get back together, but he hasn't changed in the slightest since the divorce. In fact, he's gotten worse. He's mad at me because I won't even consider reconciliation. I might if I really saw a dramatic change in him. I haven't really seen anyone else since the divorce. A date or two, but I'm not really ready for anything yet."

"Gwen, why did you two get divorced?"

"It was mainly over money. He refused to get a real job and was always chasing some new idea which would supposedly produce big money overnight. But they were always pipe dreams. I wanted him to get a real job and he just wouldn't. We argued over it a lot. And finally, he moved out and sued me for divorce. A no fault divorce, obviously. Well, he's still chasing dreams, doesn't have a job, and now he's begun to drink heavily. He doesn't pay his child support very often. He's just a mess. Do you really think that the judge would award a man like that custody of Casey?"

"Probably not. With a drinking habit and without a job, probably not. But what you tell me makes me think it is more likely that he can be helpful to us and come to court and testify on your behalf. We can use the failure to notify him as legal grounds to set aside this morning's order. Then we can try to turn him into our witness to get him to refute the idea that you would ever bruise Casey. He could testify that he has never seen bruises on her during your marriage or during any of your visits. I think it's worth a shot."

"Well, okay. Especially if he will get notice eventually anyway. I certainly would rather you talk with him before that Corliss woman gets to him."

"Fine," Peter said. "He is step one. I've got three other steps I want to try for sure. Maybe more later. I want to subpoena the other social worker and the police officer. I'll get their names from the prosecuting attorney. She'll have to give them to me as well as a copy of all reports. I want to see if their story holds up under cross-examination with only one of them in the courtroom at a time.

"And then, I am going to bring Dr. Davenport in for live testimony. I am sure he will be much more convincing in person than in a short affidavit. I'd be surprised if Walinski even thoroughly prepared Davenport's affidavit giving a complete history of absence of bruises."

Gwen smiled. This was aggressive. This man seemed like he really wanted to fight for her. But then, she remembered a problem area—money. "How am I going to pay you for all of this? I simply can't afford to pay very much at all. And my parents went to their financial limit giving Walinski $500."

Peter smiled and sighed a little. "You know, if it weren't for what happened with Walinski, I would offer to do this for free. But you might suspect my motives if I did that. Here's my best offer, take it or leave it. I will charge you $75 an hour for all the work after this lunch. This has been truly free. I won't charge more than $1250 for doing your case in Juvenile Court. I know that may sound a lot to you. But here's the kicker. You can pay me as little as $25 a month, and I'll never charge you a dime of interest. That way I figure I might get to keep you as a regular client in case anything else ever came up."

Gwen smiled in obvious approval. A thought of doubt shot through her mind like a rifle.

"Mr. Barron," she began.

"Please. Call me Peter."

"OK, Peter. Well, what I was going to ask is this: Why are you doing this? Why are you being so nice? After this morning I don't know if I can trust anybody. What's in this for you?"

Peter looked at her. Something inside him wanted to sigh. She was indeed beautiful, and he had always been a sucker for a damsel in distress. He stared off at the River for a moment, and then turned back and looked her squarely in the eyes.

"Gwen, I'm trying to decide how to tell you this. Some of it's a little personal."

Gwen immediately thought he was going to tell her, "I'm gay." She braced for the worst.

"Gwen, I'm a born-again Christian."

This is really weird, she thought, *Why is he telling me this?*

"My faith is based upon the Word of God. And, as a side note, one of the reasons I want to help you is that the Bible says a lot about helping widows and orphans. But the Bible also gives a number of principles for daily living, which I do my best to follow because I want to please my Lord Jesus."

It was all sounding like church camp, but Gwen continued to smile pleasantly and occasionally nodded in apparent understanding.

"Because of my beliefs—I'll explain them more to you some other day—you can be guaranteed I won't be coming after you—at anytime. I'll treat you like a sister, nothing more. OK?"

Gwen caught herself staring back at Peter in confusion and quickly reached for her drink. After the earlier events of the day it was a comparatively mild shock.

She shook her head a little from side to side.

"Peter, I'm sorry. I really don't understand. After all that's happened . . ." She paused and stared at her half eaten salad.

"You seem so nice, but this has been such a strange day. I guess I just can't take anything for granted. Why don't you explain it to me now? About your beliefs or whatever it is."

Peter began to wish he hadn't opened the entire subject. He knew he wasn't another Walinski, but in trying to prove it he had made a verbal mess for himself. But he mustered up a smile and launched in.

"Gwen, it's just this," he said with a hush in his voice.

"I believe that the Bible teaches that as a single man I am unable to marry a woman who was divorced under circumstances like yours. Not all born-again Christians believe this. But I do. So because of that . . ."

He paused for a moment, looked down briefly, and continued, "Because of that I would never begin to pursue a relationship with you. I would like to be your lawyer and your friend, but . . . nothing more. I shouldn't have brought this all up. I just wanted you to know that you could trust me to do you a favor, without an ulterior motive. OK?"

"OK, I guess. Just help me get Casey back. That's all I want." Gwen surprised herself at feeling a hint of rejection in what Peter had said. She couldn't sort it all out but was relieved to find a lawyer who seemed to have a better idea of how to fight for her beloved Casey.

Gwen glanced down at her watch. It read 1:20. "Oh my goodness!" she exclaimed. "I've got to meet Casey and my parents in ten minutes."

Peter threw a $20 bill quickly on the table and said, "Let's go. Barron's shuttle service at your command."

As they neared the courthouse, Peter said, "One last thing. I need you to write down every single word and action you can remember about the two CPS visits to your home and bring them to me in my office tomorrow at 9:00 A.M. sharp."

"OK," Gwen replied. "I'll write you a prize essay."

Peter could tell she was feeling better under his care. He liked it whenever a client expressed confidence in him. But despite his lecture about scriptural principles, there was something else mingled in his mind about this particular client.

6

~

Gwen and Peter made it back to the conference room before Casey and her grandparents. Peter stepped out to the clerk's office, used the phone to tell Sally that he would be about twenty minutes late, to apologize profusely to the clients, and ask them to begin reading their wills.

He stepped back into the conference room only moments before Casey and Stan and June Mansfield entered the room. Stan was carrying a small blue suitcase.

"Gwen, what happened to Bill Walinski?" her dad began. "And, I don't mean to be rude, but who's this?" he said gesturing toward Peter.

"Mr. Mansfield, I'm Peter Barron. I'm an attorney and Gwen just kind of ran into me in the parking lot here at the courthouse after an unfortunate incident with Mr. Walinski. Gwen should probably tell you about the incident with Mr. Walinski at a more private moment," he said with a knowing glance directed at Casey.

"Mr. Barron is going to be taking over our case," Gwen said. "He's got some really good ideas. I'll tell you about it in a few minutes."

"Gwen, will you introduce me to your daughter?" Peter asked.

"Of course. Where are my manners? Casey, this is Mr. Barron. He's a lawyer, a new lawyer who is going to help Mommy against those ladies who scared you so much."

Without approaching the little girl, Peter crouched down to her eye level, and smiled warmly at Casey. He raised his right hand and waved as he gently said, "Hi Casey. I just wanted to meet you so I can know such a special little girl. Your Mommy and I are going to

65

work together to protect you from those ladies. We're going to work really hard."

Casey barely understood a word he said but felt no impulse to shrink back from him. She did understand that he didn't like those ladies either. She smiled, and not knowing what else to do, just looked at her mother.

Peter stood up and said, "I think it would be best for you to spend the rest of the time until two with just family. I'll get right to work. Gwen, I'll see you in the morning."

⌣

The transfer of Casey was tearful, but without hysterics. Casey simply could not understand why her mommy could not come with her. And no explanation they offered could suffice.

The foster parents, Tom and Brenda MacArthur, were kind people who seemed to understand the trauma of all concerned. Brenda repeatedly promised Gwen that she would take good care of Casey. They also arranged a time for Gwen to call each day to talk with Casey. CPS hadn't told them to do that; the MacArthurs simply took the initiative out of compassion for both Casey and her mom.

As soon as the door shut behind the MacArthurs, Gwen fell into her father's arms for her most violent cry of the day. She had been trying her best to be calm for Casey's sake, but as soon as she was gone, all restraint gave way.

When she had calmed down a good deal, Stan said, "Gwen, she'll be all right."

"That's right, honey," June added. "They seem like real nice people."

"Gwen, I am dying to know what happened with Walinski and all about this new guy. What in the world has been going on for the last couple hours?" her dad asked.

After Gwen related Walinski's indecent proposal, Stan was glad that he was not in the courthouse. He might be the next one in trouble—for murder. His fury abated to controllable anger after Gwen related Peter's idea of pursuing a complaint with the bar association after the child abuse case was completed.

Gwen explained Peter's plan to approach Gordon and to use his lack of notification to blow the case wide open. His plans to subpoena the CPS worker, the police officer, and to obtain all the reports.

"Well, sounds like you found a real go-getter. Where did he come from anyway?" Stan asked.

"When I ran out of here to get away from Walinski, I ran to the parking lot to catch you guys, but you were too far away. I was leaning on his car crying. He either had to help me or else wait until I got done getting his door all wet," Gwen laughed.

Her mother spoke. "Well, he seems like a wonderful young man and a very competent lawyer. But who can tell these days? Are you sure that he is on the level? He's very handsome. Maybe he's on the make as well, but just more subtle."

"That's something that's a bit confusing," Gwen replied. "I said something to him that brought up the same issue you're asking about. He went into this long explanation that he's a born-again Christian and can't marry divorced women—or something like that. But he said he was only telling me all this so that I would know he is safe after the incident with Walinski. I didn't understand all his Bible talk, but he seems totally sincere, very aggressive as a lawyer, and just very, very nice. And what other choice do I have?"

"How are you going to pay him?" her dad asked.

"He told me that he might have done it for free but after Walinski, he didn't want me to question his motives. He said he would charge $75 an hour, and no more than $1250."

"But that's a lot of money. We can't afford it and neither can you," her dad countered.

"He told me that I would only have to pay him $25 a month and he would never charge me any interest."

"Well, that's pretty generous really," Stan said, seeming convinced.

"What are we supposed to do next?" her mom asked.

"I'm supposed to write down everything that happened at home when those CPS witches came out both times. He's going to start gathering their reports and subpoenaing witnesses. In one meeting he's already got more plans than Walinski was able to figure out in days," Gwen said.

"I think he spent his time plotting something else," Stan said with jaws clenched. "That bird is going to pay for that."

"Now, Stan," his wife said, "let's not do anything in anger that will only cause us all more trouble with Casey."

"Humph," Stan replied. It was the standard answer he had developed in over forty years of marriage when he was giving in to his wife's position in an argument, but still wanted to cling for another minute to his own view.

∿

Peter Barron's office location was strategic for small firms or solo practitioners. It was in the core of the business district connected to the skywalk system. The Paulsen Building was an older, but well-maintained building which did not demand unreasonably high rent. And more importantly for beginning firms, the Spokane County Law Library was located on the tenth floor of the building. This saved an enormous expense of buying one's own legal collections in the early days of a practice.

The prestige firms of forty to sixty lawyers had their offices consisting of whole floors—sometimes two floors—in the newer bank building towers. They maintained substantial libraries in their own suites. If they needed anything extra, a law clerk or associate was quickly dispatched to the Gonzaga Law Library with its exhaustive collection.

Peter had opened his solo office in the Paulsen Building three years earlier. It had been six years since he first began practicing law. The first three years after graduating from Gonzaga law school were spent across the street in the Old National Bank Building. He had been a promising associate with the firm of Parker, Thompson, Traughber & Darling. Like most associates in Spokane, he had clerked part-time for the firm during his last two years of law school. About a year before he would have normally been offered a partnership in the firm, he decided to leave and go into solo practice.

It was an amicable parting. Peter merely wanted to avoid the impulse of a large firm to cause a partner to become too specialized.

The pay would have been fantastic, but he wanted a wider range of practice.

The parting had been so amicable that occasionally the firm would send Peter a case which they couldn't take because of a conflict of interest. Once there had been a major business case that Peter felt was beyond his resources, and he had gone to the firm and asked them to take over as lead counsel while he continued to work with them on the case.

The second reason he left the firm was one which Peter kept to himself and his closest personal friend, Aaron Roberts. Peter's Christian faith occasionally came into conflict with the firm's practices. The issues were not unethical in a conventional sense—Parker, Thompson, Traughber & Darling practiced the highest standard of legal ethics. Peter simply was bothered by the idea of being a partner with a firm that was deeply involved in divorce work and the defense of criminals whether or not they were really guilty. He knew that his views were not shared by all other born-again Christians, but his own inner being simply was not comfortable being directly involved in breaking up marriages and defending the truly guilty. He was happy as an associate because he was never required to work on such cases. But if he became a partner, he felt he would have a moral responsibility for all the work of the firm.

Peter's practice had grown steadily over the last three years. And last March 25, when he celebrated his thirty-second birthday, he hired his first associate. Joe Lambert had been out of law school for two-and-a-half years—a University of Idaho graduate. He had been an assistant United States Attorney since passing the bar, but after the Clinton administration replaced the Republican who had been Joe's boss, he decided to leave even though he officially had the right to remain. He met Peter through the Spokane chapter of the Christian Legal Society during their monthly luncheon meeting.

～

Joe had just begun to discuss the clients' wills with them when Peter burst into the office twenty-five minutes late.

He thanked and excused Joe and apologized profusely to the couple, telling them the truth. He had run into a woman at the courthouse who had a legal emergency involving the custody of her child. The retired couple, who attended Peter's church, Valley Fourth Memorial, were sympathetic and understanding.

When they were signed, notarized and gone, Peter called Sally and Joe into his office for an emergency conference.

"I have just taken on a case with a great deal of urgency," Peter began.

"I hope it pays well," said Sally who was not only the firm's secretary but also the bookkeeper. The firm was doing reasonably well, but there were months that it took until the 30th to come up with all the necessary revenue to cover the bills.

"It'll be OK, don't worry about it," Peter replied.

Joe and Sally looked at each other and grinned. "Another time payment case," they said in mock unison.

"Ha, ha," Peter replied with an annoyed voice but smiling eyes. "In any event the case will be over, or at least probably will be over, in seven days. I've got a lot of work to do and I really want to win. I want the two of you to get together and scrutinize my schedule. Joe, I want you to take over anything you believe is within your experience level, and look at everything else to see if it can be continued, postponed, or cancelled. Come back to me in an hour with a list of everything that I simply must do between now and next Tuesday. The hearing in this case is Tuesday at ten and I want to focus as much time as possible on it. OK?"

"Aye, aye, Sir," Sally said, standing with a tongue-in-cheek salute.

"What's it about, Peter?" Joe asked.

"A single mom lost custody of her child this morning to CPS in a hearing before Judge Romer. She's a nurse at Sacred Heart and I think she's innocent. Bill Walinski represented her."

"No wonder she lost," interjected Joe, who had prosecuted a couple of drug dealers Walinski had represented in federal court. Joe sent them to the federal pen with maximum sentences.

"And to top it off, when the case was over, Walinski had the audacity to tell this grieving mom that he would do the rest of her case for free if she would sleep with him. I found her crying in the parking lot, leaning against my car."

Joe's sense of righteous indignation was ignited. "Good grief! No wonder some people rate lawyers below pond scum. Why don't we do her case for free?"

"I have every intention of forgiving her obligation to pay me $25 a month once the case is over. I didn't want her to think I was another Walinski by offering to do it for free."

"Did Walinski have a good reason to make his pitch, or was he bottom fishing?" Joe asked out of Sally's hearing.

"She *is* gorgeous. Incredibly gorgeous."

"And available?" Joe asked, goading Peter just a bit. Joe was happily married with a three-year-old son.

"Not for me," Peter replied. "She was divorced without scriptural grounds. You know my rule."

Joe shrugged and smiled, wishing his highly eligible boss would find the right Christian woman to marry and settle down.

"There actually may be a way to make some real money off this case after we win this round. If the facts develop right, I am thinking about a federal civil rights lawsuit against the CPS investigators. They strip searched a four year old girl without a warrant."

"You know how hard civil rights cases are to win against social workers. When the courts hear 'child abuse' all the normal rules of constitutional law just seem to sail out the window," Joe replied.

Peter appreciated Joe's substantial federal court experience in evaluating such cases.

"I hope you didn't build up her hopes about such a lawsuit," Joe continued.

"Not one word. Didn't say a thing," Peter answered. "I only focused on this next hearing. If we don't win her child abuse case, any thoughts of a civil rights case will fly away. I know a federal jury would never award damages to a convicted child abuser."

"You're smarter than you look," Joe replied with a laugh. "We'll clear the decks for you, Peter. This may not be the most important case we ever get involved with legally or financially, but after what happened to this lady with Walinski, it may be one of the most noble things our firm will ever do."

"Get to work," Peter said in mock anger.

∽

Peter's first call was to Bill Walinski. Before he could officially begin work on the case he had to secure Walinski's withdrawal.

"Bill Walinski, please, this is Attorney Peter Barron calling."

"I'm sorry he's on another call, but I'll slip him a note to let him know that you're holding if you would like," said the secretary while flicking her cigarette. Walinski wasn't really on another line, but the I-will-slip-a-note answer was part of the regular drill to make Walinski seem important to the caller, and at the same time make the caller feel important as well.

I've trained that girl well, Walinski said to himself as he put his feet up on his desk while reaching for the phone.

"Peter, this is Bill Walinski, how can I help you?" When another attorney called Walinski he was usually happy. It normally meant he was being called about some case in progress and this meant he got to bill someone for talking on the phone.

"Bill, I need you to immediately prepare and fax me a substitution of counsel in the Gwen Landis case," Peter said going straight to the point.

"What? What are you talking about?"

"You know very well what I am talking about. I found Gwen in tears in the parking lot after your— let's just call it your unusual offer."

"I have no idea what you are talking about," Walinski retorted.

"I don't want to argue about this. And realistically I don't expect you to admit any wrongdoing to me over the phone. Just sign the substitution, fax it to me, and I will take over without further fuss, at least for now."

"If Gwen calls me and asks me personally to withdraw, I will," Walinski countered.

"It's your right, of course, to have the client personally discharge you. And I will tell Gwen to do that if you insist. However, if you make her call you for this, I will first give her the number of the ethics office of the state bar in Seattle."

The phone went dead for twenty seconds. Walinski finally said, "What's your fax number?"

"555-3022. Ten minutes. I'm giving you ten minutes. Good-bye."

~

He placed another call.

"Prosecuting Attorney's Office."

"Gail Willet, please. This is Attorney Peter Barron calling."

"Just a moment."

Forty-five seconds later a stern voice said, "This is Gail Willet."

"Ms. Willet, my name is Peter Barron, I'm an attorney calling about Gwen Landis."

"Ms. Landis already has an attorney. I was just in court with him this morning. Walinski I believe the name was."

"Mrs. Landis has decided to substitute counsel and I'll be appearing on her behalf next Tuesday at the hearing."

"I can't discuss anything about the case with you until I get the substitution of counsel."

Just like a Seattle lawyer, Peter thought. *Hypertechnical.*

"You'll have the substitution form by fax within half an hour," Peter said tersely. "And along with that, you will get a written request for all reports by social workers and police officers. I understand there were three people who entered the Landis home. I would like all three of their reports. This case is of the utmost importance, as I am sure you will agree, and I'm coming in late and must hustle. I'd like to pick these up by 4:30 at your office."

"That's pretty quick. Hey, I will give you a continuance for an extra week if you need more time to prepare," Willet said.

"That would be fine if you return custody of Casey to her mother in the meantime," Barron rebutted. "No, we want to go forward as soon as possible to get this mother reunited with her daughter."

"I'm not sure that I can get all the reports by four-thirty. I only have the Corliss report now."

"Since we haven't met," Peter began, "you wouldn't have the opportunity to know that I normally try to extend every courtesy to opposing counsel. And when we deal with each other in the future, I'm sure I'll have a chance to show you that I'm easy to work with. But I really must move quickly if I'm going to properly represent this lady next week. Please have your people fax the report to you, and I will pick them up personally at 4:30. OK?"

"I'll try to do what I can, assuming I get the substitution of counsel."

"You'll get it in just a few minutes," said Peter, who could hear his fax phone ringing in the background. "Thanks so much for your cooperation. I look forward to meeting you on Tuesday if not before."

Gail Willet immediately knew that she would be challenged by a much more aggressive lawyer at the next hearing. She smiled at the idea. She didn't just like winning. She liked beating the best. *Maybe this Peter Barron will be a worthy adversary. He'd have to be better than that half-witted idiot this morning,* she thought.

～

At three-thirty the white Explorer pulled up in front of an apartment complex on the corner of Euclid Avenue and Northwest Boulevard. Peter looked at the directory, chose the building on the right and went down a half-flight of stairs to the first floor units. At the first door on the left, he paused and rang the bell.

A man about his own age answered the door. He was a fairly good looking man, slightly taller than Peter, with sandy hair. He was a little too thin, and his eyes revealed that all was not well. The chief color was neither brown, nor blue, nor green; red was the dominant effect.

Peter noticed the eyes, *There's more of a drinking problem here than Gwen seemed to indicate,* he thought.

"Yeah?" Gordon Landis said after he had looked the well-dressed stranger up and down.

"Mr. Landis? I'm Peter Barron. I'm an attorney and I'd like to talk with you."

"About what?"

"About your daughter and former wife."

"Hey, it's not my fault I'm behind in my support. I just can't find steady work." He began to shut the door. Peter reached out his hand and blocked the door.

"No, no. It's not about child support. I'm not here to give you a hard time. There's a bit of trouble, and I'm here to see if you will be willing to help them."

"What?" Gordon said opening the door again part-way.

"Mr. Landis, I think it would be better if I came in and told you about all this in private. I assure you I am just here to seek your support for Gwen and Casey."

Something in the way Peter said their names shot a pang of jealousy through Gordon. But he said, "Come on in—for just a minute."

The apartment wasn't in a terrible mess as Peter half-expected. A couple of shirts, a few newspapers, a couple dozen beer cans sitting here and there.

The living room was behind the kitchen and a sliding glass door looked out on a bit of grass and the apartment parking lot. The curtain was half-open and a fair amount of sunlight came in. Gordon sat heavily on the couch and gestured for Peter to sit in the only chair.

"Mr. Landis, your daughter and wife are having trouble with the child welfare authorities."

Gordon replied with a quizzical look.

"Someone called the child abuse hotline and claimed that Gwen spanks Casey excessively, some CPS workers charged in the home, strip searched Casey, and claimed they found some bruises. Gwen and Dr. Davenport, Casey's pediatrician, deny that there have ever been any bruises."

Gordon blushed, but Peter ignored it, assuming the color in his face was induced by excessive alcohol.

"This morning, a judge took custody away from Gwen for seven days so she could be evaluated by another doctor and a psychologist. A foster family has custody in the meantime."

It was far more than Gordon had bargained for. He didn't want this much trouble. And he knew that if it was ever discovered he had made the call, the chances of Gwen returning to him would be gone forever.

"You're kidding," Gordon said. "Gwen's a good mom. She would never do that. We don't get along about everything, but she's a good mom to Casey."

Peter exhaled heavily with relief. "That's what I was hoping you would say. I just met her this morning after the hearing and that's my impression as well. But obviously, you can give us a real opinion, not just a superficial impression."

"What happened in the hearing? why did she lose custody?"

"First of all, she had another lawyer who probably mishandled the case. And afterward he was extraordinarily rude to Gwen. She literally ran into me in the parking lot, and after some discussion, I agreed to take over."

"So what do you want from me?"

"Mainly, your cooperation. One of the chief legal mistakes made in this morning's hearing was the failure to notify you of the proceedings. You had an absolute right to be notified about the hearing. No one brought you any legal papers telling you of the hearing, did they?"

"No way."

"That's what I thought," Peter said with a half-smile. "That's really helpful."

"What I'd like to do, is prepare an affidavit for you to sign. That's a written statement you sign before a notary. I just want you to make two points: one, that you didn't receive any notice of the hearing and that you demand your rights of notice; and two, that Gwen is a good mom and has never bruised Casey by spanking her. That's all true isn't it?"

"Sure it's true," Gordon said with conviction. "But how do I write this affidavit thing?"

"Don't worry, I'll write it for you. I'll just put down what you have told me and you can read it to make sure it's all correct."

Gordon nodded with a semi-audible grunt of acknowledgment.

Normally, Peter would have asked Gordon to come to his office to sign the affidavit. But this was too important and Gordon seemed of questionable reliability, so he said, "OK, I'll bring you the affidavit tomorrow. What time will be good for you?"

"Oh, anytime. I'm out of work right now, been lookin' real hard though."

"How about 10:30?"

"Fine with me," Gordon said with relief. He didn't want to be awakened too early.

Peter got up, shook Gordon's hand and walked to the door. "Your cooperation will really help your daughter and wife, I mean former wife—sorry."

"I'm sorry she's my former wife, too. I'd like her back anytime," Gordon said with discernible sadness. "Anytime," he repeated closing the door.

~

At four o'clock Gail Willet was in her office carefully scrutinizing every word of the written reports of Rita Coballo and Officer Donahue. After a third reading, she concluded there was nothing remarkable in them and that she would turn them over to Barron without a fight.

She handed them to her secretary to make copies and leave them on the receptionist's desk for Peter Barron. The secretary assured Ms. Willet that the receptionist would recognize Barron by sight—asking for his Bar Identification Card would not be necessary. "He's something of a minor heartthrob here in Spokane. All the receptionists know him," the secretary laughed with a touch of disdain.

Gail picked up the phone and called Donna Corliss. She asked about the schedule for the psychological assessments of mother and child, and the physical screening for Casey. The physical had been scheduled for Wednesday at 2:30 P.M. with Dr. Stratton. The child would be taken to Dr. McGuire for psychological evaluation on Thursday at 10:00 P.M. Corliss had decided to use McGuire to do the psychological and parenting assessment of Gwen Landis as well. She was expected in his office Thursday at 5:00 P.M.

Willet concluded the call and quickly dictated an appropriate notice to require Gwen Landis to present herself to Dr. McGuire as scheduled. She wanted the paper served on Barron when he arrived at four-thirty. The receptionist would now be required to obtain Barron's signature on a proof of service as well.

Willet, satisfied everything was under control in the Landis case, turned her focus to a stack of cases which also called for her attention.

~

At five o'clock, Peter was back in his office with the reports and the notice requiring Gwen's examination by Dr. McGuire. He dialed the number for Sacred Heart Hospital and after two transfers, got his newest client on the phone.

"Gwen, this is Peter Barron. I just wanted to update you on the case and tell you about a scheduling issue."

"Peter, I appreciate you being so quick to respond, but I really can't talk for more than a minute or so right now. I have my lunch break at seven for thirty minutes. Can I call you then?"

"Well, that will be difficult. After six our incoming phone calls are intercepted by an answering service. What if I meet you in the cafeteria at seven, and bring you up to speed?"

Gwen was about to decline, preferring a phone call. But then Peter added, "I went and talked with Gordon. I thought you'd want to know."

"OK. Seven in the cafeteria," Gwen replied decisively. "It might take me a minute or two to get there. You know where it is?"

"I'll find it and I'll wait."

～

Peter read and reread the three reports. Corliss's report was essentially identical to her affidavit. He got the copy of the entire court file from the clerk after filing the substitution of counsel. The clerk's office was just the other side of the judicial complex from Gail Willet's office. While he was there, he asked them to copy the tape recording of the hearing. It would be ready tomorrow by midday.

Peter found little on which to build his case in the reports. But after thirty minutes of pacing, reading, and staring out his window, he noticed a few issues that bore investigation.

Why was there no mention of bruises in the police officer's report?

Why were there no pictures taken of the bruises? Pictures of bruises were a CPS trademark.

Why was there no description of the bruises in either the Corliss or Coballo reports? Both noted the existence of bruises, but other than the term 'fading bruises' any particular description was missing.

Peter was hoping for a smoking gun, some clear discrepancy. The best he could do for now was find some unanswered questions to focus on. It was better than nothing, but not yet very much to go on.

～

Peter pulled into the Sacred Heart parking lot at 6:45 P.M. With the help of some giggling high school Candy Striper volunteers, Peter easily found his way through the maze of corridors to the cafeteria. He leaned against the wall, just outside the entrance for the serving line, and waited.

A couple of doctors who passed by gave him cold stares as they entered the serving area. They could smell any lawyer for miles and especially detested lawyers who hung around hospitals.

Presently Gwen Landis came striding down the hall in her nursing whites. Peter couldn't help staring at her. A smile broke out on his face involuntarily. And with the smile, there came a momentary pang of spiritual conviction. He realized that he was not guarding his heart very well. Not only was Gwen divorced, he had no reason to assume she was a believer. He had very strict standards and had not dated a nonbeliever in years. He focused his mind quickly on his legal mission, and greeted Gwen with a mix of warmth and professionalism.

"Hi, Gwen. Two meals in one day," he said with a soft laugh.

"Hi. Thanks for being here, but this is hard for me," Gwen said quietly. "I'm going home in a few hours and my baby will be gone." Her lower lip was trembling slightly.

Peter shifted his weight uncomfortably. "I'm sorry, Gwen. I get so wrapped up in strategy and trying to win I sometimes forget the human costs of lawsuits. But I do have some good news for you."

Gwen did her best to smile bravely and turned to go through the food line. Peter paid for both their meals after a brief protest and they found a fairly secluded table in a far corner of the cafeteria.

"What happened with Gordon?" Gwen demanded as soon as they sat down.

"It went really pretty well. He had not been notified as we guessed. And he assured me that you were a good mom and had never bruised Casey."

"Great. But will he testify in court?"

"I think so. He promised to sign an affidavit for me in the morning. He seems very eager to be in your good graces."

This was a touchy point with Gwen. "What condition did you find him in?"

"It was obvious he had been drinking," Peter said with a sad shake of the head. "A lot. His eyes were awful. But he spoke clearly and I don't think he was drunk at the time. Both he and his apartment showed signs that he does not go for long stretches of sobriety."

"Pooh. And I suppose he was home in the middle of the day because he still doesn't have a job."

"You're a good supposer. But, don't be so hard on him, I think he's going to be very helpful to you next Tuesday."

Gwen stared at her tray of food. She looked up at Peter, and said with measured words, "I'm sorry to be so bitter. And I certainly don't like being divorced. But Gordon simply let me down far too many times and it hurts a lot. He was more committed to his dreams of quick riches than he was to me and our daughter."

Peter was anxious to change the subject. "There are two other developments I need to discuss with you, and we don't have a lot of time. Half an hour? That's all they give you?"

"Normally I just have to eat, not tell my life history," Gwen replied brightening just a bit.

"On Thursday at 5:00 you are expected to be at the office of a psychologist named Dr. McGuire for an evaluation. I assume that the judge ordered that today."

"Oh. I had forgotten that. Do I have any choice?"

"Probably not at this point. I think our best strategy is to cooperate as much as possible with this judge through the week and try to win his favor in the next hearing."

"I have to go to work at 3:00 on Thursday. Can't you change it?"

"Perhaps. If not, can you change your shift and work mornings that day?"

"Probably. Normally, I'm reluctant to do that because I want to spend the day with Casey, but that's not an issue right now." Tears were visible in Gwen's eyes, but they didn't spill over.

"OK, why don't you pursue that first. I'm also going to have a friend of mine who's a psychologist do an independent evaluation. Jean Schram—she's a good friend and a good psychologist."

"How much will that cost?"

"I think Dr. Schram will do it pretty inexpensively, and whatever it is, I'll pay and just add it to your bill. Three or four more months of twenty-five dollar payments, that's all."

Gwen smiled and looked at Peter with genuine gratitude. He seemed so eager to help and please her. He really was an interesting guy. But she quickly dismissed the thought when she remembered Peter's "Bible speech" at lunch.

"One last thing," Peter said. "I read the reports of both CPS investigators and the police officer. No smoking guns, but some interesting things are left out."

"Like what?" Gwen asked with genuine curiosity.

"Three things have surfaced so far. First, there is no mention of pictures of the bruises. CPS almost always takes pictures of the bruises. Second, neither CPS worker described the bruises in any detail in her report. I find that unusual. Finally, the police officer's report is silent about bruises."

"Bruises, bruises. My life hangs on the issue of bruises. We see bruises in here all the time. A bruised child is possibly abused, but bruises can come from so many sources. Some children bruise so easily that a light swat that would not be truly damaging will leave them with a substantial bruise."

"Is Casey like that?" Peter asked.

"No. She has very normal skin and it was flawless on the day those witches invaded my house."

"Well, you've got to go, I guess," Peter said looking at his watch. "Don't forget. I need your written recollections by nine in the morning."

"Oh yeah, I started it this afternoon. I'll get up early and finish it in the morning. I hope it helps."

"Me too," said Peter as they stood and left the table.

The handsome couple turned heads as they passed without a word through the corridors and up the elevator to Gwen's floor. Her fellow surgery nurses tried to ignore Peter as he said good-bye to Gwen at the elevator landing. But as soon as he was gone, they cornered Gwen saying, "Who was *that*?"

"He's just my lawyer," Gwen replied.

Normally they would have teased her, but everyone at the hospital knew about Casey. They simply dropped the subject and went about their business.

7

~

It was their usual meeting place for such a rendezvous—the Ram's Head Tavern just south of the intersection of 57th and Regal. It was a pickup truck type of tavern and Randall's BMW and Gerald's Celica were conspicuous when they arrived.

The tavern was located on the far south side of Spokane, outside the city limits. Close by were a conglomeration of radio and TV towers, just on the edge of the metropolitan area and less than five miles from where serious agricultural operations began.

Randall arrived first and waited in the corner with a Coors while Clint Black serenaded the patrons from an old juke box. A redheaded waitress in her late thirties came by three times in ten minutes. Randall glanced up at her but wasn't interested in what she was selling. The years had not been kind to her.

Gerald finally arrived and ordered a Coors Light and ignored Lila's efforts to gain attention. They immediately got to work.

"I understand you have another special case for me," Randall said.

Gerald nodded, sipping his beer. "It's very important to us."

"They always are," Randall replied. "Who are we dealing with?"

"The mother's name is Gwen Landis, her daughter is Casey, age four. She's accused of spanking the girl and leaving bruises. The mother admits spankings with a wooden implement, but denies the bruises," Gerald said.

"You know how I feel about parents who hit their children," Randall replied, shaking his head in disgust.

"That's why we come to you. We know you are on our team . . . and are reasonably willing to do what it takes to advance the cause of children," Gerald replied.

"If we were in Seattle or Portland or San Francisco, we could do this openly. Most juvenile judges there share our convictions. But these Spokane judges live too close to the boonies. Bruises are their threshold. No bruises, no action."

Randall nodded in agreement.

"Well, what do I need to do?"

"You are going to interview both mother and child on Thursday. We want the report to be professional, but spun in such a way that these yokel judges will bite."

"No problem. I can spin with the best of them. You understand I must tell the truth, but whenever our arrangement is in place I am willing to tell it creatively."

Gerald pulled the envelope out of his inner jacket pocket and laid it on the table. "I need the report by ten Friday morning."

"It's half written already," Randall said with a laugh. "I'll bill you for the official fee in due course."

Gerald stood. "You'll take care of the tab for the beer?"

"It's the least I can do to show my gratitude," Randall replied, raising his glass to Blackburn.

Gerald Blackburn, "Top Child Advocate of 1993," left quietly, got into his Celica and headed south. Randall McGuire, Ph.D., sat at the table for another ten minutes, counted twenty one hundred dollar bills in the envelope, then got in his BMW and headed for his spacious home on the seventh hole of the Manito Country Club, only ten minutes but a world away from the Ram's Head.

~

Peter returned to the Paulsen Building from his "fine dining" experience at the Sacred Heart cafeteria. Using his pass key, he entered the Spokane County Law Library located two floors below his office.

His first selection was with the Revised Code of Washington, the series of books containing all laws for the Evergreen State. Lawyers aren't expected to have the law completely memorized, but they are expected to know how to find it. Within two minutes he had found and marked for copying, the controlling statute. It provided that the kind of hearing scheduled on Tuesday could not remove custody for longer than thirty days. A final hearing would have to be scheduled within the thirty-day period.

Thirty days maximum. That's what the statute said. Peter, however, knew the practical realities as well. If a judge ruled against a party in a child abuse case twice, it was highly unlikely that another hearing thirty days later would have a different result.

He copied the "thirty day" statute as well as the one which provided that Gordon was entitled to notice.

Peter turned next to the Rules of Juvenile Court. He made copies of three rules he found particularly relevant. It was only a twenty-minute foray into the library, but it was twenty minutes more than all the research that Walinski had bothered to put in on the case.

He jogged up two flights of stairs and returned to his office. Flipping on the computer, he reviewed the written list of "must do" assignments from Sally and Joe which had been placed on his desk while he waited for the program to go through its startup paces. A mandatory settlement conference on Friday at two with Judge Goodlate—a real estate fraud trial that Peter had filed thirteen months earlier and was on the August trial docket. That would take an hour to an hour and a half—but the preparation was all complete. And there was a deposition Monday at three. His client was being sued for breach of a covenant not to compete. It had been continued twice before and just shouldn't be continued again. Fortunately, he had his list of questions for his client's former employer all prepared from the prior occasions on which it had been scheduled. An hour's review would bring him fully up to speed and ready to do battle.

Not bad. He was proud of Joe and Sally. He knew that most of the work had fallen on them rather than simply being put off. It was a good team he had in place.

The blue word processing screen was ready and Peter began to type. MOTION TO COMPEL INDEPENDENT PSYCHOLOGI-CAL EVALUATION were the words at the top of the screen. Tomorrow morning Sally would add all the technical words needed at the top of the page to make it official. He began typing in the meat.

Willet would have the motion in-hand before noon. "Two can play the psychological game," Peter said aloud as he finished the third document—the proposed order for Judge Romer to sign. It had taken him less than fifteen minutes, but Sally would need another half hour in the morning to put on the finishing touches and clean up his mistakes.

He rode the elevator to the ground floor, stepped outside and into his car which was parked right in front of the building. *With parking this good, I should come to work this late every day,* he thought smiling.

As he began the drive to his home out to Liberty Lake in the far eastern edge of the valley, he picked up his car phone and punched the number for his friend Aaron Roberts.

Aaron was forty and was an elder in Peter's church. He had been discipling Peter for five years. As brothers in the Lord, they had developed a deep love and appreciation for each other. Aaron was one of the top computer programmers in the Northwest and was on demand as a consultant all over Washington, Oregon, Idaho, and western Montana. Occasionally, he would venture into northern California and British Columbia. Aaron's wife, Lynn, was home schooling their four children.

"Aaron, I'm glad you're home," Peter said when he answered.

"Me too. Doesn't happen enough. What's up?" Aaron answered.

"I got a new case today that I would like you to pray about. A mother lost custody of her four year old daughter this morning. Probably was mishandled by another lawyer. After the hearing he had the wild notion that this lady would be willing to trade sexual favors so that he could continue on the case for free."

"Good grief! Who are they?"

"You know I can't tell you the names of clients, but I'll be happy to tell you the name of the lawyer as soon as I'm off this cellular phone," Peter said. "This lady has been accused of bruising her child by spanking and I think it's a phony deal."

"What makes you think so?"

"Well, for one thing, she's a nurse at Sacred Heart and obviously knows bruises. And something in my spirit just tells me she's innocent."

"You know better than to rely on hunches. Our intuition is not always the Holy Spirit. Have you prayed about all this?"

"Not really. I need to do that. But anyway, this lady is really upset and needs prayer. She's probably not a believer either. And we can certainly pray along those lines too."

"Sure, Peter, I'll pray," Aaron said. "How's everything else?"

"Well, this week everything else will probably be set aside so I can do her case. There's a critical hearing on Tuesday."

"Don't forget our time Friday morning at seven. You aren't planning on being too busy for that, are you?"

"No way," said Peter. "See ya then."

～

Gwen's night had not been pleasant. The empty home worked strangely on her mind. The previous evening she was able to talk with Casey for about three minutes just before the MacArthurs put her to bed. It helped Casey a lot. For Gwen it accentuated her own helplessness.

Her responsibility to finish the written narrative of the events of May 11 and 12 for Peter was good for her spirits. It made her feel she was really doing something positive to bring an end to the madness and get Casey back home. After she finished her assignment, she stepped out on the back porch and fixed her gaze on the swing set. Casey's face and giggle were all too real—memories from the morning when Donna Corliss first invaded her life. Gwen's mind began to drift. . . . *What if Peter failed to regain custody? I can't let that happen. It cannot happen,* she thought as tears filled her eyes once again.

As she let her mind wander, a plan to kidnap her own daughter began to take shape in her clouded mind. *Perhaps we could go to California and live with Pam and Josh,* Gwen thought. She quickly rejected that idea, realizing it would put her sister and brother-in-law in jeopardy. She also correctly perceived that it would be one of the first places the authorities would look for her if she became a runaway "child abuser." A better plan would have to be made.

Gwen started and sat straight up in bed when the alarm sounded at 7:00 A.M. She felt as if she hadn't slept at all. After showering and dressing quickly she headed down the South Hill to Peter's office downtown. She arrived early, but was not surprised Peter was already there. Nor was she surprised when she was ushered into his office immediately. For whatever reason, Peter was obviously going out of his way to place her case as the highest priority on his schedule. She both appreciated and puzzled at this fact.

"Good morning, Gwen," Peter said brightly. "I see you've met Sally."

"Sort of," Gwen replied.

"Well, let's do this right," Peter said with a flourish. "Sally, this is Gwen Landis, our newest client, and Gwen, this is Sally Finley, the best legal secretary in Spokane."

Sally blushed modestly. She had heard the line before but was glad of Peter's praise. She wasn't sure she was the best in Spokane, but very content to have a boss who made her feel that way on a regular basis. "I'm happy to meet you, Gwen," Sally replied. "Please feel free to call me any time. I can usually locate Peter anywhere in the world."

"Thanks, that's reassuring," Gwen said, a bit uncomfortable with all the attention.

Sally quickly left, shutting the door behind her.

"Were you able to finish the chronology of events?" Peter asked.

"Yes, it's right here," Gwen replied handing over a nine-page hand-written document.

"Boy, if the microfiche machine ever goes on the blink at the law library, you could get a job," said Peter staring in amazement at her tiny, precise penmanship.

Gwen laughed.

After a minute of silent reading, he spoke up. "Well, this looks pretty thorough. I won't try to memorize it in your presence."

"Fine with me," she replied with relief. She had thought he might keep her there for a long time, grilling her on details she had already given him yesterday over lunch.

"Well, today I'm going to get Gordon's affidavit signed, pick up the tape of yesterday's hearing, and see if I can get Judge Romer to sign an order allowing us to take Casey to Dr. Schram for our own examination."

"Won't that be a lot of exams for a four-year-old? Two psychologists and a physician in one week," Gwen said with real concern in her voice.

"You're right," Peter said shaking his head. "But I'm afraid it can't be avoided. You never know how their exam is going to come out and we must be prepared."

"But the psychological tests they give are so routine. Couldn't we just have our doctor review the test results and not give a whole separate battery?" Gwen asked.

"Well, I'll talk with Dr. Schram. We'll do whatever we can to limit the examination time, yet do a thorough job," Peter replied. It was obvious that Gwen had a mind of her own and he would have to be ready to explain decisions in clear terms and not simply try to blow past her with a stuffy "its-my-professional-opinion" kind of answer.

Gwen stood up, ready to leave. "Well, I'd better let you get to all of this work you are doing to get my daughter back. I really appreciate it." Her smile was genuine and warm.

"Oh, OK," Peter replied surprised at her suddenness. Normally clients like to chat all day even if it is their own case they are delaying.

"Please check with me this afternoon before work. I'll let you know about your examination time with Dr. Schram. And Casey's as well if the judge lets me."

Peter picked up the phone after a moment of staring at the door Gwen had just closed.

"Ms. Willet, Peter Barron again. I'm calling to see if I can get your consent to an order allowing us to have Casey undergo a second psychological exam with a psychologist we have chosen."

"Why do we need a second opinion? We haven't even seen the first one yet," she replied.

"There's obviously not enough time to wait for your man's report, evaluate it, and then try to decide if we need a second exam. And we're entitled to the exam under JCR 23.2," he said, citing the juvenile court rule he had copied the prior evening.

"You're entitled to an exam for 'good cause shown' according to the rule," said Willet quoting the rule from memory. "And I don't think you've got good cause."

"Well, that's why we have judges. I'm going to present a motion asking Judge Romer to order the examination at two this afternoon. This is your phone notice of the *ex parte* hearing. I'll fax you a full set of the papers in a half hour or so."

"See that you do," Willet replied curtly.

Peter said, "Good-bye," and chuckled at Willet's rudeness as he set the receiver down, shaking his head.

⌒

Dr. Ron Stratton examined a timid little girl that morning. Brenda MacArthur, sat by trying to encourage Casey as much as possible. Brenda was a merciful soul who quickly connected to every child she met. Stratton was a thorough professional and took child abuse allegations very seriously. He asked questions of Casey, knowing the limitations of a four-year-old's ability to report a medical history. He tried to ease Casey's mind by humming a tune while conducting the exam, pausing long enough to listen to her heart and chest. He examined her buttocks, legs, and back very carefully.

After about ten minutes of checking and humming and listening and poking, Dr. Stratton said, "Well, Casey, you can get dressed now." Turning to Mrs. MacArthur, he shrugged his shoulders and said, "Perfectly healthy little girl. I can't find a thing."

Brenda smiled, wanting to believe the best, but was experienced enough through her own years as a social worker conducting adoption interviews to wait for the psychologists' report before she would be able to reach a more final conclusion.

~

Peter's second encounter with Gordon went more poorly than he had planned. He came to the door only after three minutes of off-and-on ringing and knocking. Clad in an old T-shirt and gym shorts, Gordon stood in the doorway and looked straight through Peter, making no indication that he wanted Peter to come in. "I've come back to have you sign the affidavit," Peter said, trying to be as cheerful as possible.

"What's it say?" Gordon demanded, his speech more slurred than at their first meeting.

"Just the things you told me yesterday. Why don't we sit down at your kitchen table and you can read it?"

"I can read it here," Gordon barked, quickly looking at the document without actually seeing anything.

Peter looked at his shoes, the hall, the doorbell, and the ceiling a time or two, trying to avoid an awkward meeting of the eyes.

"I guess it's OK. Do I sign it here?" Gordon said suddenly.

"Yes, right there." Peter lifted his briefcase for a hard surface to write on and handed Gordon a pen. Gordon scribbled his name.

Peter took the papers and pen saying simply, "Thanks, Gordon. See you later, next Tuesday if not before."

"Whatdya mean next Tuesday?"

"That's when the hearing is. You're entitled to be there. And it'll help Gwen and Casey," Peter replied.

"Uh. . . we'll see. I'm not sure if I can make it."

Peter silently hoped that the nearest Albertson's would run out of beer and wine next Monday. "Lord, please help this man show up sober on Tuesday," he prayed silently.

Gordon closed the door and collapsed back on the couch in his dimly lit apartment.

～

At five minutes before two Peter entered the chambers of Judge Romer's courtroom in the main courthouse. The Judge, like all superior court judges have, had chambers located just off his own courtroom. During each of their turns presiding over juvenile court, the judges would hold hearings in the juvenile building, but conduct all chambers matters in their normal chambers.

Peter informed the judge's clerk that he was present for an *ex parte* hearing on the Landis file but that he was waiting for Ms. Willet to arrive. The clerk pulled the file, placed Peter's original documents on top, and walked in to give it to Judge Romer for his review prior to the meeting with both counsel.

Willet appeared precisely at two. Surprisingly, Donna Corliss was at her side. Before anyone else could speak, the clerk said, "I'll tell the judge you're ready."

Peter took the initiative. "Ms. Willet, I'm Peter Barron. Happy to meet you." He expected that Willet would introduce him to the woman at her side who Peter had never met.

"Thank you," said Willet, tersely ending any chance for further conversation.

Fortunately, the clerk promptly ushered them in to see the judge. He was sitting in his shirtsleeves, reading glasses on, with Peter's papers in his hand finishing a quick read of this motion. "Come in and sit down. Mr. Barron, I take it you've met Ms. Willet and Ms. Corliss here."

Peter smiled, grateful that the judge had cleared up the mystery of the second woman. "Yes, Your Honor, quite briefly."

"Mr. Barron, I guess I'm a little surprised that there was such a quick substitution of counsel. But, of course, that's really none of my business," the judge said. If it had been two longtime Spokane attorneys before him, Romer would have asked him what happened and Peter would have told him the story. The whole conversation would have been off the record. But with a Seattle stranger and a CPS worker in their midst, such a discussion was simply not going to happen.

"I won't slow the case down, Your Honor. I'll be ready on Tuesday," Peter said.

"Fine," Romer replied. Leaning back in his chair, he continued, "Why are you here to see me? This looks so routine. Ms. Willet, I take it you are resisting this motion. Tell me why," the judge said, placing all the papers back on his desk, leaning his elbows on the desk and cradling his chin in both hands.

"Your Honor, the state believes this is just too many examinations for one little girl in such a short time," Willet replied.

"I see. What do you have to say to that, Mr. Barron?" the judge said, turning to look directly at Peter.

"Your Honor, if the court had selected a neutral expert, we probably wouldn't be making this motion for an additional psychological examination. In fact my client raised the same concern about too many exams in one week. But my understanding of the court's order is that this examination is by a CPS-chosen psychologist. It is simply not appropriate to have one side obtain an exam while the other side has nothing. Of course, if the state was willing to cancel their appointment with their expert and allow the court to appoint an independent psychologist the court chooses, then maybe we could forego a second examination."

Corliss grimaced.

"That's not a bad idea," the judge said, rocking gently back and forth in his chair. "What about that, Ms. Willet?"

Willet did not care about choosing the psychologist. She didn't know who was good and who was bad in Spokane. And she was unaware of CPS's special arrangement with Dr. McGuire. But she cared a great deal about losing her first encounter with Peter Barron.

"Your Honor, psychologists are busy. I doubt that it will be possible to find a so-called neutral expert on such short notice who can do the examinations, write a report, and appear next Tuesday."

The judge replied before Peter could speak. "Well, here in Spokane we've got the psychological community a bit more attentive to the needs of judges than perhaps is the case in Seattle. I am sure that with two or three phone calls I can find an appropriate psychologist to meet our schedule. What do you say?"

Corliss was about to panic. She tugged on Willet's jacket sleeve as unobtrusively as possible and pointedly shook her head "no" when Willet turned to look.

Partly because of Corliss's gesture and partly out of personal stubbornness, Willet tossed her head and said, "Your Honor, we are going to stand with our plan to use Dr. McGuire. And we will simply ask the court to protect this girl from too many examinations."

"OK," the judge replied. "If that's your position, I see no choice but to allow Mr. Barron's motion for an additional interview with the child by a psychologist of his choosing."

Embarrassed at losing even the most minor of arguments, Willet said, "Your Honor, we want it clear that Mrs. Landis should not be taking this child to the psychologist alone. She may take off for all we know."

Peter quickly countered, "Your Honor, I would be happy to accompany my client and her daughter to the interview. And I or one of my staff will stay with them through the whole interview. I would be reluctant to drive this little girl alone myself."

Before the prosecutor could bog him down in any more trivial arguments, the judge replied, "Fine, Peter. If you give me your assurance, that's good enough for me. Now if you'll both excuse me, I have another hearing very soon," Romer said, standing to politely indicate to all it was time to leave.

～

Before leaving for work, Gwen placed her second call to Casey.

"Mommy, where are you?"

"I'm at home, Casey doll."

"Mommy, come get me."

"Casey, are you OK? Are they nice to you?"

"Mommy, I wanna come home. Come get me."

"Casey are you playing with their children?"

"Sometimes."

"Are they nice to you?"

"Uh-huh."

"Did you go to the doctor today?"

"Uh-huh . . . Mommy I wanna go home. Come get me."

"Casey, I'll get you as soon as I can. Real soon."

Casey began to cry, unable to understand why her mommy wouldn't come. Gwen's tears were soft but very bitter.

8

On Thursday morning, Peter left his home on Liberty Lake at seven. As soon as he hit I-90 West toward town he punched in the audio tape of the hearing from just two days before. It proved to be cut and dried with no real surprises, as he expected. He made some mental notes, which he would translate to paper as soon as his interview with Officer Mark Donahue was completed.

Corporal Donahue arrived at the Perkins Pancake House on Division and Second precisely at 8:00 Thursday morning. Peter had arranged an interview with him through negotiations with his Lieutenant.

Peter waited in the lot for about twenty minutes for the officer to arrive at the appointed time. He had deliberately arrived early so he would have time to finish listening to the hearing. The tape was near the end when the officer pulled up. Peter turned off the ignition and stepped from his car to join Officer Donohue.

Donahue was cordial but reserved. After breakfast was ordered Peter took out his yellow pad and began. Name, rank, experience, background. Donahue gave answers that had become mechanical after testifying to essentially the same categories of facts in dozens of hearings.

"Now I'd like to ask you about the events at the home of Gwen Landis on May 12. Do you remember which family this was?"

"Sure. She's the blond. Big eyes. Red T-Shirt. Striped shorts. Yeah, I remember."

"Tell me what happened. I'd like everything you can recall."

"It was pretty routine. The lady didn't want to let us in. The one CPS lady . . . "

"Donna Corliss?"

"Yeah, Corliss—she did all the talking. Anyway, she told the lady that we had to come in and that I was there to make sure that the CPS workers could come in and do their job."

"And then what?"

"We went in. I waited in the living room with the lady, the two CPS ladies took the girl into the bedroom. The lady just sat there crying. She got really upset when we heard the girl screaming. It was obvious they were taking off her clothes to look for bruises but I don't remember the exact words. Just a lot of screaming and crying."

"What happened when they came out?"

"I don't remember too much of the exact conversation. It wasn't my investigation. I was just there for protection. But the lady answered some questions about spanking. Corliss said she should-n't spank or something. And after that it was pretty much over except for the shouting."

"Shouting?"

"Yeah, the lady called the CPS workers Nazis and witches. I felt sorry for the lady, she was upset and everything. But I remember her yelling those names."

"Did the CPS workers say anything about any bruises?"

"Not that I heard. Nothing one way or the other. Again, they weren't consulting with me, they just wanted me to stand there with my gun."

"Are you sure you heard nothing about bruises?"

"Well, at the time I didn't think they had found any. . . . " he said, pausing to think. "But I don't remember them saying anything directly. There must be some reason I thought that."

Peter just let him ponder in silence.

After staring at his coffee for a few more moments, the officer continued, "Oh yeah, I remember. Corliss said that they would probably dismiss this case if the lady would just answer some questions after they searched the girl. I guess I thought there were no bruises because of that."

Peter didn't want to highlight the answer to this question. He knew that Willet would be interviewing him later. It was standard operating procedure for the prosecutor's office. They always debriefed officers after an interview with private counsel.

Trying his best to conceal his pleasure at the last answer, and with as much false frustration in his voice he could muster, Peter asked again, "I really hate to belabor the point. But think as hard as you can. Are you sure that you can't remember any specific things said about finding bruises?"

"No. Nothing direct."

"Well, thanks anyway," Peter said while picking up the check. "Hey, I appreciate your time and your willingness to meet."

"It's my job," Officer Donohue said with a hint of a smile. Peter Barron had been cordial and professional—he could deal with attorneys like that. It was the ones who threatened and cajoled that drove him mad.

~

On Thursday morning, Dr. Randall McGuire asked Casey to draw pictures, play in a room with a one-way mirror, look at pictures, and make up a story about the characters depicted. And he did a routine interview. Casey's answers were pretty normal. The only discovery of note was that he was dealing with one terrified little girl. There were two alternative reasons for her fear. He knew how he would spin the report.

~

Gwen got off work at three and scrambled to get home, change clothes and get down to the Fifth Avenue Medical Building to Dr. McGuire's office by five. Her friend, Bonnie, had agreed to switch shifts for the day. Just before she was ready to leave her phone rang.

"Hello."

"Gwen, this is Peter."

"Oh, hi. I'm just leaving for Dr. McGuire's office."

"Fine, I just want to bring you up to date on a couple of things. First, tomorrow at 10:00 Casey has to be taken to Dr. Schram's for our evaluation. The judge gave us permission over the objection of the prosecutor earlier this afternoon."

"I guess that's good," Gwen replied, still not terribly pleased with putting her little girl through so many exams.

Peter continued, "And you get to take her to the exam. But you have to be escorted."

"Why do I have to be escorted?" Gwen demanded.

"The prosecutor was afraid that you would run away with her," Peter replied.

"It's not something I haven't thought about, but I would never do it—at least probably never do it."

"Don't tell me things like that," Peter replied.

"Who's the escort, one of the witches?"

"No, just a friendly ghost," Peter countered with a laugh. "It's me. The judge was in a hurry and I didn't want to get embroiled in a big argument with the prosecutor on every little detail, so I quickly volunteered since I knew the judge would trust me to guarantee that you wouldn't run with Casey. I promised him that either I or one of my staff would stay with you two the whole time."

"Oh, OK," Gwen replied—it finally sinking in that she was going to spend a few precious moments with her daughter.

"So you can meet me here at my office about nine fifteen, we'll drive over to the foster home, pick up Casey, and get over to Dr. Schram's before ten. The exam will last about an hour-and-a-half. And then we'll have to take her right back to the foster home."

"Can't we take her to lunch or something?"

"I'm afraid that little deviations like that might really upset the judge."

"This is so unreal! I can't take my own daughter to McDonald's without upsetting some judge. I can't drive her alone! I can't see her alone! Ooh, it makes me mad!"

"It'll only be for a few more days. I think we're going to win this case on Tuesday."

"I'd like to think so, too. How can you be so sure?"

"I'm not absolutely sure, but I am excited by what I'm finding. The police officer gave me some information I think will really help us on Tuesday."

"What's that?"

"Oh, it will take too long to explain. You've got to go to their shrink. I'll tell you later."

"Ooh. I hate to be left in suspense, but I guess I do have to run. Thanks, Peter, I really appreciate everything."

~

As she sat in the waiting room, Gwen couldn't help thinking that her Casey doll had sat on these chairs waiting for her turn with Dr. Randall McGuire. She would see her tomorrow. And hold her. And kiss her. And never let her go. Thoughts of running away crowded her mind as she contemplated the fact that she would have to turn Casey back over to the foster parents sometime before noon. Her daydream became more vivid as she imagined Peter, Casey, and herself driving in that white Explorer north for a couple of hours and escaping over the Canadian border. *The border guards would just think that we were a typical happy family,* Gwen thought. She came back to reality quickly, knowing that this semi-stranger would never do such a thing. And when it came right down to it, she didn't think she would do it either—even on her own. But she was beginning to have doubts.

Her thoughts were abruptly interrupted as the receptionist said, "Mrs. Landis, Dr. McGuire will see you now."

McGuire was a sharp dresser in his late forties. Double-breasted blue blazer, window pane pants, and a bold yellow tie with geometric patterns. His hair was stylishly long, greying, and was tightly held in place with substantial quantities of mousse.

"Good afternoon, Gwen," he began, "I'm Randall McGuire, Please sit down," he said, pointing to a comfortable leather chair.

The entire office was decorated in tasteful shades of blue-green and rose. Abstract art hung on the walls. McGuire's desk was a light oak table-style desk with no drawers or panels. He sat in a swivel chair, directly across a coffee table from Gwen.

Gwen sat on the edge of her chair still holding her purse in her lap. "Well, let's get acquainted just a little," McGuire said with disarming charm. "Obviously, I've been asked to perform a fairly routine evaluation in this matter. The court system may be adversarial, but I'm not. I'm here to ask some questions, give you a brief standardized assessment and write a report. I just give an opinion and let others make the decision. All right?"

"Uh . . . OK," Gwen stammered. She didn't know what to say or think. He seemed very nice. *Maybe this will work out after all,* she thought.

"Please tell me a little about yourself."

"Well, there's not much to tell. I'm twenty-nine. A single mom. I work in the surgery department as a nurse at Sacred Heart. And I've lived in Spokane all my life. That's about it."

"So you were born here?"

"Yes. At Deaconess Hospital. I grew up near North Central High School through most of my childhood. But my family moved to the South Hill when I was in ninth grade. I graduated from Lewis & Clark High School."

"Tell me about your brothers and sisters."

"I'm the youngest of three girls. We're very close. And I remain very close to my parents."

"So you had a happy childhood?"

"Yes, very happy."

"Were you ever abused as a child in any way?"

"No, never. My parents were very good to me."

"That's wonderful," McGuire said with a smile as he flipped a page on his yellow pad.

And so it went for about fifteen minutes of friendly, light interaction that began to totally disarm Gwen. *If I ever have a problem, maybe I'll come see this guy,* Gwen thought.

"Tell me about your divorce and your current relationship with your ex-husband."

"That's not very pleasant," Gwen replied.

"Why not?"

"Well, for one thing, my ex-husband is way behind on his child support. He simply refuses to get a job. That was the major reason we got a divorce. He was unwilling to get a real job and was always chasing after some new scheme."

"Does the way he treated you—I mean, some men just refuse to take their responsibilities seriously—does this cause you any bitterness toward him?"

"Yeah, I guess so," Gwen admitted.

"I understand," McGuire said. "At times are these feelings of bitterness pretty strong, like when you might be feeling lonely, or discouraged, or kind of abandoned?"

"I think that's right," Gwen said appreciating the fact that McGuire seemed so sympathetic to her plight.

"Um . . . OK," McGuire said, making a couple notes.

"Now, I would like to ask you about another subject. Tell me about your philosophy of discipline."

"Well, basically I try to train Casey the way my parents trained me. I try my best to explain to her what the rules are and what I expect her to do. If she breaks a rule once, I sit down and explain it to her again to make sure she understands. But if she violates my standards again, I take disciplinary action after sitting her down and explaining that such behavior is simply not allowed."

"Seems pretty thorough. What kind of discipline do you administer?"

"It depends on what she did wrong. Normally, I try to match the discipline to the behavior. If she makes a mess, I make her clean up the mess in question, plus do one or two other cleaning activities. Sometimes, I make her go to her room. I'll take away dessert for one or two days. Just a variety of things."

"And what about spanking?" the psychologist asked still looking and writing on his pad.

"I do spank Casey. Basically in situations where I don't think other measures will work well. For flagrant disobedience, I will spank her."

"How?"

"I use a wooden spoon. I don't want her to associate my hand with pain."

"How many strokes?"

"Usually one. Sometimes two. Never more than three."

"Were you spanked as a child?"

"Yes, I think I turned out pretty good, don't you?"

"Well, it would seem so, Mrs. Landis, it would seem so," McGuire said with a friendly laugh.

"Well, I think that's all my questions. I need you to step into my side office and answer some questions. It's an assessment tool I use called the MMPI, just a standard personality inventory. I can't discover your hidden dreams or anything else. It's just routine."

Gwen stood smiling. *This wasn't bad at all,* she thought once again.

"It's just over here," McGuire said, pointing to the room off to the left. "Just give it to the secretary when you're done."

Thirty minutes later she was on her way home with hope in her heart that she might really prevail after all. Everything seemed to be going so well.

⌒

McGuire flipped on his notebook computer and began to write his conclusion. He always wrote the conclusion first, and then went back and put together all the supporting details in a proper format.

> *Gwen Landis is not a child abuser by choice. She is a victim. A victim of parents who exercised the same form of corporal punishment she has now inflicted on her child. A victim of a divorce where she experiences understandable feelings of bitterness because of a husband who*

has abandoned her and her child. At times these feelings of bitterness are overwhelming. One can express great sympathy for Gwen Landis considering all that she has been through in her life.

But her victimization cannot shield us from the present realities. Her child cannot become yet another victim through this cycle of abuse, bitterness, and abandonment. We have to break that cycle.

The best course of action to break this cycle in the life of Gwen and Casey is to keep the child in foster care for up to six months. During this period of time a course of intensive psychological counseling is likely to produce dramatically improved understanding by Gwen of her need to break the cycles of victimization. In the end, we can reunite this family with a wholeness which has been missing perhaps for generations.

"A masterpiece," McGuire said aloud when he finished. "A bloomin' masterpiece. They underpaid me for this one," he cackled.

9

Peter and Aaron met at their usual spot—The Red Lion Coffee Shop just off the Pines Road exit from Interstate 90. It was about a fifteen minute drive for each of them and allowed them to hop directly on to the freeway and head for work afterwards. The waitress gave them a back table, where they could read the Bible, talk, and pray without too many stares. For several weeks they had been reading a chapter from the Book of Proverbs for their study. After reading the passage they would ask each other about the application of the principles in the passage to current issues in their lives. Today's chapter was Proverbs 21.

It was one of Peter's favorite chapters in all of Scripture. When he was a young Christian in his senior year of college, and was trying to decide whether it was God's will for him to go to law school, Peter believed that God had directed him to Proverbs 21:15. *"When justice is done, it brings joy to the righteous but terror to evildoers."* That verse was the turning point in the process of prayer, counsel, and Scriptural meditation that made Peter conclude that becoming an attorney was in fact God's will for his life.

When Aaron read the verse aloud, Peter's mind quickly raced through all those good memories of knowing that he was in the will of God by becoming a lawyer.

"Well," Aaron began when they had finished reading the entire chapter, "did any particular verse stand out to you?"

"Verse one got my attention in light of my upcoming hearing on Tuesday. *'The king's heart is in the hand of the Lord; He directs it like a watercourse wherever He pleases.'* I have been praying that God will direct the judge's heart and that my client will get her child back."

"Peter, have you given your client any opportunity to come to know Jesus?" Aaron asked. Aaron's heart was always alert for opportunities to share the Gospel.

"Not really. I made it clear to her that I was a born-again Christian, but I didn't really explain what that means," Peter replied. Seeing Aaron's unblinking stare, Peter hastily added, "But I'm looking for the right opportunity."

"Good. Remember, for him who knows to do right and doeth it not, to him it is sin," Aaron said quoting James 4:17. They had memorized the verse together several months ago.

Peter nodded and stared at his Bible hoping that Aaron would find something else to talk about. He didn't have to wait long.

"You know, verse two is one that always convicts me," Aaron said. "'All a man's ways seem right to him, but the Lord weighs the heart.' I think this means that even when we think that our motives are pure, we often deceive ourselves. I find that I constantly have to make myself look deeper and deeper into my motives to examine if anything I am doing is really being done for a motive that God would find to be wrong."

Peter felt that slight burning on his face that often accompanied a pricking of his inner spirit. He began to ask himself, *Are my motives really pure in trying to help Gwen? Am I just being a good lawyer for her by trying to win her case? Or is there something more?*

"I think it's good," Aaron continued, "to go through this kind of self-examination once in a while." Looking at his watch, he said, "Well, I guess we'd better pray if we are going to keep to our schedule."

Peter was glad Aaron didn't ask any probing questions about applying verse two to his life. And truthfully, Peter wasn't sure whether he had anything to confess. He knew for sure he would have to guard his heart more carefully toward Gwen, but for the moment he concluded that he was doing her case out of a pure desire to be a good lawyer and a good servant.

⌇

Sheriff's Deputy Wally Elrod loved serving subpoenas on government employees. It was so easy. He started his morning on Friday, by simply walking fifty yards across the public safety building and waited for Officer Mark Donahue to arrive for his shift.

"Hi, Mark," Elrod said. "Got another subpoena for you."

"Thanks heaps," Donahue said. "Landis case, whoopee!" the officer said sarcastically.

"See ya," Elrod said. And that was it.

Rita Coballo was second on Elrod's service list. Peter Barron had issued the subpoenas yesterday afternoon. As is typical in civil litigation, Peter had simply typed up the subpoena and had it delivered on the strength of his own signature as an officer of the court.

Fifteen minutes later Elrod succeeded in handing Ms. Coballo her subpoena. She did not resent being served, but when Elrod made the mistake of asking if she was *Mrs.* Coballo, her feminist ideology took over.

"I'll thank you for leaving your sexist titles to yourself. It's Ms. Coballo, if you don't mind," she fumed.

Elrod raised his eyebrows, and said, "Hope your broom is working well to fly you to court on Tuesday." He was two months from retirement and simply didn't care anymore.

⌇

Gwen arrived at Peter's office fifteen minutes early. She was anxious to get Casey as soon as possible. Peter called Brenda MacArthur, asking her to have Casey ready at 9:15 instead of 9:30.

The MacArthurs lived up on the far northside of town, about six blocks from Whitworth College in a middle class neighborhood with large yards and fences. A few, but not the MacArthurs, had pools.

Gwen was nervous and obviously excited. Peter tried to keep the conversation light. There were long lapses as Gwen would stare vacantly out the window deep in thought about her "Casey doll."

At long last Peter turned left into the MacArthur's driveway, the door burst open and the auburn-haired little girl ran toward her mother. Gwen was out of the car in a flash and swooped up the prize of her heart and squeezed tightly.

Casey giggled the instant her mother picked her up and the mood was set. There would be no tears at this meeting. Just laughter and kisses and hugs.

Peter quietly thanked Mrs. MacArthur and seated Gwen and Casey in the back of the Explorer and began the drive to Dr. Schram's.

Peter was silent the entire ride to the psychologist's office. Casey giggled and talked silly. Gwen hugged and kissed her daughter time and again.

~

Corporal Donahue walked with his subpoena across the foyer of the Public Safety Building to the Office of the Prosecuting Attorney. The main floor of this huge building houses the Spokane City Police Department, the Sheriff's Department, and the Clerk's Office for the District Court. District Court judges hear traffic cases, misdemeanors, and small time civil suits under $3,000. Their courtrooms are on the eastern half of the second floor. The entrance to the sprawling county jail is located on the western half of the second floor.

Willet was waiting for Donahue in her office.

"Morning, Ms. Willet."

"Thank you for coming so promptly."

Donahue simply nodded. He would rather be out on patrol, but he tolerated such matters as a necessary evil.

"Let me see your subpoena."

He handed it over silently.

"Just routine. No demand for documents on it. I wonder what Barron wants."

"What did you tell him during your interview?"

"I can't think of anything he would be interested in. I pretty well just repeated my report. I reread it prior to the interview."

"Did he seem to focus on any particular issues?"

"He asked me a lot about bruises. Asked me if I heard the CPS workers say anything about bruises."

"What did you tell him?" Willet asked.

"That I didn't hear them say anything directly one way or another."

"Is that it?" Willet asked.

"As far as I know. The only hard evidence I have about bruises is that I know nothing, I know nothing." He intoned the last phrase with a mock German accent to do his best Sergeant Schultz imitation from the old Hogan's Heroes television show. Willet didn't get it and wouldn't have cracked a smile even if she did.

Later that morning, Willet put the final touches on her trial preparation. She reviewed McGuire's report and prepared her direct examination and outlined ideas for possible cross-examination. She called McGuire and went over the matters she expected Barron to raise. McGuire was impressed with her insight. Indeed she was a very competent lawyer.

Willet considered the possibility of a trial brief, but rejected it, concluding that only factual issues were being raised. The judge knew well that the ultimate issue would be a determination of what is in the "best interest of the child." She knew the judge could reach that legal point automatically and saw no need for a brief.

Before noon, Willet would be completely ready for trial, except for the exchange of psychologists reports on Monday morning. Late Thursday, Peter had tried to convince her to give him the McGuire report as soon as it was ready on Friday. Willet refused, insisting on an exchange of reports on Monday at ten. She was hardnosed about everything, Peter concluded.

Jean Schram's office was on the edge of the downtown core, in a conglomeration of medical buildings that surround Deaconess Hospital, one of Spokane's three major medical facilities.

When they arrived at the office, Sally was seated in the waiting room reading a magazine. She was to be the "escort" during the hour and a half of interview and testing. Peter would return at 11:30 for the return trip.

Dr. Schram was in her mid-fifties, but had been a psychologist for only seven years. She earned her B.A. in psychology from Washington State University in 1965 and had married immediately upon graduation. She got pregnant only a year later with her first of three children.

She understood her Christian faith to require her to stay home with her children during their years of schooling. And when her third child, Marie, entered WSU as a freshman, Jean returned there as well to attend graduate school in a four year stint of commuting to gain her Ph.D. They rented an apartment. Her daughter and a friend shared one bedroom. On Tuesday and Thursday nights Jean stayed in the other bedroom. It was a very different college experience for all concerned and, while tense at times, it deepened the special commitment between Jean and Marie.

Jean divided the Landis interview into three segments. For the first thirty minutes she interviewed and observed Casey and Gwen together. Then she interviewed Gwen alone, while a graduate intern performed some routine tests on Casey. And finally, Casey was interviewed by Dr. Schram while the graduate intern gave Gwen the MMPI test to take once again.

"But I've already taken this just yesterday. Do I really have to take it again?" Gwen protested.

"Who administered it to you?" the intern replied.

"Dr. McGuire. He was very nice."

"Well, let me call his office and see if he will fax us the results. If he will, then we can skip this."

～

McGuire's secretary stepped inside his office as he was typing a report, a truthful report, for another patient.

"Dr. Schram's office is on the phone and asking you to fax a copy of Gwen Landis's MMPI results from yesterday. The report's right there in the file, is it OK?" she asked.

Without looking up, McGuire replied, "Tell them I'm in a session and have to leave the office immediately afterwards for a couple of hours and you don't think you'll have a chance to ask me about it until later this afternoon."

McGuire hoped that his answer would string them out so that Schram would decide to wait for the results which he had no intention of ever sending over—well, at least not until after Tuesday.

His secretary was used to these occasional deceptions, although she never knew when or why he would blatantly ask her to lie. She was paid well, did as she was asked, and kept her mouth shut.

Schram's intern interrupted the interview of Casey to ask her mentor for directions. In a few minutes Gwen was unhappily filling in little spaces with a number two pencil.

Peter returned promptly at 11:30 and relieved Sally of guard duty. He had used the interlude to prepare for that afternoon's settlement conference and begin review for the deposition on Monday afternoon. He was very glad that Sally and Joe had reduced the work load to only those two obligations.

Peter stepped inside Jean's office, saying to Gwen and Casey, "Wait right here, I'll just be a second."

It was actually about three minutes that Peter was inside the psychologist's inner office.

"Well, what do you think?" he began.

"They are both delightful," Jean replied. "I can't believe anyone would believe that Casey has been abused or that Gwen is even capable of such action. They react warmly together and their individual interviews are totally consistent with a wholesome, loving relationship."

"That's great! A clean bill of health. They don't have anything on them," Peter replied with glee.

"Well, Casey is clearly afraid of something. But I have no doubt that it is this incident with the two CPS workers at her home and being separated from her mother. Look at these pictures she drew for me. I would be afraid of those two, wouldn't you?"

Peter laughed at the crude monster like faces on the heads of two women standing next to what appeared to be a bed.

"If she had drawn one woman it could have been her mother. But notice the hair color. And critically, there are two women."

Casey's drawing was a little better than might have been expected. But she had some practice. She had drawn a virtually identical picture on the morning of the previous day, a drawing which was now sitting in a dumpster in back of the Fifth Avenue Medical Center.

As soon as Peter had stepped inside Jean Schram's inner office, Gwen's mind began to race. She doubted Dr. Schram's receptionist knew anything about the requirement that she be accompanied at all times. She knew the location of a rent-a-car facility just ten blocks away and cabs were probably available across the street by the hospital. The back roads to Walla Walla loomed large in her mind. From there, Oregon was just minutes away, and then Idaho, and Utah, and from there she thought she could get lost for years and years. It wasn't a bad plan. But it was a plan that was not to be, for just as her mind took her to Utah, Peter opened the door and the reality of returning Casey to the MacArthurs took control of her thoughts.

～

The ride back to the Whitworth neighborhood was very similar for two of the people in Peter's car. Peter sat alone in the front and said nothing. Casey giggled, talked, and laid her head in her mother's lap. But this time Gwen sat quietly with tears in her eyes and desperate thoughts of escape in her heart.

When Casey understood that she was not going home with her mommy, she began to cry inconsolably. Gwen was obviously shaken as well. Peter began to doubt whether it had been a good idea to let Gwen come along with Casey. Maybe he should have just waited until winning on Tuesday. But Dr. Schram had insisted on the ability to observe the two of them together and so it was simply unavoidable.

After Casey had gone inside and the door was closed, Peter saw that the crying was getting worse so he gently put his arm around Gwen's shoulder and said, "It won't be long 'til Tuesday. I'll never let them take her from you again."

These were not the words of a lawyer. Lawyers, at least honest lawyers like Peter, would never promise victory at this point. But Peter's words came from the heart of a man who simply wanted to protect and comfort a woman in distress.

As they drove away Peter let Gwen sit in silence for a few minutes. Finally he said, "Dr. Schram feels very good about what she found."

For about twenty seconds Gwen said nothing. Then turning to look straight at her lawyer she said, "Peter, it's just too hard for me to talk about the case right now. Can't we talk about something else? Anything. Anything to take my mind off Tuesday and my fears and worries."

"Sure. That's fine," Peter said. But he had no idea what to say. After an awkward minute or so, he remembered Aaron's prompting to share the Gospel with his new client. He thought he could use this time to at least plant a few seeds.

"OK. I've got an idea. It's not exactly a light topic, but it's at least different." He glanced over at Gwen. Her eyes looked so forlorn that he wanted to stop the car, hold her against his shoulder to let her cry and feel comforted. But he knew better and went on with his plan.

"When we went out to lunch on Tuesday, I told you I was a born-again Christian. My faith is something that interests me a lot and I always enjoy hearing about other people's religious background and experience. Is this OK to talk about?"

"I g-guess," Gwen stammered. "There's really not much to tell. My parents took me to church a few times a year. My mom was raised Catholic. My dad is a Methodist. They compromised by rarely taking us anywhere."

"When was the last time you were in church?" Peter asked.

"Actually, last Sunday. I was taking a walk while Gordon was exercising visitation. I slipped into this little church and sat there for a few minutes and then slipped back out."

"What did you think?" Peter asked.

"It seemed fine. Actually, it reminded me of a church camp I went to when I was about thirteen or fourteen. It was up north of Spokane about thirty miles. I can't remember the name."

"Riverside?" Peter suggested.

"Yeah, I think that's it. How did you know?"

"Well, for one thing, it's the only camp north of Spokane I know about. Also, it is owned by the sister church that I belong to. I go to Valley Fourth Memorial Church, and the downtown church that originally started our church is Fourth Memorial. They own the camp. Just a lucky guess."

"That's a pretty good coincidence," Gwen said. The conversation was having at least one intended effect. She was genuinely focused on something other than her case.

"What do you remember about the camp?"

"We played games, swam in the river, sang songs, and listened to a lot of lectures—or sermons I guess would be the proper term."

"Do you remember how you felt about the sermons?"

"I guess I liked them. I certainly can't remember anything about what the men said."

"Did they ever ask you to come forward or raise your hand or anything like that?"

"Well, I remember coming forward and saying a prayer of some kind, but it was so long ago."

"Did anyone ever follow up with you about all this after camp?"

"I don't think so. My friend who took me to camp kept asking me to come to church with her, but I don't think I ever did."

"Would you like to go to church with me sometime? After all, it is basically the same church that owns the camp you attended."

"Oh, I don't know," Gwen replied. She was uncomfortable with the idea of going to a church where she didn't know anyone—anyone except Peter, that is.

"Well, I don't want to pressure you. But if you'd like to go, I am sure the time you spend in church might really be a source of comfort for you in light of all this mess."

"Thanks, Peter. I'll think about it. Can I tell you later?"

"Sure."

They drove in silence the rest of the way. Peter flipped on the radio to break the awkwardness. He pulled in the parking garage and stopped behind her car.

"I've written my home number on the back of my card. If you decide you'd like to go to church, just call, leave an answer on the machine if I'm not there. I'll call back to confirm and I'll pick you up."

~

As he walked to the elevator, he said to himself, "It's evangelism. It's not a date. It's evangelism." Then he thought of Aaron and Proverbs 21:2, *All a man's ways seem right to him, but the Lord weighs the heart.* He hit the heel of his hand on the elevator door. *I don't know. I just don't know what is going on inside of me.*

Joe accompanied Peter to the Friday afternoon settlement conference with Judge Goodlate. It was a major case. Peter's client was seeking $250,000 in damages—not inflated damages for pain and suffering, but clear, provable economic losses arising from a fraudulent real estate transaction. Goodlate would not be hearing the case when it came on the trial calendar in August. The settlement judge reviews the file and makes an independent assessment of the merits of the case. He then tells the parties what he predicts will happen and twist arms as hard as he reasonably can to get them to come to an agreement. About one-third of the time settlements occur on the spot.

Judge Goodlate opened the session with a very insightful recitation of the relevant facts. He asked for comments or corrections, but no one said anything. Not only were the judge's mastery of the facts beyond criticism, he had a reputation as a judge with no leniency for bluffing or bravado. If a lawyer tried to puff his facts in one case, Goodlate would hold it against him for years.

Goodlate turned to a recitation of the law. He had scoured the briefs of both parties and undertook a couple hours of his own research. Again, his analysis was beyond dispute—at least Peter thought so since the judge's view of both the facts and law were very similar to those he had submitted to the court.

"Accordingly, gentleman, I think the issue of liability in this case is clear. The only real issue is the amount of damages. It is my considered opinion the jury will return a verdict very close to $200,000 one way or the other. I am going to allow each side a ten minute break to confer with your client.

Peter and Joe huddled in one conference room with Mr. and Mrs. Daniel Kling. Defense counsel and their insurance company representative found another conference room down the corridor.

The Kling's wanted $150,000 in their pockets, after attorney's fees, costs and everything else was taken out. Peter was entitled to one-third of the entire amount if the case went to trial. He had worked for a year and a half on the case without receiving a dime so far. It is the way contingency fees work. Lots of famines with a potential for feasts now and then.

The insurance company offered $125,000 initially. But after forty-five minutes of arm-twisting by the judge interspersed with huddles and conferences, the case was settled for $187,000. There had been just under $7,000 in expert witness fees and deposition costs. Peter and Joe would take home about $30,000—about half of what they would have received if the case had been tried and they had obtained a full verdict. But both the clients and Peter believed that a bird in the hand today was better than a larger amount that could be another year or two in coming after a trial and a likely appeal.

～

As they drove back to the office, Peter and Joe were pumped with excitement.

"Thirty grand!" Joe exclaimed as they were alone in Peter's car. "That'll make it easier for us to tilt a few more non-paying windmills like the Landis case."

"You got that right," Peter said happily.

They drove in happy silence for a minute with Joe beating the dash board to the rhythm of "Wipe Out" that was playing loudly on the oldies station on the radio.

"Hey, Peter," Joe said. "Speaking of the Landis case, have you done any research on the legality of the search by those CPS workers and the cop?"

"No. I thought about that for a possible civil rights case later, but what difference does it make now? This isn't a criminal case either. Do think there's some relevancy?"

"Maybe," Joe replied. "I was just thinking about the "Fruit of the Poisonous Tree" case from the Supreme Court. You know, where they ruled that if the search was illegal it could not be used for any purpose whatsoever."

"I wonder if all of that applies in the child abuse context. It seems that the courts never follow the normal law the moment someone is suspected of child abuse," Peter replied.

"I think it's worth checking," Joe said.

"Well, there goes my Saturday," Peter replied. "There may be something to it. And even if it doesn't help on Tuesday, it will help us analyze whether or not we can bring a civil rights suit against the CPS workers later."

"At the risk of popping your bubble, ole boy," Joe said, "if you don't win on Tuesday, there ain't no way you'll ever win a civil rights case. And even if you do win, there's a strong likelihood that the federal courts will dismiss the case anyway."

Sometimes Peter wished Joe was less knowledgeable about federal law. Every lawyer loves to dream of legal revenge for his innocent client. Such cases are easy to dream and hard, very hard to win.

Normally Peter would spend a Saturday in late May out on Liberty Lake either fishing or canoeing. But this Saturday he was destined to spend most of the day shuttling between his office and the law library writing a brief on the constitutionality of the search and seizure conducted by Corliss, Coballo, and Donahue.

By the end of the day, Peter felt he had gained a great deal of knowledge. He did not have a great amount of constitutional experience, but he was a good, fast researcher—especially when a deadline on an important case pressed in on him. He left the office at six, with a twenty-three page brief all ready to go.

"Let's see Ms. Willet top that by Tuesday," Peter said with relish as he snapped off his computer, picked up his keys, and headed for home.

～

Gwen spent the day shopping with her mom. They hit both downtown and the Northtown Shopping Center. June Mansfield was doing her best to fill the hours. But every time they saw a child, especially a little girl of four or five, Gwen would be reminded of the pain of separation. After a while they quit and simply went to the Mansfield home and spent the rest of the day cooking, eating, and watching old movies on television. Gwen appreciated her parent's concern and the activity. All of it helped—but not enough. She was lonely and worried.

10

~

Her night had been sleepless. Her dreams were desperate. And in the middle of the night the plan became more and more dominant in her mind.

Gwen tucked her hair up in a large straw hat. Her large, dark sunglasses were next. She had placed both suitcases in the car sometime around three the night before when no one in the neighborhood could see.

At eight-thirty she pulled out of the driveway heading north. Two sealed envelopes lay on her dash. Her path down the South Hill seemed surreal, even more than the past five days had been for her.

Spokane was quiet at this hour of the morning. A few cars heading out to one of the nearby lakes. Most of those who would be making their way to church would be underway sometime in the next hour.

She crossed the Spokane River and headed up Division toward Whitworth and the northern edge of town. At Francis, she turned left and wound her way through the neighborhood of Tom and Brenda MacArthur.

She cruised slowly past their house. There was visible activity inside the home. Two blocks away, Gwen parked in an elementary school parking lot and decided to stroll about as if she were going for a Sunday morning walk.

The first time she passed by, Gwen was on the sidewalk opposite the MacArthur home and noticed that the house next door was up for sale. She circled the block and a few minutes later passed by directly in front of the house. Her eyes were constantly on the back yard. Her ears were on alert listening for the yelps and squeals of her daughter at play.

The adjacent yard was unfenced. She found a tree in the side yard that would be a perfect shady spot to sit. From the base of the tree, few could see her from the street and she had a good view of the MacArthur's back yard.

She thought again of her mother and father. She knew she would not see them again for a long time—perhaps ever. She thought of her sisters and their families. But then she thought of Casey and the possibility that she would lose custody for something she did not do. As her thoughts swirled, tears welled up and she remembered her determination that she would cry no more. But the only thing that seemed to eliminate the possibility of more tears was to be reunited with her daughter at once.

A sound roused her from her trance. It was the voices of three children. The MacArthurs' twins and Casey came running and skipping out the back door to play.

Perhaps it was the moisture which soaked through. Perhaps it was simply breathing the fine northwest air which cleared her head. Perhaps it was the thought that occurred to her that her parents would miss their daughter as much as she would miss them. Perhaps it was the thought that her innocent daughter would become a fugitive. But whatever the reason, the would-be kidnapper got up, brushed herself off, got in her car, and drove away.

Before she had gone six blocks, her thoughts became confused again and she knew she could not spend the day alone. Gwen was afraid to go to her parents' home—afraid that she might tip them off to her secret, but now aborted plan. She wanted no one to know her intentions.

She stopped at a convenience store, got out and took the two envelopes—letters to her parents and her lawyer—tore them up and threw them in a trash receptacle. She walked to a pay phone, deposited a quarter and dialed.

"Peter, this is Gwen."

"Oh, Gwen, am I happy to hear from you. What's up?"

"Is it too late to go to church with you this morning?"

"No, the later service isn't until eleven. You have plenty of time. I'd be happy to come get you."

"That won't be necessary. Can I meet you there?"

"It's a little tough to find. Why don't I meet you in the parking lot of the McDonald's on Pines and Sprague?"

"What time should I be there?"

"Ten-thirty. Can you make it?"

"Yeah, no problem."

"This'll be great. I'm sure it will lift your spirits and be a real encouragement to you."

Gwen certainly hoped so. Anything would be better than the way she felt right then.

⁓

Gwen and Peter sat about half-way back on the far left side of the auditorium of Valley Fourth Memorial Church. Gwen hadn't really known what to expect, but it surely wasn't what she found at Valley Fourth. One thousand people attended and everything was so informal. The singing was energetic.

"These people are really vibrant," she commented to Peter during one of the songs.

Gwen felt a little awkward not knowing any of the songs, but many were simple melodies and she was able to sing along toward the end of most songs. The prior Sunday, Gwen had attracted attention coming in late to a smaller fellowship. She appreciated being a bit lost in the crowd of this larger church—although a number of people who knew Peter well immediately noticed that a striking woman was with one of their most eligible members.

One of those who noticed Gwen right away was Aaron Roberts. He was seated across the auditorium about four rows back with his wife Lynn, and their four children.

After about thirty minutes of music and prayer, Pastor Scott Lind began to teach. He was finishing a series on the Book of James. The sermon was entitled, "The Power of Prayer." Gwen was not surprised by the topic. It seemed to her like a very "churchy" thing to talk about.

As Pastor Lind began, Gwen remembered that she had prayed last Sunday for victory and that her prayer had certainly not been answered. She wanted to know why. Why hadn't God answered her prayer? The pastor had at least one visitor who was an instant skeptic.

Lind's key verse was James 5:13. *"Is any one of you in trouble? He should pray. Is anyone happy? Let him sing songs of praise."*

Peter noticed how intently Gwen was listening. The verse Pastor Lind was focusing on frustrated Gwen greatly, but at the same time she found it interesting. The pastor began talking about the "troubles of today." Some troubles are minor, he said. Some more serious, some very serious. Lind taught that all troubles of all levels need to be brought to God in prayer. And he told many interesting stories of how God had answered such prayers.

Gwen didn't miss a word, but still was unconvinced since her own recent experience had left her with an important unanswered prayer.

Finally, Pastor Lind began his second and final point.

"Friends, some of you may be facing the most serious troubles you have ever faced in your life. But as difficult and trying as those circumstances may seem, unless you have personally accepted Jesus Christ as your Savior, you face another kind of trouble which is far worse than anything we can ever face on earth. There are troubles which last forever. And such troubles are the unfortunate destiny for every person who dies without Jesus.

"We are taught in the Book of Romans that all of us are sinners. If you are honest, you must admit that your own experience confirms this is true. We have all done things that are wrong in the eyes of God.

"There is a price to be paid for sin. And that price is death. Your death, your spiritual death. That's what each of us deserves for our own sins.

"But there is an alternative. God could have been a righteous judge and just sentenced us all to go to hell. But instead He chose to pay the penalty Himself. He chose to have Jesus, his only child, pay the penalty for all our sins. Jesus was absolutely innocent. He had done nothing wrong. He had never sinned.

"Jesus could have said, "Hey this is unfair, why am I being punished for something I never did? In fact, God Himself could say, "Why should My child be taken from Me to pay for something that was made necessary by the sins of all those people?" But He didn't.

"God loved us so much, He willingly sent His son. Jesus loved us so much, He willingly died.

"It is simply up to us to respond in prayer. We need only acknowledge that we believe that Jesus is the true and unique Son of God, and ask Him to come into our lives and forgive our sins, and be our savior."

"If you are still facing those troubles that will last forever, the most important prayer you will ever pray is simply, 'Jesus, I believe in you. Please forgive my sin and live inside my heart.'"

Gwen was absolutely frozen in place. The illustrations chosen were too close to her own situation for her to miss the point. She clearly understood. But at the same time, her heart could not get over the stumbling block of last Sunday's unanswered prayer.

As the pastor gave the closing innovation, Gwen prayed only this, "God, I don't understand all this. I'm asking one more time. Please, please, help me get back Casey. Please God."

⌢

Aaron and Lynn rushed over to Peter and Gwen immediately after the last song. Lynn struck up a friendly conversation with Gwen. Aaron turned to Peter and whispered, "Who is *she*?"

"She's my new client you told me to witness to."

Aaron had watched Peter watching Gwen during the service. "You'd better be careful," was all Aaron could say without prolonging the side conversation.

Peter nodded, a bit red-faced.

Back in his car, Peter asked, "Well, what did you think?"

"It was very nice. The people were very friendly."

"Was that a different kind of church experience than you have seen in the past?"

"Sort of. It was very informal. It did remind me of camp. You were right about that."

"What did you think of what the pastor said?"

"I liked him a lot. He seemed nice and he was interesting."

Peter couldn't resist. He was, after all, a lawyer. He pounced on her evasive answer. "What did you think about the substance of his talk?"

"I'm not sure exactly. I don't know why I'm telling you all this, but last Sunday I wandered into that church on 29th. I went in to pray. I prayed that God would help me get to keep Casey. Obviously, God didn't answer my prayer. That's what I kept thinking about the whole time."

Peter didn't have a quick come-back. After a long pause, "I can understand why you would think that. I hope you will give God another chance. I've not only been working on your case, but I have been praying a lot for both you and Casey."

Their eyes met and lingered. Gwen didn't know what to think, but she was deeply touched that this man who was a total stranger to her five days ago, would care so much to take time to pray for her.

"Thank you for praying, Peter. I asked God again. I'll wait and see what happens."

"That's sounds fair," Peter said with a degree of heaviness. He realized that not only was the fate of Gwen's custody of Casey riding on this hearing on Tuesday, but Gwen's view of the reality of God might be affected for a lifetime as well.

~

On Monday morning Sally was sent out to conduct the exchange of psychologists reports. She picked up two copies of Dr. Schram's report and drove to the Public Safety Building. There she exchanged one copy for a copy of Dr. McGuire's report which had been left at the front desk by Gail Willet with strict instructions to only release the report if there was an exchange.

Sally couldn't help opening and skimming both reports. She would see them eventually anyway, but she rarely saw these things first and she was very curious.

Peter was shocked by the content of McGuire's report. He could not believe that two psychologists could interview the same people and come to such wildly divergent opinions. After a second reading, it was obvious he needed some answers from Gwen.

"Gwen," Peter said into the phone, "you need to come down here right away. McGuire's report came in and I need some answers."

"Why? What did he say?"

"I know you said he was very nice, but his report is vicious. You'd better come down here right away."

"OK. This is unbelievable. I'll get there as soon as I can."

Gwen was ashen-faced as she scurried around to get herself together to go downtown. Dressed in jeans and an oxford shirt, she was underway in five minutes.

As she drove down the winding hill past the parks, stately homes, and the hospital where she worked, Gwen began to regret she had not snatched Casey and run.

~

Sally ushered Gwen immediately into Peter's office. A copy of McGuire's report on Gwen was sitting on Peter's desk.

"Take a look," Peter said. "It's pretty awful. What did you tell this guy?"

Gwen shrugged her shoulders and scanned the front page.

"Why don't you flip to the last page and read his conclusion," Peter said.

He watched as the crimson went up her neck and across her face. Coming to the end of the page, Gwen threw the report down on the desk in anger. She sprang out of her chair. "He's lying. He's a dirty, lousy liar. I can't believe this!"

Peter watched her carefully. He was analyzing her behavior, much as juries evaluate a person on the witness stand. Embarrassed anger would reveal a person upset that they had been found out. Forceful anger, Peter believed, would reveal a person railing against injustice.

She paced in front of the windows, her fury building. "That is the most despicable thing I have ever read in my life," Gwen fumed. "He was so syrupy sweet. Portrayed himself as so understanding. I thought he was a great guy. And now this!" She walked back in front of Peter's desk, put both hands firmly on the desk, and leaned over, placing her weight on her arms. "Peter, this man is an absolute liar. I did not tell him that my parents abused me. Either he was smoking those funny cigarettes *and* inhaled, or else he is an absolute idiot!"

Peter believed her. And he was relieved she was angry rather than crying. He could work with an angry woman to get the details.

"OK," Peter said, "why don't we take it from the top? What did you tell him that might make him think your parents abused you?"

"I have no idea," Gwen replied. She walked back to the window and stared blankly at the ONB Building and Riverfront Park beyond. "The only thing I said that remotely resembles such a thing, was that my parents spanked me when I was growing up."

"Why did you bring that up?"

"I didn't. He asked me."

"Can you remember exactly what you said—or as close to it as possible?"

"I think I said something like, 'I spank Casey in basically the same way my parents spanked me.'"

"Well, that would make some sense," Peter replied. "If he is working on the assumption you spanked Casey in a manner which left bruises, then he might have concluded that your parents spanked you and left bruises as well."

"But a little bruise is not abuse!" Gwen exclaimed.

"You're right. At least in theory. But these days even a little bruise, one assumes that it is child abuse. You aren't telling me that you've left little bruises on Casey, are you?"

Gwen turned on her heel, glaring at Peter.

"Whoa. Sorry. Just checking," Peter said, ducking his head as if Gwen had thrown a punch.

Gwen smiled, a little, at Peter's move.

With a soft voice, Gwen looked at Peter and asked, "How bad is this really? I didn't say these things. Can you help me? Peter, can you help me?"

Peter pursed his lips in grim determination. "I can't guarantee anything. Basically it's going to come down to a matter of who the judge believes—our psychologist or their psychologist; you or Corliss. It will probably come down to a question of credibility. It will be my job to find every angle I can to make their story seem not believable and our version very believable."

Gwen went back to the window and stared. "This is so unfair," she said. "I am absolutely telling the truth and the other side is crazy or lying. And my child and my future hang in the balance of one man who has to look me in the eye and try to decide if I'm telling the truth."

Peter's mind said, *Any man who looks in your eyes will enjoy the experience.*

But aloud he asked, "Gwen, do you recall meeting Aaron Roberts on Sunday? You talked with his wife Lynn for a little while."

"Yeah," Gwen replied, wondering why he brought this up all of a sudden.

"Well, Aaron and I meet for prayer every Friday morning. And this past Friday, we met and read some verses from the Old Testament together, from the book of Proverbs. There was one particular verse that really seemed to stand out to me about your case." Peter stood, walked to his credenza and picked up his Bible which was lying on the top.

"Let me read it to you," he continued. "'*The king's heart is in the hand of the Lord; he directs it like a watercourse wherever he pleases.*'

Gwen, I've been praying this verse for you. This means that God is able to direct the heart of a king, or in our case a judge, wherever He wills. Sometimes our prayers are not always answered immediately. But I am praying that tomorrow God will direct Judge Romer's heart toward the truth—that he will believe you and return Casey home."

Gwen held her breath, deep in thought. "Thank you, Peter, that's very nice. I hope it comes true. You sure are different from my last lawyer. Bible verses and prayers, instead of . . . " She couldn't bring herself to finish the sentence.

"If you don't mind, I'd like to pray for you right now."

Gwen looked at him, shrugged, and nodded.

"Oh Lord God," Peter begin. "I only ask You for what is right tomorrow. I ask You that the judge believe the truth and not lies. And I ask You to direct his heart to reunite Casey with her mother who loves her so. In Jesus' name, Amen."

Gwen stood quietly—a little embarrassed. Sighing heavily, she asked, "What's next?"

"I need to study his report and prepare a cross-examination. I've also got some surprises for the other side. I spent all day Saturday in the library writing a brief that argues that the CPS workers violated your constitutional rights when they burst into your home without a warrant. If the judge agrees with me, he should dismiss the case."

"Do you think he will?"

"It's a long shot. Trial judges rarely rule anything unconstitutional. Normally you have to go to federal court or at least to the state appeals court to have a serious examination of constitutional issues. But we've got some good arguments and I think it will throw the other side off stride."

"I hope *something* works," Gwen said with a sigh.

"Me too," Peter said again pulling his gaze away from her face. "I've got to stop staring at her," he told himself. But he didn't. Finally, looking down at his desk, feeling convicted in his spirit, he said, "Well, I'd better get to work."

"What do I need to do next?"

"I guess nothing, really. Just meet me at the courthouse at 8:15, in the waiting room there."

"I'll be there with my parents. Will Casey be there?"

"Probably not. The foster parents will probably just have her at their house waiting."

"What should I wear?" Gwen asked.

"A nice, but not fancy dress in your favorite color."

"OK. See you tomorrow." She got up to leave. At the door, she turned and looked at him. "Peter, please keep praying, OK?"

⌒

Gordon Landis sat patiently in the shabby waiting area. He had an appointment with a Legal Services lawyer at eleven that Monday morning. He aimlessly looked through the week-old newspaper for the first time. Finally, his name was called and he went into the small office. Bob, a twenty-six-year-old guy with an earring, was the lawyer.

Gordon was almost completely sober, but the effects of a weekend binge were apparent. Legal Services lawyers see all types. A drunk without a job was nothing new to Bob.

Gordon explained that his ex-wife had a child abuse case filed against her and that he hadn't been notified.

"Have you received any kind of legal papers at all?" the lawyer asked.

"Only this," Gordon replied handing Bob a copy of the affidavit he had signed for Peter.

"Is all this true?"

"Yeah."

"What do you want me to do?" Bob asked.

"I want to know my rights. Should I go to court? Do I need a lawyer?"

"Do you want to get custody of your child?"

"Can I?"

"Maybe," Bob replied. "Do you think these charges are true?"

"I know they're not true," Gordon said. He was grateful that Bob did not ask him how he knew they were not true.

"They still could find against her and you have a presumptive right to custody if you want. But the court will inquire into your fitness as a parent."

"Like what?" Gordon asked.

"They'll ask about your finances, your job, and your home situation. And maybe your drinking. You got a drinking problem?"

"No . . . not really," Gordon stammered.

"What about a job?"

"I'm looking for the right thing right now."

Well, at least he's creative, Bob thought sarcastically. A day never passed before he heard that answer.

"Well, let me be honest. I don't think you have a ghost of a chance of gaining custody. If I were you, I'd stay home tomorrow unless someone serves you with a subpoena."

"Sounds good to me," Gordon said.

～

Peter sent his brief on the constitutional issue via a legal messenger service. The original was filed in the court, a copy delivered to Judge Romer's chambers, and a final copy to Willet. Peter fully expected her to be unable to respond. Normally an attorney is expected to file a brief far enough in advance of a hearing to allow the other side to respond. However, under these kinds of fast-track hearings, judges almost always accept a brief no matter how late it is filed.

Willet received the brief at three-thirty. She read it quickly, got up from her desk, walked across the room and pulled out a floppy disk containing a number of her briefs she had written in Seattle.

She pushed the disk into the disk drive and hit three strokes to get to the directory. Within minutes she selected the four portions from four prior cases which responded to all of Peter's arguments.

At 5:45 P.M., two hours and fifteen minutes after receiving Peter's twenty-three pager, Willet pulled her thirty-five page polished response from the printer. She would personally hand it to Peter Barron just before the hearing. She would relish the look on his face.

⁓

Peter's deposition lasted longer than expected. He arrived back at the office at six-thirty. He picked up the phone.

"Hello, Mr. Landis, this is Peter Barron, Gwen's attorney."

"Yeah, what do you want?"

"I just wanted to remind you of the hearing tomorrow at ten. Gwen really needs you to come and testify for her."

"Huh . . . Well I'll see if I can." His slurred speech indicating heavy drinking.

"Please do your very best to be there. Would you like a ride to the courthouse?"

"Uh . . . no."

"Try to get a good night's rest." Attempting to be as diplomatic as possible, Peter added, "A good night's rest will give all of us clear heads in the morning."

Gordon was too drunk to get it.

"See ya." Gordon said, letting the receiver drop to the floor.

11

Dawn found Peter leaning on the railing of his deck watching the sun rise over Liberty Lake. The sky was partly cloudy, a high, thin layer of white here and there. The air was still cool, but would soon give way to the gentle warmth of the mid-morning sun. His brief was complete. His expert witness readied. The adverse witnesses had been subpoenaed. Peter suddenly thought, *Too bad I didn't send a subpoena to Gordon Landis*

He went over and over the scenario of the day in his mind. Ever since Gwen left his office the day before, he had been able to completely focus on Gwen the client. Gwen the woman had only barely crossed his mind a time or two. It was time for battle and the litigator in him had arisen. The combination of instinct and experience was surging through him to allow him to focus on this hearing to the exclusion of all else.

At 7:00, Peter went inside to finish dressing. He chose the same blue suit and yellow tie he wore when he first met Gwen. It was his favorite. He grabbed his litigation brief case and headed for his car.

At 8:10, Peter walked into the juvenile court waiting room five minutes early. Gwen and her parents were already there. They had been waiting anxiously since eight.

They gathered their belongings and headed down the hall to the same conference room where Peter had met the Mansfields a week earlier. Peter gave the three of them a brief verbal outline of what he expected from each of the anticipated witnesses at the hearing. Not only was Peter more capable than Walinski, it was obvious that he really cared about Gwen and her case.

At eight-thirty, they became worried about Gordon.

"Maybe I should call him," Peter said.

"Do you think I should?" Stan offered.

"Who would have the most effect getting him to come?" Peter asked.

Both parents spoke at once. "Gwen."

"Will you do it?" Peter asked.

"For Casey, I'll do whatever it takes. Where can I call?"

～

Gwen was about to hang up when Gordon finally answered the phone on the seventh ring.

"Huh. Uh . . . Hello."

"Gordon, this is Gwen."

"Yeah."

"Gordon . . . uh . . . umm," Gwen stammered, "are you coming to court this morning."

"Oh, that."

"Yeah, it's real important."

"Not for me it isn't."

"What do you mean? Do you really want Casey in a foster home? Isn't that important to you?"

"Well, yeah. But there's nothing I can do now."

"My lawyer says it could really help if you came."

"Yeah, I know that's what he says. But I went to a lawyer yesterday and he told me to stay away if I wanted."

"Gordon, please. Please, do it for Casey . . . and for me."

"I'll see."

A surge of fear coursed through Gwen's heart. "He's not coming."

～

Shortly after Gwen returned to the conference room and told what Gordon had said, the judge's clerk knocked on the door and summoned Peter to the judge's chambers. Willet was waiting when he arrived.

"Good morning, Peter," Judge Romer said brightly.

"Good morning, Judge," Peter replied.

"Well," Romer said, glancing back and forth between both counsel, "are we all ready to go?"

Both attorneys said "yes."

"Ms. Willet, tell me who you anticipate calling and about how much time you'll need for your case in chief."

"Your Honor," Willet began, "that depends in part on whether we will be allowed to rely on the evidence presented at the last hearing. If Mr. Barron insists on all evidence coming in anew, then it could take considerably longer."

"Peter?" the judge asked.

"Your Honor, I've listened to the recording from last week, and have had it transcribed. In the interest of time, I am willing to let that evidence stand." Peter's answer was completely truthful; he was concerned about time. The judge had allotted until noon for the hearing. But there were strategic reasons that he wanted the record to stand exactly as it was as well.

"In light of that, Your Honor, I will be relatively brief. I will only have one live witness, Dr. McGuire, our psychologist. I'll need about thirty to forty minutes for my direct examination," Willet said.

"OK," the judge said, making some notes on his yellow pad. "Peter?"

"I will need about an hour-and-a-half on my direct examination of three witnesses. I would also anticipate about twenty minutes or so for cross-examination of Dr. McGuire."

"I'll write you down for forty minutes for McGuire," the judge said with a half-laugh. "Cross examinations always take longer than the estimates. And who are the three witnesses?"

"Our psychologist, Jean Schram, will take the most time. I have also subpoenaed Rita Coballo, another CPS worker, and Police Officer Mark Donahue. They both accompanied Ms. Corliss on her warrantless raid of my client's home."

"Your Honor—" Willet interjected.

Holding up his hand, indicating "Stop," Romer said, "Save it for the court room, Ms. Willet. I have read both your briefs on the issue of the constitutionality of the search, and I will hear argument in the courtroom, not in here."

"Both briefs, Your Honor? I was unaware that Ms. Willet had filed a brief."

"Here it is, Mr. Barron," Willet said, handing the thick document to him. Not only did she write thirty-five pages, but she had made copies for the judge of fifteen relevant cases. Duty required her to serve Peter with an identical copy. Peter was taken aback, but said nothing. Willet was a master of the nuance and read Peter's reaction perfectly. The faintest hint of a smile flashed across her face. It was a sweet moment.

"Anyone else to testify?"

"No, Your Honor," Peter said. "Unless something develops during the testimony of today that requires us to recall one of the witnesses from last week. I may well call my client to testify again, depending on what happens."

"Certainly, Peter. That is your right," the judge said. "Let me say, it is rare that I see so much preparation for a hearing like this. You are both very good lawyers, and I happen to believe that cases concerning the fate of children are every bit as important as car wreck injury cases. Car wrecks are always well litigated. Child abuse cases are usually pretty one-sided. You both deserve commendation for taking this very seriously. Let's get going."

Peter glanced at Willet. For a few seconds they shared a common feeling that they were engaged in one of the more noble aspects of being a lawyer. And then, their natural instincts regained control and their minds began to race again, thinking how they could pulverize their opponent over the course of the next three hours.

∾

Peter escorted Gwen and her parents into the courtroom. There were more people present than Gwen anticipated. Gail Willet and Donna Corliss were seated at the counsel table on the left side of the court room. Officer Mark Donahue and Rita Coballo were both seated in the front row behind Willet. Randall McGuire was in the last of four rows on the left hand side. His hair was perfect. And he was at his dandy best wearing a blue silk, patterned jacket, navy wool slacks, and an Italian silk tie. Gwen winced when she saw him, and immediately looked at the floor until she was well past his row. Gwen looked two or three times around the courtroom and confirmed her suspicions. Gordon was not there. But she thought he wouldn't be there for a little while in any event.

"No Gordon," Gwen whispered to Peter.

"You're right," Peter replied grimly.

Without warning, the judge entered, and both lawyers again jumped to their feet.

"Please, please be seated. We're in juvenile court. All right, I understand we are ready to begin. Are there any preliminary matters?"

Peter sprung to his feet. "A couple of things, Your Honor. First, I'd like to ask for the exclusion of witnesses."

"Very well, it is your right to do so," the judge replied. Looking around the courtroom, the judge said, "Ladies and gentlemen, Mr. Barron has invoked a court rule which requires that all people who may take the witness stand today be excluded from the courtroom until it is time for them to testify. The rule is designed to make sure we get just your own testimony and not get things all confused with one witness listening to another witness and trying to reply or adapt. It's simply routine, so I will ask Dr. McGuire, Officer Donahue, Ms. Coballo, and Dr. Schram to leave the courtroom if they are here."

McGuire, Donahue, and Coballo began to leave. Peter stood and said, "Your Honor, Dr. Schram is not scheduled to be here until ten-thirty."

"That's fine; is there anyone else who may testify who is present?" the judge asked. "Obviously, the parties may remain. Mrs. Landis, this rule doesn't apply to you since it is your hearing. And Ms. Willet, I assume that you are designating Ms. Corliss as your representative for this hearing."

Willet stood. "That's right, Your Honor. I'm entitled to one person to assist me from CPS and obviously, Ms. Corliss is the most knowledgeable about this case."

"That's fine," the judge said with a smile, but he resented Willet's statement of the obvious. "We're familiar with the operation of this rule on this side of the mountains as well."

Willet turned red, and realized that it would be unwise for her to talk down to the judge again.

Peter stood again. "My second preliminary matter, Your Honor, concerns the constitutionality of the search conducted by the two CPS workers and the police officer. We have both filed briefs on this subject and I am prepared to argue the matter now if the court desires. First, for the record, I formally ask the court for an order of dismissal for reason the search in this case was unconstitutional, and accordingly, all the evidence concerning the alleged bruises is improper under the principle of the 'fruit of the poisonous tree' case from the United States Supreme Court. Would Your Honor like me to address the merits of this issue right now?"

"Briefly, very briefly, Mr. Barron. We only have three hours for everything," the judge replied.

"Your Honor, if you grant our motion, we can all be out of here in fifteen minutes."

Judge Romer glanced up to indicate he wanted Peter to get on with it.

"Our motion begins with the iron-clad rule that unless a government official has a warrant or exigent circumstances, any search that is made of a person's home is illegal," Peter said. "In this case there was no warrant, nor has there been any claim to date of exigent circumstances—no emergency justifying the immediate entry into this home.

"It seems apparent that CPS is not relying on either a warrant or the doctrine of exigent circumstances. Rather, CPS appears to be arguing in their brief that when CPS workers are investigating child abuse, they are not required to obey the Constitution of the United States.

"We rely primarily on two cases which make it clear their position is a gross misunderstanding of the law. First, the U.S. Supreme Court of *Wyman v. James* which we cite in our brief. In that case, the Court held that social workers who were making routine inquiries regarding families who receive welfare need not obtain a warrant. But in the course of the Court's discussion, the majority explicitly held that when social workers enter a home to conduct an adversarial investigation, the normal rules of the Fourth Amendment are to be followed.

"The second case is *H.R. v. Alabama*, a 1993 case. In that case a social worker obtained a court order from a trial court based on nothing more than an anonymous tip from a child abuse hotline. The mother who was being investigated appealed that order claiming that an anonymous tip was not sufficient to justify the court order.

"The appellate court agreed with the mother's position and held that it would be illegal to allow a court ordered search of a home if there was no greater evidence than an anonymous tip.

"If an anonymous tip is insufficient to obtain a court order, it is also insufficient to justify a search where there has been no court order." Peter sat down and waited.

Willet sprang to her feet. "Your Honor, Mr. Barron makes two factual assumptions which have not been proven in the record. He assumes that the search was made based on an anonymous tip. There is nothing in the record which says that the tip was anonymous. All reports are confidential, which means we are not allowed to tell others the identity of the caller. It does not mean we don't know who the caller was. Or to be more precise, it does not mean Ms. Corliss does not know who the caller is. I have no idea personally whether the call was anonymous or not. Mr. Barron has simply failed to prove the tip was anonymous.

"His second factual assumption was that there were no exigent circumstances. He does not know whether or not our information included information about the existence of bruises. If we had a report of a child being beaten with a stick, and the child was bruised, it is our position that we have exigent circumstances—a real life emergency—and we are going to go into that house to save that child no matter what.

"Accordingly, Mr. Barron cannot go anywhere with his constitutional argument because he has no factual proof of his contentions. However, let's assume for the moment that he gets around the issue of proof. Mr. Barron is simply wrong when he contends that child abuse workers must have a warrant to conduct an investigation of this nature.

"This is not a criminal case, this is a juvenile case which crosses the bridge between civil and criminal law. We are not expected to follow the strict rules of criminal procedure in the conduct of juvenile cases, including child abuse investigations.

"The job of CPS workers is to protect children. If we have to comply with the technicalities of all the rules of searches and seizures which apply in the ordinary criminal context, we are going to have tens of thousands of additional children—innocent children—who are going to be hurt, maimed, or killed, while Mr. Barron wants us to demonstrate exigent circumstances. Millions of children are dying across this country. That is exigent circumstances. And child abuse investigations done in good faith need not comply with all of the technicalities Mr. Barron desires.

"We rely on the case of *Meyers v. Contra Costa Department of Social Services.* This is a decision of the U.S. Court of Appeals for the Ninth Circuit. Mr. Barron relies on the H.R. case from Alabama. Alabama decisions are not binding in Washington. Decisions of the Ninth Circuit are binding on this jurisdiction. And the Meyers case approved the actions of social workers who allegedly violated the Fourth Amendment rights of a California family.

"Our position is simple. Social workers who act in good faith are immune from constitutional challenges of this sort."

Peter stood to reply. The judge, however, had heard all he cared to hear.

"Mr. Barron, there is no need to reply. I am going to deny your motion for now and we are going to go on with our hearing today. Even if I were to agree that the search was illegal, I am not inclined to dismiss this lawsuit. If you want to discuss the legality of that search in some other context or at a later point in this litigation, we can re-examine the issue. I may be a bit too simplistic, but I simply want to find out what is happening with this little girl. Your motion is denied. Is there anything else before we get to the evidence?"

Peter glanced at his watch. Nine-eighteen. "Just a minute, Your Honor." Leaning over to Gwen he whispered, "Gordon hasn't come in, has he?"

Gwen shook her head no.

"We have a final preliminary matter to discuss. And again we are asking the court to dismiss this case. Our ground for this motion is RCW 26A.04.050."

Willet grabbed her statute book and flipped to the section Peter had just cited.

"This section requires," Peter continued, "that in any juvenile case where the custody of a child is at issue, it is the responsibility of Department to notify both the custodial and non-custodial parent of the lawsuit and give each parent a chance to respond. Simply put, CPS has failed to notify Gordon Landis, Casey's father and Gwen's ex-husband, of this lawsuit. Accordingly, both today's hearing and last week's hearing were conducted illegally. We ask that Casey be returned to my client and the decision of last week vacated because of this major procedural failure."

"Ms. Willet," the judge said, "this motion merits serious consideration, what do you have to say?"

"Your Honor, I agree with part of what Mr. Barron says, but I disagree with his conclusion. He is correct in saying that Mr. Landis, and this is the first I have heard there is a Mr. Landis, is entitled to notice. And he is right that without Mr. Landis here in the courtroom today, this hearing cannot go forward. However, it does not mean that last week's hearing is void. Mr. Barron is apparently unaware of the decision of the Washington Court of Appeals in *Freed v. Rose* last January. In that case, the court held that a procedural failure concerning notice can only be raised by the party who was not notified. I know that this case has not yet made it into the statutory pocket part updates, but I know that the case was decided since I was the winning lawyer in that case, Your Honor, and I can supply the court the citation if necessary."

"Ms. Willet," the judge said, "why has Mr. Landis not been served?"

"The truth is, Your Honor, I was unaware of the existence of a Mr.

Landis as I mentioned a moment ago. We'll be happy to postpone this hearing until next Tuesday and give him the proper notice," Willet replied.

"I'll be out of town next week," Romer replied. "It will have to be two weeks from now. I do not approve of your failure to check into the existence of Mr. Landis, but I may have no alternative but to continue the matter."

Gwen was about to panic. This Gordon maneuver was supposed to help her, but all of a sudden she was staring the prospect of two more weeks without her daughter as a result. She looked at Peter with desperation in her eyes.

Turning to Peter, the judge asked, "Mr. Barron, have you had any contact with Mr. Landis?"

"Yes, Your Honor, I have. I have an affidavit he signed which says that he received no notice of this lawsuit, that he finds Gwen to be a very good mother, and that he has never known Casey to be bruised from spanking. If I may approach the bench, I'll hand up the affidavit."

"Fine," the judge replied. He paused to read the two page document. "Well, Mr. Barron, it looks like I'm going to have to—"

Just then there was a loud stumbling sound at the courtroom door. Before anyone could say anything else, a head peered in the door and said, "Is this the Landis hearing? I'm Gordon Landis and I guess I'm supposed to be here."

For the first time in years, Gwen wanted to hug Gordon.

"Well, Your Honor, I guess our problem is solved," Peter said, hugely relieved.

"Not so fast," Willet said, jumping to her feet. "Just because Mr. Landis is present does it mean that he is prepared for a hearing? He has the right to obtain counsel and argue his position fully."

"Mr. Landis, come forward," the judge said. "You have come in belatedly in this matter and since you were not served by the Department it's not your fault. What is your desire? Do you want a lawyer? Would you like to have this hearing later? What would you like? Because you haven't been officially notified you pretty well get to call the shots for today."

"Well, judge, I talked to a lawyer yesterday. I don't think it would do any good to talk to another one. I'm just here to speak up for Gwen. She's a good mom. That's all. Nothing has to be put off because of me. I don't have much else to say."

"Well," the judge said, "in light of this, I think we can go ahead. Let the record reflect Mr. Landis is now present and has waived the procedural failures. Ms. Willet, be more careful next time. I want you to always assume there is a second parent and in my court, at least you should make some effort to comply with the law."

The prosecutor squirmed in her seat. It was obvious the judge did not like her personally. But, she had prevailed on the constitutional issue, and seemed poised to prevail on the second issue even though it had been her error in failing to serve Gordon. *I'd rather win than be liked,* Willet thought to herself.

"We've already spent just over a half-hour on the preliminaries; let's get going," the judge said. "Ms. Willet, call your witness."

～

Randall McGuire adjusted his tortoise shell glasses as he walked to the witness stand. He turned, faced the clerk and solemnly raised his right hand.

"Do you promise to tell the whole truth so help you God?"

"I do," said McGuire.

Willet dutifully marched him through the preliminary questions establishing his credentials.

"Now, Dr. McGuire," Willet said, "did you have occasion to conduct an examination of Gwen Landis and her daughter Casey?"

"Yes, last Thursday."

"Can you tell us the nature of the examination process which you employed?"

"I interviewed Casey and Gwen individually and performed certain standard psychological tests on each of them."

"Which tests did you perform on Gwen Landis?"

"The MMPI, the Minnesota Multiphasic Personality Inventory."

"What is this test designed to reveal?"

"The MMPI gives reliable insight into basic personality traits such as truthfulness, anxiety, self-confidence, and so on."

"And what did the MMPI reveal about Gwen Landis?"

"Gwen is a sensitive, caring individual who has internalized a great deal of anxiety, frustration, and bitterness. These are the conclusions relative to my overall diagnosis."

"What did the MMPI reveal as to her truthfulness?"

"The results were inconclusive," McGuire answered with a concerned expression. "Gwen's original scores were quite conclusive as to her veracity." But McGuire knew three answers to change on the test to change the results. Six changed answers would have made Gwen out to be a serious liar.

"What degree of reliance did you place on the MMPI in making your diagnosis?"

"Almost none in isolation. But the MMPI results were quite compatible with my clinical findings through interview. Adding the two aspects of the process together yields a very reliable diagnosis."

Very clever. Peter thought while making a note on his yellow pad. *Don't attack the MMPI results independently of the interview conclusions.*

"What test did you perform on Casey?" Willet continued.

"I performed the draw-a-person test which is a standard psychological assessment tool. I also gave Casey the Piers-Harris Self-Concept assessment."

"What did these tests reveal?"

"Casey is quite a normal little girl in almost every aspect. Almost every aspect except one."

"What is that one area of exception?" Willet asked.

"Fear. Casey exhibits an extraordinarily high level of fear."

"Did your clinical interview corroborate these assessment results?"

"Absolutely. Casey is a wonderful little girl, but she is gripped in fear that is quite detrimental to her well-being."

"Were you able to ascertain the cause of the fear?"

"Casey is afraid of her mother," McGuire said.

Gwen winced and shot an angry look at McGuire.

Peter jumped to his feet. "Objection, his answer was non-responsive and there has not been a sufficient foundation to jump to this conclusion."

"Sustained. The answer will be stricken," Romer said. "Your question was fine, Ms. Willet. Your witness just jumped ahead a bit, if you could just rephrase the question."

"Dr. McGuire, we are still going through a description of the process," Willet said. "Without telling me the nature of your conclusion, my question is this: Were you able to ascertain the cause of Casey's fear?"

"Yes, I was."

"What is the standard you used for reaching your conclusion?"

"I employed the standard I believe you lawyers call 'reasonable medical certainty,'" McGuire answered. "It is my opinion that a clear majority of qualified professionals would reach the same conclusion based on the observable symptoms."

Willet stood and walked across the court room. "Dr. McGuire, I want to ask you to give us your opinion as to the cause of Casey's fear and the facts which support your opinion."

"Objection," Peter said. "Compound question."

"It is compound," the judge said, "but, I'm going to let it stand. Dr. McGuire you may answer the question that way if you can."

"Certainly Your Honor," McGuire said, turning to face the judge and flashing a perfect, yet humble smile. "It is my professional opinion that the cause of Casey's fear is her mother. Not her mother's relationship in general. In general terms, their relationship is quite positive. But there is a pathological aspect to the relationship—the area of discipline.

"There are four critical facts which lead me to this conclusion. First, Casey's interview revealed clear fear of discipline. Second, the CPS professional observed bruises. Third, Gwen admitted that her parents spanked her in a similar fashion. Fourth, Gwen revealed a great deal of bitterness and anger toward her ex-husband and frustration with her perception that he does not give her proper financial support. It appears that her frustrations, and her own experience as an abused child, lead Gwen to spank Casey in an improper fashion."

"What do you recommend to restore the relationship between Casey and Gwen on a sound basis?"

"Let me emphasize that I think their relationship is basically sound and I strongly recommend therapy that I believe will yield a very positive result. But it is simply far too dangerous for Casey to be in her mother's care until this cycle of abuse that appears to have been going on, perhaps for generations, is arrested," McGuire said.

"How long do you recommend for this course of treatment?"

"I believe that five to six months of foster care will be necessary to achieve the desired results. If she cooperates under my care, I believe that we can make the necessary gains on this time table. If she doesn't cooperate, then it may take a year or more."

"Your witness," Willet said shooting a look of satisfaction at Peter.

Willet had walked McGuire through a flawless performance. McGuire congratulated himself on mixing just a bare minimum number of lies with heavy doses of the truth to achieve the desired result.

Peter stood and grasped the back of his chair. "Dr. McGuire your conclusion is that Mrs. Landis is first a victim of abuse who is locked in a cycle of abuse, and that is why she is, in your view, abusing Casey. Is that a fair summary of your opinion?"

"Yes, counsel, I think that's fair," McGuire said with an upbeat tone.

"What makes you think she was abused when she was a child?"

"She told me so."

Peter paced across the courtroom with his hands clasped in front of him. "She told you so. Hmmm. What, precisely, did she say?"

"I don't remember the exact words. I just remember making a note that she had also been abused by excessive spanking."

"Do you have those notes with you?" Peter asked.

"No, I'm afraid I don't. They're in my office."

"Convenient, isn't it? Dr. McGuire, do you have a fax machine at your office?"

"Yes, of course."

"Your Honor," Peter said, "I would like the good doctor here to be directed by the court to call his office and have these notes faxed here to the juvenile clerk at once. Can we have a five minute recess for this purpose?"

"Any objection, Ms. Willet?" the judge asked.

"Yes, Your Honor," Willet said standing at her table. "This witness did not testify on direct from his notes and I see no need to waste time in a fishing expedition."

"Your Honor, it is our position," Peter began, "that Mrs. Landis never told this psychologist she was abused as a child, because the simple fact is she was not abused. I think I'm entitled to see this man's notes to find out what she really said. It is my belief there is some misunderstanding. I believe I'm entitled to see these notes."

"OK, Dr. McGuire, I'd like you to step into my chambers and use my phone to call your office."

"Of course, Your Honor," McGuire replied calmly. *My secretary will just have to 'discover' the fax machine is broken*, he told himself while making his way to the judge's chambers.

"We'll take a five minute recess," the judge said. "Come with me, Dr. McGuire; I'll get the fax number for the juvenile clerk's office off my rolodex."

McGuire followed the judge into the juvenile court chambers. The judge walked to the rolodex, flipped it a few times. "The number's 555-3458. Here's the phone," he said taking the receiver off the cradle and handing to the dapper psychologist.

McGuire paused, hoping the judge would leave so he could make the call in privacy. Romer just stood there, looking at McGuire, waiting for him to place his call. He dialed.

"Hello, Nancy, this is Dr. McGuire. I'm here in Judge Romer's chambers and he would like you to fax a copy of my notes from the Gwen Landis interview here. Just her interview notes."

"I don't want any more interruptions. Have her fax you the whole file. Let's get the whole file in case something else comes up," Judge Romer said, interrupting.

"Uh, Nancy, you need to fax the entire file." Turning to look at the judge, McGuire said, "There will be a lot of pages, are you sure you want it all?"

"I think it's a good idea. Let's get it all," Romer replied, still studying McGuire.

"Nancy, fax the whole file," McGuire said, rapidly trying to remember if he wrote anything in the file that would reveal the exact nature of his actions. "Fax it as soon as you can, I know how busy you are."

"Tell her to fax it immediately," Romer commanded with obvious irritation.

"Uh. . . Nancy, we're going to need that immediately . . . Uh . . . 555-3458 . . . Yeah. Thanks. Bye."

"Thank you so much," Judge Romer said with a smile. "Shall we?" he said, gesturing toward the door.

At ten minutes after ten, the court reconvened with Randall McGuire perched nervously on the edge of his chair.

"The clerk informs me the pages are still coming in on the fax," the judge said. "Mr. Barron, do you have other questions we can cover while we are waiting?"

"Certainly, Your Honor," Peter said standing with a yellow pad in his hand.

"Dr. McGuire, do you spank your own children?" Peter asked with a fixed stare at the psychologist as he paced across the room behind counsel tables.

"Objection," Willet called out. "I fail to see the relevance of this."

"Sustained, unless you can show some relevance," Romer said.

"With the court's permission, I'll ask a couple of questions to lay a foundation to demonstrate the relevance."

"First of all, Dr. McGuire, do you have children?"

"Yes, I have a son, age eleven."

"And does your own practice of discipline reflect your professional philosophy of how parents should raise their children?"

McGuire saw the trap coming. "To a certain degree," he said hedging as best he could.

"To a certain degree," Peter repeated, pacing, staring. "Well, let me ask it this way: You wouldn't practice a form of discipline that you believed to be abusive per se, would you?"

"That is correct."

"And so your professional philosophy about child rearing and discipline can be revealed in your own practices with your own son, isn't that true?"

"Well, I guess you could say that."

Peter paced and stared. He glared at his pad. Turning to McGuire he said in a soft voice, "You don't spank your son, do you, Dr. McGuire?"

"Objection," Willet said, standing to argue.

"Overruled, I think the foundation of relevance has been laid," the judge said, leaning back in his swivel chair.

"Please answer the question," Peter said.

"No, I do not spank my son," McGuire replied.

"And isn't it true that your decision to not spank your son reflects your own philosophy of what is right and what is wrong in parenting?"

"It's not that simple," McGuire countered. "I don't believe that discipline is one-size fits all. What is good for my family may not be good for others and vice versa."

"I see," Peter said pacing some more. "I assume that you have counseled a great number of families who come to you with concerns about child discipline. Am I right?"

"Mr. Barron, I hate to interrupt, but I believe that the young woman at the back of the courtroom has the fax you wanted," McGuire said, hoping to distract Peter from his current line of questions.

"Thank you. Let's look at them in a moment, doctor," Peter said refusing the bait. "My question right now concerns the families coming to you for counsel. Is it true that you counsel families who come to you with concerns about discipline?"

"That is true. Hundreds of such families."

"Fine," Peter said stopping behind his chair, grabbing the top with both hands. "Dr. McGuire, in these hundreds of cases have you ever counseled any family to begin spanking their children as the most effective means of solving their discipline problems?"

"I'm not sure," McGuire lied. "But it would be rare," he said getting a little closer to the truth.

"Dr. McGuire, when we strip it down to its bare essentials, you believe that all spanking of children is inappropriate, don't you?"

"I wouldn't say it that way," McGuire said trying to hedge his answer as best as possible.

"All right, doctor. How *would* you say it?"

McGuire stared straight ahead. Gathering his composure, he said in a warm self-assured voice, "Mr. Barron, I would put it this way. I simply believe there are better ways to achieve proper behavior in children than spanking them in most cases."

Peter was satisfied that he had made as many inroads on this subject as possible. He walked to the back of the room and held out his hand to the court clerk who had been sitting quietly with the file folder. Peter whispered, "Thank you," to the clerk, turned and headed back toward the courtroom clerk.

Peter approached the courtroom clerk and held the file out. The clerk took the file, put a sticker on it, and wrote on the sticker, "Respondent's Exhibit 1." Peter walked back toward McGuire and paused about ten feet from the witness stand, faced the judge and said, "May I approach the witness, Your Honor?" It is an ancient ritual still practiced by a diminishing number of the members of the bar. The judge granted permission with a wave of his hand.

As he handed the as-yet-unopened file folder to the increasingly nervous psychologist, Peter said, "I'm handing you what has been marked for identification as Respondent's Exhibit 1 for identification. Can you identify this document?"

McGuire said nothing but took a great deal of time looking through the document. In reality he wanted to make sure he didn't see anything in the file that shouldn't be there. When the pause became embarrassing, he said, "Since this is a fax, and not my original file, I just wanted to make sure my secretary got everything. It will take me just a few more moments."

He continued to scan the file frantically, doing his best to look as cool as possible. A quick once-over revealed nothing of his secret arrangement. He looked up, smiled at Peter, and said, "Yes, it appears to be all here."

"Fine. Dr. McGuire, I would like you to look at your notes and ascertain for us, what they reveal as to Gwen Landis's exact words which led you to the decisive conclusion you mentioned earlier concerning her alleged history as a victim of child abuse," Peter said.

McGuire skimmed quickly and found it a second time. He had located the spot in his earlier scan through the file. McGuire looked up at Peter, indicating that he had found the place.

"Dr. McGuire, you told us earlier that you could not remember the exact words Gwen Landis used to lead you to your conclusion she had been abused as a child. Having looked at your notes, can you now tell us more precisely what she said on this subject?"

"Yes, what I wrote was this, 'Dad spanked G in a similar manner.'"

"I see, a similar manner. Why did this statement make you think that Gwen had been abused by her parents—or more precisely, by her father?"

"I was, of course, working with the history of events supplied to me by Child Protective Services. CPS revealed a history of Gwen spanking Casey in a manner that left bruises. And, Mr. Barron, you questioned my philosophy earlier, but I know of no mental health professional who will have a contrary view about bruising a child. That is abuse—period."

"I see," Peter said. "Let me see if I understand you correctly. CPS told you that Gwen bruised Casey. Gwen told you that she spanked Casey in a manner similar to the manner she had been spanked by her father in childhood. You added those two things together and reached your conclusion about a cycle of abuse. Is that about right?"

McGuire brightened. "That's pretty close to my process of reasoning."

"Dr. McGuire, what happens to your analysis if you remove the bruises CPS claims they saw. If there were no bruises, doesn't your entire analysis about the cycle of abuse crumble? Without verification of the bruises, your theory of abuse simply vanishes, doesn't it?"

McGuire was scrambling. He was not about to give Peter a straight admission, but the best he could do was to say, "Mr. Barron, I have worked with CPS many times before. They are highly trained, committed professionals and very reliable. If they observe bruises, I feel that I am on solid ground to proceed with an analysis on that basis."

"Dr. McGuire, I hate to prolong this, but let me try once again. If there were no bruises, your analysis is just plain wrong, isn't it?"

"I refuse to make an assumption that CPS professionals would make an error of that magnitude."

The judge had grown tired of McGuire's evasiveness. He was sympathetic with the doctor's reliance on the veracity of CPS workers, but he was annoyed McGuire would not simply admit that the presence of bruises was crucial to his theory. Romer interrupted the process saying, "Mr. Barron, you've made your point. I understand that if the report of bruises is erroneous, this witness's analysis would have to be rethought completely. Do you have anything else for this witness?"

"No, Your Honor," Peter said, feeling good that the judge had indeed gotten the message.

"Any redirect?" Romer asked.

"Just one question," Willet said. "Dr. McGuire, were there any other findings in your reports that support your conclusion Mrs. Landis abuses her daughter?"

"Yes, indeed. Her anger, her frustrations, and Casey's extreme fears all add up to support this theory. Indeed it is a perfect match."

"That's all, Your Honor," Willet said.

Judge Romer looked at Peter. "Any brief recross, Mr. Barron?"

"Just one question. Dr. McGuire, all these symptoms are also consistent with a family that has been severely traumatized by the separation of a mother from her daughter, aren't they?"

"There certainly would be some trauma associated with such a separation, but I don't believe that the degree of emotional response can be adequately explained by a few days of separation."

"Dr. McGuire, how would you feel if a court took your child away from you for a few days and falsely accused you of child abuse?"

"Objection," Willet said loudly.

"Sustained."

But Peter had made his point. The judge, who was also a father, understood completely.

"May the witness be excused?" Judge Romer asked both attorneys. They both nodded.

McGuire rose, took his file and started to leave. Peter stood. "Your Honor, I would request that the witness leave exhibit 1. Even though it wasn't admitted, it was referred to in the record, and since the court can possibly have on-going jurisdiction in this matter, I think it would be appropriate to retain."

McGuire glared at Peter. Peter held out his hand, smiled, and took the file from the psychologist. He walked over and handed the document to the clerk.

"Do you have any other witnesses at this time, Ms. Willet?" the judge asked.

"No, Your Honor. For the record, we rely on our affidavits and the testimony at the prior hearing."

"Mr. Barron, for the record, you have agreed to this process?" Romer asked.

"Yes, Your Honor. In the interest of time, we so stipulate," Peter replied.

"OK," the judge said, "the state rests. Mr. Barron, it is your turn."

"Fine, Your Honor. I would like to call Rita Coballo," Peter said standing, flipping his notebook to the right page.

The clerk went out into the waiting area, and shepherded Ms. Coballo back into the courtroom.

After she was sworn, Peter asked. "Ms. Coballo, you are an investigator for CPS, is that right?"

"Yes," Coballo answered warily.

"You accompanied Ms. Corliss here," Peter said gesturing toward her co-worker seated beside Ms. Willet, "on May 12, when the examination of Casey took place at the Landis home, didn't you?"

"Objection. Leading question," Willet called out.

"Overruled. Ms. Coballo works for the prosecuting agency, she is obviously called as an adverse witness, which entitles Mr. Barron to ask leading questions," Romer said.

"You accompanied Ms. Corliss to conduct the investigation at the Landis home on May 12, didn't you?"

"Yes, I did."

Peter began pacing again behind the counsel tables. "Ms. Coballo, did you see any bruises on Casey?"

"Yes, I did."

"Ms. Corliss called the bruises 'fading bruises' in her report. Does that comport with your recollection?"

"Yes, it does."

"Ms. Coballo, can you describe the location, color, and nature of these 'fading bruises'?"

Coballo froze. "They were on the lower back, just above the buttocks, and on the buttocks themselves."

"Was there a greater prominence on one side or the other?"

"No, not really."

"Ms. Coballo, are you sure of your description of these bruises?"

"Yes, I am virtually certain, but I do see a lot of bruises."

"Speaking of seeing a lot of bruises, isn't it your policy at CPS to take photographs of bruises?"

"Yes. We usually do."

"Was that done in this case?"

"No, I don't believe so."

"Why not?" Peter asked.

"I believe we simply forgot the camera. Human error."

"Human error, huh? I see, how often does that happen?"

"Not often. We're careful to follow policies and regulations."

Peter smiled, put his pad on the table, and pulled out his chair. "No more questions of this witness, Your Honor."

"Any cross, Ms. Willet?" Romer asked.

"No, Your Honor." Willet said.

"Very good. We're picking up a little speed," the judge said glancing at his watch. "Mr. Barron, is your next witness another short witness?"

"Yes, Your Honor. It is Officer Donahue. It will be a similar amount of time as Ms. Coballo."

"Good," the judge replied. "Let's get his testimony, and then we will take our morning recess."

Officer Donahue was brought into the courtroom by the bailiff, duly sworn, and identified himself as an officer employed by the Spokane City Police Department.

"Corporal Donahue, you accompanied Ms. Corliss and Ms. Coballo to the Landis home on May 12?"

"That's right."

"Did you participate in the actual strip search of Casey Landis?"

"No, I wasn't even in the room. I waited in the living room, while the two CPS workers went into the bedroom with the little girl."

"Where was Mrs. Landis?"

"She was in the living room with me."

"Why was she there rather than in the bedroom with her daughter?"

"The CPS workers did not want her in there. My assignment was to keep her away from their investigation."

"This may seem obvious, Corporal Donahue," Peter said. "But did you see any bruises on Casey?"

"No, I did not. I saw the little girl. But she was fully clothed when I saw her."

"Did you hear the CPS workers say anything about bruises?"

"Objection. Mr. Barron is asking for obvious hearsay," Willet said.

"Your Honor, I am not seeking the information for the truth of the statement."

"The objection is overruled."

"Let me rephrase the question. Did you hear the CPS workers say anything about bruises?"

"No, not directly."

"Did they say anything that indirectly related to the subject of bruises?"

Donahue remembered his earlier discussion with Peter. "Oh yeah. At the time, I didn't think they found any bruises, because the lead worker, this lady here—" Donahue said pointing at Donna Corliss, "she told Mrs. Landis she would close the case if she would answer some questions."

"I object," Willet cried out. "The officer can testify to what he heard. The inferences he draws from that are pure speculation."

"Overruled," the judge said, not because of any particular rule of evidence but because he was interested in the testimony.

"When did this happen?" Peter asked resuming the inquiry.

"After they had examined the little girl."

"Corporal Donahue, have you accompanied CPS workers on other such occasions?"

"Yes, many, many times," Donahue said shaking his head.

"Have you ever heard a CPS worker say anything about dismissing a case when they had found bruises?"

"No. And that's the reason I didn't think they had found any bruises. If they had found bruises, it would be very strange for them to say anything about closing the case."

"Thank you very much, Officer Donahue. I have no further questions."

Willet knew she had been wounded. She stood with a pad in her hand.

"Officer, you didn't hear the CPS workers say one word about bruises one way or the other did you?"

"No, I didn't."

"Your opinion about there being no bruises is pure speculation, isn't it?"

"Well, sort of."

"You're just guessing about that, aren't you?"

"It's an educated guess, I would say. All I can say is that I was surprised to hear they found bruises *after* they told the lady they would close the case if she would cooperate."

Willet saw she was losing ground rapidly and decided to quit. "Nothing more, Your Honor."

"Any redirect, Mr. Barron?"

"No, Your Honor. That's all."

"Very well," the judge said. "We'll be in recess for fifteen minutes. I want to start again promptly at eleven."

Gwen reached over and squeezed Peter's hand. It was obvious to her that he had scored well with Officer Donahue and she was greatly heartened. He smiled at her, stood and said, "He was great wasn't he? Couldn't be better if I had written him a script. But it's not over yet."

~

Gwen, her parents, and Peter spent the short break outside. There had been no conversation, only glares, at Donna Corliss and Gail Willet as they passed out of the courtroom into the waiting area. Coballo and Officer Donahue were gone—excused after their testimony.

At five minutes before eleven, Jean Schram pulled her car into the parking lot. Peter introduced her to the Mansfields and then the two of them stepped aside for some last minute instructions.

Promptly at eleven, Judge Romer re-entered the courtroom. "Call your next witness, Mr. Barron," he said.

"I'd like to call Dr. Jean Schram, if it please the court."

The bailiff went to the hallway and escorted Dr. Schram into the courtroom.

"Do you promise to tell the whole truth and nothing but the truth so help you God?" intoned the clerk.

"Yes, I do," Dr. Schram replied.

Peter began. "Please tell us your name for the record."

"I'm Jean Schram."

"And your occupation?"

"I'm a clinical psychologist."

"Where and when did you get your various college degrees?"

"I received both my bachelor's and Ph.D. in psychology from

Washington State University. The bachelor's was in 1965. The Ph.D. was in 1987. I was a mom in between. I went back to school after my youngest graduated from high school."

"How long have you been a licensed clinical psychologist?"

"For seven years."

"And do you have an area of specialization?"

"Not in a formal sense, but the vast majority of my work involves family issues, marital problems, or children."

"Did you have occasion to interview Gwen and Casey Landis?"

"Yes, I did, last Friday."

"Please describe the interview process you followed," Peter said, glancing at his notes for the first time since he asked the question.

"I broke the interview into three phases. First, I interviewed and observed Casey and her mother together. Then, I interviewed Gwen while my graduate intern gave Casey some routine psychological exams. And finally, I interviewed Casey, while my intern gave a standard test to Gwen."

"Please tell us about the qualifications of your intern."

"She has just received her Ph.D. from WSU and is doing a one year stint under my supervision as is the normal practice in our profession. This is the third time my alma mater has asked me to supervise an internship. She is fully qualified to perform these standard tests, but I did the scoring and interpretation."

Peter resumed his pacing. "Dr. Schram, what was your assessment of Gwen and Casey Landis based upon your interview and tests?"

"Objection," Willet said. "I don't think she can testify based on tests she did not perform herself. These exams are not like simply taking a temperature where a nurse can report a simple fact to a doctor. Psychological tests are much more complex and the person doing the scoring must observe the person being tested."

"Overruled," the judge said before Peter could say a word. "I have psychologists in here all the time looking at tests other doctors have performed and they comment and interpret based on these tests. I am sure your Dr. McGuire would feel quite competent to interpret the results given by Dr. Schram here. Overruled."

Dr. Schram looked at the judge. "Shall I continue?"

"Yes, ma'am. Do you remember the question?"

"Yes. My findings were that the relationship between Gwen and her daughter is warm, loving, and quite positive. I found no area of abnormalities between them."

"Did you find any psychological problems in either of them?" Peter asked.

"Gwen has some understandable feelings of bitterness and anger toward her ex-husband, but nothing out of the ordinary. And she is certainly quite upset with this whole process, especially the strip search and removal of her daughter. But, as a mother, I certainly think this is quite understandable and within normal limits one would expect."

"And what about Casey?"

"Casey is a very fearful little girl right now. Very fearful. It is outside the normal ranges for a child her age. She's going to need some counseling."

Peter stopped pacing and resumed his second favorite position—standing behind his chair, gripping the back. "Dr. Schram, were you able to ascertain the cause of the fear?"

"Yes, I was. In my opinion her fear reactions were brought on—"

"Objection," Willet called out. "Mr. Barron needs to lay a proper foundation."

"Sustained. Turn-about is fair play, Mr. Barron. You made the same objection with Dr. McGuire."

Peter smiled and bowed his head. "Fair enough."

"Dr. Schram, you told us you were able to reach an opinion as to the cause of Casey's fear reaction. In reaching this conclusion, did you employ the standard of 'reasonable medical probability?'"

"Yes, I did. I believe the vast majority of mental health professionals would reach the same conclusions I reached if they were supplied with the same data."

"What data did you rely on?"

"The interviews, the tests, and especially the time of interview with mother and child together. But there was one outstanding piece of data we gathered, which provides what I believe to be the singular best insight into the fears of this little girl."

"And what evidence is that?"

Dr. Schram reached into a file folder and pulled out a picture—a picture drawn by a child with crayons. "This picture was drawn by Casey in the draw-a-person test. My assistant directed her to draw a picture of some people and this is what she drew."

Peter had the picture marked and identified as Respondent's Exhibit No. 2.

"Please describe the picture."

"It shows two women, one can tell they are women because they are wearing dresses, with quite scary looking faces or heads. They are standing by what appears to be a bed."

"Did you ask Casey any questions about this picture?"

"Yes, I did. My assistant brought it to me after the testing, and during our interview time I asked Casey to tell me about this picture."

"What did she say?"

"She said it was the mean ladies in her room."

Peter began to pace once again. "All right. Based on your interviews with both Casey and Gwen, your tests, and your evaluations of these tests, and employing the standard of reasonable medical probability, what is your opinion as to the cause of the fear you observed in Casey Landis?"

"I believe it is a reaction brought on by the forced strip search by the two CPS workers and the subsequent removal from her home."

"Dr. McGuire testified earlier this morning he believed that Casey's fear was caused by her mother's excessive spanking. How does this comport with your findings?"

"I considered this as a possibility. But, it simply did not coincide with the observations I made—particularly when I observed the two of them together."

"Thank you, Dr. Schram. I have no further questions."

"Ms. Willet?" the judge asked, looking at the prosecutor.

"I have some questions, Your Honor."

"I assumed you would," the judge said with a smile.

"Dr. Schram, do you know Dr. McGuire?"

"Yes, I know him, mainly through his professional reputation, but we have met a few times."

"He testified this morning he has been in practice for seventeen years. And you testified that you have been in practice for only seven years, is that correct?"

"Yes, it is correct."

"And you testified that you were a 'stay-at-home mom' between your two colleges degrees, did you not?"

"Yes, those were the most important years of my life."

"At one point in your testimony, you said—and I think I am quoting you almost word-for-word—'that as a mother you can understand the reactions of anger experienced by Gwen Landis in reaction to the removal of her daughter.' Do you remember that testimony?"

"Yes, I do," she replied with confidence.

"Dr. Schram, you are called as an expert witness. A psychologist. There is no category of expert witness called, 'experienced mother.' Isn't it a fact that your entire opinion is colored with your mothering experience? You are not giving us a straight-forward professional opinion, are you? Aren't your opinions nothing more than home-spun theories?"

"Objection, the question is argumentative," Peter said.

"It is," the judge replied. "But I'm going to let her answer this one."

"Well, Ms. Willet, you are right in one sense. My experience as a mother does blend into my overall thinking as a psychologist. And it is my belief that a person who practices in this profession in a way that is totally separated from normal human experience has only a textbook understanding of psychology. Human experience, plus professional training is what enables us to understand people's problems and help them resolve them."

"I see, Dr. Schram." Willet said with a note of triumph in her voice. "Your Honor," Willet continued, "in light of this admission, I ask the court to strike the entire testimony from this witness. It is simply inappropriate to mix her profession with what she calls 'human experience' in the manner she has described herself."

"Your objection is noted, Ms. Willet," the judge said making some notes on his pad. "However, I believe your objection goes to the amount of weight I will ascribe to Dr. Schram's testimony, not to its admissibility. But your objection is duly noted."

"Thank you, Your Honor. I have nothing further."

"Mr. Barron?" the judge asked.

"I have nothing more for this witness," Peter replied.

"Thank you, Dr. Schram. You are excused," Romer said with the smile he gave to almost every departing witness. "Who's next?"

"I would like to call Gordon Landis very briefly," Peter replied.

"Fine, very briefly though. We only have fifteen minutes left."

Gordon Landis walked, without a stagger, to the witness stand.

After Gordon had been properly sworn and identified, Peter got quickly to the substance.

"Mr. Landis, how long were you married?"

"Four years."

"How long have you been divorced?"

"About two years."

"Do you exercise regular visitation?"

"Yes, every other week."

"Did Gwen spank Casey during your marriage?"

"Well, not at first. But around age two we would both swat her lightly on the bottom when she needed it."

"Did you ever observe bruises on Casey's buttocks or in the near vicinity at any time?"

"Never. At least never where there was not a reason other than spanking that we knew about."

"Such as?"

"Kids fall hard sometimes. You know, just normal kid stuff."

"Have you observed any bruises on Casey's buttocks at any time for any reason since the divorce?"

"No, I haven't."

"What is your evaluation of Gwen's parenting skill?"

"I think she is a very good mom. She really loves Casey. It's the reason I didn't ask for custody. I wish Gwen would resolve things with me. But that's another story."

"Thank you, Mr. Landis. No more questions."

Willet stood. "Mr. Landis, can you say for a certainty that some of these so-called normal childhood bruises were not bruises left from spanking that your ex-wife just explained away?"

"I can't say very much for a certainty. But I certainly don't remember ever thinking that a bruise I saw was caused by anything other than Casey falling or something like that."

"But it is possible that some bruises were caused by spanking, isn't it?"

"I guess anything is possible. But I don't think so."

"Nothing more, Your Honor," Willet said.

It was three minutes until twelve. "Are we all through?" the judge asked.

Peter stood. "Your Honor, I would like to recall Ms. Corliss and ask her one or two questions."

The judge looked at his watch and sighed. "I have another hearing at one-thirty and we all have to eat and I have to announce my decision, and you both will probably want to make a closing argument. One or two questions, that is it."

Corliss took the stand and was sworn to tell the truth.

"Ms. Corliss, you heard Ms. Coballo's description of the bruises this morning. Was it accurate?"

"Yes, it was very close to the way I remember the bruises."

"Fine." Peter pulled out a tape recorder from his litigation case. "I'd like you to listen to your own testimony from last week."

Peter pressed the button and Walinski's voice began.

"Can you please describe the bruises for me?"

"They were fading, kind of green and discolored a bit. They didn't look like they had been terribly severe when they were fresh, but I believe that any bruising caused by a parental spanking is child abuse."

"Where were they located?"

"On her buttocks."

"Can you be more specific?"

"On the lower half of the buttocks with a prominence of greater bruising on the left hand side."

"Are you sure you are not mixing this up with some other case?"

"I am absolutely certain of what I have told you."

Gwen caught herself having a positive thought about Walinski. But it was quickly choked off.

"Ms. Corliss, how do you explain the discrepancy between your testimony last week and Ms. Coballo's testimony this morning?"

"We both see lots of bruises. And I think the descriptions are pretty similar."

"Oh, I see," Peter said. "Nothing more, Your Honor."

"Any questions, Ms. Willet?" Romer asked.

"Just one," the prosecutor replied. "Do you have any doubt there were bruises?"

"None whatsoever."

"Fine," Romer said. "It is seven after, and I have to make and announce my decision. I do not want to delay beyond today making this decision. I'm going to ask you both to keep your closing arguments to two minutes each. Then I'll ask you all to come back at one, and I'll announce my decision. Ms. Willet, you may proceed."

"Your Honor, I'll be brief. Two professional CPS workers found bruises on this girl. If her mother had come to court and said, 'I'm really sorry' my recommendation would be to send Casey home and put the family under supervised counseling. But she continues to deny the existence of bruises. All professional witnesses agree this little girl is in need of serious psychological help because of fear. An angry, upset mother is not what this child needs. She needs a mother who will cope with reality, break the cycle of abuse and get on with life on a positive basis. Our plan of six months of custody, with ongoing therapy is what is needed. Dr. McGuire's analysis is sound. His recommendation is sound. I strongly recommend that the court retain Casey in her current placement and order a psychological program for both mother and child."

Willet sat down and shot Peter a look which said, "Beat that."

Peter rose and once again stood behind his chair.

"May it please the court. It is crucial to remember who has the burden of proof in this case. That proof rests squarely on the shoulders of the prosecution to demonstrate by clear and convincing evidence that child abuse has, in fact, occurred.

"I would respectfully suggest that the CPS workers, for reasons I simply cannot explain, are wrong about the existence of these so-called 'fading bruises.' There are no photographs; CPS routinely takes photographs of bruises. The police officer believed they found no bruises because they told Mrs. Landis that they would close the file if she would cooperate. Gordon Landis testified there were no bruises. And last Tuesday, this court authorized a medical and psychological exam, yet there is nothing offered today by the prosecution from the physician. It is proper to infer their doctor found nothing. Dr. Davenport, the child's regular pediatrician also reported by affidavit last week the child was not bruised. Dr. Davenport is a mandatory child abuse reporter. It is reasonable to infer Dr. Davenport has never observed bruises—otherwise a mandatory child abuse reporter would not sign an affidavit even when it is addressing a particular incident.

"The two psychologists present a totally different interpretation out of the same operative facts. Both report a scared little girl, but one assumes bruises because CPS told him so. The other psychologist, Dr. Schram, concluded that Casey is frightened by the two CPS workers. Both theories are plausible on their face. But only one theory is supported by the tangible evidence of Casey's own drawing; Respondent's Exhibit 2. Dr. McGuire also administered the draw-a-person test. He was required to fax his entire file, but there is no picture in the file. For whatever reason, the picture is missing, and McGuire's theory is just theory.

"There were no bruises. There is no abuse. A great injustice needs to be rectified by returning Casey Landis to her mother at once."

"Thank you both. This matter was well tried. I'll announce my decision at one. We'll stand in recess until then."

Gwen walked over to Gordon. "Thank you, Gordon. I'll never forget what you did today."

Gordon smiled, "Maybe things can get better for us."

"Maybe," Gwen said. "But you know what you have to change first before I would ever consider it."

"Yeah," Gordon said hanging his head. He stood and quietly slipped out of the courtroom and away from the courthouse.

⌒

Peter, Gwen, and her parents knew they couldn't eat until the decision was announced. It wasn't merely that they had only forty-five minutes, they were far too nervous to try to even attempt eating.

Peter suggested the four of them go for a walk in Riverfront Park. They all agreed. They walked to Peter's car, drove five blocks, and got out on the northside of the park. Gwen was holding tightly to her father's arm. June Mansfield walked alongside Peter.

"You did a very good job," Mrs. Mansfield said to Peter.

"Thank you, ma'am. You've got a great daughter and grand-daughter. They're pretty easy to defend."

"I like to think they're pretty great. But you were so much better than the last lawyer."

"The proof is in the pudding. We will find out at one," Peter said with a shiver. He was as nervous as he had ever been about any decision.

"You do think we'll win, don't you?"

"I know that we should win," Peter said. Gwen and Stan were both listening intently as well. "And that's my best judgment looking at the evidence as objectively as I can. But you really never can tell. I have walked out of cases convinced I won and ended up losing. Other times I was convinced I lost and ended up winning. Judges and juries both can be so unpredictable. They will seize some little point of evidence or some argument or some theory and go off and make a decision you could not have foreseen."

"What a crazy profession," Stan replied. "How do you stand it?"

"At times it really does bother me. But far more often than not, in the long run, with appeals and so on, things usually get sorted out pretty much according to some sense of justice. And if good people who don't believe the right things aren't in the system trying, the evil side will win every time." Peter laughed, "There I go again. Explaining everything in terms of good and evil. I try not to do it, but in this case it seems so applicable. Except for the police officer, I just couldn't stand all the people on the other side."

"I hate 'em," Gwen said without a smile.

Stan patted his daughter on the shoulder. "We'll deal with that when you get Casey back."

They walked and talked and eventually all fell silent. As the hour approached, their emotions were just too strong to talk about anything. They returned to the courthouse and were in their places at ten minutes before one.

Peter sat at the table silently praying. Gwen was lost in thoughts of escapes and victories and revenge and her desire to embrace her daughter so tightly she would never let go.

Just before one, Willet and Corliss slipped into the courtroom without a word.

At three minutes after one, Judge Romer entered from the door behind the bench.

"Thank you for waiting. A case like this one is a terrible burden on a judge. We want to do what is right for children and parents but sometimes those are not the same thing."

Gwen's heart sank. Peter felt a knot in his stomach. He did not like the way it sounded.

"First, let me say," Romer said, "that I always give great credibility to the testimony of CPS workers. If they tell me there are bruises, I give great weight to their testimony because of their experience and advocacy for children."

"And I also note Dr. McGuire's analysis makes perfect sense to me, if in fact there were bruises found on Casey."

"I will say I was very impressed with Dr. Schram. The fact that she was a mother before she was a psychologist only enhances the legitimacy of her analysis in my mind."

Gail Willet turned slightly red.

"I attach a great deal of weight to her testimony especially because she interviewed mother and daughter together and was able to watch them interact."

"This brings me to what I believe to be the crucial issue in this case—the existence of bruises."

Gwen looked at Peter trying to gauge his reaction. He didn't appear to be panicking, but she was on the verge.

"As I said earlier, I always attach a great deal of credibility to the testimony of CPS workers. But there are some troubling things I must consider as well. It would have certainly been better for all concerned if there had been photographs taken according to the usual policy. But, human error does happen, and I accept that explanation."

Peter's heart began to sink. "Please God, please," he said silently.

"But the description of the location of the bruises was quite different from last week to this week. That is quite troubling. Based on the normal credibility I attach to CPS workers, I view this whole thing as basically neutral. The normal credibility is undermined to some degree, but not conclusively by this discrepancy alone."

"For me, the conclusive factor was the testimony of Officer Donahue. These CPS workers see a lot of bruises, he sees some. He is not as likely to mix up two different cases. The fact that he believed they had not found bruises based upon the comment the case would be closed if Mrs. Landis cooperated, is for me the evidence that tips the scales."

Gwen's heart was racing wildly. She glanced at Peter. He was doing his best to maintain the poker face lawyers are expected to maintain when a judge is making a ruling.

"I am not making a finding that the CPS workers made up anything. I know Mr. Barron has inferred this. I reject this inference. But Mr. Barron correctly pointed out the burden of proof rests upon the prosecution, and I find that it simply was not carried in this case. Accordingly, the charges are dismissed. Casey Landis is ordered to be returned to her mother forthwith."

"Oh, thank you, thank you," Gwen blurted out loud, tears streaming down her face.

Peter grabbed her hand to hush her up. The judge just smiled and said, "You are welcome, and now if you will all excuse me, I have to prepare for another hearing in ten minutes. We are in recess."

Gwen jumped to her feet, grabbed Peter around the neck and squeezed him tightly in pure joy. Her parents came up and joined in the hugging and happy crying.

"Oh, Peter, thank you. This is the happiest moment in years. I can't believe it. I was so scared. Oh, thank you, thank you." She grabbed him again and held on. Peter knew he probably shouldn't, but he hugged back with enthusiasm.

12

~

Gwen and her parents drove the few miles north to pick up Casey. A few tears were shed but there was mostly laughter and hugging and kissing all around. Gwen expressed sincere appreciation to Brenda MacArthur. Casey seemed to be as happy as was possible under the circumstances.

Casey, Gwen, and her parents returned to Gwen's home for the balance of the day. Gwen would return to work tomorrow. Life seemed back to normal in almost every way. Then Casey's first nightmare came at ten-thirty while Gwen's parents were still at her home. It was a grim reminder that not everything would be resolved immediately.

Even Casey's nightmares could not dampen the great joy that had swept over Gwen's mind and soul. As she lay on her bed at midnight, relishing the thoughts of the day, it suddenly occurred to her that God had indeed answered her prayer.

"God, thank You for answering my prayers about Casey," she said softly, as she lay staring at the ceiling. "I was so worried. I don't understand how You work exactly. But thank You anyway. And thank You for sending Peter to be my lawyer. Maybe that's one of the ways You work, I don't know. Oh well. Amen."

Gwen let her mind dwell on Peter and all he had done for her. And the more she thought, the more Peter the man began to stand out more than Peter the lawyer. She was genuinely impressed with his character, his sincere desire to help the helpless, his stability, and even his religious commitment—though she didn't understand that yet.

Gwen had never really contemplated Peter's statements to her in their first conversation about not being able to marry a divorced woman. Her mind was so focused on getting Casey back that she never even tried to understand. Now, it puzzled her. She knew he was handsome and had been exceedingly kind to her, but her thoughts had not developed much beyond that stage. For the first time she realized that it was apparently not even a possibility she and Peter could see each other in a new dimension, and the thought left her feeling strangely empty.

Seventeen miles to the east, Peter lay on his bed, reliving the events of the day as well. His curtain was open and moonlight shone through the window that overlooked the lake.

It had only been a week, but virtually every waking moment of the last seven days had been focused on Gwen and Casey. They had even managed to invade his non-waking moments and had played prominent roles in his dreams.

The legal victory was bittersweet. He had poured his heart and soul into winning, but winning meant less contact with Gwen. That thought was both disappointing and troubling. He was disappointed because he wanted to keep seeing her. Yet he was troubled, because he knew his desires did not mesh with the lessons he believed the Bible taught. Gwen was not a believer. But Peter believed that her spiritual condition might well change anytime. Her status as a divorcee was unchangeable—absent the unlikely possibility Gordon would drink himself to death sometime soon.

Peter rolled on his side, flipped on his light, walked downstairs and got his Strong's Concordance. He returned to bed, took his Bible off the bedside table and with the two books in his lap began an earnest study. Maybe he had reached the wrong conclusion about marrying a divorcee, he thought. Just before two, Peter fell asleep in a half-sitting position with the light still on and the books fallen askew the bed.

Peter had more than enough to do when he arrived at the office Wednesday morning. Client meetings, which had been rescheduled from the previous week, would take up most of the morning. The afternoon would be spent preparing for two depositions later in the week. It was time to earn some money and stay in business.

At lunch time, Peter decided to grab a sandwich in a deli on the ground floor of the Paulsen Building and spend the rest of his lunch hour researching the possibility of a civil rights lawsuit against the social workers. After twenty minutes of searching he settled on the *Meyers v. Contra Costa Country* case Gail Willet relied on in court.

It was not a child abuse prosecution but a civil rights case against social workers—just like the one he contemplated.

The Ninth Circuit's decision left no doubt. He simply could not sue Corliss or Coballo for anything that happened after they filed the child abuse charges. They were absolutely immune.

But everything that occurred earlier could give rise to a civil rights claim—if the social worker violated rights that were "clearly established." Peter rolled the two-word phrase over and over in his mind. The sole claim he could make for damages would be to sue for the invasion of Gwen's home. Peter was glad that the real damages—the fear which had gripped Casey—could be traced primarily to the incident of May 5. The removal of Casey from her home would not give rise to any claim for damages, based on the facts and law as Peter could discover so far.

At two-thirty, Sally buzzed Peter on the intercom, "Gwen Landis on line two," she said.

"Hello, Gwen, I was just doing some research for you at lunch."

"Why? I thought everything was over."

"Well, their case for child abuse is over—although they could appeal. But that's unlikely. I was researching the possibility of a federal civil rights suit against CPS. You remember, we talked about suing them after we got Casey back. Well, we got her back and I was making plans to go ahead. Do you still want to?"

"I certainly do. Sue them for a gazillon dollars, especially that Corliss woman."

"That's not what you were calling about, is it?" Peter asked.

"No, it isn't. But I am glad to hear you are still working on things for me. The reason I am calling is to invite you to dinner at my house on Saturday night. It'll just be my parents, Casey, and me. Would you like to come?"

"You bet," Peter responded. "I wouldn't miss it for anything."

Gwen was pleased with his enthusiastic response. "Fine, seven o'clock. You know how to get here?"

"Yes, I think I can find it."

"See you then."

"Bye," Peter said casually. As soon as he hung up the phone he clenched his fist and said, "Yes!"

Peter got up from his desk and the notes on the deposition he was supposed to study. He paced in front of his windows, staring at the ONB Bank Building, a parking garage, and a sliver of Riverfront Park three blocks away. He was definitely going to talk with Aaron about a certain blond client on Friday.

~

On Wednesday afternoon, Donna Corliss was summoned to the office of Gerald Blackburn.

Corliss knocked on his door.

"Come in, Corliss," a stiff voice called from behind the door.

Blackburn was away from his desk closing the shades. It was a habit he had developed whenever he discussed a Code B file in the office.

"So you lost it anyway."

"I wouldn't characterize it as my loss exactly," Corliss replied.

"Well, it certainly wasn't my loss," Blackburn said coldly. "You know we have never lost a Code B case before."

"I know, I know," Corliss replied nervously. "We could always appeal."

"That's very risky. I don't want to bring any more scrutiny on this case than is absolutely necessary."

"But the appeal would be on the record. There wasn't a hint of any of our activities brought out in court," Corliss said.

Blackburn picked up the pair of Chinese worry balls he kept on his desk. He rocked back in his chair and jangled the two balls for a moment, lost in thought.

"I understand McGuire was forced to fax his entire file to the court," Blackburn said. "Did you scrutinize it to see if there was anything in there that shouldn't have been?"

"No, but that wasn't admitted into evidence. I'm telling you the record is clean," Corliss said. "I really think we should appeal."

"Now you listen to me carefully," Blackburn said leaning forward in his chair. "I'm giving you two assignments. And there will be no more talk of an appeal until you have completed them."

Corliss sat motionless.

"First, you will go to the clerk's office and review the McGuire file very carefully. If there are problems, you are to do nothing but report to me."

Corliss nodded. "Yes, sir."

"Second, you are authorized to go to Gail Willet and ask her for her opinion about an appeal. You are to tell her that your supervisor and only your supervisor is authorized to make a decision. You got that?"

"Yes, Mr. Blackburn, I'll report back to you immediately."

"See that you do. Immediately."

Corliss went directly to her state car and drove to the courthouse.

"I'd like to see the Landis file, including the trial exhibits," Corliss said to the clerk.

"Fine, I'll get it," the clerk replied. "What's up?"

"Oh, we just want to make sure we have everything we need to prepare the final order," Corliss lied.

"I thought Peter Barron would prepare the findings of fact and order of dismissal since he won," the clerk replied.

"I don't know," Corliss answered. "I just do as I'm told. Maybe they want to make sure he gets it right."

A minute later the clerk returned with the file. "You'll have to examine it right here," she said. "Only attorneys can take the file out of our office. You can sit at that table over there," the clerk said gesturing. For the next forty-five minutes Corliss pored over the file. She actually handled every document in the file, but kept going back to the McGuire exhibit. She didn't want to be conspicuous in case the clerk was watching.

Corliss didn't see anything that seemed to give away McGuire's arrangement with Blackburn. However, there were a lot of abbreviations strewn throughout the document she didn't understand. It appeared to be a kind of short-hand McGuire used to detail regular items he encountered in an interview. Corliss was able to decipher a few of the more obvious codes. The letter "G" appeared to stand for "Gwen", "C" for "Casey", and "pnt" for parent. But many of the codes eluded her.

Corliss took the file back to the clerk. "Is there any way I can get a copy of the two exhibits? We appear to have everything in the file, except for those two. Always like to keep complete records, you know."

"Sure," the clerk said. "It'll be twenty-five cents a page if you take them. If I give them to Gail Willet, she can get them for free since she works for the prosecutor's office."

"Oh, that's OK. It'll only be three or four dollars. I'd like them right now."

Corliss paid the clerk $3.75 and made a bee-line for Gail Willet's office across the courthouse compound, taking care to stash the exhibits inside her leather portfolio.

"I'd like to see Ms. Willet," Corliss said to the receptionist.

"I'm sorry, she's on the phone. Do you have an appointment?"

"No. I'm with CPS, my name is Donna Corliss. Ms. Willet was the trial attorney on one of my cases yesterday. I just want to check a couple of things with her."

"Oh, OK. When she gets off the phone, I'll see if she can talk with you."

Ten minutes later, the receptionist looked up at Corliss. "Ms. Willet can see you now. Do you know where her office is?"

"Thanks. I do."

Willet's door was closed. Corliss rapped tentatively.

"Come in."

Corliss opened the door and leaned in to be recognized.

"Oh, Ms. Corliss, come in. What's up? Another sure-fire-winner for me?" The sarcasm in her voice was unmistakable.

"No, not really. I just wanted to ask a few follow-up questions," she said, standing awkwardly in the doorway.

"Alright," the prosecutor said with a sigh. "But I've only got a few minutes."

"First of all," Corliss began, "let me say that you are one of the very best prosecutors our department has ever worked with. I thought you did a great job."

Thoroughly uninterested in the praise of a CPS case worker, Willet snidely remarked, "Yeah, bang up job—that's why we lost."

"Well, I thought you were great—really."

"Why did you come to see me today? I'm sure it wasn't to tell me how wonderful I am."

"OK, I'll get to the point. My supervisor wants your opinion about an appeal."

"Appeal! Are you serious? For what?"

"Well, we lost, and we think we should have won."

"But the case turned on purely factual issues and that is a pretty slim ground for any appeal," Willet said. "If we had some legal issue the judge messed up on, then perhaps. When it is purely factual, it is extraordinarily difficult to overturn a decision of a trial judge."

"What about the judge's ruling letting that homemaker parading as a psychologist testify? Isn't that a legal issue?"

"Well, perhaps. But it is extraordinarily weak."

"What about the issue of letting that police officer testify he thought there were no bruises because I supposedly said I would close the case if she would cooperate? Isn't that hearsay or something?"

"No. It's not hearsay—at least not the kind of hearsay we can object to. But," Willet continued as she turned to stare at the wall, "

. . . it was pure speculation. And I did object. And that's what the judge appeared to rely on most of all. Maybe you've got something there."

Corliss smiled and said nothing.

"So why do you and your supervisor want to appeal?"

"I didn't say we wanted to. At least I didn't say *he* wanted to. I'm only authorized to ask for your opinion. As for me, I don't like setting a precedent of judges disbelieving our testimony."

"I can understand that," Willet replied. "But frankly, I was a little troubled about some of the holes in your testimony. You and Ms. Coballo gave completely different versions of the location of the bruises. I tried to cover the best I could. And why no pictures? What's the deal with that?"

Corliss tried to not react. But her neck turned crimson involuntarily. She hoped Willet did not notice.

"Oh, I don't know. This Landis chick called us a bunch of vile names. And her unruly child was in hysterics when we just tried to do a routine exam for bruises. I guess we just got distracted. I know the bruises were there. You can count on that."

Willet thought over her prospects. Cloudy. Dubious. But she was sure that she would like to get revenge sooner rather than later on Peter Barron, Esq. In her humble opinion, she was the best appellate lawyer on child abuse in the state—and she wasn't far from wrong.

"OK, I'll think about it for a few days. We have thirty days to appeal. I'd like to take a fresh look at some of the cases. I did most of the recent ones myself, but I've never done an appeal on this precise issue. It'll take some time."

"When should I check back with you?" Corliss asked.

"Early next week."

"Sounds good to me. I'll let my supervisor know."

⌒

Peter arrived at the Red Lion coffee shop five minutes early on Friday morning. He wanted to get his notes and arguments lined up before Aaron arrived for their weekly Bible study. When Aaron arrived, Peter was still writing on a legal pad.

"Preparing for a big case?" Aaron asked as he slipped into his chair.

"If this is a case, then I have a fool for a client," Peter said.

Aaron gave him a puzzled look.

"You know," Peter explained, "the old saying that he who acts as his own lawyer has a fool for a client."

"Oh! I get it," Aaron said with a chuckle.

"I know. I know," Peter replied. "If you have to explain a joke, it ain't funny."

"Well, what's all this about, anyway?" Aaron asked.

"I've got something important to talk with you about," Peter said.

"It wouldn't be about a certain blond client who came to church last Sunday would it?"

"I'm that obvious?" Peter asked.

"Not exactly. I guess it was the two of you together that made a certain impression. Standing side-by-side, you looked like the models on a wedding cake."

"Oh, get off it," Peter laughed.

"OK," Aaron said, "time to get serious. What's all this about?"

"I guess the best way to say it is I need your counsel. I am having real difficulties sorting out my emotions relative to Gwen, and I need you to help me understand some scriptural principles."

"Go on," Aaron said.

"Gwen is not a Christian as far as I know, although she did walk an aisle and say a prayer when she was a teenager at a camp up at Riverview."

"Fourth Memorial's Riverview?"

"Yes. The same camp. Anyway, I think it is very likely that she may become a Christian very soon."

"What makes you think that?"

"Well, last Sunday, we talked for a good bit after church. The prior Sunday it seems that she just 'accidentally' wandered into

South Hill Bible Church. While she was there, she prayed for God's help with her first hearing. She lost, of course. That's why we had a trial this week."

"Oh, how did that go? I've been out of town and haven't heard."

"We won. Big time. Casey returned to her mother on Tuesday."

"Congratulations! I am sure it was your consummate legal skills once again," Aaron said with a smile.

"Thanks, but I'd be a fool to take the credit. It was a long way from a slam-dunk. The Lord was with us every step of the way," Peter said seriously.

Aaron nodded somberly.

"In any event," Peter continued, "she told me she had a hard time responding to our pastor's invitation last Sunday, because God had not answered her first prayer. So I told her: 'Why don't you put God to the test?' She agreed, and then we won. I expect she will respond very favorably when I get a chance to follow up."

"Or when someone gets a chance to follow up," Aaron said with one eyebrow raised.

"Uh . . . yeah," Peter replied.

"There's more, isn't there?" Aaron asked.

"Yes," Peter said, lowering his eyes. "I am very attracted to Gwen, and it's not just her looks, although her looks are obviously very appealing. But I know more than enough to curb that attraction unless and until she becomes a real believer."

Aaron, "You got that right. So what's the issue?"

"The issue," Peter replied, "is that she is divorced, and she didn't have scriptural grounds. And you know I have a commitment to not marry a divorced woman under those circumstances."

"Why did she get a divorce?"

"Her husband divorced her because she kept complaining he wouldn't get a real job. Now he's an alcoholic. I've met him—he was a witness in the hearing. Her complaints were obviously valid. He wants to get back together and she refuses because of his continued irresponsibility. To say it simply, I believe Gwen probably will become a Christian. But there is no way that she can change her status as a divorcee. What I want to know from you is whether I have read Scripture correctly when I made a commitment to never marry a divorced woman?"

"Wow, that's a real tough one," Aaron replied.

"You're telling me. I've been up late every night searching the Bible for the right answer. It's a lot like the law. There's enough material to use to argue either side of the issue," Peter said.

"Well," Aaron said sipping the coffee that had appeared at his elbow. "You are right in saying this is an issue where Scripture is not crystal clear. Very solid men of God have come to divergent views on this point. And when it comes to such issues, it is great to have personal convictions, but it is difficult to draw a blanket rule."

Peter looked at his friend with hopeful expectation.

"So, you've got a different kind of issue than pure Scriptural interpretation. You've reached a conviction in the past about the meaning of Scripture and made a commitment to God based on that understanding. And now, when a very attractive alternative interpretation of Scripture comes on the scene, you are rethinking your convictions. I don't think that's the way that God wants us to operate. Sure, there are times we should change our views. None of us interprets Scripture with one-hundred-percent accuracy. But I don't believe that we should change our convictions in the heat of the moment—especially when the reason for the change is not some new insight in Scripture, but simply a very attractive temptation to vary what we have believed."

Peter sighed deeply and fiddled with his coffee cup. "I was afraid you were going to say something like that. You're probably right."

"Well," Aaron replied, "I don't feel that it is appropriate for me to give you a blanket answer about divorce. If God changes your mind, that's one thing. But if it is a beautiful woman responsible for the change, I fear you set a very dangerous spiritual precedent in your life."

"Well, thanks. I think," Peter said with a weak smile.

~

Lila was on duty Friday night at the Ram's Head. McGuire did not recognize her at first because tonight her hair was jet black. She remembered McGuire from a couple of weeks back. A sharply dressed, good-looking guy was etched in her memory forever—or for a month or two, whichever came first.

McGuire did not have to wait long for Blackburn to appear.

Blackburn sat down without so much as a hello. He pulled a manila folder from his briefcase before speaking.

"This is a copy of your file that lawyer Barron got you to fax straight to the court."

"So," McGuire said.

"So!" Blackburn said sternly. "We are concerned that it may contain some reference to our arrangement on this case."

"Have you read it?" McGuire suggested, his own voice growing testy.

"Of course, I've read it," Blackburn snapped back. "But you've got so many initials and abbreviations, that I can't figure it all out."

"Well, if you can't figure it out and you know what's going on, what's the worry?"

"That pesky lawyer," Blackburn said.

"He did nothing but glance at it during the trial."

"Yeah, and I hear he destroyed your theory that we paid good money for you to develop."

"He did no such thing," McGuire replied.

"I'm not going to argue about it. We need to decide whether we are going to appeal this case. And we need to know if anything is going to jump out and bite us from these notes. We're giving you an assignment. I want a full version for my eyes only. I want a literal, correct, word-for-word translation. Hand written. No photocopies. One original—that's it. Then I want a safe version. I want you to make a plausible interpretation of anything in this report that opens us up in any way. Normally you're a head doctor. Now we're going to see how good a spin doctor you are. Make all the copies you want of the second version. Leave them lying in a park for all I care. But I want both versions on Monday. Right here at seven."

Blackburn immediately stood to leave.

"Hey, what's your rush? And where's my envelope?" McGuire demanded.

"There is no envelope. And there will be no more envelopes until we get these follow-up documents. You helped mess up this case. Now you're going to help clean it up."

"I will not be threatened," McGuire said with indignation.

"Think what you will. Just do what I tell you," Blackburn said coldly. He turned his back and was gone.

McGuire sat for a long time. Lila continued serving him beer until she actually started to look good to him . . . but not good enough. He walked to the door, hitting the wall only once on his way, and drove his BMW slowly through the housing developments that encroach on the city-side of Moran Prairie and on north to his home.

13

~

It was another Saturday in the law library and the office for Peter. He wanted to finish the federal civil rights complaint and take it to dinner that evening. After his conversation with Aaron, he realized that when he really focused on his responsibilities as Gwen's lawyer, his mind did not wander as much. Having the lawsuit completed would give him something substantive to talk about—at least at some point in the evening.

He was dressed in sweats and tennis shoes while he shuttled back and forth between his twelfth floor suite and the library two floors below.

At four-thirty, the last edit was finished and he printed out the sixteen page complaint, dropped it into the automatic document feeder on his copier and printed four copies—one for each of the adults scheduled to be at dinner.

Peter had his clothes for the evening in the back seat of his Explorer. He drove a few blocks to the Spokane YMCA where he and Aaron regularly played racquetball. Even though he was a decade older, Aaron was his stiffest competition. Today there would be no games at the Y, just a quick shower and on to dinner.

His navy wool trousers, blue and white striped shirt, and light-blue patterned sports jacket were perfect to bring out the color of his eyes, he thought with a touch of vanity. It was difficult not to think about trying to impress Gwen with his attire and looks.

Peter stopped at the flower shop on Grand on his way up the hill to Gwen's house. It was the polite thing to do, he convinced himself. Peter selected a brilliant spray of late spring flowers. While making the purchase, his eye wandered over to the cooler where the fresh roses were kept.

Thinking that Peter hadn't settled on the spring flowers, the clerk said, "Have you changed your mind sir?"

"No, these will be fine."

～

"Come in," Casey said when she opened the door. "Thank you for coming to our dinner."

The lines had been rehearsed at least fifteen times throughout the day.

Gwen was just a few feet behind her daughter when Peter stepped through the front door. She was wearing a long-sleeved pink cotton sweater and a long, flowing silk skirt patterned in shades of pink and light green. Peter swallowed, said "Hi Casey," then looked at Gwen, completing his thought, "Don't you both look beautiful."

"Thank you," Casey beamed. "It's my new dress."

"Good evening, Peter, thanks so much for coming," Gwen said extending her hand. "And thanks even more for making this victory dinner possible."

"Hey . . . thanks for inviting me. I wouldn't have missed it for anything. These are for you," he said, presenting the flowers he had been concealing behind his back.

"Oh, they're beautiful," Gwen replied.

An awkward silence was interrupted by the appearance of Gwen's father from the kitchen.

"Good evening, Peter," Stan said. "I was just in the kitchen lifting the roast out of the oven for the ladies."

"My mom is a great cook; you're going to love dinner," Gwen said.

"You and your mom are equals in the kitchen. You're both great," Stan said.

Stan's statement sounded a bit too much like a sales pitch, exactly as he intended it, and a second awkward moment followed.

"Well, how's my favorite client?" Peter said, squatting down to Casey's eye level. "I am really glad you are back with your mommy."

Casey smiled shyly, grabbed her mother by the knee, twisting her body back and forth.

"Please sit down," Gwen said. "Casey and her grandpa will keep you company while Mom and I finish getting dinner on the table."

"OK," Peter said. "If it is half as good as it smells, I'm in for a real treat."

Peter and Stan chatted casually. Peter did most of the talking, answering Stan's questions about his childhood, schooling, and his career history.

Dinner was soon ready, and Stan's culinary predictions had been modest. The conversation was mostly light. Peter quickly discovered they did not want to talk about the lawsuit in Casey's presence. But the entire family did accept Peter's invitation to join him at church tomorrow at eleven. Gwen had told her parents of the discussion she and Peter had about prayer. Tonight's dinner was a one-time event to thank Peter. A one-time visit to church to thank God seemed to Stan and June the right thing to do.

When the meal was finished, it was nearly Casey's bedtime. June served her a dish of ice cream—a more elaborate dessert was yet to come for the adults.

Within minutes Casey was dressed in pajamas and sent by her mother back into the living room to give everyone a goodnight kiss. She readily threw her arms around each of her grandparents who kissed her playfully. Casey ran over to Peter, but then suddenly became shy.

"It's OK, honey," June said. "You can give Mr. Barron a goodnight kiss. He really helped you and Mommy this week."

Casey shyly pressed her cheek against Peter's then turned and ran to her mother's waiting arms.

Peter and the Mansfields talked about Casey's current problems with nightmares. Peter's interest was both personal and professional.

A little girl's continuing nightmares could really motivate a jury to return a serious verdict for damages.

When Gwen emerged from the bedroom and sat next to her mother on the couch, Stan said to Peter, "Well, we would certainly like to hear about your ideas for a lawsuit against these awful CPS people."

"Sure," Peter said. He walked across the living room and retrieved the file folder he had placed on the hallway table. "I have copies of my final draft for each of you. Of course, if there's anything we need to change as we look at it, I can do it first thing Monday morning. I'm hoping to file the suit early next week. I want to keep their heads spinning."

"Sounds good to us," Stan said smiling. "Can you give us some background on what this will involve?"

"Of course. This past case was in the state court system. It was a civil child abuse case brought by the state against Gwen, supposedly for the protection of Casey. It did not technically charge her with a crime.

"This new lawsuit is one we are going to file against them on behalf of Gwen and Casey. We are going to bring it in federal court rather than in the state court system. We could file it in the state court system, but I'm afraid of the fact that all of the Superior Court judges we would go before routinely interact with these CPS workers. I want to go before a judge who never sees them at all—someone who is truly neutral."

Stan and Gwen gave each other affirmative nods.

"This is a civil rights case brought under federal law. It allows us to seek three kinds of court orders against the CPS workers and the State of Washington. First, we are asking for the court to award Gwen and Casey money damages for many of the things that have happened to them. Second, we are asking the court for an order which prohibits CPS workers from ever going into anyone else's home without a warrant and causing all of this trouble again. And finally, we are asking the court to award you attorney's fees," Peter said looking at each of them.

"Speaking of attorney's fees, can we make them pay you for the fees Gwen is going to owe you for the first case?" Stan asked.

"That's a difficult question," Peter answered. "I'll explain all that in a minute. They will have to pay all my attorney's fees for this federal case if we win. Everything. Gwen won't have to pay a dime for my fees. And unlike most cases, I won't be working for a percentage of the damages. Whatever damages you are awarded, you keep one-hundred percent. In most cases, the only way a lawyer can get paid is to take a percentage of the recovery, but in civil rights cases, the defendant has to pay both full damages and full attorney's fees both if they lose."

Stan glanced at the complaint. "So who's this third person you are suing? I know Corliss and Rita—the two CPS creeps—but who's this Gerald Blackburn?"

"He's their supervisor at the CPS office. I called there anonymously and got his name. I am going after him because he undoubtedly sets the policy which allows these people to go into homes without a warrant."

"Sounds good to me. The more the merrier," June said.

"There is an important limitation on this lawsuit. Under the existing federal cases, we cannot sue CPS workers for anything that happened after they filed the lawsuit. So the fact that they made you go to court, took Casey away for seven days, or anything else that happened after the first court papers were filed—I can't sue them about any of that. It is called the doctrine of 'quasi-judicial immunity.' You can't ever sue judges for what they do in the line of duty. And the same rule applies to prosecutors or other investigators, like CPS workers, but only for actions taken after they file a case in court. So the only thing we really can go after is their raid of your home and the strip search of Casey. But from a lawyer's perspective, that's quite enough because that is where most of the emotional damages to Casey were caused anyway."

"It just doesn't seem fair that I have no right to sue them for taking my daughter away for seven days with their lies," Gwen said.

"It isn't fair," Peter agreed. "But, unfortunately, that's the law right now. It would take an act of Congress or a decision of the United States Supreme Court to change that rule. Our federal judges here in Spokane couldn't give you a dime for those seven days under any circumstances."

"That's really a stupid law," Stan said.

"It was a rule made by lawyers and judges to protect lawyers and judges," Peter said with a shrug.

"Yeah. Every time I start to like you, I remember you're a lawyer," Stan laughed.

Peter chuckled good-naturedly.

"What are our chances?" Gwen asked.

"It is always an uphill fight to sue the government. They've got so many rules stacked in their favor. But this case looks really promising. The basic rule is, no government official may come into someone's home without a warrant. And that applies to social workers, just like police officers. But there are two complicated rules which affect all of this."

"Figures," Stan said. "It was sounding too easy to understand."

"The first is the rule of exigent circumstances."

"I'm afraid you've started talking like a lawyer," Gwen laughed. "Exa—what?"

"Exigent circumstances," Peter replied, avoiding any hint of condescension. "It means, basically, emergency circumstances. If they had good reason to believe that Casey was in immediate danger, they could come in without a warrant to protect her from imminent harm. If they believed that Casey was being beaten with a stick and they had reason to believe you were really hurting her—bruises, broken bones, anything like that—they could come in warrant or no warrant."

"But wasn't that what they were claiming?" Gwen asked.

"Yes, after they raided your home they were claiming bruises. They said nothing about bruises at all before their little raid."

"Boy, this is complicated," Gwen replied.

"Sort of," Peter replied. "Just keep in mind that what they find cannot be used to justify the raid. The issue is what they knew before the raid. In any event, we've already gotten one judge to cast severe doubts on whether there ever were any bruises."

"There were no bruises—ever!" Gwen said forcefully.

"Easy, Gwen. I believe you. We won that in court. Remember?" Peter said.

"Sorry," Gwen said with an embarrassed smile.

"Exigent circumstances is one of the important issues. The other is whether or not their information was based on an anonymous tip," Peter said.

"Yeah, I'd sure like to know who started this mess in the first place. Can't we sue them, too?" Gwen asked.

"I'm afraid not," Peter answered. "They can never be required to tell us the identity of the person even if they know—and they may not know. Even if we found out on our own, we could never sue such a person because child abuse reporters are exempt from any liability. It's a good rule sometimes, but a lot of vindictive people use hotlines these days to phone in bogus charges."

"Somebody phoned in a bogus lie against my daughter, Stan said. "I'd like to meet them in a dark alley if I can't take 'em to court."

"They will be required to tell us whether or not the caller was anonymous. If all they had was an anonymous call, they probably won't have the right to argue the exigent circumstances rule. If the caller was anonymous, before they could raid your home, they would have had some reason to believe the caller was reliable. An anonymous tip alone can almost never pass the standard of reliability."

"Well, I don't understand it all," Gwen said. "But it sounds like you do."

"I do now," Peter said. "These kinds of lawsuits are very rare, and hard to win. I've never done one exactly like this before."

"How do you know all this stuff then?" Stan asked.

"Research, basically. And I have an associate who used to be a federal prosecutor. He helped me with a lot of preliminaries. Lawyers don't always know all the rules, but we are expected to be able to find them and understand them. I think I've got it all down, but there are people more experienced than me."

"I don't care if there are," Gwen said looking Peter in the eye. "You believed in me and got my daughter back, and I'll never use another lawyer for anything as long as I live."

"Boy, I wish I did television commercials," Peter said with a gentle smile. "I'd like to put that endorsement on TV."

Everyone laughed.

"Well, I think it is high-time we had some of this strawberry angel food delight," June said, standing. "Gwen, come on and let's get the dessert and coffee."

Stan sat reading the complaint muttering, "that's right" and "you got them on that one," when the phone rang. Peter could hear June answer. She stuck her head through the kitchen door and said, "Stan, it's Gordon. Gwen doesn't want to talk with him. He's drunk."

Stan got up to take the call. At first Peter could hear Stan's voice trying to calm Gordon down, when suddenly the only thing he could hear was a child's piercing cry coming from Casey's bedroom. Instinctively, Peter dashed into the room and found Casey screaming, "They're under my bed. They're under my bed. Mommy! Mommy! Don't let them get me!"

He scooped Casey up in his arms and began to talk soothingly to her. Gwen appeared at the door with Stan not far behind. She paused to see how Casey would react.

"Your Mommy is right here, Casey," Peter said in his most soothing voice, rocking her gently. "Nobody is going to hurt you. Nobody is under your bed. And I'm way bigger than those mean ladies. Way, way bigger."

Casey stopped her crying as Peter repeatedly said, "Way, way bigger. Nobody is going to hurt you. I'm way, way bigger."

In about three minutes, Peter had rocked her back to sleep and laid her gently back in bed. Stan had retreated from the doorway so he did not inadvertently wake his granddaughter. Gwen just stood there in amazement. As Peter made his way to the door, it was obvious that Gwen was not going to move. As he approached her, he reached out his hand, grasping her arm gently to rouse her so they could both leave the room.

"Peter," she whispered. "You are wonderful. You are truly wonderful."

Peter's head was swimming. It was the closest he had ever been. He could smell her hair and feel her breath. He lingered. If only her parents had not been in the outer room . . . how he desired at that moment to kiss her with reckless abandon.

"I think you're more than wonderful," he whispered.

⌢

Stephen Stockton was wakened by the sound of soft crying. He glanced over at the clock. It was two-thirty. He had only been asleep for an hour after yet another long night of studying for the Bar. Even his Saturday nights were not immune from the necessity of study. He turned over in bed.

"What's wrong, Donna?"

"Oh . . . oh, nothing."

"Right. You don't expect me to believe that do you?" he asked.

"I don't know what you want to believe anymore," Corliss replied.

"OK. We can do this the long way or the short way. Do you want to tell me what's wrong or do I have to cross-examine you and force it out bit by bit?"

"Oh, all right. I'm scared and I'm lonely," she replied.

Stockton cuddled up next to her.

"I think I understand the lonely part. I have not been very good company lately. This bar exam has got my attention. There are so many details to memorize and theories to understand. I guess I shouldn't worry so much and spend more time with you."

"It's not just the bar exam," Donna replied. "I guess in a way I think you're already gone. As soon as the exam is over, you leave for Washington—for two years."

"You can still come with me. It's not too late."

"Oh, there's no time for a wedding and everything," she said with an exasperated sigh.

"So you would marry me if there was time?" Stockton asked tightening his embrace.

Corliss wiggled free and sat up. "Oh, I don't know. There's so much pressure."

"I guess you could come to Washington without marrying me, just keep on like we are now."

"But I thought you said that your job wouldn't permit us just living together."

"Obviously that's not an official rule. But unofficially, it won't look good at all. At least not for long. But we could probably get married at Thanksgiving or something. I think they'd ignore us if a wedding was imminent. So are you coming with me?"

"Oh, I don't know. I don't think so." She flung her pillow against the wall in obvious frustration.

"OK. OK. I'll drop it . . . for now. But what are you afraid of?"

"You wouldn't understand."

"Try me."

"It's stuff at work and I don't want to talk about it."

"What kind of stuff at work?"

" . . . Blackburn. He's really on my back about this particular file."

"It wouldn't happen to be that case you told me about a couple of weeks ago, would it? The one where you . . . uh . . . stretched the facts a bit?"

Corliss flopped backwards on the bed and gave a loud moan. "Yes, that's it exactly."

"So what happened? Did he find out about you fudging a bit and now he's giving you a hard time?"

"Are you kidding?" Corliss replied. "He does it all the time. In fact, he invented the whole idea. He even calls it Code B, like we were some kind of secret agents or something."

"So why is he on your case if he condones this sort of thing?"

"We lost the trial. The kid went back to her cutesy, cutesy mother, when her new obnoxious attorney got involved. We've never lost a Code B case before. Blackburn is furious."

"OK, he's upset. But why are you afraid? Is he threatening you or something?"

"No, not directly. He is investigating an appeal and he wants everything sanitized before he makes a decision. He says that I have to make sure the file is absolutely clean if there is a problem."

"Did something happen during the trial that revealed the . . . the Code B stuff?" Stephen asked.

"Not really, but the lawyer made some strong attacks on our credibility. He didn't find out what was really going on, but he managed to get one document in the record that may reveal some data when it is interpreted."

"Please, don't tell me anymore factual secrets, Donna. It's really best that I don't know."

"I thought you couldn't tell anyone no matter what."

"I won't tell. But it's just awkward and there might be some ethical problems I really can't anticipate. Hey, I'm not even really a lawyer yet. These are the kind of nuances you only learn by experience."

Corliss felt even more abandoned. She stared at the ceiling, feeling not just alone, but stripped of all protection and comfort.

"How can you sanitize a file that's on appeal? Once you are in the appellate courts the file cannot be opened. This guy sounds crazy." Stockton rolled over and put his arm around Donna's shoulders and held her tight. "Listen, I want you to come to Washington with me. This sounds weird. I want you away from all this stuff. Do you hear me? I don't know how to protect you from this Blackburn creep if you keep working there, but I know how to get you out of town."

Corliss said nothing, but tears streamed down the sides of her face as she lay flat on the bed. After about fifteen minutes of silence, Stockton noticed she had fallen asleep. He quietly turned off the light, glad to be finished with the topic, and attempted to go back to sleep.

～

Peter waited anxiously in the church parking lot for Gwen, Casey, and the Mansfields. He had barely slept all night, even though he left Gwen's by ten-thirty. His heart and his spirit did battle as he replayed over and over Aaron's counsel from Friday morning. He knew it was right for Gwen to come to church. But, nonetheless, he was worried about what Aaron would think. Deep down, he was worried that he was going down a path that was not God's best for him, but he tried not to think about it.

About three minutes before the service began, the Mansfields' Pontiac Bonneville pulled into one of the front-row parking spaces reserved for first-time visitors.

Peter greeted them all warmly and hustled them to the back of the auditorium. During the first hymn, Peter saw Aaron, Lynn, and the Roberts children seated toward the left front of the auditorium.

The entire routine of church seemed different to the Mansfields. Casey had never sat through a church service before. The people seemed happy, the music was relatively lively, and it seemed to the Mansfields a fine and noble exercise despite the unfamiliarity.

Pastor Lind rose in a continuation of his series on the book of James. Last week he had preached on the first half of James 5:13, "Is any one of you in trouble? He should pray." This week the whole sermon was devoted to the second half of that verse. "Is anyone happy? He should sing songs of praise."

"You will notice the stark contrast in these two phrases in the same verse. In the first half, we are dealing with troubled people. In the second half, we are dealing with happy people. The reality is that we all experience trouble in our lives. And we will all experience happiness in our lives. In fact, some of you may have been here last week in desperate trouble, and this week you are brimming over with happiness."

Gwen looked at Peter, gave him a shy, knowing smile, and turned her head back to listen.

"One might be tempted to think that the responses to trouble and happiness would be different in the lives of believers. In reality, they're not that different. When we have trouble, we direct our attention to God and talk to him. That kind of talking with God is prayer. But when we're happy, we are to do essentially the same thing. When we have happiness, we again direct our attention to

God and talk to Him. This kind of talking with God is praise. When we are in trouble, we pray. When we are happy, we sing songs of praise.

"If I were to take a survey of all of you," Lind continued, "I would guess that I would find a high percentage who regularly pray whenever you face trouble—at least serious trouble. But it is my experience that far fewer of us turn to God during the happy times and praise Him in any form, whether that is singing, or just ordinary prayers of thanksgiving.

"Why is it that we recognize that God can solve our troubles when we are facing problems? But we are not nearly as quick to praise God when he solves those troubles and brings us happiness.

"Brothers and sisters, I believe it is just as important to sing songs of praise when we are happy as it is to pray when we are in trouble.

"Someone might ask: 'Why should I praise God when I am happy? What has God got to do with my happiness?' The answer, I hope is clear: God is responsible for your happiness.

"He created you. He created the things we love and bring us happiness—our children and the beautiful world we live in. He is the one who intervenes for us when we are in trouble. And, most importantly, He is the One who gives us the opportunity to have eternal happiness. I am talking about salvation. Jesus died for you so that you might have forgiveness of sins and live in heaven with Him forever. Ladies and gentlemen, that is true happiness, and when we are there, we will sing songs of praise."

Gwen could not hold herself back when the Pastor gave the invitation. "Peter, I want that. Will you walk with me?" she asked.

He nodded, tears barely visible in his own eyes.

Two other people came forward and reached the pastor just before Gwen and Peter arrived. The pastor talked with them, then came to Gwen. After a few whispered words, he motioned for a counselor to come forward. Aaron and Lynn Roberts slipped out of their seats and came up to Pastor Lind. Gwen brightened when she saw that the counselor was someone she had at least been introduced to previously. After a few more whispers, Lynn quietly told Peter that she and Gwen were going to a side room together. Aaron slipped beside Peter and put his arm around his friend and gave him one strong squeeze. The two men stood side-by-side singing the last two verses of the hymn of invitation while a new citizen of the kingdom of God was receiving a few words of counsel and prayer.

Peter told Aaron that he felt he needed to get back with Gwen's parents and Casey immediately after the close of the hymn. Aaron knew the discussion that was obviously necessary would take a long time and should not even be attempted now.

Gwen came out, hugged Peter modestly as a new sister in Christ and said, "Thank you for bringing me here. You continue to do good things for me. Thanks so much."

Stan looked about uncomfortably. He and June were confused about everything. They decided that Gwen was simply walking forward to demonstrate her thankfulness for getting Casey back.

Peter was actually glad that the Mansfields had plans for Gwen and Casey for the afternoon that pragmatically couldn't include him. Aaron noticed Peter leaving the sanctuary alone. He purposed to call soon.

14

Joe had some minor changes he suggested in the civil rights complaint on Monday morning. Sally finished the civil cover sheet and summons, and got the check ready for the filing fee for Peter's signature. At two o'clock, it was all ready to go.

Peter walked the eight blocks down Riverside Avenue, Spokane's main business street, to the United States District Court for the Eastern District of Washington on the top floor of the federal building. At the time of filing the complaint, the case would be permanently assigned to one of the two full-time federal judges based in Spokane. The system of assignments is kept secret from all but the clerks and judges so that attorneys cannot pick their own judge by timing the filing of the case in accordance with the schedule. Another possibility, although a bit more rare, was the assignment of a case to a former full-time judge who had gone into the semi-retirement plan federal judges call "taking senior status."

The clerk who filed the case was tight-lipped and simply stamped the paperwork and assigned the case a file number. When he was done, Peter asked, "Which judge got the file?"

"Judge Stokes," the clerk replied.

Stokes was a senior judge. He had gone into semi-retirement two years earlier after serving fifteen years. He had been appointed to the bench by Jimmy Carter in 1977, after a twenty-year career as a flamboyant litigator for a variety of liberal causes—including a number of cases where he had been a volunteer attorney for the American Civil Liberties Union.

Stokes was no-nonsense on procedural matters and expected every case to be moved through his court promptly. Peter had appeared before him three or four times in the past, but was not a regular in his court by any means. Peter was unsure how to evaluate Stokes's propensities on this case. He immediately returned to his office to find Joe hard at work on a bank fraud case.

"We got Stokes on the Landis file," Peter said as he stuck his head in the door.

"That's great," Joe replied.

"Great? He's such a lefty. Why is that great?" Peter asked.

"Precisely for that reason," Joe replied. "You've got a very strong constitutional rights complaint against the government. Better a former ACLU lawyer appointed by a Democrat president than one of the Republican appointees who spent their careers defending corporations."

"I never thought of it that way," Peter said.

"Stokes will not let you win automatically. I have no idea how he feels about child abuse cases. He may go off on some left-wing bleeding heart binge because the case involves the so-called need to protect children. But if this were any other kind of case where the government busted into somebody's home without a warrant, Stokes would hang the government's hide on the wall."

"I guess my job is to get him to want to follow the normal rules of law, even though we are dealing with child abuse workers," Peter replied.

"You got it, buddy," Joe said looking back at his own file.

Wally Elrod returned to the sheriff's office at three-forty-five. He had found ten of his twelve intended targets that day. The *Landis v. Corliss, et al.*, complaints had arrived at three-thirty. The sheriff's office was not required to serve federal court complaints, but for a fee they did.

Elrod almost never went out a second time to begin service of new documents which came in during the course of the day. He liked his day planned out. And being just a few weeks from retirement, he would not prolong his day more than absolutely necessary.

When he found that the lawsuit included one Ms. Rita Coballo, however, he decided to make a little visit to the CPS office on the way home. He could serve all three summonses and complaints on Corliss, Blackburn, and Coballo at one time. He laughed to himself thinking about Coballo's comments at their last interaction.

Elrod asked for Blackburn first. He was ushered into his office by a secretary.

"I got some legal papers for you," Elrod said handing him the summons and complaint, making a note on his pad of the exact time of service.

"What are these?" Blackburn asked in an irritated voice.

"Don't explain 'em, just serve 'em," Elrod said for the sixth time that day.

"Humph," Blackburn snorted as he glanced at the document and began to understand its purpose.

"You got a Corliss and Coballo in this office? I assume they are here from these papers," Elrod said.

"Yeah . . . they work here," Blackburn replied distractedly, his nose still buried in the papers.

"Can you tell me where their offices are so I can give 'em these papers and get out of everybody's way?" Elrod asked.

"Uh . . . " Blackburn looked up and focused on what Elrod had just asked. "I guess they have to get them. I don't want any more people in the office than necessary to be tormented by all this. Let me just call them in here and you can serve them both right here."

"Fine with me," Elrod said with a smile. He leaned against the wall by the door and waited as Blackburn called both women.

Corliss showed up first.

"This is Ms. Corliss," Blackburn said as she entered the door.

"Well, Ms. Corliss, as this fine gentleman told you on the phone, I got some legal papers for you. Here you go," he said, thrusting the papers into her outstretched hand.

Corliss just rolled her eyes without a word and started to leave.

"Donna, wait here. I want to discuss this so-called lawsuit after this man leaves," Blackburn said, emphasizing each word.

Corliss turned and sat in the chair furthest from the door and the Deputy.

About two minutes later, Coballo appeared. Before Blackburn could speak, Elrod grinned broadly and handed her the papers saying, "*Mrs.* Coballo, here are some *more* legal papers for you."

"You sexist pig," Coballo said.

Blackburn shot her an angry look.

Elrod feined a shocked expression and turned to face Blackburn. *I deserve an academy award for this performance*, he thought to himself.

"He did this same sexist bit the last time he served me a subpoena," Coballo said to Blackburn, ignoring everyone else in the room. "He also called me a witch."

"Officer, I will thank you to not harass my staff when you are serving papers," Blackburn said, glaring at Elrod. "I'll have your job if you ever do this again."

"From the looks of these papers, you're going to need a second job to pay for the damages this Peter Barron is planning to take out of your hide. And in just three weeks, I'm retiring, so I'd be glad to see that you get my job, mister," Elrod said as he turned and walked out of the office and left for home.

Blackburn glared after him, and then, pointing his index finger at one and then the other woman, he threatened, "You two better be covering your bases. Now get busy on this case."

Thirty minutes later, Corliss was summoned back into Blackburn's office. She knocked on his door with the utmost reluctance, hoping that somehow he had left the office, although he had called only two minutes earlier.

"Come in, shut the door, and sit down," Blackburn growled. The curtains were completely drawn. The Chinese worry balls swirled past each other in his left hand.

"I assume you have read this lawsuit that you have brought on this department," Blackburn said.

∽

Corliss knew better than to point out that he had approved every action and had created the Code B procedure in the first place.

"Yes, sir. I have read it."

"They have not yet discovered us, but they are on our trail," Blackburn continued. "It is your responsibility to get them off our trail."

"I don't know how to get them off the trail. I mean I did go into that house without a warrant. I can't do anything about that," Corliss said.

"Oh yes you can, but that is secondary. Let me make one thing perfectly clear—if our Code B operation is exposed in this case, you will regret the day you ever suggested that you use Code B in the Landis case."

"I'll do what I can," Corliss countered.

Blackburn stopped his whirling of the Chinese balls in his hand. In a quiet but menacing voice he said, "The price of failure will be extraordinarily high. Extraordinarily high."

Corliss thought her heart was about to stop. She could feel the tears welling up. "Uh . . . uh . . . OK," she stammered.

"But I also fully expect you to cover us on this present lawsuit which is based on what they already know," Blackburn said, resuming the clinking of the balls in his hand.

"Mr. Blackburn, I really need your help on this. I don't know what to do. I just followed policy and did what I have been trained to do," Corliss pleaded.

"All right, let me explain it to you again. If I had known you were such a rookie I would never have let you employ Code B. This lawsuit is focused on your entry into the home. There are two key issues raised in the complaint. One is the fact that the tip was anonymous. And second they claim we did not have exigent circumstances—that there was no immediate emergency or imminent threat to the child's well-being."

"But we go into homes all the time on anonymous tips, and we go in whether or not there is an immediate threat. All we require is a report of child abuse and we go in—period."

"Of course, we do. But it is far better if we cover our backsides by pleading that we had information suggesting an emergency and I want us to be able to say that we were acting upon the tip of a known, reliable source."

"But the hotline record says otherwise and they will certainly get that record somehow."

"You are absolutely right. They will get the record that is in our computer at the time of their subpoena. Your job is to make sure that our computer records reflect an emergency and that tip had better not be anonymous," he thundered.

"OK. OK. I get it. Any other suggestions?"

"Yes. See if you can pull that off first, and we'll have another little chat tomorrow."

"OK, I'll get it done," Corliss said standing.

"By tomorrow. I want results in the morning," Blackburn said. "One more thing. Not a word to anyone. Not Coballo. Not that boyfriend of yours. No one. You got that?"

"Yes, sir," she replied closing the door behind her.

It was well after five as she walked down the corridor to her office. She saw and heard no one. The tears started to flow as she walked hurriedly down the hall. She did not want to be seen. She entered her small windowless office and shut the door. Since it did not have a lock, she moved a chair against the door and piled some books on it. It would do nothing to stop a real intruder but somehow it made it easier to cry.

After regaining her composure, Donna logged on to her computer. She quickly hit the keys to take her to the hotline reporting database. Corliss had never "edited" a hotline report before. But she knew how it could be done. The CPS manuals from Olympia made it clear that hotline reports were to be considered original records which should not be substantively changed. But if the CPS investigator found that an address or phone number had been entered incorrectly or other simple clerical error, the investigator was authorized to correct the clerical errors in the original report. A second entry was supposed to be added to the end of the file to indicate that the change had been made.

As Corliss peered at the screen, she found that she could fulfill most of Blackburn's command with three minor changes. First, she changed the date of the hotline report. The computer record now reflected that the original call was made May 9th, the night before her original visit to the Landis home, rather than May 5th. Next she changed the nature of the injuries. The word "unknown" was easily erased and replaced with the words "severe bruising reported." Finally, the case became a Code 1, rather than a Code 2 priority with two simple strokes at a computer keyboard.

The final change would necessitate a little trip. Corliss, gaining courage by the moment, got her keys and left the building. She got in her personal car, headed north across the Spokane River on Washington Street and wound her way up the first few blocks of the South Hill to the Sacred Heart Hospital parking lot.

She entered at the main door, and quickly located the sign for the cafeteria without needing to ask at the front desk for directions. She followed the directional arrows in the hallways until she came to the eating line. Three nurses were standing by the menu board chatting. Corliss looked at their name badges. Nanette Gray was a fortyish woman with flecks of silver in her hair. "She'll do," Corliss said to herself.

Corliss put a quarter in the newspaper rack, bought a Spokane Chronicle, the city's evening paper, and turned to retrace her steps down the hallways. As she exited the hospital she threw the paper in a receptacle by the front door.

She was careful to obey all the speed limits as she retraced her route back to her office across the core of downtown Spokane. She thought if she were caught for speeding, somehow a policeman would figure out what she was doing and expose her.

She walked quickly down the silent corridor. Blackburn's door was closed and no light emanated from the crack under the door. Corliss was relieved that even he was gone by now. She entered her office, logged on once again, and retrieved for a second time the Landis hotline record. She scrolled the cursor down to the line which called for the name of the complainant. She knew that what-ever name was put there, it would never be revealed. A general description might be disclosed. But, never, ever would the name of the actual person be disclosed.

The letters u-n-k-n-o-w-n were removed and then Nannette Gray, R.N. Sacred Heart Hospital, had become the informant of child abuse for a case involving a co-worker she had never met.

"It's perfect," Corliss said out loud. "Co-worker and a medical professional. She's absolutely perfect."

Corliss then pulled up all her own notes she kept on the computer and made sure that all references in her reports matched the details as she had just concocted them. She also deleted all references to the Code B procedures. Her internal notes had never been revealed in any prior case, but she had never been in a federal civil rights case. No chances could be taken.

Corliss clicked off the computer, walked out the door, and drove home to an empty apartment. Stockman would not be there until midnight or later. She opened her first bottle and proceeded to drown her fear of the Washington State Top Child Advocate of 1993 in a cheap California wine.

~

Click, jingle. Click, jingle. The Chinese worry balls were being worked rapidly as Blackburn sat at his desk Tuesday morning reviewing the "new and improved" documents Corliss had brought him that morning. He liked them. In fact he liked them so much, he actually returned the worry balls to the felt-lined box which held them when they were not in use. Blackburn rocked back in his chair.

"Very good, Donna. Excellent. I like the touch with the nurse. Is she real?"

"Of course she's real. I went over to the cafeteria last night and spotted her in line for dinner."

"Brilliant. Good work."

"And I made sure all of my own internal notes match up."

"Very thorough. Very thorough, indeed," Blackburn replied. "I got McGuire's sanitized report last night. It's fine. He only made one stray reference to our arrangement, but it was in code and he had a brilliant explanation for it. I think everything is going to be fine. Just fine."

~

Gordon Landis opened the front door of his apartment at eleven. He had gotten desperate for cash again and had taken a job working the three to eleven shift at a 7-11 five blocks from his home. He bought two large bottles of beer and drank them as soon as he got home most every evening. Last night had been no exception.

He stooped over—the dizziness wasn't too bad—and pulled the Spokesman Review newspaper off the green indoor-outdoor carpeting that lined the hallway of his apartment building.

Gordon thoroughly devoured the newspaper every day. He had been a good student in high school. Having always been bright, he didn't have to work hard to do well. He could discuss current events of Spokane or the nation with the best—when he was sober.

While scanning the Metro section for items of interest, his eye caught the headline of a small article: "Child Abuse Search Challenged in Civil Rights Case." It was buried in the midst of a series of short articles giving a two- or three-line description of all court cases of any significance which had been filed the previous day in both the state and federal courts in Spokane. Lawyers and people with too much time on their hands were the only ones who read the section regularly.

Gordon walked over, picked up his phone book, found the number for the clerk's office for the federal court, and dialed.

"Hello," the voice said.

"Uh . . . hi. I saw an article in the paper about a case filed in your court yesterday. I'd like some information about it."

"Do you have the name of the case?"

"The person who filed it is Gwen Landis . . . let's see, the defendants are—"

"That's OK, I can look it up from the plaintiff's name. Landis, yes. I've got it. What do you want to know?"

"Oh, just what it's about and everything."

"Sir, the file is public record. If you want to know general background, you should just come down here and get a copy. Copies are fifty cents a page."

"Uh . . . OK. How do I find out when there are hearings on this?"

"You can ask the lawyers if you'd like."

"I really don't want to talk to the lawyers or anything. Is there some way I can be notified?"

"No, not really. The best I can suggest," the clerk said, " is to come into our office once a month or so and pull the file and look to see what hearings are scheduled."

"Once a month? Won't there be hearings more often than that?"

"Look, sir. If you are this interested in this case, maybe you should get a lawyer. I really can't advise you about all the details. You can come down and look at the file every day as far as I care. But if you looked at it every two weeks that really should be often enough so that you don't miss anything."

"Two weeks. OK. That sounds good. Thanks a lot."

"You're welcome, sir."

〜

Matt Bartholomew had been the Chief Deputy Prosecuting Attorney for five years, but had a falling out with his boss and had moved on. Fortunately for Matt, at the time he was looking to make a move, the Washington Attorney General's office had an opening in Spokane for the Chief Deputy to run the Spokane Office. Matt was fully qualified for the job, and besides, he had helped Allen Radcliff in his election for the Attorney General's position in 1992. The job was his for the asking.

Bartholomew's office would be required to defend the civil rights suit against Corliss, Blackburn, and Coballo. He was a little concerned about the ability to cover the case. No one in the Spokane office had substantive experience in child abuse law. This was no mere defense of a suit for tort liability. It was a constitutional challenge to the practices of the Child Protective Services.

"Willet here," the phone said.

"Ms. Willet, I'm Matt Bartholomew. I'm in charge of the AG's office for the Spokane Branch. Nice to talk with you."

"Sure. What can I do for you?" Willet said, typically brushing off small talk.

"We've gotten a copy of a federal lawsuit filed against some people you represented in court a week or two ago. Have you seen the lawsuit?"

"No, I have no idea what you are talking about. Who does it involve?"

"It is filed by Gwen Landis against Donna Corliss, Rita Coballo, and Gerald Blackburn. A child abuse case gone bad or something."

"Amazing." Willet said, sitting up in her chair. "You say this is a federal lawsuit?"

"Yep. Civil rights case. Section 1983."

"I wonder why I didn't get a copy."

"Well, we represent CPS in all civil litigation filed against them or one of their people. It's just routine."

"Yes, but I'm surprised these people didn't tell me. I was researching an appeal for them and was supposed to talk with them later today."

"Yeah, I've heard about your appellate work. It's an impressive record," Bartholomew said.

"You've got good sources," Willet said with an uncharacteristic laugh.

"Well, the reason I'm calling is that I hope to ask you to help defend this civil rights lawsuit filed against our CPS workers. The core legal issues are the ins-and-outs of child abuse law—and you're the expert. I'd like to make you lead counsel, and someone from our office would assist primarily on the issues of damages and so forth. What do you think?"

"I don't understand exactly. Are you offering me a case or a job?"

"Just this one case. I will go to your boss and ask him for permission to associate you as Special Assistant Attorney General. And our office would reimburse the Prosecutor's Office for an appropriate portion of your salary," Bartholomew replied.

"Special Assistant Attorney General. I like the sound of that," Willet said. "Sure, if my boss gives the green light, I'd really like to do this case."

"Thanks, I'll be in touch."

Charles Sexton, *the* Spokane County Prosecuting Attorney, was only too happy to have Gail Willet serve as Special Assistant Attorney General. He was glad to do Matt Bartholomew a favor and revive their relationship. After all, he thought, the next election was not too far off and it would be better to have the former Chief Deputy Prosecutor and current Deputy Attorney General for Eastern Washington as a friend than as an opposing candidate.

～

Gwen was looking forward to her visit from Lynn Roberts on Wednesday morning. She found Lynn to be very personable when they spent twenty minutes in the counseling room after the invitation on Sunday morning. Lynn had made good on her promise to call Gwen every day since Sunday. And Gwen had made good on her commitment to read three chapters from the Gospel of John.

Lynn's home schooling was over for the year and her oldest son was fifteen—plenty old enough to watch his three younger siblings.

Lynn and Gwen sat at a small table on the back deck and visited, as Casey played on the swing-set in the back yard. At first they exchanged small talk and life histories. Lynn later gave Gwen a Bible study book that Valley Fourth used in follow-up for all new believers. Gwen happily agreed to meet with Lynn once a week for eight sessions over the summer. A couple of interruptions would be necessary for some planned vacations.

Eventually, their talk came around to the subject of Peter Barron. Lynn brought him up first.

"You know that my husband and Peter are best friends, don't you?"

"Peter said they were good friends," Gwen answered. "I didn't know exactly how close."

"Yes, they meet once a week a lot like we are planning to do," Lynn answered.

"I'm just curious. I thought Peter had been a Christian for a long time. Why would he be in a Bible study like this now?" Gwen asked.

"You're right, Peter has been a Christian since he was in college, I think. The Bible study they do isn't exactly like the one we'll be doing. Our study will be covering the basics. I'm not exactly sure what they are studying right now, but they wouldn't be using an introductory book like this. But, Gwen, we never outgrow our need for studying God's Word, no matter how long we have been Christians. I'm sure that the Bible study is just as much for Aaron as it is for Peter. And Aaron's been a Christian for over thirty years and is an elder in the church. We always need to keep growing."

"My . . . there's a lot to think about," Gwen said, a bit surprised.

"No matter how many times I read or study a particular passage in the Bible, when I read that passage again, there is usually something new that God shows me to apply to the issues I am facing at the time," Lynn said.

"What passage in the Bible talks about marrying divorced women?" Gwen asked suddenly.

"Boy, that's a question out of the blue. Why do you ask that?"

"Well, the first time Peter and I met, he told me that I didn't have to worry about him because he was a Christian, and he believed he wasn't supposed to marry a divorced woman," Gwen replied.

"That is a very strange thing for him to say. Why did he bring that up?" Lynn asked.

"It's a long story. And it's not totally strange. I had another lawyer before Peter. He made an extremely crude pass at me, and I was leaning on Peter's car crying about that—not to mention I had just lost Casey a half hour earlier—when I first met Peter. That whole story came out in the course of our conversation, and I think Peter wanted to reassure me that he was genuinely different from that first jerky attorney."

"All right. That makes a bit more sense," Lynn said. "Well, Gwen, the Bible says quite a bit about divorce. And I would have to do a little preparation to really give you a proper answer to that question. Would it be OK if I do that and give you a full answer next week, rather than trying to guess right now?"

"Sure," Gwen said. "And I assure you that Peter has been a perfect gentleman the whole time. But . . . " She changed her mind and didn't complete her sentence.

"But what?" Lynn asked. "You can feel free to talk with me. I won't tell Peter anything."

"Well, it's just that Peter has said and done some things that normally I would interpret as suggesting that he was interested in me as a woman, and not just as a client," Gwen answered. "I really can't give you specifics. It just something I sense."

"How do you feel about that?"

"Well, it really confuses me. I think Peter is absolutely wonderful. The way he got Casey back won me as a lifetime client. There are many other things I like about him, as well. And the other night, he was here with my parents for a dinner celebrating our victory in court when Casey had a nightmare. He swept Casey up in his arms and rocked her to sleep in a way that really touched me. He's really a great guy. But I guess he feels he can't be interested in me because I'm divorced. I'm really confused."

"Gwen, I don't know everything to answer your questions completely. But I do know that God forgives us completely when you ask Jesus into your heart. There is nothing in your past that God has not forgiven. Divorced people are not second class Christians. I don't know how that relates to Peter. But as it relates to God, He accepts you as His child."

"Thanks," Gwen said softly, lowering her eyes. Lynn seemed to understand how she was feeling inside.

"I'll try to get you a better answer when I see you next Wednesday morning. OK?"

"That'll be fine. I'm looking forward to learning, and you are so nice to teach me," Gwen answered.

"It will be fun for both of us," Lynn answered, standing to leave. "I'll still call every day for a couple of minutes if that's OK."

"Sure. I look forward to your calls."

Lynn prayed for Gwen and Casey as she was getting ready to leave. And she prayed silently that she would figure out how to answer this difficult question about Peter and divorce before next Wednesday.

⌒

On Thursday, Peter received a mailed copy of the formal Notice of Appearance signed jointly by Matt Bartholomew and Gail Willet. "Figures that *Ms.* Willet would find a way to butt into this case," Peter said to Sally when she handed him the notice.

"You don't like her, do you?" Sally asked.

"What was your first clue?" Peter asked, his eyes crinkling with a mischievous smile.

"Just the way you say 'Ms.' Admit it. You can't stand her, can you?"

"I refuse to answer that question on the ground that you already know the answer," Peter laughed.

"Is she a good lawyer?"

"Very competent," Peter said quite seriously. "It'll be a real test. And Bartholomew is no dummy, either."

"I can see the headlines now: 'Spokane's Best Litigators Duke It Out in Civil Rights Case.'"

"On a serious note, I think having Willet on the case will make it move more rapidly than normal. In our last hearing, I never thought she would have a brief ready in time to respond to me. She did it, and it was good."

"You'll beat her again. And this time you can earn a fee. We need it, so get to work," Sally said, backing out of the office and closing the door.

Peter didn't get to work, but sat deep in thought, holding the Notice of Appearance in his hand. He hadn't contacted Gwen all week. He was doing his best to just be her lawyer and nothing more. And since nothing had happened on her case, he had no reason to call.

A notice of appearance is a very minor event in litigation. He knew that ninety-nine times out of a hundred, he wouldn't bother to call his client to give them such an update. But Peter had the additional excuse that this was an unusual situation where a prosecutor was appearing as counsel in a federal civil rights case. At least it seemed unusual enough to Peter to justify a call. He dialed the number despite some nagging doubts about his motives.

"Hi, Gwen, this is Peter."

"Long time no see, Peter. How have you been?"

"I've been great. I'm calling because of a small development in your case. But first things first. How are things going with the Lord? I was really thrilled with what happened on Sunday."

"I'm really happy, Peter. Thank you for taking me to church. Lynn came by and gave me a Bible study we're going to do. She's called me every day. If her husband is half as nice as she is, I can see why you like him so much."

"They're a neat couple, that's for sure." Peter fell silent, wanting to continue, but not knowing how to carry on the conversation without going down paths that bothered his conscience.

Finally Gwen said, "So what happened in my case? Isn't that why you called?"

"Oh . . . right. Well, it's kind of complicated to explain the significance of it. The short version is that we got a notice of appearance. Gail Willet and a man from the state Attorney General's Office are both going to be representing the three social workers."

"Is that unusual?" Gwen asked.

"Willet works for the Prosecuting Attorney's office. They only do criminal and juvenile court cases in state court. The Attorney General's Office defends all state agencies and workers in civil rights cases filed in federal court. I have never seen a prosecutor appear in federal court ever. I'm sure it has happened, but it's rare."

"Why do you think it has happened here?"

"The best reason I can figure is that Willet is a true legal expert on child abuse cases. She has argued many of the reported appellate decisions on the subject in the state in the last four or five years. I think the AG's office just wanted her legal expertise."

"I am even more impressed with your win last week. You beat the best, huh?"

"Well, the Lord gave us the victory," Peter said softly. "He really did."

"I know you're right," Gwen replied. "I'm just beginning to understand that. But I am still very grateful to you."

"Thanks. Well, that's all I have to report. I guess I'll see you on Sunday in church."

"Casey and I will be there. My parents probably won't come. But let me ask you one more thing about my case. What's next? What can I expect to happen when?"

"I'm sorry. I should have explained all that to you before. They have thirty days to answer the complaint. They could file an ordinary answer saying we admit part of these facts and we deny these other facts. They'll never admit anything important. Or else they could file a motion asking the judge to dismiss the case. If I were a betting man, I'd bet on the motion to dismiss on about the twenty-eighth day. We're going to have to get through that motion to know what to expect for the rest of the case."

"Can we win that motion?" Gwen asked with concern.

"It is not a slam dunk for us, but I feel good about our chances overall. I can't even give you a very educated guess until I see whatever paperwork they file."

"So they have thirty days to get this in? Why so long? They didn't give me thirty days."

"Who said courts were fair? You are fighting the government ,and the government writes the rules," Peter answered. "But I'll push them as hard as I can."

"I have no doubt about that. I've never seen anybody so dedicated to a cause as you are to my case."

In Peter's mind he said, *And I've never seen anybody as beautiful as you*, but he stifled the thought and said, "I'll move things as fast as I can. See you Sunday, OK?"

"Sure. Bye, Peter. I miss seeing you."

"Bye, Gwen . . . Me, too."

Peter held the receiver a long time. Then he paced and stared out his windows. Being just her lawyer was not going to be easy.

Peter was five minutes late for his Friday morning session with Aaron. He quickly ordered a cup of coffee and his standard granola with strawberries and skim milk. Peter did his best to stay in shape.

"Sorry, I'm late, Aaron," Peter said.

"It's OK,; I was a couple minutes late myself. How's everything going?"

"Fine. I'm always busy just like you."

"Get four kids *and* a busy job, and then you can talk about being busy just like me," Aaron said with a smile.

Peter's mind flashed to Casey. He certainly wouldn't mind having one child right away, and maybe more later. "You got me there. What can I say?"

"I've been anxious to talk with you since last Sunday. But I've been gone again. Missoula is pretty nice this time of year. I wanted to talk with you about Gwen."

"I knew you would," Peter said, holding his breath in anticipation of a gentle, but effective tongue-lashing.

"She really seems like a wonderful lady. Lynn has talked with her on the phone every day since Sunday. Wednesday she went to her home and began our new believer's Bible study with her. Lynn thinks she is really great."

Peter was afraid to agree out loud, so he said nothing.

"Peter," Aaron said a bit more seriously, "I can really understand why this is so difficult for you. If she weren't divorced, I would be encouraging you to make a reservation to use the church some Saturday afternoon in about six months."

Peter sighed. Aaron, he realized, wasn't a cruel task master. He was just a friend who encouraged him to stick by his own convictions. Neither Aaron nor his church had been the source of his belief about marrying a divorced woman—Peter had first heard the material at a seminar and had done a lot of reading and studying before reaching the conclusion that he should not marry a divorced woman.

"Thanks," Peter said. "I appreciate your understanding, I've never met anybody who affects me the way she does. It's obvious that she is really pretty, but there's a lot more as well. She seems so vulnerable and open. I just feel like I want to protect her. Her personality is so warm and she has these little flashes of fieriness when she lashes out at the social workers that show she's got a lot of spirit. Now she's come to know the Lord . . . I could go on, but I shouldn't."

"Peter, I told you last week that you shouldn't change your convictions merely because an attractive alternative came along. And I stick by that. Obviously, God does give us more insight from time to time. I have changed my views on some issues over the years."

Peter felt a rush of hope in his heart.

"But, Peter," Aaron continued, "I cannot stress enough how important this is to you. Not just in terms of a marriage partner—which is obviously one of the most important decisions in your whole life. This challenge for you concerns your fundamental relationship with God. Will you obey what God has shown you no matter how attractive the alternative is?"

"The question I have," Peter began, "is whether what I have believed in the past is what God showed me, or just my own conclusion. There is at least a possibility that I missed the correct answer initially, isn't there?"

"That's certainly true," Aaron said. "I just have one question for you. Down deep, what does your spirit say to you about all this? Not your heart, not your head. What does the witness of the Holy Spirit say to your spirit?"

Peter looked out the window of the coffee shop with a fixed stare. He was silent for about thirty seconds. He turned back to the table, picked up his coffee cup in his hand, swirled it around a bit, and looked Aaron straight in the eye. "That's the problem. To the best of my understanding, I don't think I'm supposed to change. I don't actually feel like God is dealing with me about the substance of the issue of divorce—although that is still plenty important to me. What you said last week has really been resonating inside of me. If I would change my views of God and His Word because—when you boil it right down—because I want to, I feel that I might turn my back on God for anything."

"I feel for you, Peter, I really do," Aaron said.

"This is the hardest challenge I've ever faced in my Christian life," Peter said. "It would be so easy for me to be completely in love with Gwen. . . ."

"I am sure it is hard. But faith in God is not merely about following Him when it's easy. Real faith involves following God when it's hard."

"What should I do?"

"I think you should just keep going forward with your commitment. Treat Gwen as a client and as a sister in Christ. And keep asking God to use His Word to speak to your spirit."

"I'll do my best. You've got to pray for me."

"Sure. I really will—more than ever."

〜

Gwen and Peter talked briefly at church on Sunday. They sat in the same pew—on opposite ends of the Roberts' family. They caught each other's eye once or twice and smiled. The bulk of the week went by without any contact. Peter received nothing on the case, so he did not call—at least until Thursday when he got Gail Willet's motion to dismiss in the mail. It was two weeks earlier than he expected. He called Gwen immediately and arranged to have her come in the following morning to review the documents.

At eleven on Friday, Gwen showed up right on time. Sally had gone to the office supply store for a few minutes, so Joe and Peter kept their doors open and listened for the phone. Gwen saw that Sally was gone, so she walked over to Peter's open door, tapped lightly, and stuck her head inside.

Peter looked up, startled to see her standing there. But he recovered quickly, "Gwen, don't you look nice!"

And indeed she did. She had her hair back in a loose pony tail tied up in a bright red ribbon. She was wearing white denim jeans, a blue button-down oxford shirt, with a red and white striped sweater tied over her shoulders.

"I was beginning to think you weren't working on my case any more. I hadn't heard from you in so long," Gwen teased.

"With this latest load of garbage from Willet and Corliss, I think we'll be seeing each other quite a bit for a few days," Peter replied.

They both secretly hoped it was true.

"Here's your copy of their latest papers," Peter said handing her a half-inch stack of documents. "Let me walk you through them."

"Phew," Gwen sighed. "That Ms. Willet can sure produce paper in a hurry."

"There are basically four different documents: a motion to dismiss, a brief supporting the motion, an affidavit from Donna Corliss, and a copy of their initial intake report."

"Am I supposed to understand what you just said?" Gwen asked.

"Not yet," Peter laughed. "Those are just the names of the documents. Let me explain them."

"The motion is their official request to the judge to dismiss the case. It gets everything going, but it's only two pages and basically just a technicality that's required. The brief explains their legal and factual arguments. It tells the judge why they think he should dismiss the case. The final two documents—the affidavit from Corliss and their intake report—contain their version of the facts."

"OK. I think I understand," Gwen said, flipping pages.

"Basically they make two arguments that are important. The first is a factual argument. They claim that Corliss believed that Casey was in immediate danger of real abuse and so they were justified in coming into your home without a warrant. The second is a legal argument. They are arguing that social workers are immune from civil rights suits whenever they are acting to protect children. And Willet cites twenty-five or thirty cases to prove that particular point."

"What can I do about all this?" Gwen asked, a bit panicked. "I don't know how to answer twenty-five or thirty cases. Isn't that your job?"

"Exactly," Peter replied. "I'm going to take care of the immunity issue and find thirty-five or forty cases to answer them—or maybe just one if it is from the Supreme Court. You are going to see a lot of paperwork which talks about this "immunity" issue, and I just wanted to explain it as best I can. Where I need your help is on the factual issues. I need you to remember, with as many details as possible, exactly what happened."

"But I've already told you everything I can remember. I wrote you that big long paper."

"I know. I know," Peter said, smiling. "Let me ask you a very specific question. Did Corliss ever tell you when they first got the call from the hotline?"

"Whew. That's a tough one. I'll have to think. Did I say anything about this in my paper?"

"Yes, you did, as a matter of fact," Peter replied, holding her handwritten document in his hand. "You gave two different versions. And it could have been that you got mixed up. Or that Corliss told you two different stories. I want you to try to remember it for me fresh if you can."

"I really can't remember anything one way or the other right now. Am I not supposed to look at my own paper?"

"No. It's OK to look. I just wanted to see if you had an independent memory. It's not a big deal. I just need to know what I am dealing with," Peter said, handing her a photocopy of her own statement. "Look at the two different spots I have highlighted in yellow. On the first day—the day when Corliss came alone—you wrote down that she said they had received the hotline call on Thursday, which would have made it six days earlier. Now flip over to page eight. This time, after Corliss had strip-searched Casey, you wrote that she said the call had come in 'night before last'—that would have made it on Tuesday night. Now what I—"

"Hang on. Let me read this again," Gwen interrupted. She flipped the pages back and forth and read each section two or three times.

Peter sat silently to let her think.

"I am sure I wrote this correctly. As a nurse, I am required to record the details right on people's medical charts. And I have good short-term recall of a lot of details. I am positive that I got this right. She had to tell me two different stories. And now that I think about it, I can remember her telling these two contradictory pieces of information. I was just so upset, I didn't compare them to one another at the time."

"That's what I was hoping you would say," Peter said, standing. He loved to pace whenever he was on an important trail of thought.

"I am glad this makes you excited," Gwen said with a smile. "I don't see why it is so important."

"It is *very* important," Peter replied. "If they got the call on Thursday—six days before her first visit—there is no way that the tipster gave them information there were severe bruises and so on. If they had received that kind of information, they would have been out to your house the next day, pronto."

"I hate to take up Corliss's side. But. . . . " Gwen paused to focus her idea. "Didn't she say—at least the second time she came to my house—that they had just got the call the night before last?" Gwen asked with a grim look on her face.

Peter stopped his pacing and looked Gwen straight in the eyes. "That's exactly what she was saying—on the second occasion. But not on the first. And my gut tells me that something stinks about all this. It's just all too cozy. And if you tell me that you are sure she gave you two different stories, I believe you, not her."

"No offense, Peter," Gwen said, "but you're my lawyer. You're supposed to believe me. Even if I am right, how can we prove it? Isn't just my word against hers?"

"Not exactly, it's a little worse than that, " Peter replied soberly. "They've also got this CPS intake report prepared by some unnamed hotline operator. They've got her word—or his word—against yours as well. This hotline report says that the call came in on Tuesday, and they could argue, 'well, even if Ms. Corliss did say the wrong thing during the first visit, it was a mere slip of the tongue. The intake report establishes the correct date of the hotline call.'"

"It all sounds pretty bad, doesn't it?"

"Yes, it does," Peter admitted.

"Does this mean it's all over?"

"No, but it is a big hurdle, that's for sure."

"What can you do?"

"Two things are possible. Corliss could be lying. I think she was lying about the fading bruises bit, and the police officer helped me smoke her out. This is going to be tougher because she's got this intake report to back her up. The other possibility is we can argue that the report was legally insufficient and the reporter was unreliable. Therefore, she shouldn't have been allowed to go into your house without a warrant. But those are pretty tough arguments for us to win on."

"It sounds hopelessly complex."

"Why do you think lawyers get paid so much money? They make up complex rules of law and then get paid big bucks to explain them to people."

"Oh sure! You are going to get really rich on my twenty-five dollars a month," Gwen said smiling. But a moment later, the smile was gone. "Peter," she said with a quiver in her voice. "Peter, what are we going to do?"

He walked around to the front of his desk and turned his chair around to face Gwen's. Peter sat down and reached out and took both her hands in his. "The first thing we're going to do is to pray about this. From a lawyer's perspective we have definitely got an uphill fight—with a very steep incline. But you are now a child of the King, and we need to talk to your Heavenly Father about this."

Gwen smiled and bowed her head—partly because that's what she thought she was supposed to do, and partly because she was a little embarrassed and confused to be holding hands with Peter— even for prayer.

Peter prayed first and then Gwen prayed, as well. Peter was struck by the clarity of her prayer. She was just talking to God without all the routines and formulas that Christians develop after years of listening to other people pray in public. He could tell that Gwen's love for God was real and growing. While he was happy to see signs of real spiritual vitality in her, it made him ache inside all the more.

After they both said, "Amen," Peter's hands held hers a little longer than necessary. They both knew what was happening, but neither said anything. Finally, Peter stood up, turned the chair back into its place and said, "I'd better get to work finding some cases to answer her brief."

"When do our papers have to be filed?"

"Technically within ten days. But I think we can get some extra time. Lawyers almost always give each other extra time to file briefs in situations like this."

"Do you think that Ms. Willet will agree to anything you ask her?"

"Uh . . . you've got a point there. Even if they don't agree, I can always ask the judge for more time, and he will almost certainly grant it."

"I'm glad you're the lawyer, not me. I could never do this."

"And I would be terrible taking care of patients after surgery. Sacred Heart would have a lot of people with severe complications, if I was watching after them."

Gwen just smiled. She appreciated Peter's self-deprecating style. She could tell he was self-confident, but she liked the fact that he was so self-confident that he found it unnecessary to brag on himself. She didn't know many lawyers. If she did, she would have realized how rare an attribute that really was.

She left the office and got in the elevator alone. As she glided down the twelve stories, she spoke her thoughts aloud. "God, what's wrong with me? Why am I not good enough for Peter?" Tears were starting to form in her eyes, when the elevator stopped. Two men and a woman were waiting to go up. Gwen quickly brushed her eyes, moved out of the elevator, exited the building, and got swallowed up in the lunch time crowd on Riverside Avenue.

15

It was six A.M. Saturday. The Red Lion coffee shop was nearly abandoned. It was the time Peter and Aaron used to make up for missed meetings on Friday. Peter would have been happy to meet at a more leisurely hour, but Aaron wanted to spend all of Saturday with his family, so they had to be finished by seven.

Peter arrived first, and was on his second cup of coffee when Aaron rolled in about ten minutes late.

"Sorry I'm late. Bed gravity got me for a couple minutes," Aaron said.

"No problem, it gave me a chance to inject some coffee into my system," Peter replied.

"How's your week been—especially with Gwen?" Aaron asked.

"You don't beat around the bush, do you?" Peter responded with a slight smile. It was an increasingly sensitive subject—one he had begun to dread talking with Aaron about.

"Sorry," Aaron said, looking hard at Peter, trying to discern his emotional condition. "But I've really been praying for you this week about all this, and I just want an update."

Peter sighed. He knew Aaron was truly concerned for him.

"Well, on the personal front, things are going OK, I guess. It's hard for me, but I haven't changed my views."

"How's her case going?" Aaron asked, giving Peter a momentary reprieve.

"Not so good, actually," Peter replied.

"Why? What's happened?"

"Nothing significant has happened—yet. But the attorney for the CPS workers has filed a motion to dismiss that is going to be difficult to overcome."

"Tell me about it," Aaron said.

"I'm glad to," Peter said, "but I thought we were supposed to be talking about spiritual issues."

"Well, the way I figure, this is a spiritual issue. Handling your relationship with Gwen is the most important thing that is going on in your spiritual life right now, and I think it is good for me to get some idea of the context."

"OK. That makes sense. Well, we are suing the CPS workers for violating Gwen and Casey's civil rights. I am arguing that when the CPS workers came into her home and strip-searched Casey without a warrant, they violated their constitutional rights."

"I'm still amazed they have the power to come in someone's home like that. But your case sounds good to me. So what's the problem?"

"There's an exception to the rule about warrants. If the CPS investigators had a legitimate reason to believe that there were exigent circumstances—that's lawyer-talk for an emergency—then they can go in basically to rescue the child, and they don't need a warrant."

Aaron nodded. "I'm following. Go on, professor."

"Well, the CPS workers—Donna Corliss is the chief culprit—they are now claiming they had evidence that there was an emergency— that the hotline tipster had told them there were severe bruises."

"Would that be enough to satisfy that exi-. . . . exi-"

"Exigent circumstances," Peter said helpfully.

"Yeah. That rule. Would bruises be enough?"

"Severe bruises? Probably."

"What can you do about that? If they got the report, aren't they entitled to rely on it?"

"Personally I think they shouldn't be able to rely solely on an anonymous call, but it's tough to get a court to agree with that perspective."

"Are there any holes in their arguments?"

"Just one. The CPS worker came out twice. Once by herself. Once with another worker and a cop. On the first visit, Gwen remembers her saying that they got the hotline call six days earlier. On the second visit, Gwen believes the CPS lady said they had received the call the night before her first visit."

"What's the significance of that?"

"If they got the call six days before the visit, there is no way the tipster told them there were severe bruises. They would have been out to her house in a flash. I think they are lying. I caught them in a lie in the first hearing. It wasn't really clear to the judge that they were fabricating evidence, but he believed Gwen, not the CPS worker, in the end. And I think she is lying again."

"Well, can't you use that? Gwen, who has been shown to be believable says one thing, while the CPS worker, whose credibility has been damaged, says another."

"I could," Peter replied, "if it were just Gwen's word against Corliss's word. But they've got this hotline report from the operator which reports the severe bruises and records the date of the hotline call as the night before Corliss's first visit. I think the report is phony, but I have no way to prove it."

"Is the report computer generated?" Aaron asked.

"Sure," Peter answered.

"Too bad I can't see the hard disk of their computer," Aaron said.

"Why? What good would that do?"

"I could tell you if they made any changes in their report after the original information was keyed in," Aaron replied.

"You could? How? I thought that once a file has been saved, it overwrites the old version of a file and only the new file is saved."

"That's what my fellow computer geeks and I want you to believe," Aaron said smiling broadly. "In reality, in most word-processing type systems, when you save a file, you are only saving the modifications to the old file. The old file is still there in its original form. It's just kind of buried underneath a bunch of computer codes, which direct your computer to make the necessary modifications."

"And you can retrieve the original, if I can get a copy of the file?"

"No. Not from a copy of the file. But if I can have access to the actual hard disk, the answer is yes. I can unravel the codes and show you the original file, the date of the changes, what was changed, and perhaps even who changed the records."

"You've got to be kidding! This *is* spiritual talk. You have just given me an answer to prayer. Gwen is going to be thrilled. I sat her down yesterday and prayed with her about this, and we asked God to open up a way to get to the truth to vindicate her."

"That's great," Aaron replied, "provided. . . ."

"Provided what?" Peter asked.

"Provided that they changed the records. There is a possibility that the hotline report has never been changed, isn't there?"

"I guess there is," Peter answered a little more soberly. "There's always a possibility. But, A, I can't believe that Gwen ever harmed Casey, let alone having caused severe bruising; B, Even if the records were not tampered with I can still smell a rotten fish; and C, those CPS workers are lying again. I can feel it."

"There's only one way to prove it. Get me that hard disk."

They only had time to read the assigned chapter in Proverbs, have the briefest discussion and quick prayer. As they walked together, Aaron said, "Would you like to come over and tell Gwen what we talked about?"

"To your house?" Peter responded with too much enthusiasm.

"Yes. Gwen is coming over for most of the day. I guess Casey's dad is going to exercise visitation today and Lynn didn't want Gwen to be alone. And she wants to ask Lynn all about home schooling. She seems intrigued with our kids, and Casey is starting kindergarten this fall, so she's got a ton of questions."

"Sure, I'd love to come over and tell her."

"And I can keep an eye on you when you do," Aaron said, throwing his arm around his friend, giving him a quick jostling hug.

⌒

Casey zipped down the slide from the huge Radio Flyer Wagon on the southern edge of Spokane's Riverfront Park to Gordon's waiting arms. The ten-foot high, Paul Bunyan-sized wagon was a favorite with kids for obvious reasons, and a favorite for parents, because, unlike other attractions in the park, play on the wagon was free.

Gordon had just barely enough money to let Casey ride a couple times on the elaborate carousel — the centerpiece of the park's attractions for kids.

After a couple hours of walking, playing, and throwing bread to the ducks, Casey and her father settled down on a park bench to a lunch of a hot dog with ketchup and a small coke. The purchase had emptied Gordon's reserves.

"Havin' fun, Casey?"

She giggled and nodded her head, bouncing the curls her mother spent half an hour creating that morning.

"It's too bad your mommy can't come with us today. What's she doing anyway?"

"She's going to Lynn's house," Casey answered.

"Who's Lynn?"

"She's the lady from church."

"Church?" Gordon said astonished. "What church is that?"

"It's Peter's church," Casey said, chewing her hot dog.

"Peter, the lawyer?"

"Uh . . . I dunno. Just Peter."

"Is he a tall man with black hair?"

"Uh huh," Casey nodded affirmatively.

"Does Peter come over to your house a lot?"

"Sometimes."

"Lots of times or just once or twice?" Gordon asked, with jealousy building by the second.

"I dunno. Just sometimes."

"Is he nice to you?"

"Uh huh," she said nodding again. "One time he rocked me when I was scared."

Gordon had heard enough to arouse his envy. But he couldn't help asking one more question.

"Is Peter with your mommy at Lynn's house?"

"I dunno," Casey answered.

Gordon assumed the worst, bit his lip, and tried to concentrate on the little girl whose affections might not be exclusively his for very much longer.

⁓

Gwen arrived at the Roberts' home around ten. She was surprised and yet perplexed to see Peter's Explorer in the driveway. She didn't think that Lynn would have had Peter over without telling her. Lynn answered the doorbell.

"Come in, Gwen. It's good to see you."

"Uh . . . hi, Lynn. I see you already have company," she said gesturing to Peter's truck.

"Oh, Peter. He's not company. He's practically family. But he's not here right now. He and Aaron went to watch Joey's baseball game. It started at nine and the baby was still sleeping, so I stayed here."

As they talked, Lynn led Gwen through the house, into the kitchen and they sat down at the table where the fresh-brewed coffee aroma filled the air.

"Oh, that coffee smells so good."

"It's Starbucks French Roast. We think it's the best. I forget, how do you take your coffee?"

"Black," Gwen said, still distracted by Peter's presence, unsure of whether to be relieved or disappointed that he was not there now.

"Anyway, the reason he came over this morning was to tell you some good news about the case."

"Really? What good news?"

"I don't know. They didn't have time to tell me. It's just something he and Aaron apparently figured out at breakfast this morning."

"That's great. When will they be back?"

"In about an hour. We'll have plenty of time to talk. And I don't think Peter is planning to stay."

"Oh," Gwen said, now feeling genuinely disappointed.

The two mothers chatted freely about children and the events of the week. Lynn transitioned the conversation naturally into spiritual issues. She was thrilled with Gwen's spiritual progress. Gwen asked good questions and showed obvious signs of having spent regular time in the Word. She was doing their planned Bible studies and was obviously reading on her own as well.

Gwen asked and Lynn answered all of the typical questions concerned parents have about home schooling. When Gwen asked, "What about socialization? I've heard a lot of criticism about home schooling because of the lack of interaction the kids have." Lynn laughed out loud and said,

"How do you think my kids are doing? Furthermore, look around you and ask yourself if you approve of the socialization that is taking place. And now that you've got me on a roll, where is Joey right now? Socializing with twenty-five boys and their fathers at the baseball diamond. Fifteen years ago the jury was out on this issue. Now, however, the results are indisputable."

Gwen had to admit Lynn's children were doing fine. She was intrigued with the idea of home schooling, but it was a little too new for her just then.

"Mom, we won!" Joey's voice rang through the house. A moment later he appeared.

"That's wonderful! How did you do?" Lynn asked her eleven year old boy.

"I did pretty well," he replied modestly.

"Pretty well indeed," Aaron's voice boomed in from the hallway. Poking his head in the kitchen, he continued, "Two singles and a double, and four flawless innings at second base."

"Sounds great, son," Lynn said. "Joey, isn't it time for you to say hello to Mrs. Landis? Home schooled children may be good," Lynn said turning to Gwen, "but they are far from perfect."

"Sorry, Mom," Joey said. "Good morning, Mrs. Landis."

"Good morning, Joey," Gwen said with a big smile. "And congratulations. Sounds like you did great."

"He did indeed," Peter chimed in, peeking in the now-crowded kitchen from behind Aaron's shoulder.

"Mom, can I go outside?" Joey asked.

"Sure. Get out of that uniform and leave it in the laundry room on the way out," Lynn replied.

Aaron motioned to Peter, and the two men joined Lynn and Gwen at the kitchen table. While serving coffee, Lynn spoke.

"We've both been dying to know what this good news is that the two of you discovered this morning at breakfast. What's going on?"

"Well, it involves my best friend, the computer genius," Peter said. "He has figured out a way for us to find out if the CPS workers have falsified their reports. He can work some computer magic and tell us if they ever changed the files."

"Really?" Gwen gasped. "That's amazing."

"Sure can," Aaron said. "If Peter can get me access to the actual hard disk which has the records on it."

"Can you do that?" Gwen asked turning to Peter.

"Well, I've never tried to get a court order for something like this. And I am sure that our opponent, *Ms.* Willet, will put up a huge stink—something, I have a hunch, she's really good at. But I think we've got a shot at it. A good shot."

As Peter explained to Lynn why they suspected that the reports may have been falsified, Aaron sat back and took stock of the situation. It seemed so natural for the four of them to be sitting around as couples, talking and chatting as friends. As he watched Gwen watching Peter, he realized more fully just how difficult it would be for Peter to maintain his commitment. *They did seem perfect for each other*, he thought. Aaron began to wonder whether he had given Peter the right advice. But as he sat and thought, he remembered that it was Peter's own spirit that was convicting him, not merely his advice. Aaron made an inner vow to be very careful not to substitute his personal opinions for the leading of the Holy Spirit in Peter's life.

Peter stayed for lunch, but left soon afterwards.

Gwen was home at four, an hour before Gordon was scheduled to return with Casey. He was twenty minutes early, having run out of money and ideas.

Casey burst into the house and ran into the kitchen, where Gwen had begun dinner. She hugged Gwen around the legs. "Hi, Mommy. We had fun."

"Good, Casey. Is your Daddy still here?"

"Yeah," Gordon answered from the front doorway, which Casey had left wide open.

"Hi, Gordon," Gwen said a little tersely, walking into the living room wiping her hands on a kitchen towel.

"Yeah, we had a great time. We went to Riverfront Park and had a blast. Too bad you couldn't join us." Gordon was not normally this testy, and Gwen was taken aback.

"I'm sorry, Gordon, but you know that is simply not going to happen. And it doesn't help to say this kind of stuff in this setting," Gwen said with a subtle head nod in Casey's direction.

Gordon was not to be deflected that easily. "Oh, that's right, you had a pressing engagement with some lady from church."

"How did you know—" Gwen stopped before finishing, instantly discerning that Gordon had been pumping Casey for information.

"And I imagine that lawyer of yours was there, too. Getting pretty cozy aren't you?" Gordon asked sarcastically.

Gwen burned inside. She knew the meeting with Peter was happenstance, but she also knew there was an element of truth in Gordon's underlying accusation.

"That is none of your business," Gwen said emphasizing each word.

Gordon knew her answer meant that Peter had been present.

"Pretty cozy, I'd say."

Gwen's anger flamed. In a soft, but emphatic voice she said, "Out. Get out now."

Gordon turned and headed out the door.

Gwen stood at the door and glared as Gordon walked to his car.

"You are a free woman, I guess," Gordon said opening the car door. "But if I ever find out that he is spending the night here, I'll call CPS myself."

Gwen started to launch a steaming verbal counter-attack, but something inside changed her mind.

"Gordon, I'm really sorry you said that," she said softly. "It disappoints me greatly. But I can assure you that Peter is my lawyer and my friend. There is absolutely nothing romantic between us."

Her words didn't convince him. But Gordon was surprised at the tone of her answer. He was expecting fire. It suddenly occurred to him that her answer might actually be true.

Without another word, he slammed the door and headed down the South Hill, to his favorite tavern on Maple Avenue only a few blocks from his apartment. After all, it was Saturday night.

∾

On Monday afternoon Gerald Blackburn summoned Donna Corliss into his office. There was a knot in her stomach as she glided down the hall, stopping for a moment in front of his door. The sound of the Chinese worry balls was discernible through the door. The knot in her stomach grew tighter. She knocked.

"Come in," he barked.

She opened the door slowly and stuck her head in.

"Come in here and shut that door."

"Uh. . . . hi," Corliss said timidly.

Blackburn was agitated, but she had seen worse.

"Look at this," he said, throwing a single sheet of paper down on the far side of his desk."

She picked it up and read. It was a copy of a "subpoena duces tecum" issued to "Gerald Blackburn, Supervisor, Child Protective Services." It commanded him to appear for a deposition to be taken at his own office, next Tuesday, June 28. Peter Barron had, of course, issued the subpoena. It also commanded him to produce for inspection the computer on which the records concerning the Landis case were kept.

"What do you make of this?" Blackburn demanded.

"I guess they suspect that the records we gave them aren't accurate," Corliss replied.

"Exactly." The two worry balls were a constant blur in his left hand.

"But there's nothing for them to find except what we already gave them," Corliss said.

"Are you sure?"

"I'm positive. Check it for yourself."

"You show me," Blackburn said motioning for Corliss to come behind his desk. He stepped aside so she could sit down at the terminal on his desk extension.

Corliss hit the keys forcefully.

"See, here is the intake report. Just what we printed up. There is no other file. I'll show you."

She typed the name "Landis" in the search field and it located a single intake file.

"See," she said growing more confident.

"Yeah, what about your personal files?"

"Watch," she said.

A few more key strokes produced her word processing directory. She typed the command to search all of her personal files again for the name "Landis." A single file was produced.

"Here. Read it yourself."

Blackburn scrolled through the record. He read. He nodded. He grunted. And then he would repeat the process—reading, nodding, and grunting his way through six pages on the computer screen.

Blackburn sighed heavily and slowed the pace of the movement of his worry balls. "You're right. You haven't missed a thing. I don't think Barron will be able to find anything that you haven't shown me."

"But can he do this?" Corliss asked. "We wouldn't want someone in our computers in any case, not just a Code B case. An attorney could come into our files and find out the names of confidential informants and other confidential information. Shouldn't we stop him so that he doesn't start a bad precedent—even if we're clear on this one?"

"I knew I liked you for a good reason. You think a lot like me," Blackburn said, smiling. "I've already called Willet and told her precisely the same thing. She is preparing a motion to stop Barron's effort to look in our computers. I just wanted to test your thoroughness in case she's unsuccessful with the motion."

～

With fresh papers in hand from Gail Willet, Peter got Gwen on the phone Wednesday just before noon.

"Hi, Gwen, we've got some new paperwork in on your case. Willet is living up to our expectations—she's filed a motion to stop Aaron from looking at their computer. I still don't think they know what we really are capable of doing."

"But aren't you going to have to tell them sometime?"

"Probably. In fact we are probably going to have to tell the judge directly tomorrow. She's scheduled a hearing to try to stop me from taking the deposition and looking into their computer."

"Tomorrow? Isn't that quick?"

"Not really for this sort of thing. We're under time pressure to respond to their motion. And federal judges like to move their dockets quickly."

"Will I have to be there?" Gwen asked.

"No. You don't have to—but you should if you can. It's scheduled for 11:45. The judge will knock off his trial fifteen minutes early and take our motion just before lunch."

"Well, I guess I'll be there."

"Good. Aaron will be there to testify, and maybe Lynn will come along to watch."

"That will be great."

As he hung up the phone, it occurred to Peter, once again, that he was treating Gwen differently than just any client. He prided himself on keeping his clients well-informed on the progress of their case. But Gwen had to have set a record—he never had called a client this quickly or this often. It was a thought he wouldn't share with Aaron.

Peter spent the bulk of the afternoon in the law library. There were no cases about gaining access to computer hard disks. If this had been done before, it had been very recently, and the cases had not gone to the appellate courts. This hearing would open new legal ground. As he was closing the last law book, Peter wondered whether Gail Willet had found any cases on point. Given her experience, Peter thought, she had probably argued such a case three months ago, and the decision was just too new to be published.

Peter's brief was only four pages, contained only general principles, and was delivered by four that afternoon—as the judge had directed.

～

Peter, Gwen, and Aaron met at eleven in Peter's office. Lynn was going to meet them at the federal courthouse. Her oldest two sons were going to come as well. She thought it would make an excellent home schooling field trip.

They went over Aaron's testimony and answered questions. Peter repeatedly encouraged Aaron to talk normal English, not computerese. And he had to keep his answers short—the whole hearing would last only fifteen or twenty minutes.

The trio decided to walk the eight blocks down Riverside to the federal building. It was late June, but it was only in the low 80s, with high, thin clouds.

The nine-story federal courthouse was much newer than the castle-like Spokane County courthouse. It was a modern design of light-red brick. The courtrooms were on the top floor.

Lynn and her sons were waiting on a bench in the hallway outside Courtroom No. 2. Peter stuck his head inside the door and found that Judge Stokes's trial was still in progress. They would wait in the hall.

Willet showed up five minutes later, with Matt Bartholomew along for the ride. They had agreed that she would do all the talking. Bartholomew had been before Stokes many times. It would be Willet's first experience before this particular judge.

Peter walked over, shook hands with Bartholomew, and turned to extend his hand to Willet in a similar greeting. She looked at him and glared. The wounds of losing the last round to Peter were too fresh for her fiercely competitive spirit. If Bartholomew had not been present, she would have simply turned her back and ignored him. But she grudgingly stuck out her hand and muttered, "Good morning, Mr. Barron."

At 11:40, Donna Corliss and Gerald Blackburn walked out of the elevator. Gwen reacted in surprise.

"Why are they here?" Gwen whispered to Peter.

"You sued them. Remember?" he answered.

"Oh yeah. I just didn't expect to see them. I think of Ms. Willet as the opponent."

"She is," Peter replied with a friendly wink. "But so are they."

The trial participants began to trickle out of the courtroom into the hallway. Peter looked at his group and said, "Let's go quickly. The judge will want to start right away."

Judge Warren Stokes did not leave the bench between hearings. He sat at the end of the massive courtroom on the bench twirling his gavel in his hand. He was thin, balding, and wore glasses that he had cocked up on the top of his head. He would put them down on his nose when it was time to read a document. The courtroom was lined in oak from floor to ceiling. It was at least four times larger than the juvenile court, and the twenty foot ceilings made it seem even larger.

"Mr. Barron, please come in quickly and let's get going. Is Ms. Willet here?" the judge asked.

"I'm right here, Your Honor," Willet said. She was halfway down the aisle with Bartholomew a half-step behind.

Peter quickly took his papers out of his briefcase and turned to sit down next to Gwen. In the back of the courtroom, the door opened. Gordon Landis tentatively stuck his head in the door and quickly slipped in the last of the fifteen rows in the courtroom. Peter sat down, leaned over and whispered, "Don't look now, and don't react, but Gordon is in the back of the courtroom."

Gwen couldn't help herself. She whipped her head around and caught his eye. He quickly looked down.

"What is he—"

Peter put his hand on her arm and gently squeezed. "We'll talk later. We have more important things to do right now," he whispered firmly.

"Ms. Willet, I know this is your motion," the judge began abruptly, "but frankly I'd like to begin by asking Mr. Barron a few questions."

"Fine, Your Honor," Willet replied.

"Good. I'm glad you approve," he said. "Mr. Barron, let me get to my main point. Why do you want to look in their computers?"

"To see if they have changed their records after this case was filed. We have reason to believe that their records have been altered," Peter answered.

Blackburn shot a worried look at Donna Corliss. She mouthed the words, "Don't worry."

"And why do you think they have altered their records? You realize that is a very serious allegation against anyone—especially a government agency, don't you?" the judge asked.

"Yes, Your Honor. And we don't make it lightly. Basically there are two reasons we think the records *may* have been altered. I stress the word "may" because we are just engaged in discovery here. I do not have to prove that the records have been altered at this stage of this case. But I do understand that I have to make a preliminary showing to demonstrate to the court that my theory is plausible."

"I think we all know this is discovery, Mr. Barron. Get on with it," Stokes replied.

"The first reason we think the records have been altered is that Ms. Corliss, the lead CPS investigator, told my client two different stories concerning the date that CPS received the hotline call. And the date of that call is crucial to the case."

Blackburn glared at Corliss. She wanted to melt and disappear under the crack in the door.

"The second reason is that we believe we caught them lying in the trial in state court. Ms. Corliss claimed to have found 'fading bruises' on my client's child. But this fact was disputed, albeit by inference, by the police officer who accompanied the two CPS workers when they strip-searched Casey Landis."

"Do you have any documentation of this second theory of yours?" the judge asked, flipping his glasses down on his nose in anticipation.

"Yes, Your Honor, I do. If I may approach the bench, I can hand up copies of the transcripts of the hearing in state court. I have marked passages in yellow on pages 25, 30-36, and 49."

"OK, let me see that exhibit," the judge said, reaching for the papers.

Peter took his seat. The whole courtroom sat frozen while the judge read and flipped pages and then read some more and flipped more pages. After two minutes of complete silence, save the sound of pages loudly being turned, the judge put the transcript down abruptly and said, "OK, Mr. Barron, I get the idea. Let's move on to the second issue."

Willet stood up tentatively. "Your Honor, I'd like to be heard on the first issue before you make a decision."

"All in good time, counsel. I don't believe you've been in my court before, have you? Everyone gets a chance. I just run things the way that seems to get the point most expeditiously in each case. Sometimes that's the traditional back-and-forth method. And sometimes, like today, I like to get straight to my questions. Be assured you'll get a chance to talk. And if you'd like, you might even get to join the exclusive club of lawyers who have made speeches that have convinced me to change rulings that I intended to make in favor of their clients."

Willet turned bright red and sat down. It was exactly the response the judge had hoped for.

"All right, Mr. Barron, back to you. I want to know why you think you could find something if I let you look at their computer hard disk. I know a bit about computers. Even if someone changed a file, once that change has been saved, doesn't it supersede the original version?"

"That's what I thought until last Saturday, Your Honor. That's when my expert witness, Aaron Roberts, explained the way the system works. He says he can take a file that has been altered and decipher the original version from the changes."

Donna Corliss took a deep breath and thought her heart would stop beating. She looked straight ahead, not daring to look at Blackburn.

"This sounds interesting," Stokes said, flipping his glasses back to the top of his head and rocking back in his leather swivel chair. "I might have use for this technology in the future. Let's get this witness on the stand for a quick explanation of how he does this."

Aaron sat on the edge of his front-row seat. Peter motioned for him to come inside the swinging door and railing that lawyers call "the bar." The bailiff motioned for him to stop in front of the witness stand.

"Please raise your right hand," the clerk intoned. "Do you promise to tell the whole truth, so help you God?"

"I do indeed," Aaron replied.

"Please state your name and address," Peter commanded.

"My name is Aaron Roberts. And I live at S. 2964 Kennewick Avenue, Spokane, Washington."

"What is your occupation?"

"I am a computer consultant. My training and experience is primarily as a systems analyst."

"Where were you educated?"

"I have a Masters in Computer Science from the University of Washington. My bachelor's was in physics from the University of Montana."

"Please tell us the names of some of your clients for whom you provided computer consulting services."

"I do consulting for the University of Montana in Missoula, Deaconess Hospital here in Spokane, and Potlatch Corporation in Idaho, and I do some specialty work for Boeing. Those are some of my larger accounts. I have others."

"Please tell us about your responsibilities with Boeing."

"Uh . . . well, actually I don't think I can. At least not specifically. It is connected to a Defense Department account that Boeing services. And all of my work is classified."

"Fine. Mr. Roberts, are you familiar with the type of computer system that Child Protective Services operates here in Spokane."

"Not the specifics of it. But the nature of the system has to be very similar to any large institutional system which runs on a network."

"Do you have any doubt that you can understand and operate the CPS computer systems?"

"By asking relatively few questions of their systems analyst, I can certainly understand their system sufficiently for the purposes you have in mind. What we are talking about is not that complex and does not vary much from system to system."

"Can you decipher a file that has been changed to decode the original portion from the changes?"

"Yes, I can."

"Can you please explain how that works?"

"Basically, it is very straightforward. In any word-processing or data system that is based on words and not merely mathematical calculations, files are not truly changed the way they would appear on a computer screen. On a screen, a person can take an original document, hit the correct keys, wipe out one word, let's say 'chocolate' and replace it with another word, for example, 'strawberry.' As far as the user knows, the original word 'chocolate' is gone forever. But, in reality, the changes that are made are codes on the hard disk. In effect, the code says, 'forget about chocolate, and replace it with strawberry.' By running a specific program on the hard disk, I can break through these codes and separate the original portions of the document from any changes which have been made."

"Fascinating," the judge said aloud. "Can you do the same thing with files that have been erased?"

"Basically, yes, unless all of the available space on the hard disk has been used. Then you might actually start to lose some files beyond any person's ability to retrieve them. But ordinarily, all one has to do is to remove the codes which say 'erase this file' and the file can be restored."

"I think I'm through, Your Honor," Peter said.

"Fine. Fine. Fascinating stuff. All right, Ms. Willet. Now's your chance," the judge said, smiling and rocking back and forth in his chair.

She decided to avoid a direct confrontation with Aaron. His knowledge on the relevant subject was far beyond her own. She decided to attack on her turf.

"Mr. Roberts, if you have access to a CPS computer, would your ability to rummage around in the files be limited to the files concerning the Landis case?"

"No. Theoretically at least, I could read everything on the disk."

"And if the name of confidential child abuse informants are on those files, could you discover those names as well?"

"Certainly. Any information on the files, I would be able to see and read."

Gordon Landis turned white—but no one noticed.

"I have no further questions, Your Honor. Just a brief argument when it is my turn."

"It's your turn right now. And please be brief," the judge replied.

"Your Honor, one of the most important principles in child abuse detection and prevention is the confidentiality of our files—especially the confidentiality of our informants. State and federal law require that we protect the confidentiality of our informants. If we can have a computer consultant for every litigant come into court and run their deciphering programs, no informant will be protected. And once that word gets out, we will have thousands of children suffering from increased abuse because legitimate informants will be afraid of retaliation."

Peter stood to speak.

"Mr. Barron, please sit down, unless you want to lose," the judge said without a smile.

Peter sat and smiled.

"Ms. Willet, I have no intention of letting Mr. Barron look into your computer records for precisely the reasons you raise."

Gwen gave Peter a confused look. Peter just shrugged, he didn't get it either.

"However," the judge continued. "I am going to look at your computer records. I am going to make Mr. Roberts here an expert under the control and supervision of this court. He is going to perform his programs under my supervision. We are going to print out—we can print out what we find, can't we, Mr. Roberts?"

"Yes, Judge, we can," Aaron replied, still sitting on the witness stand.

"I will see to it that the names of any confidential informants are blacked out. I will also require Mr. Roberts to take an oath of confidentiality. But I figure if he has a security clearance to do Defense Department work, I can trust him to keep a confidence in this case as well. Will you do that, Mr. Roberts?"

"Yes, sir," Aaron replied.

"Fine," the judge said. He picked up his calendar, and flipped his glasses back to their "down position" on his nose. "All right, let's see. Monday at 4 P.M. Counsel any problems with that?"

Both attorneys shook their heads "no."

"Mr. Roberts, I should check with you. You are not under any compulsion here. Are you willing to do this under the terms I've outlined? And are you available on Monday?"

"Yes, Judge. On both counts, the answer is yes."

"Fine, fine. Anything else, counsel?" Stokes asked.

"No, Your Honor. Nothing for me," Peter replied.

"No, Your Honor. It was just the one issue," Willet responded.

"All right, we are in recess." And the judge was gone before anyone could breathe twice.

"He's amazing," Gwen whispered to Peter. "Is he always like that?"

"Not always. But whenever you are in his courtroom, there is no doubt as to who is in charge."

"I can see that," Gwen whispered. Just then she noticed Gordon slipping out the back of the courtroom.

"Why in the world was Gordon here? Did you call him and tell him to be here?"

"No way. I had no idea that he even knew this case had been filed, much less that we had a hearing today."

~

Blackburn grabbed Corliss's hand when the judge was making his ruling and squeezed hard—a maneuver clearly intended to inflict pain and instill panic. His move had its intended effect—Corliss had never been more scared in her entire life. "You're coming with me," he whispered in a menacing voice. Corliss had no choice but to go with him. To this point she had been worried that he might get mad and fire her. For the first time she genuinely became afraid for her own life.

16

Lila was back to being a redhead when Randall McGuire arrived at the Ram's Head Tavern Thursday evening. Blackburn had called just after lunch and demanded a meeting—or else. McGuire vowed this was it. He would never get involved with Blackburn again; it simply wasn't worth it.

Ten minutes later, Blackburn arrived and immediately went to the corner where McGuire was waiting. McGuire had already downed a double scotch and was working on his second.

"Thanks for coming," Blackburn said with a smile seemed more sinister than friendly.

"I want you to know," McGuire said, "this is the last time I am ever coming to one of these meetings or working on one of your 'special' cases. So state your business and be quick about it."

"You have stated my sentiments exactly. This *is* our last case together. But we do need one more very short meeting."

"Explain yourself," McGuire said tersely.

"Surely you remember Peter Barron, Esquire? He managed to get a federal court to order a computer guru to have access to our computer and to go rummaging through our records."

"Surely you are smarter than that," McGuire said. "You've gone in and changed all the records to make sure everything appears normal, haven't you?"

"Of course we have. Days ago. But Barron has come up with a computer wizard who says that he can go into our system and decipher our documents and can tell the judge exactly what has been changed in any files."

"Can he really do that?"

"I checked with our systems analyst and the answer is 'yes.'"

"You've got to be kidding. Did you have anything in the Landis file about our arrangement?" McGuire asked in a panic.

"Of course I did," Blackburn lied.

"Oh, no! no!" McGuire leaned back in the booth and closed his eyes, shaking his head. "A lousy two thousand bucks! A lousy two thousand bucks may cost me my career," he moaned.

"More like fifteen thousand bucks. That is how much we have paid you from our special account over the last four years."

"Whatever. The amount is not important. In any event, it's not that much money compared to the risk."

"I am very glad to hear you say it is not that much money," Blackburn said tapping the ends of his fingers against each other.

"What do you mean?" McGuire asked.

"I have a plan to fix your problem. But there's a little fee involved. And it just so happens that the fee is fifteen thousand dollars."

"What are you talking about? I thought you said this computer guy could find files that have been changed. How are you going to fix this problem?"

"He can only decipher a computer disk if the disk and the computer still exist. Dynamite has been proven to be very effective in scrambling a computer disk so that it is unreadable no matter how smart your computer expert may be."

"You are going to blow up your own computer? Won't they figure that out and come back and get you?"

"I don't plan to be around for anyone to find me," Blackburn replied. "I'm leaving the country—this weekend. And I am going to need a little traveling money. The way I figure it, I can leave without taking care of the computer and you will be found out. Or before I leave I can, shall we say, erase our records and you will not be discovered. The only difference between those two scenarios is a fee that is—as you've already said—not that much money. I want you here Saturday night at 11:00 P.M. with $15,000 in cash. We'll meet in the parking lot. As soon as you have paid the fee, I will take care of the computer."

"You're crazy. I should have you committed to Medical Lake," McGuire replied.

"You won't commit anyone to any place for long if I don't have fifteen thousand in cash by tomorrow night."

McGuire stared hard at his glass. Finally, he looked up and said, "OK. Tomorrow at eleven. Now get out of here and leave me alone."

"Gladly," Blackburn said coolly. He stood, winked at Lila and walked out into the dark.

～

Donna Corliss was at her bank when it opened on Friday. Her "fee", payable in cash to Blackburn, was $2500. Rita Coballo had been blackmailed for a similar amount for her involvement in this and other Code B operations. Corliss withdrew $1500 from her savings, leaving less than $50 in the account. She left that bank and drove across town to a different branch of the same bank to get a thousand dollar cash advance on her Visa card.

She was at the office by ten-thirty. Her scheduled time with Blackburn was thirty minutes later. She hadn't slept at all the night before. It had taken Stockton only five minutes to go soundly to sleep after midnight. He knew something was bothering her, but he was too tired and too distracted by the bar exam to ask her any questions. After he was asleep, she had spent the night pacing, watching television, and crying.

～

It seemed like it took forever for the half-hour to pass. Finally, the dreaded moment came and she walked down the hall one last time. She would spend the afternoon getting most of her personal things packed in a suitcase. Blackburn told her the explosion would be confined to the computer room, but Corliss was unsure if the building would be standing on Monday.

She knocked.

"Come in," Blackburn called out. He sounded almost cheerful.

She opened the door and walked in slowly. She was surprised to see Blackburn's worry balls sitting in their container on his desk.

"Oh, good morning, Donna. Thank you for coming."

"Yeah. . . . sure."

"Oh don't be so unpleasant," Blackburn said. "I am really sorry I have to ask you for a little funding, but really this is going to be better for us all. I am certain the folks in Olympia will elevate you to my spot and you'll make back this insignificant little amount in less than six months with the raise you'll get."

"I'm not sure I'll have a job after Monday," Corliss replied.

"Oh, nonsense. This is going to look like a little electrical explosion in the computer room. My friendly explosives expert assures me no one will suspect a thing. I might even be able to come back some day. I'll just claim I had a stress attack and couldn't handle things for a while. But all those nasty computer records will be gone for good."

Corliss actually felt a little better. "Well, I hope so." She reached in her purse, and threw a brown envelope containing twenty-five $100 bills on Blackburn's desk.

"Well, thank you so much," Blackburn said, picking up the envelope with a flourish.

"Sure. As if I had a choice," Corliss replied.

"Let's not get ugly, Donna. Just be a big girl and run along. And forget you ever knew me."

"*I wish,*" Corliss said to herself as she stood and left Blackburn's office for the last time.

~

Randall McGuire had met Eddie Hodder three years earlier. Hodder had been on trial for the rape and murder of a seventeen year old girl. His lawyer raised the defense of insanity—claiming it was a Vietnam War flashback that had caused him to commit the acts.

McGuire had done the evaluation. Hodder's father, a wealthy businessman, made sure that McGuire was well-paid.

Hodder was found not guilty by reason of insanity and spent over two years in a mental institution. He had just been released, but was required to have twice-monthly counseling sessions. He, of course, chose McGuire, who knew that nothing was wrong with Hodder other than a very mean streak and a flashpoint temper.

Hodder knew something was up when McGuire called him. He knew that whatever it was, McGuire was up to no good when he asked him to meet him in Comstock Park at six on Saturday morning wearing jogging clothes. McGuire had promised him that it would be worth his while.

⌐

McGuire had already taken one lap around the park when Hodder pulled his '87 Chevy pickup into the diagonal parking spots in front of the swimming pool. He half-jogged over to McGuire and followed his signal to begin running. After about two-hundred-and-fifty yards, McGuire slowed to a walk, as if he were merely taking a break from running.

"I've got a special job for you," McGuire said, looking straight ahead.

"It figures," Hodder replied.

"I want you to get my money back from someone, that's all."

"Explain what you mean."

"I don't want you to know too much for your own good, but what you need to know is that I'm being blackmailed. And tonight at eleven, I have to pay a certain scoundrel $15,000. All I want from you is to pose as an armed robber and relieve him of my fifteen grand. He can't call the cops or they will want to know why he was out on the street with fifteen big ones at midnight. You get the money, bring it back to me, and a third is yours."

"Sounds too easy. Anything you're not telling me?" Hodder demanded as they continued to walk.

"No. That's it. All I want you to do is follow this guy from the drop off point. From there he will probably go to his office. I want you to make sure he goes in the office. Then when he returns, you relieve him of the cash."

McGuire began to run again to let Hodder think it over. After about two minutes of jogging, Hodder slowed down, puffing.

"OK. I'll do it. But if anything is not exactly like you said, I'll simply disappear into the night."

"Fine. I promise you it will work perfectly."

∼

Blackburn spent Friday and Saturday gathering as much money as he could. By cleaning out his own savings, and taking all the cash advances his three credit cards would allow, he managed to accumulate eighteen thousand dollars. With the five thousand he had coerced out of Corliss and Coballo, he had a total of twenty-three thousand. With fifteen grand coming from McGuire, there would be enough for a reasonably good start in Canada, especially with the favorable exchange rate, he thought.

Blackburn obtained a thorough portfolio of fake identification and determined that Toronto would provide a nice place to live. He would slip across the border in British Columbia in the early hours Sunday morning, and drive the Hertz rental car he had rented for two weeks. He would abandon the car somewhere along the way, and take the train to Toronto. He thought it was a magnificent plan.

Hodder arrived at the Ram's Head at ten. He downed two beers and made a date to meet Lila when she got off work at one.

He went outside at 10:45 and sat slouched down in his truck which was parked on the far edge of the parking lot.

McGuire's BMW turned north on Regal off 57th and pulled into the Ram's Head parking lot at 10:57. He turned off the headlights and remained in the car. McGuire watched nervously as car after car came south on Regal, passed by the parking lot and turned, one direction or the other, onto 57th. Finally, a Celica turned left into the Ram's Head lot and pulled into the open spot on the left hand side of the BMW.

Blackburn motioned for McGuire to get in his car. McGuire got out, opened the passenger door of the Celica and threw a small packet on the front passenger's seat.

"Why don't you get in?" Blackburn asked.

"I have nothing to say to you," McGuire replied. "Besides, I'm allergic to certain forms of powder."

"Oh, it's safely in the trunk," Blackburn replied, sticking the envelope into a small travel bag on the front seat.

McGuire turned away without a word, got in his car, and left rubber on the pavement in his haste to get away.

Blackburn watched McGuire's rapid departure and laughed. He shifted his car into reverse and began the trek to his office building on the northern edge of downtown.

Hodder gave him a twenty second head start. He had been briefed on the office location by McGuire. Even if they got separated, he would know where to go. But as they passed down Regal, past the strip malls, apartments, and churches on 29th, and then down the stately Grand Avenue and into downtown, Hodder kept the Celica in clear view.

Hodder had figured out an "improvement" on McGuire's plan during the afternoon. Why should he settle for five grand when he could get fifteen? What would McGuire do? Tell the cops that he had asked Hodder to do an armed robbery? There seemed no reason to give any of the money back to McGuire.

"McGuire must think I really am crazy, if he thinks I am going to give him all this money and keep only a third," he said aloud as his pickup passed over the Spokane River on Washington Street.

Blackburn turned right on Mission. He pulled his car into the parking area directly behind the building. With no moon in the sky the parking lot was completely dark and no one was in the building.

Hodder parked his pick-up a block away on a side street. He grabbed his semi-automatic pistol and dashed quickly to the parking lot, pausing about thirty yards away.

Blackburn had his trunk open. He lifted a small gym bag out of the trunk very gently.

"The money," Hodder thought. But he also remembered seeing McGuire throw a package on the front seat. Hodder recalled that McGuire had wanted him to let Blackburn go in the office first and then do the robbery. McGuire had stressed the point about six times. "What he doesn't know won't hurt him," Hodder thought.

Hodder pulled the pistol out of his pocket and quickly paced to a point about two feet behind Blackburn.

"Freeze, sucker," he growled.

Blackburn jerked involuntarily—but his fingers clutched the bag tightly.

"I want that bag—now!" Hodder said.

"No, you don't. Not this bag." Blackburn gasped, his arms shaking with fear.

"Yes, I do, plus, I want the package you got from my buddy McGuire back at the tavern."

Blackburn's blood ran cold. "McGuire? McGuire? Did he put you up to this?"

"Sort of," Hodder said, "but that is no concern to you. I want his little package as well. Just sit that bag on the ground, go back to your car and get me McGuire's little package."

Blackburn backed up slowly, reached in the front seat, and got the green travel bag which contained all of his money.

"McGuire will never be cleared unless I get that black bag into this building," Blackburn said.

"Shut up! Whatever you've got going with McGuire is your own business. Just gimme those bags."

Blackburn's mind raced furiously. If he could get the bomb back in his hands, he could threaten to blow them both up to get the robber to leave. It was his only hope. He walked back toward the first bag and sat the money bag down on the ground and kicked it toward Hodder. "Here's the money."

Suddenly, Blackburn darted for the bomb. Instinctively, Hodder fired. He didn't miss. Blackburn fell with a gaping hole in his chest. Blood was gushing from the wound.

Hodder grabbed both bags and ran to his truck. He drove as rapidly as he dared. He went north, keeping to residential roads and avoiding the main arteries.

Twenty minutes later he was on the Nine Mile Falls highway and headed away from the city. He pulled off the highway, onto to a deserted side road. There was nothing in sight.

"All right, let's see what we got for our efforts," Hodder said aloud, his heart beating furiously. He opened the money bag. Although it was dark in his truck, he didn't want to turn on the dome light—he could see well enough to discover there was obviously more than $15,000. Much more.

"Yeah!" he said, with his fist clenched in a sign of victory. He reached for the second parcel.

"And I got two bags full," he said. He carelessly opened the second bag, but couldn't make out the contents because of the darkness. He reached in and tried to ascertain its contents by touch. His hand felt some wires. "What the—" he said, quickly pulling his hand back. It was his last move.

The explosion woke people and pets for a two-mile radius. The truck, the money, and the man were eliminated in a spectacular instantaneous fireball.

Hodder had a record as a certified crazy man. The Spokane County Sheriff's Department wasn't terribly intrigued with the fact that he had managed to blow himself up. Gerald Blackburn appeared to the Spokane City Police Department to be nothing more than an unfortunate victim of a random, and unsolved, robbery. The two deaths were never connected by the two sister police agencies.

17

Peter Barron and Gail Willet were able to agree to put everything in the case on hold for three weeks as a result of the murder of Gerald Blackburn. Judge Stokes summarily approved their request. The inspection of the computer by Aaron and Judge Stokes was to be the first event in the new schedule and that would take place on July 20. The deposition of Donna Corliss would follow the week after.

Peter and Gwen talked on the phone a couple of times about the death of Blackburn. The calls were relatively short and somber. Other than at church, Peter had little justification to call or see Gwen. His spiritual struggle seemed better with her out of the daily details of his life, but he never passed a day without thinking about her at least a half-dozen times.

Gwen spent the early part of July enjoying her daughter and her new found life in Christ. Her studies with Lynn were both enjoyable and helpful. But Lynn's explanation of Peter's position on divorce still left her confused. Gwen knew that someday she would have to hear the reasons from Peter himself.

On July 5—three weeks before the Washington State Bar Examination—Stephen Stockton left for Seattle. His father wanted him to study in the city where the examination was held, free from all distractions. A suite in the exclusive Westin Hotel became his temporary residence, thanks to his father's golden checkbook.

Corliss spent her nights alone, living in fear of the coming examination of the CPS computer by Aaron Roberts. She slept little and drank much—something she had never done consistently before.

One week before the impending computer analysis, Rita Coballo knocked on her door.

"Come in. What's up, Rita?" Corliss asked sitting in her same old cubicle. No one had yet been promoted to take Blackburn's place. "Can I shut the door so we can talk?" Coballo said.

"Uh . . . s-sure," Corliss answered nervously.

"I suppose you've been thinking about this upcoming computer deal," Coballo began.

"I can't think about anything else. I'm so scared. Do you think we'll go to jail?"

"Not if we use our heads," Coballo answered.

"Not another bomb. You can forget that."

"No, of course not. But if we keep our stories straight, I think we can lay the blame where it really belongs—on the head of a dead man."

"What do you mean?" Corliss asked.

"I mean that we testify that all the changes in the documents were apparently made by our beloved Blackburn."

"Do you think it will work?"

"If we think it through carefully, I think so."

"Go ahead and explain," Corliss said eagerly.

"Well, you could testify you never saw the actual intake report prior to going out to the Landis house. Blackburn just gave you an oral summary. Weren't you sick or something the day after it really came in?"

"I was. Go on."

"We could say that he was responsible for just sitting on the report until you got back and apparently lied to you as to the date of the intake report to protect his own sloppiness in management."

Corliss was beginning to feel a gradual easing of the knot in her stomach.

"And we can say that he made up all the other changes after the lawsuit was filed, just to protect his own backside. And that we knew nothing about it," Coballo continued.

"But how are we supposed to make these explanations if we knew nothing about it? If we knew nothing, we don't know that there were any changes."

"Good point. Let me think," Coballo said rocking in her chair rubbing her temples. "Well, first of all, we have to act genuinely surprised when they spring any changes on us. Even with Willet. Then, I think we say something like, 'We had a meeting with Blackburn shortly after the lawsuit was filed. He told us that we weren't going to have to worry about the lawsuit and that he was going to fix everything.' Something vague, but that clearly suggests he was the culprit."

"It might work. It might actually work."

"You know, I don't care whether this blasted Department loses this lawsuit or not. And if a jury awards damages against us, the state is going to pay for it anyway. All I care about is keeping my backside out of jail," Coballo said.

"You got that right," Corliss replied, smiling for the first time in days.

～

Aaron Roberts was told to meet Judge Stokes in his chambers forty-five minutes before their nine o'clock appointment at CPS headquarters.

The clerk greeted him warmly and ushered him into the Judge's chambers.

"Please come in and sit down, Mr. Roberts. Thank you for coming so early," the judge said, standing up and motioning toward a couch in the corner. The judge walked across his expansive office and sat down in a leather chair in front of an enormous wall of law books.

"Impressive office you have here, Judge," Aaron said cheerfully.

"Yes, yes. The taxpayers treat us well." The judge leaned forward and picked up a yellow pad from a coffee table between the two men. "I wanted to go over a few ground rules with you before we go over there."

"Great. I'm glad for your direction. I know the technology, but I'm unsure of all the legal implications."

"Good. We'll make a good team," the judge said smiling. "Frankly, one of the reasons I'm going with you personally is that I want to learn as much as I can about the technology you are using. I think this may open up a whole new area of legal inquiry. Before computers were widespread, any changes in a document usually could be detected by some tried and true methods. Changes on a computer record are a brand-new legal issue. There may be none in this case. But if there are, I think we will be plowing new legal ground."

"You make it sound like an adventure," Aaron replied.

"OK. Let's get to our rules. First, you are not allowed to tell your friend Peter Barron about anything we find. Understood?"

"Yes, sir."

"OK. This is very important. You seem like a man of character and you've got a government security clearance, so I am going to leave you on your honor."

Aaron smiled and nodded.

"Second, I want you to confine your search as much as possible to documents relating to the Landis file. I don't know how these things work, but if you inadvertently discover information about other files, you are not to disclose that to anyone. You understand?"

"Yes, Your Honor, I think I do."

"And finally, you are to give the printed documents as I direct you today to me and to me only. You are not to make extra printed copies of the documents and you are not to make computer copies on disk, unless you give me those disks right then and there."

"That's fine, Judge. I am happy to do all of this."

"Good. Good. All right, let's go. We can take my car."

Jeremy Bowden, the CPS chief systems analyst from Olympia, was waiting in the reception area when Judge Stokes and Aaron arrived.

"Good morning, Judge. And I assume that you are Mr. Roberts," Bowden beamed. He had been given strict orders by the Secretary of Health and Human Services to comply fully with all of the judge's requests. The Department would not get caught in a cover-up if they did have some investigators who had gone too far, he had been told. "The computer room is just down this corridor. I am sure you want to get right to work."

"Thank you," the judge said, smiling. "Please lead the way."

The computer room was small, but the CPS staff had managed to arrange three chairs so that the keyboard and screen for the main file server were visible. Upon direction from Bowden, Aaron sat in the middle in front of the keyboard, the judge was on the left, and Bowden took the right hand chair.

"The system is up and going, and I will assist you with anything you need," Bowden said helpfully.

"Great, let's get acclimated a bit," Aaron said.

He stroked the keyboard and ran some initial diagnostic commands to understand the basic nature of the system. Then with the assistance of Bowden, they located the sectors on the hard drive where the Landis files were supposed to be located.

After a few more minutes, he pulled a 3.5" floppy disk out of his briefcase and put it in the A: drive in the body of the computer.

"We're getting there, Judge," Aaron said. "The preliminaries are just about over."

Aaron typed the strokes to run the sectors on the hard drive through his "deciphering" program. He spent about ten minutes scrolling through files, until he said, "Bingo. This looks like one of the Landis reports." It was the intake record. After twenty seconds of slow scrolling Aaron said, "And here are your changes."

"Can you print those out?" the judge asked.

"It would be easier to copy them on a floppy and print them later," Aaron answered.

"OK, fine. Is that it?"

"I would guess they would have more files than their initial report," Aaron said. "Wouldn't that make sense?" he said turning to Bowden.

"It certainly would. Standard practice is to keep records of every step along the way," Bowden answered.

After another twenty minutes of search commands and scrolling, Aaron found the investigative notes. "Here's something about Landis," he said. "And . . . yeah, there are some changes to this as well."

"Copy those records and keep looking," the judge said in a voice brimming with excitement.

Another half hour of searching yielded no other records.

"That's all I can find right now," Aaron said. Turning to Bowden he said, "where can I print this?"

"I've got a printer ready to go in an office right down the hall," Bowden said. "Can I get a copy?"

"Not from us," the judge said. "They're your records. I can't stop the Department from using their own records, but I will say that if any further changes are made, I will jail whoever makes them for contempt of my court."

"I won't risk it, Your Honor. I won't even go back and look. You've got a clever man here in Mr. Roberts," Bowden said.

"I think you're right," the judge said beaming.

The copies were made. And the disk and the printed copies were handed over to the judge, who took them with a flourish. "Very good. Very good. I can't wait to get back to my chambers and figure out what all these changes mean. Will you be available, Mr. Roberts, if I need any translations later today?"

"Yes, Judge. I'll be returning to my office as soon as we're finished."

～

On Friday, July 22, two days later, Judge Stokes issued a ruling. He made a finding that there had been four changes made in the relevant documents:

(1) The date of the intake call had been changed from May 5 to May 9;

(2) The nature of the injuries had been changed from "unknown" to "severe bruises;"

(3) The name of the reporter had been changed from "anonymous" to the name of a medical professional—the new name was not specified in the order; and

(4) The coding of the call had been changed from a Code 2 to a Code 1.

He also found that the changes had been made the same day that the federal lawsuit had been filed. Aaron had been unable to determine which computer in the system had been used to make the changes.

～

Gail Willet's face turned ashen white when she got the judge's order. Her first call was to Matt Bartholomew, who was floored.

"What have you gotten us into, Ms. Willet?"

"What are you talking about, Bartholomew?" Willet answered angrily. "Your agency—and I remind you—*you*, represent this agency. *Your* agency apparently thinks it's OK to tamper with government records. I had nothing to do with this."

"I'm sorry. The changes had just seemed too well-informed. Right down the lines of the legal theories."

"I did tell Mr. Blackburn my off-the-cuff analysis of our best defenses the afternoon the suit was filed, but I never advised him to change any records. And I never dreamed that anyone would do such a thing!"

"I'm sorry for questioning you. OK, OK. What are we going to do now?"

"I am going to the library. I remember some cases that say that even when government agencies use knowingly forged documents or knowing perjury in trial to convict someone, the government is still immune from damages," Willet replied.

"I hope you're right," Bartholomew said. "But I want you to get hold of our other two clients and find out what in the world is going on."

～

Peter wasn't able to reach Gwen with the news of the judge's order until after she left for work on Friday afternoon. They agreed to meet Saturday morning at ten for brunch and discuss the case. Gordon would be exercising visitation of Casey starting at nine.

～

Donna Corliss and Rita Coballo reported to Willet's office at four-thirty as ordered. They were ushered into an empty office by a receptionist. Willet was expected back from the law library any moment. An anxious ten minutes passed and then the door opened, Willet walked in, and the door slammed shut.

"What in blazes were the two of you thinking of?" Willet yelled.

Corliss was frozen. Coballo spoke first. "If you are talking about the two of us—we didn't do anything."

"I suppose little mice got into your computer and changed the documents," Willet said contemptuously.

"No. But it appears that our former supervisor did," Coballo said calmly.

"Well, of course. The dead man did it. Now, explain to me why I don't believe you?"

"Think what you want, Ms. Willet," Coballo said forcefully. "The two of us are innocent in this matter. We were just doing our job. I don't like to speak evil of the dead, but Mr. Blackburn was no "Mr. Nice Guy". He pushed and shoved us to have a high conviction rate. And it is certainly consistent with the way he ran his department that he would go in and change records to get the results he wanted."

Coballo was able to deliver the argument with a ring of truth. Blackburn had pushed them, but they had also been willing participants.

Willet said down in her chair and fumed. She eyed one woman, then the other.

"You've been awfully silent, Ms. Corliss," Willet said suddenly. "What do you have to say about all this?"

"Rita's right. It's just the kind of thing Blackburn would have done." She was glad to have something to say that felt close to the truth.

After another minute of silent glaring, Willet said, "All right. I might as well go with it. I think I can make it add up. But, wait— one last thing. Neither of you have any idea about his death do you?"

"Absolutely not!" "No way!" They said, talking over each other.

"OK. I guess I'll go with it. Let me tell you what I've found. There are a number of cases which are going to be helpful to us. The basic idea of these cases is that people cannot file successful civil rights lawsuits for events that have occurred after the filing of a social services complaint for child abuse."

"Even if officials change the records?" Coballo asked.

"Yes, that's right. Even if officials commit perjury, use forged records, or anything else like it," Willet answered with a smile. "Our friend Mr. Barron has found a factual bonanza but it has no legal implications whatsoever."

"Are you sure?" Corliss asked—her spirit becoming more buoyant by the minute.

"Yes, the lead case is a decision by the United States Supreme Court in 1983. The name of the case is *Briscoe v. LaHue*."

"Forgive me for asking this kind of question. But why do they have such a rule? Doesn't that mean that social workers could do literally anything and get away with it?" Corliss asked.

"It reassures me when you ask a question like that," Willet said. "Blackburn probably did make the changes."

Corliss hoped that her burning ears weren't visible through her hair.

"Well, the answer to your question," Willet said, "is the Supreme Court doesn't want police officers, prosecutors, and social workers having to always defend these kind of lawsuits. Every time we get a conviction, they could sue us claiming we committed perjury, or that we introduced forged evidence, or some such charge. The vast majority of these cases would be frivolous where it's just the convicted person's word against the word of the official. So rather than put any of us through the hassle, the Supreme Court has said no such civil rights suits will ever be allowed. They figure prosecutors, police officers, and social workers would lose their jobs and go to jail if they ever really did this sort of thing. That's a sufficient deterrent to stop people from doing it."

"You mean Blackburn could have gone to jail if—if—." Corliss couldn't finish the sentence.

"Yes, that's right. If Blackburn were still with us, he would be looking at some serious jail time for tampering with these documents."

Corliss's stomach fell to her feet.

"What happens next?" Coballo asked, sensing that Corliss had her nerves rattled by that last exchange.

"The next thing is that Peter Barron is going to take the deposition of Donna here, and then, he will probably want to take your deposition as well, Rita. Then after that, I will file a renewed motion to dismiss the whole case. I will argue that even if someone committed perjury or tampered with documents, this line of cases says the case must be dismissed anyway."

"How do you think our chances are of winning?" Coballo asked.

"Well, you can count on Judge Stokes being furious with our agency and he won't trust anything we say. But, Supreme Court cases are hard to ignore. I think he'll rule our way. And if he doesn't, I can almost guarantee you the Court of Appeals in Seattle will reverse his decision."

"Sounds great," Corliss said.

"Just once more, just between us," Willet said softly. "You swear to me that neither of you had anything to do with these documents being changed?"

"On a stack of Bibles," Coballo lied.

Corliss just shook her head "no" and smiled.

⁓

On Saturday morning, Peter picked Gwen up at her house and drove her to the Spokane House Restaurant, an upscale restaurant on the eastern edge of town with a magnificent view of the river and downtown, and a legendary weekend brunch.

Peter noticed a number of men doing double takes as he walked by with Gwen. He couldn't suppress the pride welling up within him. How he wished their envy was really merited.

"So this has to be really good news for our case," Gwen said as they got their food and settled in.

"The best," Peter replied. "Not only does it show they tampered with the documents, but it also means that Judge Stokes is going to believe you in any factual dispute that develops between the CPS workers and us. Their credibility is toast."

"Can't we sue them for anything else as a result of this? Isn't forging documents a violation of my civil rights?" Gwen asked.

"One would think so," Peter replied. "But it's not going to be easy."

Peter had been in the law library reading the same cases that Willet had found.

"I'm going to amend the complaint," Peter continued. "But there are some cases, including Supreme Court cases, that seem to rule out these kind of suits."

"You're kidding, aren't you? When people are victimized by intentionally forged documents, you cannot sue the officials for *that*?"

"No such suit has been successful so far—especially not in the Supreme Court. But we can argue two things to try to get around it."

"Like what?"

"First, we can argue that the other cases involved mere allegations of forgery and perjury; here we have absolute proof. And second, we can argue the Supreme Court decision is wrong and it should be changed."

"Can Judge Stokes do that?" Gwen asked.

"He can't change a Supreme Court rule, but he could go our way with the first theory."

"I can't believe the Supreme Court's rules are so against people like me," Gwen said in despair.

"I fully understand what you are saying. I know it doesn't seem fair. But, all of this does help us with our original suit. They are still liable for things they did at your house before they first filed papers in court. And secondly, I don't mind the idea of standing in front of the Supreme Court and saying to them, 'Your rule is wrong. You should change it.'"

It was the perfect segue. She hesitated, but couldn't help herself.

"Peter, speaking of rules that are unfair and that I don't understand, I want to talk with you about . . . about . . ." She sighed and paused and looked intently out the window.

"About the two of us?" Peter said.

"Yes," Gwen replied.

When she looked up, Peter could see a tear glistening in her eye. He wanted to crawl under his chair and die.

"Peter, the first time we met, you told me that you couldn't marry a divorced woman because of your faith. I didn't know anything about your faith then, but I do now. Lynn has tried to explain your position to me—but I just don't get it.

"I wouldn't have said anything," Gwen continued, "except for the way you treat me."

"Have I done something to offend you?" Peter interrupted.

"No, no, nothing like that. You treat me like a princess. You shower me with attention. You go out of your way to be concerned about me. And the way you look at me . . . Peter, I can't take it anymore. You say you can't marry me. But you act like you could fall in love with me at any moment."

Peter knew better, but the words escaped from his mouth. "I'm afraid that moment has already come, Gwen. I *am* in love with you. Despite everything I've tried to tell myself about my convictions; I simply cannot stop feeling the way I feel. You are the most wonderful person I have ever known."

Peter sighed deeply. Tears were streaming down Gwen's cheeks.

"I don't know what to say," Gwen said. "I really don't. What does this mean about all your convictions?"

"I am really confused. I don't know what to think. On the one hand, I don't feel free to change what I've always believed. But on the other hand, I can't stop thinking about you. You're on my mind night and day," he replied.

"Peter," Gwen began, "this is really hard for me, too. If you told me that you felt free to marry me, it would be almost impossible for me to resist your love. But as it is, this is really unfair to me. I wish you would just make up your mind whether or not you believe that God would allow you to marry me."

"I wish I could, too. I have really wrestled with this. I just can't figure it out. My mind is so confused that I have even found myself wishing that Gordon would have an accident or something. But that is obviously an evil thought. Whenever it crosses my mind, I try to pray for him and his salvation."

Gwen sat silently. She stared into Peter's eyes. She knew she would love to fall in love with this man. But his indecision hurt her more than anything had in a long time.

"Gwen, what do you want me to do?"

"What do *I* want you to do?" she asked with emphasis. "I really don't know. I am tempted to tell you to leave me alone unless you get this spiritual debate resolved."

Peter swallowed hard and felt a surge of panic.

"But, I don't want to stop seeing you. You've been a Christian for a lot longer than me. If you don't know the right answer, how do you expect me to figure it out?"

"You're certainly right about one thing. I have been terribly unfair to you. It is selfish of me to string you along, and keep telling myself that I am only your lawyer. I stopped being 'only' your lawyer when you hugged me the day we got Casey back. I knew at that moment you really loved your daughter deeply. I have always wanted to find a woman who could love me that way."

Gwen smiled broadly, remembering that moment, but a few seconds later just shook her head.

"Peter," she said, "as hard as it is, I think we should stop seeing each other unless God gives you the green light."

Peter hung his head. He knew she was right. He couldn't look her in the eye for the moment.

"OK. Unfortunately, I think that's the right thing to do."

For the first time in fifteen minutes, Peter became aware there were other people in the restaurant. He quickly laid some money on the table, and quietly escorted Gwen out the door.

They rode silently in the car until Peter stopped in front of Gwen's home.

"Gwen, I'll tell you what. I will give you a final answer by the end of October. I am going to seek counsel from Pastor Lind and I am going to pray about it. If I don't get a green light by the end of October, I'll set you free for good. But you have to make me one promise. Promise me that you won't fall in love with anyone else until then."

"Peter," Gwen said smiling, opening the door, "you are certainly worth waiting for. I promise, Peter—I promise."

18

Peter's conference room was rather small—a conference table, six chairs, and one wall of bookcases which were about half-full.

But it was large enough for the deposition of Donna Corliss, scheduled for Wednesday, July 27, at 9:00 in the morning.

On Tuesday evening, Peter spent three hours going over all the documents and pleadings to make sure he didn't forget anything. After the last order by Judge Stokes, Peter was extremely anxious to get the opportunity to ask a number of questions about the alteration of the documents. But he couldn't let the glamour of that issue distract him from the many other areas of inquiry.

Corliss spent the evening in agony worrying about her upcoming session with Peter Barron. At nine-thirty, she received an unexpected and pleasant surprise. Stephen Stockton called her from Seattle. They hadn't talked in over a week.

"Oh, Stephen, I am *so* glad you called," Donna said. "I was beginning to wonder if you remembered me."

"Oh, I remember all right. I'll be home in just two more days. I can't wait to see you."

"Me too. How did it go today? You started the Bar Exam, didn't you?"

"Yes, we started this morning, and let me tell you it was grueling. I'm really happy my dad made me study so hard. I think the legacy of Raymond Wolff is about to be buried. This Gonzaga valedictorian is not going to flunk this exam."

"So you think you did OK?"

"Well, I had nine essays to answer today. I know I aced seven of them. On the other two, I am pretty sure that I at least got a passing score."

"That's great, Stephen. I wish you were a lawyer right now."

"What's going on? Has that civil rights case flared up again? I thought Gail Willet was going to file a motion to dismiss."

"A lot has happened. I don't want to tell you everything right now. It's too complex and too distracting. Tomorrow I'm having my deposition taken."

"Oh, OK. Well, I wish I could be there to help. But, it won't be long now."

She thought about Stephen's impending move to Washington, D.C. "Yeah, you're right, Stephen, it won't be long now."

～

On Wednesday morning, Gwen showed up at 8:35. It had taken her a few minutes longer than planned to get ready and to take Casey over to her parents. Other than a brief hello at church on Sunday, it was the first time she and Peter had talked since the brunch on Saturday.

Peter went over the planned areas of questions he had for Corliss and asked Gwen if she had any comments or thoughts on the topics. Gwen had little to say. Peter had clearly mastered the facts and circumstances surrounding this case.

When they finished their discussion of the case, Peter glanced nervously at his watch. It was ten until nine. He was not nervous about the deposition; but about being alone with Gwen.

"After I blurted out everything on Saturday, I don't want to go into territory I shouldn't," Peter said, "but I just want to know if you are doing OK?"

"I'm OK, Peter," she replied with a hint of a smile. "How about you?"

"I'll make it. I'm glad for this deposition, it gives me a lot of work to focus my mental energies on."

The intercom buzzed. "Everyone's here and all set up in the conference room," Sally said.

"We'll be right there," Peter replied, standing up with papers in hand. "Well, let's go find out if they've decided to tell the truth today."

⁓

The court reporter was seated at the far end of the conference table with her back against the bookcase. Corliss and Willet were seated at the side of the table closest to the window. Corliss was seated at the end of the table next to the court reporter. Peter was seated directly across from Corliss with a stack of papers in front of him. Gwen was to his right with a blank yellow pad and a pen lying on the table in front of her.

"Shall we begin?" Peter asked.

"That's why we're here," Willet answered.

Turning to the court reporter, a dark-haired man in his thirties, Peter said, "Would you please swear in the witness?"

"Please raise your right hand," the reporter said to Corliss. "Do you promise that the testimony you are about to give will be the whole truth, so help you God?"

Corliss hoped she would not have to lie very much or at all. But she was not about to tell the whole truth. "I do," she answered.

"Please tell us your name, business address, and occupation," Peter said.

"Donna Corliss, my business address is West 245 Mission, Spokane, and I am an investigator for Child Protective Services."

"Ms. Corliss, in order to save time in this deposition, I would like to ask you one preliminary question. You previously testified in two hearings on a related matter involving the same parties in state court, did you not?"

"Yes, I did."

"You were under oath on both of those occasions, and you promised to tell the truth, isn't that right?"

Corliss was already becoming nervous. Questions about her truthfulness were her deepest fear. "Yes, that's right."

"OK. So in order to save time today, if I were to ask you to answer any questions about your background, training, or even the basic facts of this case involving Gwen and Casey Landis, would your answers be the same as in those state court hearings or would you give different answers today?"

"They would be the same as far as I know. Certainly anything about my background would be the same. Are you saying that I didn't get something right in those hearings?"

"Yes, counsel," Willet interjected. "If you are trying to discredit her by showing that she said one thing one time and something different now, I think it would be more appropriate to have you ask her about something specific."

"I agree," Peter said. "My question really was only intended to relate to her training, background, and experience."

"We'll stipulate that her background and experience have not changed, counsel," Willet said.

"Fine. Let's move on," Peter said, taking note that Corliss was very touchy about the issue of her personal credibility.

"When did you first learn there was a report that Mrs. Landis allegedly had abused her daughter Casey?"

"I personally learned about it on the morning of Wednesday, May 11, when I reported for work around eight or eight-fifteen."

"How did you first become aware of the report?" Peter asked.

"I read about it on my e-mail, and I also got a call from my boss, Gerald Blackburn. I can't remember which came first, they were both so close. But I think Mr. Blackburn gave me a verbal report about the case first."

"Why did you learn about the case on Wednesday, May 11? Now that Judge Stokes and Aaron Roberts have deciphered your original documents, we know that the call actually came in on the prior Thursday, six days earlier. Why the delay?"

"I have no idea about any of that. I do know I took a day of sick leave on Friday, May 6. On Monday, May 9th, I was out of the office all day teaching an in-service class for new CPS investigators, and on Tuesday, May 10th, I was in juvenile court all day. So I can't tell you what happened between the evening of May 5 and the morning of May 11. I wasn't there."

"What happens if an emergency case comes in and is assigned by the hotline operator to you, and you are not in the office that day for some reason?"

"Then my supervisor, Mr. Blackburn, would be responsible to check my e-mail and make sure that any emergencies were covered—either by himself or another investigator."

"Oh, I see. So at least in theory, Mr. Blackburn would have checked on the Landis matter some time between May 5 and May 11, right?"

"Yes, proper protocol would have been for him to check on it the morning of May 6, assuming that the call really did come in on May 5."

"Do you still have any doubt about that?" Peter asked with a sharp look.

"I have no doubt that's what our report said," Corliss answered. "Hotline operators do make clerical mistakes from time to time."

"Oh, they do? Do you have any reason to believe that they made a mistake in this case?"

Corliss saw herself creating a trap she might fall in. She quickly went a different direction. "No. Not really. I was just pointing out the theoretical possibility."

"Let's skip theoretical issues for now," Peter said impatiently. "What date did you think the call had come in when you went to see Gwen Landis, the first time, on May 11, 1994?"

"I don't remember. I think Mr. Blackburn told me that it had come in just the day before or something. I don't remember looking at the date of the report on my e-mail, and the only reason I wouldn't have done that is that I must have been told a 'date of report' by Mr. Blackburn."

"On your first visit, on May 11, did you tell Gwen Landis when the report came in?"

"I can't remember. But it's very doubtful."

Peter looked at Gwen. Her eyes flashed in anger.

"Why do you say that it's very doubtful?" Peter continued.

"Because Mrs. Landis refused to cooperate with me that day. If she had cooperated with me , this whole thing probably would never have gone any further. She made a big federal case out of something that should have lasted only ten or fifteen minutes."

Peter paused while he made some notes. He looked at the reporter and said, "Please mark that last answer."

The reporter nodded and hit the key that placed a red square in the column of the continuously fed paper that came through his stenographic machine.

"OK. How about on the second day, May 12? Did you tell her the date the call came in then?"

"I don't remember her asking me that question." Corliss answered.

"It is possible that you could have mentioned it yourself, isn't it?"

Corliss nodded. "Sure, it's possible. But I don't remember mentioning it on my own, and I don't remember her asking about it either."

Willet looked at Corliss with an "attagirl" expression on her face.

"All right." Peter said. "So if Mrs. Landis tells me that on the first visit you told her the call came in on May 5, and the second visit you told her the call came in on May 9, you wouldn't have the memory to contradict her testimony one way or the other, would you?"

Corliss was not going to give up easily. "I don't remember saying anything about it at all. But I can guarantee you that I didn't tell her two different stories."

"Isn't it interesting that the two different stories Mrs. Landis remembers are the two different dates that appear on the intake report? On the original intake report the date of the hotline report is recorded as May 5, and on the version that was tampered with, the date was May 9. How do you explain that remarkable coincidence?"

"Counsel," Willet interrupted. "Your question is both argumentative and assumes facts not in evidence."

"What do you mean it assumes facts not in evidence?" Peter shot back. "I am doing this deposition because the facts of document tampering, as discovered by Judge Stokes, are fully in evidence in this case. Do you disagree with that, Ms. Willet?"

"No. Obviously not. But your question assumes Ms. Corliss was the one who did the tampering. I think it would be more appropriate for you to ask the question directly than to imply it in a compound question she might not understand."

"Oh, I didn't think it was that difficult to understand," Peter snapped. "All right, Ms. Corliss, what role did you play in the changes which have been made on the intake report?"

"None whatsoever."

"None whatsoever, huh? Do you know who made the changes?"

"I don't *know* who did it. But I have good reason to guess as to who it was."

Willet was waiting to object if Peter asked her to guess.

"Tell me who you think it was and all your reasons for thinking that and we will let Judge Stokes decide if it is a guess or not," Peter said.

Corliss looked at Willet for instruction. They had obviously talked about this point in advance.

"I think the way he asked the question, you probably better go ahead and answer it," Willet said out loud. Turning to Peter, "We do reserve our objection to this question as we do to all of your questions."

"Of course," Peter replied. "Now Ms. Corliss, what's your answer? Who do you think tampered with the documents and why do you think that?"

Corliss looked at Willet for reassurance again. Willet nodded.

"I believe it was Mr. Blackburn who made the changes in the file."

"Why do you think that?" Peter repeated.

"I hope I've made it clear I don't know who did it. But it seems like something he might do."

"I hope you can be more specific than that," Peter said.

"Mr. Blackburn was a hard-nosed investigator. He didn't like to take no for an answer. And he didn't like to lose. He was really upset when we came back after we lost the hearing you handled for Mrs. Landis. And he wasn't just upset when we got served with the civil rights lawsuit—he was furious. Then we called Ms. Willet on the speaker phone and she explained some of the legal issues involved in the case and he calmed down some. Later in the day he said we shouldn't worry about the federal lawsuit, that he was going to fix everything so it would be OK."

"Did you ask him what he meant by 'fix everything?'" Peter asked.

"No. I didn't want to be yelled at anymore."

"Have you known Mr. Blackburn to tamper with documents in any other case previously?"

Corliss debated about which lie to tell. "Not that I know of," she said.

"But it's possible, isn't it?"

"Counsel," Willet interjected. "You're asking her to speculate about a dead man's action she does not have knowledge of. You don't think the judge would ever let that in, do you?"

Peter knew she was right, but he simply said, "It's not worth arguing about. Let's move on."

"So your testimony is that Blackburn said he would "fix everything" regarding this federal lawsuit?"

"That's right."

"When did he say that?"

"Late in the business day, it could have been after five, on the day we were served with your federal lawsuit."

"Did you ever have any other discussions with him that relate to your belief that he altered the documents?"

"No, I didn't."

"Was anyone else involved in the conversation where he said he would fix everything?"

"Yes, there were three of us in his office: Rita Coballo, Mr. Blackburn, and myself."

"All right, Ms. Corliss, I'd like to talk about something different for a little while. Why did you leave Mrs. Landis's house on the first day you were there, Wednesday, May 11, without having performed a search of the premises?"

"She wouldn't let me in."

"OK. When you came back the next day, Mrs. Landis still did not want you to come in, isn't that right?"

"That's right. She still refused to cooperate."

"She refused you entrance both days. Why did you go in on one occasion and decline to go in the other?"

"I was just following CPS policy. Whenever entrance is refused voluntarily, we are required to get a police officer to accompany us, plus an additional social worker if possible."

"So your decision to enter the Landis home against her will and without her consent was made in accordance with CPS policy?"

"Yes, that's right."

"Does CPS have a policy about getting warrants to enter people's homes?"

"No. At least I've never heard of such a policy."

"On what basis do you go into someone's home?"

"Whenever we receive a report that could be child abuse or neglect, if the allegations are true, we are required by law to do a face to face investigation. That means, when a child is in the home, we are required to go into the home and look at the child and the child's physical circumstances."

"Did you believe there was an emergency in this case—that Casey's life or health was in imminent danger?"

"I wasn't sure. That is what I was there to find out. The allegations were certainly serious. And the fact that she twice refused to cooperate made me very suspicious that she was hiding something."

"Didn't Mrs. Landis say that if you would simply let her know what the nature of the allegations were she would consider cooperating? Wasn't it you and not her who was hiding something?"

"Mr. Barron, I was simply following CPS policy. In fact, I teach new investigators about the policy. We never disclose the nature of an allegation in advance. It might give a guilty parent a reason to change their story."

"Your agency has demonstrated its expertise in changing stories, so I guess you would know," Peter replied, flipping the pages in his notebook. Willet just glared at him.

"All right, Ms. Corliss, let's talk for a couple minutes about those mysterious fading bruises," Peter said. "Are you sure you saw them, or are they another one of those fabrications that Mr. Blackburn made up?"

"Your question is highly argumentative, counsel, and I will direct my client not to answer," Willet said contemptuously.

"All right. Ms. Corliss, did you or did you not see any fading bruises?"

"I saw what I saw. There were bruises there."

"You teach CPS policy, right?"

"That's right."

"Your policy is to take pictures of bruises, right?"

"Yes, Mr. Barron, that's right."

"And you are asking us to take your word for it, that you simply forgot the camera that day, right?"

"We forgot the camera."

"I am handing you two portions of the transcript of the two hearings in the state court. The first is your testimony in the first hearing. You will see there highlighted where you gave a physical description of the bruises. And in the second transcript, Ms. Coballo gave her description of the bruises. Those two descriptions don't match, do they?"

"Not very much. But the differences are superficial. And again we see hundreds of beaten, bruised children each year. And this child was wiggling and yelling and screaming while we were trying to search her. We wanted to be as humane as possible, so we didn't pin her down and draw pictures. We saw some bruises and we wanted to get her back to a situation where she would calm down as soon as possible."

"I see," Peter said. "All right, do you have a nice, neat explanation for why you told Mrs. Landis that you would probably close the case if she would cooperate? The police officer recalled you saying that. Would you have said that if you had found bruises?"

Corliss was ready for the question. She and Willet had practiced the answer several times. Willet genuinely believed that Corliss was about to tell the truth in a smooth and creative way, but still the truth.

"Mr. Barron, I cannot explain why Officer Donahue said what he said. If you will recall, at the trial he did not remember this until after you prompted him with the information. He did not come up with it on his own. If his memory is that bad, I doubt that we can take the precise words he says he heard as literally true. I am sure that he heard something. I have no reason to believe that Officer Donahue is making anything up. He probably heard me say something like, 'Mrs. Landis, things will go much better for you if you cooperate.' That is what I think I said to her. That's what I would usually say under the circumstances."

It was a clever answer, but Peter was ready.

"OK, Ms. Corliss, that sounds very plausible. Would you have closed the file if you found bruises?"

"No."

"Under any circumstances, if you found bruises that you believed were related to spanking, would you ever close a file at that point?"

"No, I would not. We would seek voluntary treatment or go to court under such circumstances."

"If I can phrase it another way, would you ever have closed this case in fifteen minutes if you had found bruises?"

"We did find bruises, but the answer to your question is no. The case was certainly going to last longer than fifteen minutes."

"Ms. Corliss, isn't it the truth that you never found any bruises, but you simply were angry at Mrs. Landis because she stood up for her constitutional rights and refused to let you in her house? It was her so-called lack of cooperation, and not any bruises, which led to her being charged in state court. Isn't that true?"

"No, Mr. Barron, that is not true. And I resent your remarks."

"You can resent them all you want, Ms. Corliss, but you still have to answer them. You told me just a minute ago that if you found bruises, you would never close the case in fifteen minutes. And you also say that you definitely found bruises. But today you told me, and this court reporter, that if Mrs. Landis had cooperated that first day, this whole thing would have been over in fifteen minutes. How does your early statement today square up with your later statements today?"

Corliss looked at Willet bewildered. Willet leaned forward, "You are taking what she said earlier out of context. And we don't have time for you to have this fine reporter hunt through two and a half hours of deposition to find an isolated statement."

"Oh he won't have to hunt. I had him mark it, remember? How long will it take you to find it?"

"A few seconds," the reporter replied with a sly smile. "I've got it here. Mr. Barron was speaking. 'On your first visit, on May 11, did you tell Gwen Landis when the report came in?' Ms. Corliss answered, 'I can't remember. But it is very doubtful.' Question, 'Why do you say that it is very doubtful?" Answer: 'Because, Mrs. Landis refused to cooperate with me. If she had cooperated with me that day, this whole thing probably would never have gone any further. She made a big federal case out of something that should have lasted only ten or fifteen minutes.' Was that the one you wanted?" the reporter asked innocently, knowing full well it was.

"Well, Ms. Corliss, you heard it yourself. Why did you tell us that this should have lasted for only ten or fifteen minutes if in fact you found bruises?"

Her ears burned. Her cheeks were flushed. Peter could see the redness and wished that Judge Stokes could see her right now. It would be obvious to him that she had just been trapped in a lie. For almost a minute, the room remained silent.

Peter looked at his watch and said, "Let the record reflect that it has been a minimum of forty-five seconds since I asked the question and the witness has still not answered." Her silence would condemn her, but not in a typed transcript.

"Oh, I thought you were just making another one of your nasty comments," Willet said. "Did you ask my client an actual question?

Please restate your question and we'll both synchronize our watches."

"Please read them back my question," Peter said turning his head to the reporter.

"The question was," the reporter said, pulling up his strip of paper and deciphering the shorthand, 'Well, Ms. Corliss, you heard it yourself. Why did you tell us that this should have lasted for only ten or fifteen minutes if in fact you found bruises?'"

"Mr. Barron, you are reading things into my comments. When I said that, I had my mental state on the first day in mind. I didn't expect to find bruises at first. And given that expectation, if she would have cooperated, it would have lasted only ten or fifteen minutes. I didn't have the bruises in mind when I said that. You are taking it out of context."

"I see," Peter said. He was happy with the results, but there was no certainty that the judge would be convinced she was lying. He leaned over to Gwen and whispered, "Can you think of anything else?"

"I'm just glad you're on my side, Peter Barron," she whispered back.

∼

Peter spent the balance of the day attending to other matters. After a quick supper from the deli downstairs, he went back up to his office and worked on amending the complaint in light of the events of the last week.

He added a new count against Donna Corliss and Rita Coballo for violating the due process rights of Gwen and Casey by making the deliberately false statements that they had seen "fading bruises." And the second new count was against Corliss, Coballo, and Blackburn—now changed to "the estate of Gerald Blackburn"—for another due process violation: falsifying the computer records. Peter believed that it was best simply to blame the trio and let them fight among themselves over individual responsibility for tampering with the documents. He knew that preserving these counts was going to be an uphill legal fight; but he was certain that Judge Stokes wanted to permit such a claim if it was legally possible for him to do so.

By ten the next morning, Sally had the Amended Complaint ready for Peter's signature. He debated the alternative of signing the document himself alone or asking Gwen to sign the new complaint as well. The rules permitted either method, and he decided to sign it alone since he realized the only real reason he was considering having her sign was to gain another opportunity to see her. He was trying to be better.

Joe had a hearing in federal court at 11:00, so he left ten minutes early to allow him time to file the papers with the clerk's office. Copies went to Bartholomew and Willet by courier that afternoon.

～

Willet was surprised by nothing other than the speed of Peter's action. She was angry at the department—for now she was reasonably certain that Blackburn acted alone—but in a strange way she enjoyed the additional challenge of defending a case with bad facts. She knew that the court precedents were on her side, and her job was simply to make Judge Stokes realize that he had no alternative but to dismiss this entire case—even the perjury and tampering counts.

She was in the prosecutor's private library until midnight that night, copying cases, making notes in the margins, and writing an outline for her revised brief.

She had two hearings on Friday, so she would be unable to sit down and write the new version of her briefs and moving papers until the weekend. She was as dedicated to this case as Peter. Gail Willet would love to set legal precedents advancing the cause of government programs to protect children. She loved winning, and, now with these new discoveries, wanted to beat Peter Barron more than ever.

Donna Corliss began her vacation on Friday. She had long planned to take off as soon as Stephen Stockton finished the bar exam and would spend a full week with him at his parents' lake home until he left for his new job in Washington, D.C.

The first night after his return, their time together was as happy and enjoyable as any point in their relationship. But day-by-day the reality that he was leaving and she would be left alone to deal with this lawsuit began to creep deeper and deeper into her soul.

By Wednesday, Stockton began to notice the change in her countenance and tried one last time to talk her into going with him to Washington, D.C.

"Donna, you really should come with me. We can get married there or back here at Thanksgiving. I think I could slide things along with the boss until then. They wouldn't be that nosy right away."

"Oh . . . I don't know. I have so many doubts and so much confusion."

"Well, you certainly don't have to worry about loyalty to Blackburn keeping you here anymore. Have the police ever found a suspect?"

"Not yet. We hardly ever hear from them any more."

"You don't know anything about how he died, do you?"

"No, I really don't."

"Was he involved in anything peculiar just before he was killed?" It was a question the police had never asked her.

Corliss's heart sank. She knew she could not lie convincingly to Stephen, but she could not bring herself to tell him the truth. And she felt certain he would feel responsible to tell the police if she revealed the details of the blackmail plot. She knew that Blackburn had coerced a payment out of Coballo, and she had begun to wonder if someone else had been blackmailed as well.

Stephen's question prompted her to think, for the very first time, that the murder might actually have been committed by someone who had been blackmailed. The thought scared her. Tears rolled down her cheeks.

"Donna, hey, what's wrong?" Stephen asked softly.

She recovered her composure enough to say, "I'm really sorry. It is still so fresh. I have a hard time talking about it right now. Especially with the thought of you leaving."

"If my questions make you cry, how were you able to withstand the deposition by that Barron guy if this still bothers you so much? Why didn't Willet get it postponed for you?"

"It was postponed for a while, but she said the judge insisted we go forward. I simply made myself do it. It wasn't easy."

"Did he try to pin all the forged documents on you?"

Corliss didn't want to let Stephen see her eyes. She got up from the deck chair overlooking the mountain lake and went to the corner of the deck and rocked back and forth as she continued to talk.

"The whole thing is so upsetting. He tried to pin it on me. But when I told him what really happened, he seemed to accept the fact Blackburn had made the changes."

"Is that what really happened?" Stockton asked.

"Yes it is. Why don't you believe me?"

"Who said I didn't believe you? I was just asking if you knew what really happened. I remember that one time you were involved with Blackburn in embellishing some facts on a case. I just wanted to know what you knew."

"I don't know anything for sure. It looks and smells like something Blackburn did or ordered done by someone. It certainly wasn't me."

Despite the inability to see her eyes, Stockton had doubts about her story. She protested way too much. He knew her well and had good lawyerly instincts. He decided to change the subject. For the first time he was secretly glad she was not going with him to Washington, D.C. He would not ask her again.

Donna and his parents were by his side when Stockton left Spokane International Airport the following Sunday morning, August 7—First Class to Chicago and then on to National Airport. The First Class tickets were one of his father's final presents for his high achiever son. Normally he would have wanted Stephen to come straight to work for the law firm. But frankly, the Washington, D.C., job was not only good for Stephen, in the long run it would be good for the firm as well.

～

On Monday afternoon, Sally buzzed Peter on the intercom.

"Peter, line two is someone named Morgan Howard, says he's a reporter with the *Spokesman-Review*."

"OK, I'll take it," Peter replied.

Peter cradled the receiver on his shoulder. "Hello, Mr. Howard, how can I help you?"

"I guess your secretary told you I was a reporter for the *Spokesman-Review*."

"You guess well," Peter replied.

"I was at the federal court today and checking some recent filings and I saw a brief being filed signed by a Gail Willet—I guess she's a new Deputy Prosecutor. Anyhow, I was intrigued by her brief and so I pulled the file. It looks very newsworthy. I'm surprised we missed it to this point. What is going on in this case?"

"Newsworthy? I'm not sure of that," Peter teased. "All you've got is document tampering by state agents uncovered by a computer guru and a federal judge. Plus some perjury in state court, a little warrantless strip search of a four-year-old-girl, and a mysteriously murdered defendant. I'm not sure why you think it's newsworthy. I've got six other cases just like it."

"Very funny, Mr. Barron," Howard said dryly. "If you knew we weren't doing our job, why didn't you call us?"

"I'm sorry. I didn't mean to make fun of your work. It's just such a bizarre case. And I didn't call because I'm not the kind of lawyer who tries his cases in the newspaper."

"You are willing to talk, aren't you?"

"Sure, fire away."

"Frankly, I'd rather do this in person. I can be there in five minutes. You're in the Paulsen Building, right?"

"You got it. And it would be fine for you to come by. But I've only got about twenty minutes."

"I'll take it," the reporter said.

～

It took seven minutes for the fiftyish, thin man in an olive corduroy sports jacket and khaki pants to present himself to Sally Finley. He had grey curly hair, slightly long and disheveled. He wore gold wire-rimmed glasses that he would peek over when he was trying to make eye contact with an interviewee. Even if Peter had not told her that Morgan Howard was coming, she would have known he was a reporter.

Peter greeted him at the door and ushered him into his office.

"So you're interested in the Landis case?" Peter asked.

"Yes. Tell me a little about your client," Howard began.

"Well, it will be very little. Because of the nature of the case I am reluctant to go into details that go beyond the public record. I will tell you that Mrs. Landis is a single mom and is employed as a nurse in the surgery unit at Sacred Heart."

"What happened in the state court proceeding?"

"This is awkward because the juvenile court proceeding itself is confidential, and I can get in trouble with the Bar Association, not to mention the judge, if I reveal details about that. I think I can repeat what we have alleged in our Amended Complaint. There were child abuse charges brought, and now we contend in the federal suit that those charges were based on deliberate falsehoods concocted by the Child Protective Services. CPS succeeded in removing my client's daughter for seven days, but when the full hearing was held, that decision was reversed and Casey was returned to her mother and the case was dismissed by the juvenile judge."

"Was the juvenile judge aware of the falsified computer records?"

"No. I see you have a copy of Judge Stokes's order about that," Peter replied. "You'll notice that the records were falsified the same day I filed this federal lawsuit. The juvenile case was over when that happened. But you'll notice in the Amended Complaint that we contend that CPS was already involved in perjury in the initial court action."

"What kind of perjury?" the reporter asked, still scribbling notes from Peter's last response.

"Basically they claimed to find bruises that never existed."

"Do you have any reason to believe that CPS have ever falsified information in other cases?"

"I have no evidence of that—only suspicions."

"Tell me about this Gerald Blackburn. How was he involved in this whole deal?"

"He was the supervisor of the unit that did all these things. He wasn't an active participant in any of the state court hearings. As far as I remember, I only saw him once sitting in the federal court hearing when Judge Stokes issued the order opening up their computer records."

"Do you think that his death was related to this case in any way?"

"I have no evidence nor any theories about that. It's really bizarre."

"So who do you think falsified the computer records?"

"I really don't know. They appear to be claiming that Blackburn did it. I think you ought to ask them to answer that question."

"I will. When do you think this case will go to trial?"

"We're not at a stage where I can answer that. The first thing we have to do is get past their motion to dismiss."

"You don't think Stokes will dismiss this case after that order of his, do you? I mean, there is fire coming off the pages. He knows he caught them with their hands in the cookie jar."

"If I can tell you something off the record, I completely agree with your assessment of Stokes's attitude. However—and now I am back on the record—Gail Willet has filed a brief which points to a number of cases which say that social workers cannot be sued for actions taken during a child abuse lawsuit—even if they commit perjury. That rule stinks and I think it is unacceptable for the State of Washington to come to court and argue that its employees should be shielded from liability even if it is clear that the employees have committed deliberate perjury."

"Just a minute, I want to get that one down," Morgan Howard said, scribbling furiously. "Yeah. I think I'll call the Governor and Attorney General to get their opinions on that one."

"Good idea," Peter replied.

"Anything you want to add?"

"No. I always tell witnesses to duck that question in court. I think I'll follow my own advice."

The reporter stood up and reached in his jacket pocket. "Here's my card. Please let me know if there are any developments on this, and I especially want to know if there are any hearings scheduled."

"No problem," Peter replied, "We'll certainly let you know about the hearings."

"Can I get a photographer out to the house to take a picture of your client and daughter?"

"Hmm. I'll have to think about that one. Let me call her and talk it over. Off the cuff, I'm a little reluctant to do it because this little girl has been traumatized by this whole deal and I'm not sure I want her picture plastered all over the paper. Call me back in a couple hours and I'll let you know."

"Fair enough."

Morgan Howard gave Sally a business card and asked her to remind her boss to let him know about any hearings. She just smiled and nodded.

⁓

"Hello," Gwen said.

"Hi, it's Peter."

"Good to hear from you, Peter. Something new going on with the case?"

He was glad she directed the conversation toward business right away. "Yes. Are you ready to become famous?"

"What are you talking about?"

"I've just spent half an hour with a reporter from the *Spokesman-Review*. They finally woke up to this case and sent one of their senior reporters, Morgan Howard, to get up to speed on your case."

"Is that good or bad?" Gwen asked with concern.

"I'm not sure. It might be good. For one thing, it is certainly unavoidable. You've got state agents caught forging documents and a dead man. It's news."

"Do I have to talk with them?"

"Not if you don't want to."

"Then I don't want to."

"That settles that. I'll tell them I have advised you not to talk to the press. It's the advice most lawyers give to their clients."

"Good. I knew I kept you around for some reason," Gwen laughed.

"How about pictures? Do you want to see that beautiful face of yours all over the papers? They want to send a photographer out to your house." As soon as the words were out, he knew he shouldn't have said them.

Gwen turned a little red, not from embarrassment, but from the turmoil such words created inside her—wanting to hear them, but knowing that Peter was a bit beyond the edges of his commitment to her.

"Oh, I don't think I want photographers in my house."

"That's what I told him I thought you'd say. I'm sure you don't want Casey's picture in the paper—and that's clearly what they want."

"Yeah, you're right," Gwen replied.

"There's one thing that might come out for the good from the newspaper getting involved," Peter said.

"What's that?"

"I told the reporter that I thought it was wrong for the State of Washington to argue in court that its agents can't be sued for deliberate perjury and tampering with documents. Even if the law technically gives them a defense, I suggested that honor would require them to waive the defense. He said he would bring that up to the Governor and Attorney General."

"Could they actually do anything to stop Willet from making those arguments?" Gwen asked.

"Sure they could—especially the Attorney General. But their reasons would be entirely political, not legal. We would have to create a stir that lasted a good while for them to feel enough pressure to make them take action."

"It sounds like a long shot," she said.

"It really is. At least we can make them squirm for a few minutes. And who knows, maybe God will use it in some way to bring about a good result for us."

"Maybe He will," Gwen replied softly.

"Gwen?"

"Yes?"

"One more thing," Peter said in a subdued voice. "I'm sorry I went overboard a few minutes ago flattering you. Of course, I do think you are very beautiful, but it doesn't do any good for me to keep throwing lines like that into our conversation. I'm sorry. Will you forgive me?"

"Sure, Peter. I forgive you."

～

Peter spent three or four hours every evening that week researching and writing his reply brief. Sally edited it Friday morning and Joe looked it over for an hour or so just after lunch. Peter did his final revisions Friday afternoon. It was twenty-nine pages—just one page under the limit specified by the local court rules for briefs. He had until the next Wednesday to get the brief filed.

After all his research, Peter felt better about his chances of prevailing on at least parts of his case. The doctrine of official immunity—which prohibits most suits against government officials involved in the legal process—is so strong that it takes great facts and creative lawyering to ever prevail in such a case.

It infuriated him the courts had steadfastly refused to allow suits against government officials when it was alleged that they had perjured themselves in order gain a conviction against ordinary citizens. Congress could have changed the law to allow suits against government officials who tell deliberate lies, but government officials have a tendency to protect each other in the rules they write.

~

Peter was awakened on Sunday morning by the phone ringing. He looked at his clock. It was 7:00 A.M. It was Gwen. It was only the second time she had ever called him at home.

"Peter, have you seen the paper? We're on the front page of the Metro section."

"No, I haven't seen it yet. I'm surprised you've seen it already," he replied.

"My dad woke me at six with the news. He liked the article a lot."

"What do you think?" Peter asked.

"It's OK. I just feel strange reading about myself in the paper."

"Well, maybe I should go get my paper and call you back after I read it."

"Good idea, talk to you soon," Gwen said hanging up the phone.

Peter slipped on jeans and deck shoes. The newspaper delivery box was attached to his mailbox across the road from his home. He stood by the side of the road, pulling sections of the paper apart. "Murdered CPS Official Accused Of Tampering With Documents" the headline screamed. Peter tucked the paper under his arm and went into the kitchen and turned on the coffee maker.

Morgan Howard's article took about an eighth of the front page of the August 14 edition of the *Spokesman-Review* and spilled over to the next page. They managed to find a picture of the ambulance drivers loading the draped body of Gerald Blackburn into their vehicle. The *S-R* night photographer took the photo after listening to his police scanner. The original article on his death had not seemed prominent enough to justify a picture.

Peter was pleased with the article when he finished. The facts were mostly correct, and he and Gwen were both presented favorably. The article left no doubt Gwen had been absolutely innocent of the charges.

He read the quote from Allen Radcliff, the Attorney General of Washington, three times, "Our office will review the suitability of employing immunity defenses in light of the very special circumstances of this case." Howard had even managed to get a quote from Tim McGranahan, a Republican state senator from Yakima, widely rumored to be Radcliff's likely opponent in the next election. "If our current Attorney General insists on protecting officials who have trampled on the rights of innocent citizens by employing tactics like these, we may have to hold legislative hearings to review this matter when the legislature reconvenes next January."

Peter smiled and shook his head in disbelief when he reread that quote. The coffee was ready. He poured a cup and picked up the phone and dialed.

Gwen picked up the phone and without even saying hello said, "Well, Peter, what do you think?"

"You were pretty confident it was me, weren't you? Well, it's great. The stuff from the Attorney General and that Senator from Yakima will put tremendous pressure on Willet. You can't ask for a better article than this."

"Peter, do you think the murder of Gerald Blackburn was related to our case in any way? The article seems to hint at that."

"Yes, it does, but it doesn't come out and say anything directly. I think if anyone had any current evidence of a connection, you would probably see it in print right now. The police will probably start looking again to check that possibility out after reading this."

"But what do you think?" Gwen asked again.

"I still don't know. Who would do it?"

"Maybe one of his trained witches."

"What would be their motive?" Peter asked.

"To have a permanently silenced person to blame for tampering with the documents," she replied.

"Not bad," Peter said, rolling the idea around in his head.

"Can you look in to that in our case?" Gwen asked.

"I don't see how it fits. Willet would be all over me with relevancy objections. But I'll keep my eyes open. I am curious. And by the way, it would be better for you to stop calling them witches in private. You might slip and say it in a deposition. And it would be really a mistake for you to ever suggest that those two CPS workers may have had something to do with his murder. They could eat you for lunch in a defamation suit. You can say whatever you want to me—attorney-client privilege. But no one else should ever hear those words out of your mouth."

"Thanks for the tip. At least I have one person I can tell my secrets."

Peter was silent.

"Sorry," Gwen said.

"It's OK," Peter replied. "You said it with an innocent heart. When I shoot my mouth off, I usually know exactly what I'm saying and what it implies."

"You're a little too hard on yourself," Gwen said cheerfully. " I'd better get ready for church. See you soon."

"Be ready to be a celebrity at Valley Fourth," Peter replied.

"You and Aaron are the stars of the article. I'm just along for the ride."

"Right," Peter said. "Bye, Gwen."

~

"Dear Lord," Peter prayed out loud as soon as he hung up the phone, "Help me to keep my heart inclined toward you. Please reveal what you want me to do about Gwen. And whatever you tell me, give me the strength to obey your will. Amen."

19

Peter and Gwen were not the only ones who discerned the Morgan Howard article would prompt the police to begin looking at the connection between his death and the pending civil rights case. Donna Corliss got sick to her stomach reading the article when she awakened around noon. She knew she was innocent of any connection to Blackburn's death, but she was terrified that somehow the detectives might stumble into the blackmail plot and implicate her in the perjury and document tampering.

She tried all day to reach Stephen Stockton on the phone at his new apartment in Washington, D.C. He finally answered around seven-thirty Pacific time.

"Stephen, it's Donna."

"Oh, hi, Donna," Stockton said with as much enthusiasm as he could muster.

"Where have you been all day? I have been trying to get you for hours."

Stockton motioned to the young woman co-worker who had been his companion for a day of sight-seeing that she should sit down in the living room. He mouthed the words, "I'll be a few minutes."

"Oh, I've just been out sight-seeing. This is really an interesting town. Lots to see."

"Sounds great," Corliss said. "In fact it sounds so great that I've decided to join you there—take you up on all those offers you've made time and time again."

The young woman got up off the couch in Stockton's apartment. She walked across the living area and started looking at his bookshelf in earnest. Stockton thought that she was clearly better looking than Donna Corliss and didn't come wrapped up in a pile of ethical problems that he neither wanted nor needed right now.

"Well, that's a surprising development," Stockton said. "What made you change your mind?"

"Oh, I guess I just miss you, Stephen."

It was a true enough answer, but Stockton suspected it was not the whole truth. "Anything else going on?" he asked.

"No, not really."

"How about that case of yours? Anything happening there?"

"Nothing really new. There was an article about it in the newspaper today. That's the only major development."

"Really? Could you get my dad's secretary to fax it to my office in the morning? She has the fax number."

"Stephen, here we are talking about faxes and newspaper articles and everything under the sun. I've just agreed to marry you and you haven't said anything about that. What is going on?"

"I don't know. I really don't. I can't talk right now. I'm with some of my co-workers."

"Oh yeah? What's her name?" Corliss asked angrily.

"Let me call you back soon. OK? It really would be better."

"You pig! You use me for three years and then dump me in less than a week! You're a pig!"

"You're jumping to conclusions. Please let me call you later. Bye." He hung up the phone before she could speak again.

Corliss was not only furious—she felt like she had just been kicked in the stomach. She flung herself on the couch and screamed for a few minutes and then changed to a brokenhearted cry that lasted for hours, or so it seemed. She stayed up until nearly midnight—Pacific time—and her phone didn't ring .

On Monday morning, Peter personally walked the reply brief over to the Federal Courthouse. As soon as the clerk saw the case name on the papers, the whole office came alive with activity.

Photocopies of the Sunday article were waiting on every desk on the ninth floor—including Judge Stokes's.

The clerk who accepted the brief for filing took the extra copy Peter supplied for the judge and said he would deliver it personally ASAP. And he did, after a short stop at the copy machine where he burned off three quick copies for the clerk's office staff to read when things weren't terribly busy that day.

The judge's law clerk, a young woman lawyer who had graduated from the University of Washington near the top of her class a year earlier, called Peter within forty-five minutes of his return from the courthouse. Oral arguments on the motion to dismiss would be held a week later, Monday, August 22, at 9 A.M. Each side would be given thirty minutes for oral argument—"just like arguments in the Supreme Court" the clerk had said when she informed Peter of the judge's ground rules.

Peter's morning was interrupted with six other calls which were generated by the article. All were from people who believed they had been the victims of CPS. None of the six remembered any involvement by Corliss, Coballo, or Blackburn. All six were eventually reunited with their children. He took some notes and promised to contact them if he discovered anything relative to their cases.

~

Donna Corliss called Conner Stockton's secretary around ten-thirty, Monday morning. But not to ask her to fax Stephen the article—which she had already done on her own—but to ask for an appointment with Stephen's father. Corliss had insisted that the matter was quite urgent and she needed to see him that day. He consented to a half-hour slot at 1:30. She would simply take a late lunch hour. She couldn't eat anyway.

At 1:20, Corliss entered the elevator for the ride to the twenty-first story of the Washington Trust Bank Building. Conner Stockton had the prime corner office on the top floor with the view to the northeast—all of downtown was visible, including most of

Riverfront Park, and Mount Spokane, about twenty-five miles away.

The receptionist was expecting her and she was ushered back to a small waiting alcove adjacent to the senior partner's suite. She had been with the elder Stockton many times and had visited his office several times as well. But this was the first time that she had ever seen him alone at any time, for any purpose.

Shortly after one-thirty, she was ushered in to the massive suite, tastefully decorated in a modern style. There was a separate seating area with a leather couch and two stylish arm chairs positioned around a coffee table. Conner welcomed the young lady he assumed would sooner or later be his daughter-in-law and motioned for her to sit on the couch as he chose one of the chairs.

"Heard from Stephen recently?" he asked.

"Yes, we talked last night, briefly."

"I guess he's very busy. I have only talked to him once for ten or fifteen minutes myself. His job is quiet grueling as I am sure you've heard."

"Yes," Corliss said smiling, trying to appear as normal as possible.

"Well, what brings you here today, Donna? I'm always delighted to see you, but this is a little unexpected."

"Mr. Stockton, I think I may need a lawyer."

"That is not what I would have guessed. Tell me what's going on."

"First, can I ask you something?"

"Sure. Anything."

"Can I ask you not to tell Stephen?"

"Sure. But I'm a little surprised. A lawyer cannot say anything to anyone about the confidences of his client. That includes Stephen. He used to work here and that was different. But, for two years, he's employed elsewhere and without your permission, I can't tell him anything."

"Good. Stephen knows a little of this and he's reacted quite strongly. He claimed he could protect me with this attorney-client stuff, at least until he passed the bar exam, but I wasn't sure. I didn't want to tell him something that could get him in trouble. And I'm afraid Stephen thinks less of me because he's heard part of the story. If he heard the whole story I think he would be fine."

Tears welled up in her eyes for a moment, but she regained control almost immediately.

"Please, Donna. Tell me the whole story. I'm sure I can help," Stockton said soothingly.

"I got a call from the police detective investigating the murder of Gerald Blackburn this morning. I have talked to him at least twice in the past and answered a lot of questions. It seems the article in the newspaper yesterday makes him believe there may be a connection between Mr. Blackburn's death and this civil rights case involving the Landis woman. He wanted to come over again this afternoon and ask me some more questions. I made excuses and asked to talk with him tomorrow. I didn't want to talk with him until I came to see you."

"Donna, you don't have anything to do with Blackburn's death, do you?"

"No, Mr. Stockton, I don't, and that's the absolute truth. Stephen has asked me the same thing, but I don't think he believes me."

"Then why are you concerned about answering the questions?"

"There were other things I was involved in—or at least knowledgeable of that Mr. Blackburn was doing wrong. I've been asked about that in a deposition and I didn't tell them everything I knew. I'm afraid if they go poking around trying to find a connection between the murder and the Landis suit, they may find the things I did wrong. I didn't have any choice. Blackburn forced me to be involved. He threatened me. At one point, he even threatened to kill me."

"I'm afraid you are going a bit too fast. I'm going to have to go back and ask you a number of questions if I am going to get this story straight."

"OK," Corliss responded, sighing heavily.

"What kind of wrongdoing were you knowledgeable of or a party to?"

"Did you read the newspaper article yesterday?"

"Yes, of course."

"Then you know about the falsified documents?"

"Yes," the lawyer responded.

"Well, I made the four changes the judge found in our computers. But I was acting under the direct orders of Gerald Blackburn. He threatened to kill me if I didn't."

"Can you prove that? It is hard to prove that a dead man threatened someone."

"I think I can prove it."

"How?"

"Well, two ways. He blackmailed me, for one thing. I had to pay him $2500. He said he was going to destroy the computer disk and then leave the country. He said that if I didn't give him the money, he would leave notes, telling everyone I was the one who falsified the records. I gave him the money the day before he was killed. I can show in my bank records that I did that."

"Your bank records can prove that you withdrew $2500, but how can you prove you gave it to him?"

"Oh . . . well, there's another way."

"Yes?" Stockton said.

"He also blackmailed my co-worker, Rita Coballo. She had to pay him $2500 as well the same day. She could testify to the same thing."

"Was she involved in falsifying the documents, too?"

"She knew about it," Corliss answered.

"Was there anyone else involved in falsifying the documents?"

"No. Just the three of us."

"Were there any other misrepresentations or deceptions that anybody else could have been a party to?"

"Not that I can think of," Corliss replied.

"Was there any—"

"Wait!" Corliss exclaimed. "There was someone else."

"Who?"

"A psychologist. His name is Randall McGuire."

"How was he involved?"

"Blackburn hated to lose any child custody case. Whenever he had a case that he especially wanted to win, he always made us use Randall McGuire as our expert witness. I never understood their relationship exactly, but I believe that McGuire would essentially say anything Blackburn wanted. And I would guess that McGuire got paid something extra for doing that."

"Do you have first-hand knowledge that McGuire misrepresented the facts to the Court in this case?"

"Not exactly. But his testimony was exactly what we wanted. And when the woman's attorney, Peter Barron, cross-examined him, he pointed out a lot of discrepancies between McGure's report and his original notes of the interview. I can't remember Blackburn's exact words, but there was no question in my mind that he made us use McGuire whenever we wanted to be certain the psychological report would come out our way."

"Do you think McGuire would have anything to do with Blackburn's death?"

"It would only be a wild guess on my part. But the guy has been playing fast and loose with the truth to convict people of child abuse."

"In a way, Donna, so have you," Stockton said.

There was no holding back the tears now. "You're right. But I was scared. It was my first job after college, and he threatened me so many times. I was really scared of him. Stephen can tell you that."

"I'm sure he can," Stockton said. "I'm sure he can."

Corliss hung her head and softly cried. Stockton came over to the couch, sat next to her, put his arm around her shoulder and spoke soft words of comfort.

"What am I going to do, Mr. Stockton?"

"For now, you're going to do absolutely nothing. I will call the police detective and tell him if he wants to do any more interviews with you, it's going to have to be in my office. And if he asks why, I am going to tell him we believe that the Attorney General's Office, who is representing you in the civil case, has a conflict of interest. They are trying to get the state off the hook, while my job is to defend just you."

"Oh, would you do that for me?"

"Sure I will."

"Do you think anyone will find out what I've told you?"

"It's doubtful. But if they start to get close, I think we can get them to make some kind of deal."

"That's sounds wonderful," Corliss said.

She just sat still, relishing the comfort of the senior Stockton's fatherly embrace, and even more, the security of his words.

"Mr. Stockton, can you do one more thing for me? I know it's a lot to ask, but it's the most important thing in the world to me."

"What's that?"

"Can you say something to Stephen? Not all the details—I don't want him to know something he shouldn't. But could you tell him that you've talked to me, and whatever I did that was wrong I did because I was scared by Blackburn's threats? If you told him that, I think everything would be all right between us again. You do believe me, don't you?"

"Yes, Donna. I believe you. And I'll be happy to say the right thing to Stephen."

"You're as wonderful as your son, Mr. Stockton. You really are," Corliss said.

"Hey, if we can't protect the ones who are close to us, what are lawyers for?" Stockton asked.

～

Police lieutenant Dan Greeves was not pleased by the phone call he received from Conner Stockton later that afternoon. But there was little he could do about it. Stockton's explanation that his client was already involved in a federal civil rights lawsuit where she was being blamed for document tampering and perjury that she contends were done by her former supervisor seemed completely plausible—typical legal advice any lawyer would give. He did ask whether or not the discovery of the computer tampering would have given Corliss a motive to kill Blackburn. Stockton thought he nipped that idea in the bud when he pointed out that Blackburn was murdered well before the tampering had been discovered by Judge Stokes. Conner Stockton truly believed that Donna Corliss had nothing to do with the murder of Gerald Blackburn.

∼

On Tuesday morning, Corliss was jolted from sleep by her phone ringing at six.

"Hello," she said, still more asleep than awake.

"Donna, I'm sorry I woke you, but I thought you'd want to talk. It's obviously important."

"Stephen! It's really you."

"Yeah. I'm sorry I was abrupt with you on the phone Sunday night. I just didn't want to discuss my private life in front of my co-workers. Nothing was going on, you've got to believe me."

Stockton's statement was true enough. Although he had made some suggestions to the young lady who was in his apartment, she had not responded in the way he had hoped.

"I don't know what to say. It just seemed so strange."

"Well, let me say that I talked with my father. He told me to say that he didn't tell me any details, but he did convince me that Gerald Blackburn had been twisting your arm, that whatever you were involved with was not all that serious and that you really were coerced. He thinks things are going to work out fine."

"Your father is a great man, Stephen."

"I've always thought so. Check that. Most of the time I have thought so. I was a teenager not that long ago."

"Donna, I still want things to work out between us. But I'm not sure about rushing into marriage or having you move out here.

Dad thinks that you might raise more suspicion if you end up here in D.C. suddenly. Let's get this Landis case behind you, and then we can make some decisions, OK?"

"That certainly sounds better than our last conversation. I don't know. I guess I wanted to move to D.C. right now because I was lonely and scared. Your dad has been a big help with all that."

"I'll call you and write you more often. I guess you have had a lonely summer. I'll do better. OK?"

"OK, Stephen . . . and thanks. I really love you."

"I love you, too."

The younger Stockton hung up the phone and rushed out the door to catch the Metro to work. He had called and told his supervisor that he would be in before ten and make up the time that evening. His job required about sixty hours of work a week, and a little flexibility was allowed as an offset.

While the Metro was jostling him back and forth, moving along the red line toward Union Station, Stockton decided that he would do his best to keep Corliss on the hook in case things worked out. But he would also discreetly date other women in D.C., just in case they didn't.

～

The press corps was out in force the following Monday. They were desperate for some pictures—both television and photos—of the participants in the case of *Landis v. Corliss, et. al.* There were six television camera crews—four from Spokane, and two who had flown over from Seattle after the Morgan Howard article had been reprinted in the *Seattle Post-Intelligencer*. There were also three radio reporters, four print journalists, and three photographers.

Howard himself was a part of the crowd of reporters. All his compatriots watched him like a hawk. Apparently, he was the only one who had any idea what the participants looked like.

Willet and Bartholomew were dropped off from a car directly in front of the courthouse on Riverside Avenue. A veritable foot race ensued among the reporters when Morgan Howard took a few steps in the direction of the duo.

After a few shouted questions, the reporters quieted down so Howard could ask the first question. Until he did, the rest could only guess who they were talking to.

"Ms. Willet, are you planning to use the immunity defenses in court today?" Howard asked.

"No comment," Matt Bartholomew answered.

Willet was furious with the obvious political implications that had been inserted into her handling of the case. Olympia wanted this case handled discreetly.

"We are just trying a lawsuit according to the normal rules of court. We are not going to turn this case into politics or a publicity stunt," Willet said.

Despite the fact that Bartholomew had strictly ordered her to keep her mouth shut, he was actually pleased with her answer.

"What's the Attorney General say about this hearing?" a television reporter shouted.

"Like she said," Bartholomew replied, gesturing toward Willet, "This is a lawsuit. We'll try it in court."

It wasn't much, but at least there were pictures and sound bites.

Two minutes later, a second stampede was created when Morgan Howard moved down the sidewalk toward the adjoining bank building. He had spied Peter Barron coming down the sidewalk with two others. He assumed that the striking blond was his client, Gwen Landis. He quietly whispered to his photographer, "Get all the pictures of her you can. She's going on page one." Howard was ultimately able to identify the third person as Joe Lambert, Peter Barron's associate.

"Good morning, everyone," Peter said. "We don't have anything to say right now. See you all in an hour after the hearing."

"Will your client be making a statement after the hearing?" a radio reporter shouted.

"We're just not sure. Depends on what happens," Peter replied.

"Mrs. Landis, how did you feel when you discovered the

documents CPS kept on you had been falsified?" a woman television reporter demanded, thrusting a microphone in Gwen's face.

Gwen looked at Peter, who simply shook his head from side to side. Two television cameramen blocked her path, waiting for an answer to the reporter's question. Peter put his arm around Gwen, shielded her from the onslaught, and said, "Excuse me, ladies and gentlemen. We have an appointment with Judge Stokes."

As soon as his arm was around her shoulders, the cameras flashed incessantly.

"That's the shot we'll use," Howard whispered to his camera man.

Donna Corliss and Rita Coballo were able to sneak through with a simple "no comment." Even Morgan Howard was unsure of the role they played in the case.

Gordon Landis slipped through without any questions at all. Dressed in jeans and a sports shirt, he did not look as if he belonged to the cast of players involved in Spokane's most famous current lawsuit.

Peter and Joe unloaded from their briefcases, exhibits, copies of cases, and an outline of Peter's planned oral argument. Peter was seated closest to the center aisle, Gwen was in the middle, and Joe was on the right. Willet and Bartholomew sat alone at the counsel table. Their clients were seated in the front row behind the bar. Most of the reporters—but none of the cameras—took their places near the front of the courtroom.

"Will the judge make a decision today?" Gwen whispered to Peter after it appeared to her that he was through with his preparations.

"It's very unlikely," Peter answered quietly. "In Juvenile Court, they had to decide what to do with Casey right then. That's why the judge made a decision immediately. But here, there is no time pressure on this judge to make a decision. I think he'll make it reasonably soon, but I doubt it will be done today."

Their conversation was cut short by the "All rise" call of the bailiff. Judge Stokes was a minute early.

"Please be seated," Judge Stokes said. "Ms. Willet, this is your motion. You may begin. Please keep two things in mind. First, I have read your brief. And second, there is no need to repeat what you said there."

Willet walked to the lectern at the front of the courtroom.

"Thank you, Your Honor, and may it please the Court. We have asked the Court to dismiss this lawsuit against our three individual social worker clients and the state agencies on three basic theories. First, in this circuit, the law is that a social worker is absolutely immune from civil lawsuits for actions done in connection with a child abuse prosecution. Second, the Supreme Court has definitively ruled that witnesses such as social workers are absolutely immune from a lawsuit based on alleged perjury. And third, the state agency is immune from a suit in federal court on the grounds of the Eleventh Amendment."

"The leading case on the first point, *Meyers v. Contra Costa County Department of Social Services*," Willet continued, "was decided by the Ninth Circuit in 1987. The cite is in our brief. That case clearly establishes the rule of absolute immunity for social workers in this circuit."

"Ms. Willet," the judge interrrupted, "doesn't the *Meyers* case stand for the proposition that the rule of absolute immunity applies to actions taken by social workers after they file a case? Does *Meyers* shield your client for the warrantless search which was done before the courts ever got involved?"

"We think that *Meyers* protects our clients at all relevant stages. The search was carried out prior to the formal filing of the child abuse charges, that is true. But, the search was done in contemplation of filing the lawsuit. It was all a seamless garment. The logical reading of *Meyers* is that any actions connected to the child abuse lawsuit should be considered a part of the judicial system. And the rule is that social workers are officers of the court and therefore are completely immune from lawsuits, just as judges themselves are immune from lawsuits."

"Counsel, what you are arguing is that social workers can never be sued for anything. Doesn't that go a bit far?"

"That's not exactly my argument, Your Honor."

"All right, then, please explain to me under what circumstances a social workers could be sued, Ms. Willet," the judge replied.

"If a social worker took action that wasn't connected to a child abuse suit, or in contemplation of a child abuse suit, and if the action was shown to be wrong, then a social worker could be held to be liable in a civil rights case."

"Counsel, wouldn't every investigation a social worker undertakes be in contemplation of a child abuse suit? Doesn't your rule really protect every social worker for every investigation, no matter how much they trample on the rights of people?"

"I don't see it that way, Your Honor. And more important than my opinion, Your Honor, is the way the Ninth Circuit views the relevant rules in *Meyers*."

"OK, let's hear your second point," Judge Stokes said.

"Mr. Barron's amended complaint alleges that my clients committed perjury on the witness stand when they testified that they saw bruises on the Landis child."

"Did they see them, counsel? Do you really believe them?" the judge asked.

"My beliefs are not relevant, Your Honor. They testified that they found bruises, and that is good enough for me at this point," Willet replied.

"Well, let me tell you something, counsel. Based upon the things we found in that computer record, anytime there is a question of credibility in this case, you are going to have to produce very clear evidence, or else I am going to apply the normal rule of law. I am sure you are familiar with it. If a witness has been found to be untrustworthy in one aspect of his testimony, his testimony may be considered to be untrustworthy in all other contested areas. Your people have been involved in an attempt to commit a fraud on this court, and I do not take kindly to that."

"I can understand your position, Your Honor. But regardless of the factual circumstances, the rule of law is clear, Your Honor. The Supreme Court has ruled in *Briscoe v. LaHue* that all witnesses are immune from lawsuits that arise from the substance of their testimony. This rule applies even in circumstances which involve perjury. Mr. Barron recognizes this rule in his brief and he tries to create some exceptions, but despite his attempt at legal creativity, the clear rule of law is that a witness may not be sued, even for perjury."

"Counsel, you have used up all but five minutes of your time. If you want to reserve any time for rebuttal, I would suggest you may want to stop right here," Judge Stokes said in an effort to be genuinely helpful.

"That's fine, Your Honor. I will reserve the balance of my time. I think the Eleventh Amendment issue is clear in the brief and there is no need to repeat it now."

"Good. Thank you, counsel," the judge said. "All right, Mr. Barron, let's hear from you."

"Thank you, Your Honor. I will begin with the legality of the search carried out against Gwen Landis and the strip search of her daughter, Casey. The clear reading of *Meyers* is that the rule of absolute immunity protecting social workers from all wrong-doing has a beginning point, and it has an ending point. The beginning point, according to the Ninth Circuit in *Meyers* is when the lawsuit was filed. The ending point is when the lawsuit is over. If a social worker does something that violates the rights of a private citizen either before or after the child abuse lawsuit, they can be held legally liable for their actions."

"Counsel," the judge interjected, "let's say for the sake of discussion that I agree with your reading of *Meyers* and that the rule of absolute immunity begins after the commencement of a lawsuit, and not until then. This means that social workers can be sued for unconstitutional actions taken before they formally file child abuse charges. But even if they can be sued, you still face the rule that the suit will be dismissed unless the law you claim they violated was clearly established prior to their action. That's the point I'd like to hear more about from you."

"Fine, Your Honor. Obviously, you are right. We do have to be able to show that it was clearly established it was unconstitutional for the social worker to enter Mrs. Landis's home without a warrant. There was never any claim of an emergency here. The "exigent circumstances" exception, therefore, simply does not apply at all.

I think the answer to your question is very clear, Your Honor," Peter continued. "It has been very clear since the adoption of the Bill of Rights that if the government wants to come into your home, they must have a warrant. And the various attempts to carve out an exception for social workers to this rule have simply not been successful. We cite several cases in this connection, Your Honor, the most recent of which is *H.R. v. Alabama*, where the Court of Appeals of that state held that it would violate the Fourth Amendment of the United States Constitution to allow social workers to enter private homes merely upon the report of an anonymous tip. And thanks to Your Honor's discoveries of the CPS computer records, we know that the tip here was indeed anonymous."

Gordon Landis breathed a sigh of relief. He had suspected they had not revealed his identity, but it was good to hear it said directly.

"What about the Supreme Court's decision in *Wyman v. James*, Mr. Barron? Doesn't that case seem to authorize warrantless entries by social workers?"

"The Supreme Court did address warrantless entries in *Wyman*—that is true, Your Honor. But there is a difference between a warrantless entry and a warrantless search. In *Wyman*, the case involved a woman who was receiving welfare from the State of New York. The social workers demanded the right to enter her home to check to see how she was doing. She claimed that unless they had some proof that she was doing something wrong, they should not be able to come into her home without a warrant. The Supreme Court said that kind of a visit by a social worker was not a search, but was a 'home visit' from a 'friend in need'—I believe that's the term they used for the social worker. The Court was careful to distinguish those kinds of facts from true searches where a person is suspected of wrong-doing and the entry is made to gather evidence of the alleged wrongful acts. Well, what was done here was a search by a government official looking for evidence of wrong-doing, not a home visit by a friend in need."

"All right, Mr. Barron, let's move on to the next issue. I'm frankly as upset by all of this perjury business and document tampering as you are—perhaps more upset. But here's the problem. Isn't Ms. Willet right when she says the Supreme Court has ruled that civil rights suits against witnesses are always prohibited—even if they commit perjury."

"I offer only one distinction, Your Honor. And if this court does not agree with my offer, then my response is that the Supreme Court is wrong and it should change its rule."

"What's your distinction?"

"In the case decided by the Supreme Court, and in all the cases cited in Ms. Willet's brief, the perjury has been alleged perjury. I have yet to find a case where the perjury was proven up front as clearly as the perjury and document tampering we have here. I can understand why the Supreme Court doesn't want lawsuits brought against witnesses when there is a contest about perjury—when it is an interpretation of facts. But when you have absolute proof of serious perjury up front, I think such lawsuits should be allowed. There is no public policy served by letting witnesses commit perjury and getting away with it. Perhaps the rule should be that if there has been a prior criminal conviction of perjury or proof of perjury that is so clear, that no one can reasonably contest the fact that the government official has lied."

"It's an interesting theory, Mr. Barron. I'm afraid your time is up," the judge replied.

Willet was on her feet, moving to the lectern.

"You have just five minutes, Ms. Willet. A quick point or two, OK?"

"Yes, Your Honor. On the last point argued by Mr. Barron, I would simply point out that Mr. Barron is asking this court to reverse a decision of the United States Supreme Court. Only the Supreme Court can make such a decision, and, with all due respect, this is obviously not the Supreme Court."

"Thank you for pointing that out, Ms. Willet. Sometimes I forget that fact," the judge said with obvious irritation.

"On his first argument, I think that Your Honor hit the nail on the head with the reference to *Wyman v. James*. Social workers understand that case to say that when they are in the business of protecting children, they are 'friends in need.' The Supreme Court authorized such entries without the formality of a warrant that seems to mean so much to Mr. Barron. I don't see any distinction between 'entries' and 'searches' in *Wyman* as Mr. Barron alleges. How are ordinary social workers like Ms. Corliss and Ms. Coballo supposed to know those fine-tuned distinctions?"

"They are supposed to employ government lawyers who read the cases and advise them in plain English concerning the meaning of the law," Stokes said.

"Yes, Your Honor," Willet said, taken aback.

"Will there be anything else, Ms. Willet?" the judge asked.

"Just one thing. Your Honor, if I can speak frankly, it is obvious that you are upset with the document tampering, and I have no problem with that. I was upset myself. But this motion is based upon the law, not on facts, not on one's personal evaluation of the facts. The Ninth Circuit and the Supreme Court have laid down some pretty clear decisions. The law says that this case should be dismissed, no matter what one thinks of the personal actions of the defendants in this case. Thank you for your patience with me, Your Honor."

"All right. You both are excellent lawyers, and I appreciate your zeal for your clients, and a really top-notch job on both briefs. I wish all the briefs I received in this court were as well-written and researched. But every case has to be decided, and I intend to decide this one the way I see it—according to the law." He turned and looked directly at Willet.

"This motion is going to be granted in part and denied in part. Mr. Barron, I wish I was the Supreme Court. Yours is the case I would use to reverse the rule on suing witnesses for perjury. But as Ms. Willet pointed out, I'm not the Supreme Court, and so all counts of the lawsuit dealing with perjury are going to be dismissed. I do it reluctantly, but I feel I have no choice."

Gwen looked at Peter with a puzzled look. He just shook his head and shrugged his shoulders in reply.

"But I am going to deny the motion to dismiss the parts of the case dealing with the illegal search. I read *Meyers* the same way Mr. Barron suggests. Once the social worker has filed the case in court, he or she is immune from suit. But before that time, if the social worker violates the Constitution, that social worker can be sued for violating the civil rights laws of this country."

"I also find that the law regarding warrantless searches was clearly established prior to the time of these events. Therefore, Mr. Barron has carried his initial burden, and this aspect of the case may proceed to trial. And finally, the Eleventh Amendment motion is denied."

Peter smiled at Gwen and whispered, "It was as good as I hoped."

"I will be filing a thorough opinion on these matters before the end of the week," Judge Stokes continued. "Ms. Willet, I know that you have the right to file an immediate appeal on the immunity issues. Technically, you have thirty days to appeal as I am sure you know. If you intend to appeal my decision, I would urge you to do so promptly. Otherwise, I will allow Mr. Barron to continue discovery and trial preparation until you file the appeal."

Matt Bartholomew stood. "Judge Stokes, we intend to appeal. Will it be soon enough if we file our notice within five business days of your written opinion?"

"That will be fine, Mr. Bartholomew," the judge replied. "Is there anything else?"

"No, Your Honor," the lawyers chimed in unison.

"All right, the court is now in recess."

Gwen felt like hugging Peter again—and he certainly wouldn't have minded. But she restrained herself because of all the reporters, her recent discussions with Peter, and especially because of Gordon's presence.

"It sounds good, Peter—is it?" Gwen asked in a quiet voice.

"Yes, it's good. There was just no way for him to get around these awful decisions that let witnesses get away with perjury. And since they said they are going to appeal, we can cross-appeal. That means we can keep asking the higher courts to reverse the rule that lets perjurers go free."

"That sounds good. Keep fighting, Peter. Just keeping on fighting for what's right."

∽

The reporters were not to be denied. They would get a statement from Peter Barron and they would ask questions of his client.

Peter and Joe saw the reporters huddled outside the front door of the courthouse. Cameras were prohibited from the building so the whole pack waited outside. They stopped by the elevator and warned Gwen about the feeding frenzy.

"We are about to be mobbed," Peter said.

"And they are definitely hungry," Joe chimed in. "I think you will irritate them if you don't say anything."

"Me, too?" Gwen asked nervously. "Do I have to say something, too?"

"I really think it would be best," Joe said. "It doesn't have to be complicated. Just something short, sweet, and true."

"They are going to ask you how you feel. And they are going to ask you about Casey," Peter predicted. "I think you should say that you are happy or a few words to that effect. And if you say that both you and your daughter were upset by the illegal acts of the CPS workers, they'll probably get enough. Not as much as they want, but as much as they need. OK?"

"I guess so," Gwen answered.

The trio proceeded through the door.

"Mr. Barron," ten voices shouted at once. "Are you surprised at the decision today?" one reporter asked.

"We are pleased with Judge Stokes's ruling on the whole. We are disappointed with the rule that required him to dismiss the perjury counts, but we understand we will have to make those arguments to a higher court."

"Will you appeal this case to the Supreme Court?" another voice called out.

"Not right away," Peter replied. "The next stop is the Ninth Circuit Court of Appeals. It's headquartered in San Francisco, but in all likelihood our case will be argued in Seattle. We will be filing a cross-appeal to keep the perjury issues alive."

The print reporters all scrambled to write down his last answer.

"Mrs. Landis, how is your daughter dealing with all of this?" Morgan Howard asked.

"She was upset, very upset and scared by the illegal search. But I try to keep her from the details of the case and make her life as normal as possible."

"How old is she?"

"She'll be five next month."

"Is she available for pictures?" a cameraman yelled out.

"I'm sorry," Peter said. "We're trying to protect her from trauma. And no offense to you all, but this little party might scare a four-year old. Thanks so much. That's all we have time for."

Peter grasped Gwen's left arm gently, and led her through the crowd and away from the federal building.

20

"*Mother Cannot Sue State Workers For Perjury*" the headline screamed on the front page of Tuesday's *Spokesman-Review*. It was the most comprehensive and accurate of the stories that appeared recounting the hearing and Judge Stokes's decision. The picture of Peter with his arm around Gwen as they headed into the court house took up nearly an eighth of the front page. Their looks were determined, and their images looked right out of central casting.

It had been the top story on the Monday evening news on all the local television stations. The Seattle stations even covered it, but in a later slot on their evening news.

Gordon Landis watched the five and six o'clock news shows with a slow burn. By the time the eleven o'clock news re-ran the stories, his jealousy of Peter had reached the boiling point. When he saw the picture on the front page of the paper the following morning, he slammed the paper down on his kitchen table, uttered a string of expletives, and vowed to stop this man from stealing the heart of his ex-wife.

"I'll stop him. I'm going to stop him, one way or the other," he muttered out loud in his empty apartment.

David G. Humphrey scoured the stack of newspaper articles that had been clipped and copied by his curvaceous, young secretary. He looked over his clippings each day with almost the same intensity as he watched the neckline and skirt length of the dresses Cindy Walters wore to their twenty-third story office in downtown Kansas City. His interest in the clippings was driven by his constant search for issues, controversies, cases, or situations that he could turn into a cause cèlebré through his new organization, *Heart of America.*

Humphrey was an impeccably dressed, slim, fifty year-old, with wavy white hair and perfect teeth. He had a background as a pastor, smalltime radio talk show host, and, most importantly, a fund-raiser for a variety of conservative and Christian organizations. He rarely lasted with any organization for more than two years.

The third article in his Wednesday morning stack was an Associated Press story concerning an interesting civil rights case in Spokane, Washington. The picture that had adorned the front page of the *Spokesman-Review* on Tuesday was on page ten of the *Kansas City Star* today. He was interested in the article and intrigued with the photograph of Gwen Landis.

He picked up the phone.

"Directory Assistance, for what city?"

"Spokane."

"What listing?"

"Peter Barron, Attorney. I'd like the office number please."

He dialed again.

"Barron & Associates," Sally said.

"Peter Barron, please."

"May I ask who's calling?"

"My name is David G. Humphrey," he said in his perfect radio voice. "I am the president of America's pro-family organization, *Heart of America.* I read about the Gwen Landis lawsuit in our paper here in Kansas City this morning, and I'd like to know if we can be of assistance on this important case."

Sally was impressed and excited. "Sure, just a moment. I'll get Mr. Barron."

Thirty seconds later, Peter picked up the phone.

"Good morning, Mr. Humphrey," Peter said. "How can I be of assistance to you?"

"Well, Mr. Barron. What a pleasure! Thank you for taking my call. And if I may be so bold, the question is: How can I be of assistance to you?"

"I understand you are calling about our Landis case."

"Yes. This is obviously a very important case. Probably headed to the Supreme Court, from what I read here in the Kansas City papers this morning. Very important case. And it sounds like you are doing this case out of the goodness of your heart. A single mom employed as a nurse—at least that's what the article says—cannot be paying you very much money. We'd like to help."

"That sounds very interesting. What do you have in mind?"

"I am the president and founder of this country's newest, pro-family, public interest organization. We are interested in changing government to be more sensitive to the needs of America's families. We have called the organization *Heart of America* to symbolize that we think families are the essential ingredient to change the heart of this nation."

"Is this a Christian organization?" Peter asked.

"It is a pro-family organization reaching a broad perspective of American citizens who embrace the Judeo-Christian ethic and subscribe to the importance of families. Our research indicates that over 75% of Americans hold strong favorable opinions on the issues that are the core of what makes *Heart of America* tick. Is that acceptable to you?"

"I think so. It's just that I'm a born-again Christian and I like to know where people are coming from," Peter replied.

"Well, Brother Barron, is it? Praise God. We are a pro-family organization reaching out broadly to our nation, yes. But all of our staff and all of our board members are solid born-again, Bible-believing Christians just like yourself. There are no coincidences in God's economy. This call sounds like a divine appointment."

"What is it that you are interested in doing?" Peter asked.

"We want to help with funding your case. That's it. We'll send a letter out to our members and friends. We'll tell them the facts of your case. Ask for a donation. And then we'll send it along to you. Naturally, we have to cover our mailing expenses. But beyond that, it goes to your litigation fund. Nothing complicated. We just want to help."

"It sounds too good to be true."

"We serve a miracle-working God who arranges our lives and meets our needs in a way that does seem too good to be true, but that's the kind of God we serve."

"Well, this all sounds great," Peter said. "But naturally, I'd have to get my client's permission."

"Certainly. Certainly. And we would give both of you editorial input on the packages we send out to help with fund-raising. Yes, indeed."

"It really sounds good. Thank you so much for your concern. I'm just a small operation—myself and one associate. We are going up against the State of Washington and all of their resources. And now that we are headed to the appellate courts, the out-of-pocket costs are going to be more than we can really afford. And, what you said earlier was absolutely correct. Gwen Landis cannot afford to pay us a dime. We may recover our attorney's fees eventually, but there will be a lot of lean months before this case is finalized."

"Well, I am privileged to help not only a worthy case for a brother in the Lord, but it sounds like our help will actually make a difference between doing the case on a shoe string and doing a first-class job. It's just a sign from God that all these circumstances fall together so perfectly. When can I expect to hear from you?"

"I should be able to give you an answer later today. Let's see, there is a two-hour time difference between here and Kansas City, right?"

"That's right. And later today will be perfect. We can get to work right away on this. And get you some funds in just a few weeks."

"Thanks again. This is a real surprise," Peter said, still reeling from this sudden turn of events.

~

Gwen was overjoyed with the prospect of financial help for her case. As appreciative as she was of Peter's generosity, she couldn't stop the waves of guilt that would sweep over her from time to time. She knew that Peter was going out on a financial limb for her. He was financing depositions, filing fees, expert witness fees, not to mention all his time, out of his own pocket. Gwen had been around Peter enough to know that while he was doing reasonably well, he was still in the building stage of his practice and was far from the stereotypical rich attorney.

David G. Humphrey was thrilled when Peter returned his phone call two-and-a-half hours after their first conversation. He asked Peter for only two things: a simple two- or three-page description of the case in laymen's language, and a picture of Gwen and Casey in their home to be used in telling the story of the case. He asked Peter to hire a professional photographer to take the picture and send the negatives and a proof sheet to Kansas City. In turn, Humphrey promised to overnight a check—a check for $5,000—as a token of good faith.

The next day Peter was delighted to be greeted by a UPS driver with a check—a certified check—for $5,000 from *Heart of America*. This paid off all of the $3,900 in out-of-pocket costs that had been incurred to that point. Rather than applying the balance to the over $15,000 in attorney's fees Peter had racked up in both the state and federal cases, he put the balance in his trust account to pay for the costs of appeal to the Ninth Circuit. The $1,100 would be a good start, but was far less than the amount needed to see the matter to completion.

Peter was so delighted, that, with Gwen's permission, he stood up in church the next Sunday morning and shared a brief testimony of how God had provided through this new organization—*Heart of America*.

~

Sally had never seen the tall, blond, bleary-eyed man standing at her reception desk before.

"I'd like to see Peter Barron, please," he said.

"May I tell him whose calling?"

"Gordon."

"I'm sorry, Gordon. May I ask your last name? We don't seem to have you on the appointment calendar right now."

"Just tell him Gordon is here. He'll know."

Sally got up, walked around the reception desk, went slowly behind the stranger, and slipped into Peter's office. She didn't see the bulge in the left pocket of his rumpled slacks as she passed by. She shut the door tightly.

"Peter, there is a strange man out here. Says his name is Gordon. He wants to see you."

"Gordon? That's his whole name?"

"That's all he would tell me."

"Tall guy, blond, about thirty or so?" Peter asked.

"Yeah," Sally replied. "You know him?"

"It sounds like Gordon Landis—Gwen's ex-husband. I'll see him."

"Is he safe?" Sally asked. "I've got a strange feeling about him."

"Did he seem to be drunk?" Peter asked.

"No . . . not really."

"Then I think he's probably fine. If he was drunk we might be more cautious."

Sally opened the door, stepped just outside and said, "Gordon? Mr. Barron will see you now."

"Thanks," he replied. He walked in and stood behind a chair. Sally continued to stand in the doorway.

"Sally, I think Mr. Landis may want a cup of coffee," Peter said. "Am I right?" he asked, turning to Gordon.

"Uh . . . yeah. Sure." Gordon replied.

When she returned with the coffee, Sally was able to bring herself to leave the room and close the door as was her normal practice.

After Gordon sipped his coffee for a moment, Peter broke the silence. "What brings you in for a visit today Gordon? I'm surprised to see you, but not too surprised."

"You shouldn't be surprised—the way you've been acting lately."

"Pardon me?" Peter said.

"The way you've been acting. I mean there you are on page one, with your arm around my wife. If you are doing that in public, in front of the cameras, what are you doing in private?"

Peter sighed heavily. "Oh, so that's it." He wished he could simply assure Gordon that he had the wrong idea totally and send him on his way, but he knew that such a story would fall short of the whole truth. On the other hand, Gordon's apparent conclusions were vastly different from the reality of his relationship with Gwen.

"Yeah, that's it, bub. I want to know what is going on between you and my wife."

"I hate to be technical with you. But she is your ex-wife. Right?"

"Not in my heart she isn't. I'm trying to win her back."

Peter's theology hit him squarely in the face. According to Peter's long-held view of Scripture, Gordon had the essence of the right point.

"Well, Gordon. My answer is going to surprise you."

Gordon slowly moved his left hand. He gently patted his pocket. The knife was still there. But he would wait for Peter's confession.

Peter was so caught up in his spiritual dilemma, he didn't notice Gordon's movement.

"The reality is, Gordon, that this morning and every morning for the last several weeks, I have been praying that you *would* be reconciled with Gwen. Specifically, I have been praying you would make the changes in your life that would allow Gwen to love you again. Right now, it seems it's not possible for you to win her back. But if you would change, maybe it could happen."

"What?" Gordon said. "You're not serious."

"I'm absolutely serious, Gordon. It's a long story, but let me tell it to you briefly. You see, Gordon, I'm a born-again Christian. That means I have asked Jesus Christ to come into my life and forgive my sins. And I do my best to live my life according to the principles of His Word, the Bible."

"One of those principles," Peter continued, "is that it is God's best for families to be reconciled. God hates divorce, the Bible says. And I believe that God's best for you and for Gwen, and especially for Casey, would be to have you change so that your family can be made whole again."

"You're nuts if you think I'm going to believe that. I can see it in your eyes when you are in court. You have got the hots for Gwen and don't try to pretend you don't."

"Well, Gordon, you're partly right and you're partly wrong. There is no question about my admiring Gwen greatly. And if she were free to marry, I would definitely be interested in her. That's probably what you see in my eyes. That much is true. But I can assure you there is absolutely no romantic and certainly no physical relationship going on between the two of us. And—like I said, I really am praying for you. My most earnest prayer is that you would accept Jesus as your Savior. Gwen has. And it has made a real difference in her life.

"Would you like me to show you how you can become a Christian, Gordon? There are some basic principles from God's Word I could share with you in just a couple of minutes."

Peter got up from his desk, and walked across the room to get a Bible off a small bookshelf in the corner.

"Hold it right there," Gordon said standing up as well.

Peter turned and stared at Gordon who was obviously in emotional distress.

"I didn't come here to hear Bible talk. I came here to tell you to keep your hands off my wife."

"I can assure—"

"Shut up," Gordon hissed. "I don't want to hear anymore." Peter's answers had thrown him off. He did not know how to respond. His plan swirled in his head, and the confusion was growing.

"Listen, buster. I don't want to hear anymore of your God junk. I just want you to keep your filthy hands off my wife."

"OK, no problem, Gordon. I have and I will."

"You're a nut. A freakin' nut." He spun on his heel, lunged for the door—and half-ran, half-staggered out of the office and slammed the outer door with vengeance.

~

David G. Humphrey anxiously tore open the Federal Express package. He removed the contents and placed the empty oversized envelope on the desk, right next to the photograph of his wife and two teenage sons. It was the proposed fund raising mail package which would ask the members of *Heart of America* to give money to help Gwen and Casey Landis. His direct mail consultants were in San Diego and they were very, very good at telling a story in way which would enhance the propensity of people to open their mail—always the first hurdle—read it, and then get out their checkbooks and give. He read the main letter over carefully. The "P.S." was fabulous, "*Gwen's need was so urgent, I have rushed her a check for $5,000—on faith. Faith in you, the members of Heart of America. This was money we didn't have in our budget. But our staff members have waived their salaries until we can replenish our accounts. And Gwen's case will cost ten or twenty times this amount. She needs your help—I need your help—today.*"

Next he examined the outside carrier envelope that would get the donor's attention. Gwen and Casey's picture was the prominent feature on the envelope. Below their images, printed in red, it exclaimed: "Daughter taken by Social Worker Fraud. Help Get Her Back!"

It wasn't exactly accurate now. But the direct mail gurus thought that the envelope should tell the story from that earlier time perspective. They would explain more inside. It was a small deception. Humphrey liked the results and didn't mind the methodology.

"Cindy, can you come in here, please?" he said into the intercom.

He did want her opinion of the mail package. But even more, he wanted a chance to see her walk across the room in the red mini-dress she was wearing. He was not disappointed.

"Please sit down, Cindy. I'd like you to look over this package on the Landis case."

"Sure, Mr. Humphrey," she replied, sitting and crossing her legs.

As she began to read, he got up from his desk and went behind her, ostensibly to read over her shoulder. After a minute or two of "reading," he reached out and gently put his hands on her shoulders and began to lightly massage her neck.

"Please, Mr. Humphrey. It makes me nervous when you do that. I know you are just trying to make me relax, but I don't feel right about it. What if your wife came in? I know if my boyfriend came in, he'd be furious. Please."

Humphrey removed his hands and said nothing. He liked her looks considerably. But he wished she would be more "cooperative."

"Well, what do you think of the package? After all, you found the case for us."

"I just read it in the newspaper, Mr. Humphrey. Just doing my job."

"Yes, you were. But if this package succeeds like I hope, you will learn that if you just do your job for David G. Humphrey, the rewards are sometimes quite substantial."

"What do you mean?" she asked.

"Let's just wait and see how successful it is. The mail house is going to roll out 118,000 pieces to our own donor file. And if it does as well as we all think, then we are going to rent a number of other lists and use this package to prospect and gain a number of new members. After we test it, the mail boys think we can probably roll this out to two or three million households. They think it may be our best piece ever."

"What does this part mean about waiving our salaries?"

"Oh don't worry about that. I have a little bonus in mind for those involved in getting this package for us. But we're going to have to waive those until the money comes in from the mail."

"Oh, I see," she replied innocently. "I guess that makes sense."

"Dollars and cents, honey. Dollars and cents."

～

Every year on Labor Day, Peter hosted a barbecue at his home on Liberty Lake. Over fifty people were invited to this year's event for an afternoon of swimming, boating, and, of course, eating. Peter wasn't much of a cook, but he could barbecue steaks and burgers more than adequately. The rest of the food was bought from Rosauer's deli section.

The Roberts family, Pastor Lind and his family, his associate Joe and his family, Sally, three other couples from church, and a half-dozen neighbor families were regularly invited. This year Gwen, Casey, and Stan and June Mansfield were added to the guest list.

A few weeks earlier, there had been some question in Peter's mind whether he could really afford to do a big party this year, but when the funds from *Heart of America* had come in, it relieved some of the cash flow problems and he decided to go ahead with his traditional plans.

The Roberts arrived first to help Peter with the final stages of setting up chairs and tables on the gentle sloping yard between his back deck and the water which beckoned from seventy-five feet away. The day was delightful.

Peter had not spent much time with Aaron recently because of vacation schedules. As they moved a table together, Aaron asked, "Peter, how are things going with you and Gwen?"

"Real good on the legal front, thanks to your excellent work on those CPS computers."

"But I thought the judge threw out those charges."

"He did, but it really colored his thinking on all the other issues. Your work convinced him that the CPS folks, at least the trio we're dealing with, are not to be trusted. And I've appealed his dismissal of the perjury issues. Your work will prove to be invaluable."

"Well, good. I'm glad it helped. But I really was more interested on the personal side of the relationship. How's that going?"

"Reasonably well. I told her a little too much one time, but by the end of the conversation I made a commitment to her that I would keep an appropriate distance while I seek the Lord on this whole issue. I have given myself until the end of October. If God doesn't make something clear by then, I am going to come to the conclusion that my original views were God's leading me, and I am going to stop hoping and wishing—I'll simply cut things off in my mind."

"That sounds pretty good. Are you sticking to your commitment?"

"I think I have done pretty well. I have even been praying for Gordon—her ex-husband—that he would be saved, turn himself around, and that his family would be reconciled."

"I bet that is hard to pray."

"It is—especially since the other day. Gordon showed up in my office and told me to keep my hands off his wife. I told him there was no problem there and told him that I had been praying for the reconciliation of his family. When I tried to witness to him, he freaked out, called me names, and literally ran out of the office. It was a really strange incident."

"Keep on praying, Peter. You know God is not willing that any should perish."

"Yeah, I know," Peter said, shamed by the thought that still occasionally crossed his mind that Gordon would just die and be out of his way.

Just then, two of Pastor Scott Lind's young children came running across the yard, life jackets already on, making a bee-line for the water.

"Whoa!" Peter called out. "It looks like the swimmers have arrived."

They paused long enough for Scott and his wife, Geri, to appear in the side yard. "Hold on kids," the pastor called out. "Wait 'til I can come watch you."

"Hi, Pastor Scott," Peter said. "Thanks for coming."

"We wouldn't miss it for anything. Thanks for inviting us again. I just wish you would let us help with the food."

"Oh, we've been through all that before. Just go and have fun."

The crowd slowly trickled in for the next half hour. Peter began to wonder when Gwen and her family were going to arrive. It was beyond the point of being fashionably late. But his attention was distracted by his cooking duties which, according to a quick glance at his watch, were now upon him.

Finally, forty minutes later when he was cooking the last round of steaks and burgers, he saw Casey running across in the direction of one of the Roberts children. Gwen was suddenly by his side.

"Sorry, we're late, Peter. We ran into a little trouble."

"Oh, don't worry about being late. But what's the trouble? Everything OK now?"

"Sort of," Gwen replied. "Gordon showed up and made a scene as we were leaving. Casey mentioned to him that we were coming out here when he had visitation on Saturday. He arrived about an hour ago and said he was going to stop us. He is insanely jealous of you, Peter."

No one was around. Her parents were across the yard watching Casey. Even though no one had heard any of their conversation to this point, she lowered her voice to a near whisper. "Peter, he accused us of . . . of . . . oh . . . you can guess. He thinks we're involved. And he thinks that you are the reason I won't go back to him. I was really afraid of him. There's a real change in him. Something strange and uncontrollable has come over him. I'm just glad my dad showed up when he did."

"I'm really sorry to hear that, Gwen. He showed up at my office about a week ago and made a scene with the same basic message. He made it clear he wanted me to stay away from you."

"Why didn't you tell me?"

"I couldn't think of a gracious way to bring it up without violating my commitment to you."

"Oh. I think you'd better be careful, Peter. If he shows up again, he may do something crazy. If he says anything to me again, I'm going to call the police immediately."

"Good idea. And call me too."

Gwen gave him a piercing look.

"Sorry, I guess I shouldn't be offering to be your knight in shining armor."

"Not unless you can make the offer with a clear conscience."

"I wish I could make my mouth behave," Peter said with a smile. "Your steaks are ready. Why don't you get your parents and Casey?"

"Sure," Gwen said. She patted his arm. "I like your spunk, Peter Barron. Don't you dare stop fighting for me. I hear there is a big hearing coming up in Seattle. I want your guns blazing."

⁓

The briefing schedule imposed on Peter Barron and Gail Willet left little time for dawdling. Since there was no trial to be transcribed, the briefs were due thirty days after the notice of appeal was filed. The thirtieth day, September 25, fell on a Sunday so the briefs were actually due in Seattle on the next day.

Willet had appealed the portion of Judge Stokes's decision that allowed Gwen's suit on the illegal search to continue. Peter cross-appealed the portion of the case which dismissed the allegations concerning perjury and document tampering. Both attorneys had to file an opening brief on the issue that they had appealed by the initial due date. Then fourteen days later, each had to respond to the other's opening brief.

Willet had much more experience in appellate litigation than Peter. All the rules concerning brief formats came easily to her. Peter spent three hours one afternoon doing nothing other than trying to master the rules which governed the size of paper, style of type to be used, spacing, format of case citations—all the technicalities that trial lawyers rarely have to deal with. Many an excellent trial lawyer failed to take the steps to understand the hypertechnical rules of appeals and ended up looking totally incompetent, when in fact they had an excellent grasp of the substance of the law. Peter knew Willet's experience was superior in these areas. He would have to be extra sharp.

With $225 of the money that had come from *Heart of America*, Peter took a day out of his normal routine and caught a plane to Seattle first thing in the morning. Three different panels of the Ninth Circuit Court of Appeals were hearing cases that day. By dividing his time between the three different groups of judges, he was able to watch nine different individual judges in action. He would not know until the morning of the hearing which, if any, of these judges would form the three-judge panel to hear his case. The Ninth Circuit has over twenty different judges and there is no way for lawyers to predict who will be on a particular panel. And Peter had no real idea who would be good or bad for his case anyway.

After Labor Day, Peter spent two or three hours virtually every night in the library or in front of his computer. His unfamiliarity with appellate work made him put twice as much effort into the case than might otherwise have been needed. And, like Willet, who worked hard to help forget the pain of the past, Peter's focus on Gwen's case was so intense that he began to have fewer stress-ridden thoughts about Gwen herself.

In the second week of September, Peter kept a promise he had made to himself and to Gwen, and scheduled an appointment late Tuesday afternoon with Pastor Lind.

Peter arrived at the church just before four and chatted briefly with the church secretary who was in his Sunday School class. She had no idea of the reason for Peter's appointment, but she was so tight-lipped that Peter wouldn't have minded if she accidentally found out.

A few minutes after four, a couple Peter did not know walked out of the Pastor's study. The wife had been crying. She was now clinging tightly to her husband's arm. Peter made eye contact with the husband, and both men nodded a quick "Hi."

"Come in, Peter," Scott Lind said, appearing at the door.

"Thanks for your time, Pastor," Peter said, sitting down on the couch next to the desk.

"You're welcome. Thanks again for the great time we had on Labor Day at your house. My kids really enjoy the water, and I enjoy the food."

"Glad you could come. Pastor, let me get to the point. I know your time is valuable. I want to talk with you about a very tough spiritual dilemma I am facing. It involves Gwen Landis."

"Ah, yes. Gwen. She seems like a very nice lady. Lynn Roberts tells me she is really growing spiritually."

"Yes, she really is. Here's the problem: Gwen is divorced. The reasons for her divorce basically involve conflicts over money. Her husband was clearly financially irresponsible. He now has an alcohol problem as well. But there was no infidelity involved on either side, and there are no scriptural grounds for divorce as I have always understood that term.

"Unfortunately, I have let my emotions run ahead of my convictions. I am in love with her and would marry her in a heartbeat if I could get past this issue of divorce."

Based on his experience of reading juror's faces, Peter saw a look of concern rising on the Pastor's face.

"Don't worry, Pastor, I am not about to confess some immoral activity. I have never even kissed her, much less anything more. Physically I have completely behaved myself."

"I would have really been surprised if you had said anything differently. But I am still glad to hear that in a direct way. Go on," Lind said.

"I know that some solid Christians take a different position on the issue of divorce than I have always taken. And I am confused. On the one hand, if Scripture clearly prohibits me from marrying Gwen, I am going to obey the Word of God. Or, if Scripture clearly allows me to marry Gwen, then I probably am going to ask you if the church is free for next Saturday afternoon. But, the third alternative is that Scripture is not crystal clear on the subject, in which case I have to do what I believe the Holy Spirit says to me personally through the Word of God."

"Peter," Pastor Scott said, "that is excellent analysis. Why do you need me? Those are exactly the three alternatives."

"But the problem is that, while I can state the alternatives, I have no idea what the answer is. I need your help."

"Let me start with my personal view. I believe the same thing that you apparently believe. Unless a person has been divorced for the reason of the other person's adultery, then remarriage is not appropriate. That's how I read Scripture. But let me show you a little intellectual honesty. I know men that I respect very highly who take the position that those standards apply to Christians. If the divorced person was the innocent spouse, and the divorce was before they were a Christian, there are a lot of pastors who are generally conservatives, who would say that it is OK. So where I fall is, I guess, is with your third alternative. This is a Scriptural area where I think that personal conviction based on the Word must control. If you ask me how I read Scripture, I will tell you and I can defend it. But I will give you some leeway if you read it differently. Scripture has got to be our standard. If we start making these kind of decisions based on our emotions, or our experience, then we are a ship without a rudder."

"That's what I was afraid you would say. I am so mixed up, I wish somebody would be dogmatic and just flat out tell me what to do."

"Peter, have you considered the possibility that God already has? You told me at the outset that you have held this position on divorce for a long time. I think that you should assume that is God's direction to you."

"I guess I just wanted to make sure that I wasn't missing out on a marriage to a wonderful woman because the first person who taught me on this subject happened to hold a certain view. If I had been taught by someone else, then, at least theoretically, I wouldn't be having this dilemma."

"Peter, have you ever changed your view of any Scriptural issue, based on some new teaching that you heard later in your Christian life?"

"Yes, I guess I have. Once or twice, I think."

"Did the second person present what you found to be a better interpretation of Scripture, or did you simply like the new interpretation better for some personal reason?"

"I get the point," Peter replied. "Gwen is the reason I want to change my view. It's not because I read, heard, or discovered on my own a new teaching that made more sense. It's just Gwen. That's my only reason."

"Do you think that is the way God works?"

"No," Peter replied.

"You know I feel for you, brother. It is right for you to want to be married. And from my limited contact, I can understand why you feel the way you do about her. And I know that I am basically telling you to walk away from a woman who would probably make a wonderful wife. You have to go home to an empty house tonight, and I get to go home to a beautiful wife who loves me. This is easy advice for me to give. It is hard for you to live."

"It's the hardest spiritual struggle I have ever been through. It is a lot easier to sacrifice for God when the things we are sacrificing aren't worth very much to us. I want to be married to Gwen more than I have ever wanted anything. But I have to be willing to lay it on the altar like Abraham did with Isaac."

"You understand that story now with your emotions as well as with your mind."

"Pastor, I told Gwen the other day that I was going to give myself until the end of October for God to give me an answer. If I didn't get clearance from Him before then, I was going to let her go forever. Do you think that is wrong?"

"No, I think that's probably OK. Especially if you are working on the assumption that you aren't going to change unless you get a clearly different answer you are certain is from God rather than your own desires. Let me give you a couple books written by men who take a different position than my own. Don't listen to them while you are reading these books. Listen to the voice of the Lord in your heart and search out Scripture and ask God to make it clear to you what He wants."

"Thanks. I'll read them. And if I think I am supposed to change my mind, I'd like to come back and talk it over with you first, so you can help me do a heart check to know if I am deceiving myself."

"Sure, Peter, I'd be glad to do that. You know, I rarely have someone who is struggling at this level of spiritual maturity. It's really an encouragement to me rather than hearing from people who know what God wants—things that are basic and clear—and they simply aren't willing to follow through with what they know to be right. Or they have a thousand excuses why they should be allowed a variance from God. People can invent some complex reasoning for doing exactly what they want. You are a real encouragement and, frankly, an example to me of how to approach the role of God's Word and God's Will in my life. You are doing good. You really are."

"You wouldn't say that if you knew how I shoot my mouth off or what my heart imagines."

"Sin is sin. But keep it confessed. A man of integrity is not perfect. A man of integrity simply strives to please God the best way he knows. As far as I can discern, that sounds like you, Peter."

21

⁓

Donna Corliss heard from Stephen Stockton about once a week by phone. She wrote to him two or three times a week. He wrote rarely. The girls in D.C. were interesting, but none had yet captivated his imagination. Donna still loomed somewhere in his affections, if not in his loyalty.

As Indian summer turned to fall, Donna Corliss became less and less worried about the police investigation. There was no activity that was apparent to her. She called Conner Stockton every couple of weeks just to check in. He assured her that if the police became seriously interested in her, they would call him and demand an interrogation. And like her, he had heard nothing.

A new supervisor was transferred from the Bellingham office of Child Protective Services. The scandal of the tampered documents had absolutely foreclosed any possibility that Corliss or Coballo would ever have another promotion unless it could be definitively established they had absolutely nothing to do with the document tampering.

Corliss came into Coballo's office during the third week of September.

"Rita, I just heard a rumor from Sandi down the hall that Olympia is going to send a computer team over here to do a complete analysis of all the computer records of the files in the Gerald Blackburn unit for the past three years. If they do, that they may discover all of the Code B cases we were involved in. What are we going to do?"

"If it is true, run, probably. But I don't think it is true."

"Why not?"

"It is something that they might have done if there hadn't been this civil rights lawsuit hanging around. If they were to do an internal investigation now, they would have to turn the results over to that Barron guy. You can be guaranteed they aren't going to do that. The way I figure it, he is the best insurance we have right now. When that case starts to wind down, if somebody gets the hots for the issue again, we probably should think about getting out of here."

"Don't you think if we both left this unit and left the area, or got another kind of job, there might be no interest in bringing it up again at all?"

"You're probably right, Donna. But what would you do? What would I do? How am I supposed to support my daughter?"

"There must be jobs for us somewhere that would attract less attention. The more I think about it, the more I think we should get out of here. Maybe not right away. That might look suspicious. And we probably shouldn't both quit at the same time. But I think that if either of us is here when that case is over, we are inviting an internal investigation."

Coballo sat silently for a few seconds at her desk twisting a pencil. "You try to help kids—I know we stretched a few rules—but our desire was to help when we just didn't have the hard proof all these technicalities require—and *we* end up being the fugitives while the child abusers go free."

"It just doesn't seem right, does it?" Corliss replied. "What do you think you'll do?"

"The only idea I have right now would involve a move to Sacramento. I have a friend from graduate school who is the chief lobbyist for the California Association of Social Workers. A couple of years ago she talked with me about joining their staff as a legislative analyst on social worker issues. I'd sure like to get some laws passed giving us the kind of protection we need to help children without fear of these frivolous lawsuits."

"You've got that right," Corliss replied.

"How about you?"

"I guess I hope that Stephen still wants to get married. It shouldn't raise any suspicions if I got married and moved to be with my husband in Washington, D.C. I don't know if he wants me anymore or not."

"Oh, I'm sure things haven't changed that much. He hasn't been gone that long."

"I hope you're right, but I don't know anymore. My life is coming apart at the seams."

~

Cindy Walters walked into the inner office of David G. Humphrey.

"Mr. Humphrey, we just got a fax from the mail house. The results of the Landis mailing are finally in."

"Great, great. I've been dying to see them."

He walked around his desk and pulled the two side chairs together. "Sit down here so we can look at this together. I'm sure you're going to want to see, too."

"I could make us both a copy if you'd like," Cindy said. She was uncomfortable as Humphrey seemed a little too close for the fourth or fifth time that week.

"No need for that. Just sit here and let's look."

"Let's see, we are getting a five percent response rate! That's fantastic! Average gift is $26. And we have raised nearly two dollars per name mailed to our house file. This is great."

"I can't figure all these numbers out," Cindy said. "How much have we raised altogether?"

"Our out-of-pocket costs thus far for the mailing are approximately $55,000. We have grossed $308,000, but we have some more expenses to cover."

"Like what?" she asked.

"We have our office operations for the next two months—that's $125,000. The *Heart of America* has to continue doing its important work. And then we have to pay some more fees related to the creation of this package."

"How much will that be?"

"Why don't you just go get the checkbook? I'll make out the checks and you can get them right out to the people who have done such a great job."

Humphrey watched her intently as she went into the outer office and then came back to her place by his side.

"Well, the first check should be made out to the mail house for $31,000. That's their creative fee, ten percent of the amount raised, rounded up to the nearest thousand."

Cindy dutifully wrote the check and handed it to Humphrey for signature.

"Next there will be $15,000 payable to me for a negotiation fee. The trickiest part of this whole operation is making sure that we gain access to the cases."

Cindy gave Humphrey a questioning look. Something seemed out of place with the amount. The look was not lost on Humphrey. It was just what he had hoped for.

"And the third check for $7,000 goes to . . . it goes to . . . Cindy Walters for a finders fee. You discovered this one, sweetheart."

"You're kidding, aren't you?"

"Absolutely not. You deserve every penny of it!"

"Seven thousand dollars?" It was nearly four times her monthly salary. It was more than she made in six months at the restaurant where Humphrey found her working as a bar maid.

"Yes, that's the amount. Write the check and I'll sign it."

When she handed it back for his signature, he took her by the hand and said, "I want to present this to you properly. Cindy, it is my great pleasure to present you this check as a small token of my appreciation for your excellent work."

"Oooh," she squealed. Clutching the check, she grabbed David G. Humphrey and held him tightly. "Oh thank you, thank you." She gave him a quick kiss on the cheek.

"We can do better than that, can't we?" Humphrey said and kissed her firmly on the mouth.

Walters was taken aback, but the thrill of a seven-thousand-dollar check muffled any protest she would have raised.

When Humphrey finally released her, she said, "Oh, thank you, Mr. Humphrey. Thank you very much."

"I think it is time that you call me David, OK?"

"Sure, uh . . . David," she said still smiling, but nervously waiting his next move.

Humphrey studied her carefully, correctly gauging that she was at her limit for now. He was a patient man. He could wait.

"Well, I guess that's about it. We should probably get back to work."

"Don't we have to send something to the lawyer for this case?" she asked.

"Oh, that's right," Humphrey said reluctantly. "Well, let me do some quick numbers." Punching a calculator on his desk, he looked up and said, "Sure, write Peter Barron a second check for $5,000. He'll be thrilled."

~

On Monday, September 25, there was an exchange of briefs. Both Barron and Willet had sent their original briefs, plus ten copies, off to the Court of Appeals in San Francisco by overnight delivery the previous Friday. Although the case would be heard at the branch of the Ninth Circuit in Seattle, the briefs had to be filed in the main clerk's office in San Francisco.

Peter thumbed through Willet's fifty-page effort. It was clearly a polished piece of work. Nine pages, which didn't count as part of the fifty-page limit imposed by the court rules, were devoted just to listing the cases that Willet had cited supporting her arguments. Peter knew that he had his work cut out for him to answer her arguments. She seemed so convincing when she argued that social workers were absolutely immune from any kind of civil rights lawsuit.

She presented a clever theory. If the social workers do an investigation which never results in charges being filed, then such a search may require a warrant. But if charges were filed, she contended, then the investigation was "a part of the overall effort of a court presentation" and the entire matter is exempt from scrutiny under the civil rights laws.

Willet was surprised at the quality of Peter's brief—both at his faithful adherence to the court rules for the format of appellate briefs as well as at the substance of his arguments. Despite his lack of appellate experience—she had done a Westlaw computer search to check—it was a very credible brief. On her first read through, she found what she thought were a couple of chinks in his arguments—chinks she would attempt to turn into gaps in her reply brief. She was glad that the court precedents were so strong disallowing suits for perjury. Peter's arguments certainly had the weight of moral authority behind them. No amount of moral authority and good facts that Peter mustered could overcome a single decision of the United States Supreme Court. And Willet had three cases from the high court that were clearly on point.

Both attorneys would spend four or five hours a night for the next two weeks scrambling to get their reply briefs done on time. A simple reply would not require nearly that amount of time. But given the quality of both opening briefs, the computer screens would burn brightly late into the night on both sides of the Spokane River.

~

Gwen's phone rang at 11:30 A.M. on Tuesday, September 27. She guessed it was Peter calling to tell her about the brief which he was supposed to have received the day before. She knew that he had been working hard to get his brief finished and was anxious herself to see what Peter had written.

"Hello," Gwen said.

"Hi," a tired male voice said.

"Peter? Is that you?"

"No, it is definitely not Peter."

Gwen now recognized Gordon's voice and wished she had not mentioned Peter's name.

"So you were expecting a call from that boyfriend of yours, were you?"

"He's my lawyer—not my boyfriend. But it's none of your business if he was."

"It is always my business, Gwen. I still want to come back and be a family with you and Casey."

"You just want my income. You never did want me or Casey."

"That's a lie and you know it."

"Well, you never wanted us badly enough to get a job and support your family."

"Oh, that again."

"Why am I even discussing this with you? What do you want anyway?"

"I wanted to see if you and your boyfriend were carrying on in front of my daughter."

"Gordon, leave me alone, please. I am hanging up. There is no boyfriend."

The phone slammed to the cradle.

"Fat chance," he said, tipping the bottle back to empty the last drops.

∼

The next night, Gwen noticed a car in her rear view mirror as she pulled out of the employee parking lot at Sacred Heart. The car was still there when she reached 29th Avenue. She turned right and headed down 29th. She began to really be concerned she was being followed when she slowed to five miles below the speed limit and the car was still there.

But her concern turned to relief when the car did not follow her as she turned right onto Janelle Court.

She thanked and kissed her dad as he left her home. It had been his turn to watch Casey that night.

Gordon sat in his darkened car on 29th and waited. He saw Stan Mansfield's car come by five minutes later. He waited until it was out of sight, made a U-turn in the middle of 29th, and turned left down Janelle Court. Gwen's car was the only one in front of the house.

He turned off his lights, finished off the beer which had been sitting on his floorboard, opened the door, and sauntered to the front door. Taking a deep breath, he knocked sharply on the door five times and waited.

At first Gwen thought it was her father returning, but the knock just didn't sound like his. She peeked out the front window and recognized Gordon's car parked behind hers. Gwen walked quickly to the front door and flipped the deadbolt into locked position.

"Gordon, what do you want?" she yelled through the door.

"I'm just checkin' to see if that boyfriend of yours is coming to spend the night. I don't want him hanging 'round my daughter."

"Gordon, you are crazy. Go home and leave me alone."

"I'm just gonna sit out here and make sure that you don't have any visitors later tonight."

Gwen heard his back thud softly against the front door as he settled down on the porch.

She dashed to the phone and called her dad. The phone rang and rang. Her mom had apparently fallen asleep in the family room watching TV. Her dad was not yet home.

She punched 9-1-1.

"Police. What is the emergency?"

"My ex-husband is sitting on my doorstep and says he is going to stay there all night."

"Is he threatening to break in?"

"No," Gwen said, "he's just there to annoy me all night long. I can't go to sleep, I'll be afraid as long as he's out there."

"Is he armed?"

"I don't think so."

"Well, ma'am, we'll send someone out, but this is not a true emergency. It may take forty-five minutes to an hour to get an officer to come out."

"Forty-five minutes to an hour?" Gwen cried out in exasperation. "Just send someone out now."

Gwen didn't want to be there alone with Gordon at her door—even for five minutes. She called Peter's home phone number. She wished he lived closer. It would take him thirty minutes to come, even at this time of night. Even if it were only by phone, being able to talk with Peter until the police arrived was the best solution she could devise.

His home number rang four times and the answering machine clicked on. She hung up quickly and dialed the office number. The answering service answered.

"This is Gwen Landis. I'm a client of Peter Barron's. I've got an urgent situation here. I've already tried his home number. Can you please ring through to the office line and see if he's there?"

"Ms. Landis, it is very unlikely that he would be there at this time."

"He's working late all this week on a brief for me. Can you please try?"

"Oh, just a minute."

Seconds later, Peter's voice came on the line.

"Gwen, what's wrong?"

"Oh, Peter, Gordon is sitting on my front porch. He says he wants to make sure that 'my boyfriend' isn't spending the night. I've called the police but they say that unless he is threatening to come in, they won't be able to get here for forty-five minutes to an hour."

"I'll be there in less than ten minutes, Gwen," Peter replied.

"I don't know, Peter. You showing up is sure to anger him."

"Don't worry about that. I just want to make sure that you and Casey are safe."

"But I really want to keep you on the phone until the police arrive. I'm scared, Peter."

"Look, Gwen. I'll call you from my car phone in less than two minutes and I'll keep you on the line until I pull up in front of your house."

"OK, I guess."

"Just start praying, Gwen."

"I will, Peter. Hurry."

Peter's Explorer glided up the South Hill more than a little over the speed limit. Gwen was comforted to have his voice on the phone as he headed for the confrontation with Gordon.

Peter pulled up and immediately jumped out of his truck and headed up the sidewalk toward Gordon.

"Gordon, you need to get out of here and get on home," Peter said in his deepest, most authoritative voice.

"So you showed up for a little fun and games, did you, lawyer man?" Gordon said, taunting him.

"I was at my office working on a brief and Gwen called me to come help because you were invading her property. That's it. The police are on their way. The smartest thing you could do would be to go away right now."

Gwen had cracked a window and could hear everything.

"I ain't goin' nowhere, lover boy. You gonna make me?"

Gordon closed the gap between the two men and half-shoved, half-hit Peter right in the stomach. Peter tensed just before the impact; Gordon felt like his hand had struck a brick wall.

Peter grabbed Gordon's arm and held on. "Let's go, Gordon," Peter said calmly.

Gordon jerked wildly, attempting, but failing, to get away. He swung wildly with his free left arm, but Peter ducked without difficulty. Peter quickly adjusted his hold on Gordon's right arm, jamming one forearm behind his back and holding the other arm in a half-nelson and applied just enough pressure to let Gordon know that he had only painful alternatives.

"All right, Gordon—move."

Gordon muttered vague obscenities under his breath as he marched with resistance in each step toward his car. Peter let one arm go and opened the door with his free hand. "Get in," he ordered keeping his half-nelson firmly in place.

With a final hapless struggle, Gordon plopped into the driver's seat of his car and Peter slammed the door and stepped back. Gordon started his engine and pulled away slowly. He stopped suddenly and stuck his head out his open window. "This ain't over, lover boy. It's just round one." He tried to peel out, but his car was too gutless to do anything but smoke.

Peter stood and watched until he was sure Gordon was gone. He walked to the front door, and Gwen quickly let him in. She had been terribly frightened. She grabbed Peter around the neck and held on quivering. No words were spoken for what seemed to be five minutes. Finally, still locked in an embrace, Peter said, "He's gone, Gwen. It think it'll be OK. I'll just wait here for the police."

Gwen loosened her grip, but still kept her arms around Peter's neck. She looked into his eyes. "Peter, oh Peter, I don't know what I'd do without you."

Peter smiled, but inside he felt like a knife had stabbed him. *Please God, make some sense of this for me,* he prayed silently. *I want her so much; I just don't understand.*

She awkwardly released her grip and said, "Why don't we sit down until the police arrive?" They sat on the couch a couple of feet apart.

"What I am going to do about him?" Gwen asked.

"I don't know for sure. But Gordon is really asking for it."

"I was really proud of the way you handled him. You made him get in the car without getting into a real fight. I think he was afraid of you."

Peter blushed. "I think we should ask the police to have a talk with him. If that doesn't work, I can file a restraining order against him. Then if he shows up on your property again, the police will have the authority to arrest him immediately. They won't give you the same run-around again."

"Oh, Peter, you are already doing so much legal work for me for free. I can't ask you to do that for me."

"Hey, he made it personal tonight. It's for me as well at this point. And besides, I got another $5,000 from *Heart of America* today. I guess that's just their next installment. Their letter sounded like they would raise a whole lot more than that. Not that I'm complaining about five grand. It's a real help."

"That is good," Gwen said. "How does the appeal look?"

"Well, Willet's brief is every bit as good as I expected. I'm having to work hard to be able to answer her properly. It may just depend on what judges we get on our panel."

"When will the case be heard?"

"That's the other news we got today. Oral arguments have been set for the end of October. October 26 at 9:00 A.M., to be precise. There will be a number of cases on the docket. We won't know the order until the morning of the twenty-sixth."

"Peter, I hate to bring this up, but since you mentioned the subject of the end of October, you've promised me an answer by then. Is anything happening on that?"

"Well, I've been to see Pastor Lind, and he gave me a couple of books that take a different position than I have always believed. But I still haven't been able to clear away my confusion."

"What did Pastor—"

Car lights suddenly appeared outside the front window.

"You should open the door so they don't think I'm the intruder," Peter said.

Gwen walked to the door and waited for the police officer to knock. Peter was right behind her. She opened it immediately.

"Hi, Officer. Thank you for coming. I was scared while I was waiting. So I called my lawyer, Peter Barron."

"Good evening, Mr. Barron," the officer said. Peter's name was generally known among the Spokane police force. "Is there any more trouble right now?"

"No, Officer," Peter said. "But you are probably going to have to keep an eye on him. He tried to hit me."

"You OK?" the officer asked.

"Yeah, I ducked. I guess I'm in better shape than he is, and with a little non-violent pressure, I was able to move him out of the yard and into the car. He muttered some threats about this being the first round. He's a heavy drinker. There may be trouble later."

"I'll write it up in my report. We'll look out for him."

When the officer was gone, Peter closed the door only part-way. "I should go soon. You're going to be OK, aren't you?"

"I guess you should." The fear was still resonating in her voice. She stepped close, very close, to Peter. "Peter, I don't think I have ever said this to you. And I probably shouldn't say it now. But tonight has shaken me up. Peter, I don't know what I'll do if you tell me things are over between us. I want you to love me and protect me forever."

She was so close and trembled in anticipation. Peter leaned over and kissed her ever so gently on the cheek. "Something's going to happen to work this all out. I can't stand it either. Believe me."

He tried to get out the door quickly to keep her from noticing. But she saw just a glimpse of the tears flowing down his cheeks.

"Good night, Peter," was all she said.

22

Rita Coballo marched into Donna Corliss's office with a smile on her face. "This may work out really great after all."

Donna smiled in anticipation. "Well, tell me the good news."

"I got the job in Sacramento. I start the first of December. They want me there a month before the beginning of their new legislative session. And I will get a $15,000 a year raise."

"You're kidding! That's great, Rita," Corliss said. "But isn't it a lot more expensive to live in California?"

"Sacramento is a little more than Spokane, but I'll be far enough from the Bay Area to keep the prices reasonable."

"Is your daughter excited?"

"Yeah, she really is. She thinks she can go to Disneyland every day after school."

Corliss laughed.

"Anything happening for you?" Coballo asked.

"Not really. Stephen has been calling me a little more often. He says he is looking forward to seeing me at Christmas. He will be here for ten days. I'm going to put on a full court press in person."

"Go get him. But if not, I think you can find something better than this dump."

"I sure hope so," Corliss replied.

Gordon called Gwen's house twice that week. She hung up each time. Her father waited at her home for thirty minutes longer each night. He was glad Peter had responded so effectively for his daugh-ter the other night. Why they remained romantically disengaged was a mystery to him. He knew his daughter was in love with Peter, but nothing seemed to be happening. When he asked Gwen about it, she simply said, "It's a little awkward. Maybe things will change when the case is over."

∿

On October 10, the six-week briefing marathon filing ended for both Peter and Gail Willet. Their reply briefs were both twenty-five pages long—the maximum allowed by the Federal Rules of Appellate Procedure. Joe bragged on Peter's effort. He was truly proud of his boss. He thought Peter had a real shot for a complete victory in Seattle.

Matt Bartholomew thought that Willet's brief was "masterful" and told her so. His boss, the Attorney General, was pleased that the issue of the document tampering had gotten off the front pages and the evening news. But that would briefly change when the case was argued in Seattle. He hoped that the political members of his office were all on vacation when the newspapers were printed the next day. But, as the Attorney General's personal press secretary had told him, trials make interesting news stories; appeals are only news clips. He hoped that this case would prove to become more and more invisible to the media.

∿

Joe arranged a panel of four other lawyers to join him in doing a "moot court" session a week before the oral argument. Peter needed the practice. Joe's friends were two former federal prosecu-tors and two others who had clerked in the Washington State Supreme Court. All four had fewer total years in practice than Peter, but each had substantially more exposure to the appellate process.

The moot court was assembled in the large conference room of Joe's old firm of Parker, Thompson, Traughber & Darling. Scott Winters, one of the former federal prosecutors, was a member of the firm's appellate department.

The first time through the practice argument, the panel of lawyers simply let Peter run through his fifteen-minute prepared argument. No one believed that the Court of Appeals would ever let him go for fifteen uninterrupted minutes, but they wanted to hear the flow of Peter's overall argument. A brief critique followed. Peter sat and took notes, jotting down the essence of their critiques for future preparations. Then he stood up to start again. This time the fake judges would be shooting with live ammo.

"May it please the Court," Peter began. "My name is Peter Barron, I represent the plaintiff—"

"Peter, let me stop you," Dan Henderson said. "In the Court of Appeals you are the respondent-cross-appellant, not the plaintiff. The terms have changed. This is an appeal. But, the term 'respondent-cross-appellant' is a mouthful. I would suggest that you simply say that you represent Gwen and Casey Landis. OK? Let's reset the timer and start over."

"May it please the Court," Peter began again. "My name is Peter Barron and I represent Gwen and Casey Landis in these cross-appeals now before the court. I intend to address two basic points today. First, the district court correctly concluded that the doctrine of absolute immunity does not apply to unconstitutional searches carried out prior to the formal filing of child abuse charges. Second—"

"Counsel," "Judge" Henderson said, "before you go to your second point, how can you reconcile your position with this Court's holding in *Meyers v. Contra Costa County Department of Social Services?*"

Peter was ready for that most obvious question. "Your Honor, that case held that actions of social service workers taken after charges are filed are protected by the doctrine of absolute immunity. This case involves an unconstitutional search prior to the filing of charges."

"Counsel, don't you read *Meyers* a little too narrowly? Doesn't it stand for the broader principle that any action by a social worker that is connected to a child abuse charge is fully protected?"

It was a tougher question, but Peter still felt prepared. "Your Honor, if that was the holding of *Meyers,* it would be tantamount to a rule that allowed social workers to do whatever they wanted without any regard to the Constitution of the United States. They could claim that any of their actions were protected by the doctrine of immunity. They could never be sued." Peter thought it was a great answer.

"What is wrong with such a rule?" "Judge" Joe Lambert asked. "Aren't social workers protected because of their association with the judicial process? We give them basically the same protection we give to judges, right? Aren't judges protected for virtually everything they do? Judges can only be sued if they act in some capacity other than in their role as a judge before they can be sued. Why shouldn't we adopt a rule that says that social workers can only be sued if they are acting in a capacity totally outside of their jurisdiction as social workers?"

"Wait a minute," Peter said stepping out of the role of the "moot court." "Can we stop the timer? That is a very difficult question. Willet has never raised that argument in her briefs. Do you guys think that the judges might actually ask me something like that?"

"Absolutely," two or three voices said at once.

"OK," Peter said. "You guys are the experts. How do I answer that question?"

"The way I would answer it," Dan Henderson said, "is to point out there is no such thing as social worker immunity. The doctrine is called 'quasi-judicial immunity.' There is no immunity until the social worker steps into the arena where the judges theoretically are supervising their conduct. When social workers are acting outside a judge's supervision, then they should possess no special protection."

"Good answer. Good answer," Joe called out, mocking the typical contestant on *Family Feud.*

"That is a good answer," Peter said taking notes. "OK, let's get going again. . . . "

And so it went for two solid hours. Peter had good answers for most of the questions. But every fifteen or twenty minutes, they would stump him again. When that happened, they stopped and worked together to find an answer that the group agreed was most likely to appease a panel of federal appeals court judges.

Peter had not been wildly excited about the moot court when Joe had first suggested it. After going through the exercise, he realized how invaluable the time had been. He didn't think it was possible for the real judges to ask him a question in the fifteen minutes allotted for argument that this creative team of young lawyers hadn't already thrown at him in their two-hour practice session.

⌒

Peter walked in the front door of his home and threw his jacket on a chair. He had eaten a meal from the Wendy's drive-through once again. It was 11:15. He had spent a four-hour session in his office re-reading all the briefs and many of the cases which were cited by both sides. He vowed the judges would not detect any lack of preparation or appellate experience in his presentation. The argument was two days. He would be driving over with Gwen and her parents the next day. They had booked three rooms at the Holiday Inn Crown Plaza, across the street from the U.S. Courthouse in Seattle. Casey would be staying with the Roberts.

Peter flopped down on the couch exhausted. He intended to sleep until at least nine to try and get at least one good night's sleep before the argument. He noticed the two books on divorce Pastor Lind had given him sitting on the end table. He had read them both, but still could reach no conclusion other than the view he had always believed.

"I wish I had given myself a different deadline for Gwen," he said to himself. "There's just too much to think about." He picked up one of the books and started skimming it again. It just didn't seem

356 ~ ANONYMOUS TIP

what his spirit needed. He threw it down on the coffee table. Tired of the confusion, tired of wrestling with God, and just plain tired. He got up, walked into his bedroom, retrieved his Bible from his bedside table and returned and flopped down on the couch. He kicked off his loafers and bunched up a couple of pillows under his head. Opening the Bible to the book of Hebrews, he continued his regular pattern of reading. The third chapter for the evening was Hebrews 11—the heroes of faith. *Lord,* he said silently, *help me to learn how to be a man of faith relative to Gwen. Use this passage tonight in my life.*

Nothing in the chapter seemed to particularly stand out until he got to verse 17. That verse, and the two just after it, seemed to jump off the page to speak to his heart.

"By faith Abraham, when God tested him, offered Isaac as a sacrifice. He who had received the promises was about to sacrifice his one and only son, even though God had said to him, "It is through Isaac that your offspring will be reckoned." Abraham reasoned that God could raise the dead, and figuratively speaking, he did receive Isaac back from death."

He remembered his conversation with Pastor Lind, comparing his situation with Gwen to Abraham and Isaac. He laid the Bible down on his chest and just thought. Tears were welling up in his eyes, but they did not spill over.

"I don't have any choice," he said aloud choking back the tears. "I'll have to break it off."

He tumbled off the couch onto his knees.

"God, this is the hardest prayer I've ever prayed. I don't want to sacrifice Gwen. I wanted to find a way around your Word. But I know that kind of thinking is wrong. God, I love her and I don't understand. But God, I want to love you and obey you more than anything. I can't love her anymore than Abraham loved Isaac. What I have to do is far less dramatic than the test you gave to Abraham, but it is harder than anything I've ever had to do, and I need your strength. I need your comfort. And when I tell Gwen, she's going to need your comfort. I don't know if you are ever going to give her back to me, like you gave Isaac back to Abraham, but I am going to obey you anyway. Please help me, God. Please help me."

He buried his face in the couch for a long time. Finally, when he got up, leaving a tear-dampened cushion, he resolved that he would tell Gwen after they were back from Seattle and away from her parents.

～

A grey, low-overcast morning greeted Peter as he looked out his twelfth story hotel window just before sunrise on Wednesday morning. The trip over had been uneventful, except he felt June and Stan asked a stream of questions that seemed more like an interview of a potential son-in-law than questions posed to a lawyer. He tried not to think about that subject too much and focused on the argument as much as possible.

He decided to run through the streets of Seattle for a half-hour or so to clear the mental cobwebs.

The foursome had planned to meet for breakfast at 7:30 in the hotel restaurant. He had more than enough time to run, shower, and review his final notes one last time before then. He only wished that his sleep had been adequate the night before. The anticipation of the case and the dread of telling Gwen had made sleep difficult. He guessed he had only gotten four hours.

The skyscrapers in Seattle were four, five, even six times taller than the tallest buildings in downtown Spokane. Peter felt out of his league as he ran through the core business district. But then he remembered that he had faced Gail Willet on multiple occasions, and it would be her, and not these buildings, he would be confronting in a couple of hours.

The absurdity of what he was about to do gripped him as he ran past the U.S. Courthouse, just to the west of the hotel. He had spent countless hours working on this case, and the court would give him but fifteen minutes to tell them why they should rule in his favor. The system seemed so crazy.

After his shower, Peter put on the same blue pin-striped suit and yellow tie he had worn the day he first met Gwen. He walked out of his room, punched the elevator button, and waited. The door opened revealing Gail Willet, Matt Bartholomew, Donna Corliss, and Rita Coballo all looking terribly uncomfortable as Peter entered the elevator.

"Good morning, everyone," Peter said politely.

"Morning," Bartholomew said. The women all stared silently at the lights of the passing floors as they descended.

Peter stepped aside to let the women get out first. Coballo stifled her thought to castigate Peter for his sexist manners. They were obviously heading for the restaurant as well.

Bartholomew said something to the hostess and they seated the group on the other side of the restaurant from Gwen and her parents who were already seated waiting for Peter.

"You're looking dapper this morning," June Mansfield said as Peter approached the table.

"Nice suit," Stan said.

"Brings back memories," Gwen said smiling broadly. "My legal fortunes sure have changed since I first saw you in that suit."

"Wow," Peter said. "I hope the judges like it just as much. Unfortunately, I'm afraid they're going to pay more attention to what I say."

"Are you nervous?" Stan asked.

"A little," Peter said. It was a huge understatement.

"I called Lynn to check on Casey a few minutes ago. They have called the church prayer chain to pray for you this morning," Gwen said.

"That's a real good idea. I'm glad Lynn thought of it," Peter replied.

The foursome ordered breakfast and chatted casually. Peter finished first, signed the bill to his room, and returned to his room to get his litigation briefcase. He returned five minutes later just as Gwen finished her last cup of coffee.

Peter glanced at his watch as they walked across the street. 8:10. The clerk's office would post the assignment of the three-member panel for the cases in five minutes. Peter was anxious to get there as soon as possible. But he had no idea what he would do once he found the answer.

As they turned the corner, Gwen suddenly gasped. "Oh no, Peter, look!" she said, pointing.

The car was unmistakable with its dents and rusted paint spots. It was Gordon Landis turning into a parking garage on the opposite corner, to the south of the hotel.

"What is he doing here?" Stan asked.

"Unfortunately, these hearings are open to the public," Peter answered. "For some reason, Gordon has been able to find out every time we have had a hearing in this case. He has been to every one. I guess he just calls the clerk's office regularly."

"I don't want to talk with him," Gwen said angrily.

"Join the club," Peter replied. "But I don't think we'll have to worry. There are federal marshals all over this building."

They rode the elevator silently to the fourth floor. Peter located an attorney's conference room, settled Gwen and her parents, and headed for the clerk's office. It was already 8:20.

A bulletin board just to the right of the main entrance to the clerk's office contained the schedule and listing of the judges. *Landis v. Corliss, et. al,* was the first case of the day for Judges LaSalle, Thorpe, and Boyle. Peter reached into his right jacket pocket for a folded three-page document. It was a one paragraph dossier on each of the judges of the Ninth Circuit which Joe had prepared for him earlier in the week.

Robert LaSalle was a Bush appointee who had been on the appellate bench for four years. He had been a corporate lawyer with a large Seattle firm for over twenty years. He had been an active Republican fund raiser during his years of corporate law practice and was rewarded for his efforts with a seat on the appellate bench. He had a reputation as a careful judge. "Procedurally conservative, without an apparent undergirding judicial philosophy," was Joe's quick summary.

Deborah Thorpe was another Bush appointee. She had been elevated to the federal appeals court in 1992, after ten years as a juvenile judge in Seattle. Joe correctly guessed that Gail Willet had probably appeared before her countless times in that capacity. "Dangerous choice," Joe had written after her name.

Winston Boyle was the acting chief judge for the panel. He was a Carter appointee who had been a senior lawyer for the United States Department of Health, Education, and Welfare before his appointment. He was a philosophical liberal, according to Joe's analysis. "His liberalism could cause him to go either way," Joe concluded.

Peter went into the clerk's office and reported his presence to a deputy clerk. "Be in courtroom two at 8:45," she directed.

Peter didn't like the selections. As he paced down the hall, he quickly prayed, *Lord, You are sovereign. These are the judges You have allowed to be chosen. I pray that I would present arguments that would best appeal to them. And may you guide their decisions. Amen.*

Peter had not mentioned Joe's analysis to Gwen or her parents. He decided to keep the information to himself.

"We're first up," Peter said as he entered the conference room.

"Is that good or bad?" Gwen asked.

"It probably doesn't make any difference. The only thing is that I have no opportunity to see any of these judges in action. We have LaSalle, Thorpe, and Boyle. The only one I saw when I came over here last month was LaSalle. Thorpe and Boyle weren't on any of the panels on that particular occasion, but they sure are today."

"What do you know about the judges?" Stan asked.

"Nothing very definite. Just some lawyer talk, guesses, and rumors. None of them were on the panel that decided the *Meyers* case. That is probably good news."

"Peter, can we pray before we go in?" Gwen asked. "I mean, this is a government building and everything."

"They can't stop us from praying in here—nor in there. You three can pray all you want—silently, of course, while I'm arguing."

The foursome joined hands and Peter led them in prayer.

The hour had come. They opened the door and walked into the courtroom.

The room was large, not quite as large as the federal district courtroom in Spokane, but much more elaborate. There were marble walls, a good deal of oak, and a massive elaborate bench with three black leather chairs. In front of each chair was a stack of briefs on the bench. Each judge's law clerks had placed the briefs in the order that the six cases would be called that morning. In addition to the briefs filed by each party, each judge had a memorandum written by the judge's law clerk giving his or her assessment and analysis of the case from a supposedly neutral perspective. A name plate was visible just in front of each stack of briefs. LaSalle was on the left, from the perspective of a lawyer facing the bench, Boyle as acting chief judge was in the middle, and Thorpe was on the right.

Since their case was first, Peter proceeded immediately inside the bar and began to organize the contents of his briefcase on the counsel table. Willet and Bartholomew entered the courtroom and began the same process before he was done. Gwen and her parents waited on the right hand side of the court room on the third row of benches behind the bar. When Corliss and Coballo entered, they sat in the first row on the left as they had been directed by Willet. There were about twenty other people in the courtroom, lawyers and clients for the five other cases which would be called for argument that morning.

The law clerks entered and took seats on the right hand side of the court room under a row of high windows. A moment later, Peter glanced back at Gwen, only to see Gordon Landis walking quickly into the room, slipping into the last bench on the left-hand side.

A small buzzer sounded by the bailiff's chair. "All rise!" he called out. As the three judges filed in and stood behind their chairs, he continued his cry, "Hear ye, hear ye. The United States Court of Appeals for the Ninth Circuit is now in session. All having business before this honorable court now draw near."

"Good morning," Judge Boyle said to the courtroom at large. A half-dozen lawyers responded with a chorus of good mornings.

"The first case is *Landis against Corliss and others*. Is counsel ready?"

"Yes, Your Honor," came the chorus.

"Well, Ms. Willet, you filed the initial appeal. You can go first. I understand you wish to reserve two minutes for rebuttal."

"That's correct, Your Honor," Willet said, shuffling her notes for the last time on the lectern.

"May it please the court," Willet began smiling. "Mr. Bartholomew and I represent the appellants and cross-respondents in this case. It is our position that each of the major issues in this case can be decided by reliance upon a seminal authoritative case. The decision of *Meyers versus Contra Costa County* is the precedent coming from this court which demands that the portion of the lawsuit concerning the search of the Landis home be dismissed. And the questions arising from the portion of this suit dealing with the alleged perjury and document tampering are conclusively answered by the decision of the United States Supreme Court in *Briscoe versus LaHue.*"

"Alleged perjury and document tampering?" Judge Boyle asked. "The record looks like those allegations were pretty well proven by the district judge himself."

"Your Honor, I agree that the evidence was strong relative to the so-called document tampering. But there were only allegations that my clients had committed perjury on the witness stand. We have not had an opportunity to respond to either of these areas of factual inquiry. But even the district court judge who had personally discovered the problems with the documents felt compelled to conclude that the law required him to dismiss that portion of the lawsuit on the authority of *Briscoe versus LaHue*"

"Ms. Willet," Judge Thorpe began, "can you explain to me why these CPS workers didn't go to the juvenile judge to get a court order before running off and doing this search? Surely a juvenile judge would have granted the order on the basis of her non-cooperation alone."

"I am sure that the judge would have done so, Your Honor," Willet said, smiling. She knew that Thorpe had probably signed hundreds of such orders during her stint in the juvenile court in Seattle. "But Mr. Barron would still be in this court arguing that such an order was unconstitutional, because he believes that probable cause of wrong doing is necessary to obtain a court order in a case investigating child abuse. Mr. Barron's position is that child abuse can only be investigated under the rules governing police investigation of crimes. That is the essence of what is wrong with his position and the decision of the district court. Child abuse investigations are not criminal investigations. Child abuse investigations are not merely conducted to find out who did what to whom; they are court-supervised inquiries designed, like juvenile courts themselves, for the ongoing protection of children."

Smooth, very smooth, Peter thought.

"Counsel, how does a juvenile court have any practical ability to supervise a search which is made before anything is filed in the court?" Boyle asked.

"Your Honor, as Judge Thorpe can tell you from her extensive experience on the juvenile bench, juvenile judges regularly interact with social workers inside and outside the courtroom. They have extensive discussions which are predicated on a spirit of teamwork with the goal of protecting children. It is settled law that juvenile courts are not bound by all of the rules employed in adult trial courts."

"But even juvenile courts take an oath to support the Constitution, Counsel," Judge Boyle said. "And from the facts in this case, it looks like your system of alleged judicial supervision leaves a lot of room for skull-duggery."

It looks like I've got Boyle on my side, Peter thought.

"No system is perfect, Your Honor. But it is important to remember that the principles which govern this case are principles of law, not mere factual determinations. And the principles of law on which we rely are as old as the American judicial system itself. Persons cloaked with judicial or quasi-judicial authority are immune from civil lawsuits for actions taken in their official capacity. That is the overriding principle which governs both of the issues in this lawsuit."

Willet looked down and paused for a moment. "I see that the light indicates my opening time is up. I reserve my remaining time, Your Honors."

She was polished and everyone in the courtroom, especially Gail Willet, recognized that fact.

Peter stood and walked to the lectern. Before he had settled his papers, Judge Thorpe jumped in.

"Counsel, are you seriously contending that this court can reverse the decision of the Supreme Court in *Briscoe versus LaHue?* Isn't that what your claims for perjury and document tampering are asking us to do?"

"Your Honor, I am asking this court to distinguish *Briscoe*. Never before in any of the cases cited has there been proof of perjury or document tampering as convincing as we present to this court. In the *Briscoe* case itself, there were mere allegations that a police officer had lied. We are not suggesting that you overturn *Briscoe*. Rather we simply ask this court to distinguish *Briscoe* when the plaintiff has more than a mere allegation of official wrongdoing."

"If we allow such a suit in this case," Thorpe continued, "what is to prevent other cases from being filed, and then there are motions for discovery, and depositions, and interrogatories and the like. The purpose of the rule, according to the Supreme Court, is to protect witnesses from having to go through lawsuits. Doesn't your proposed exception to *Briscoe* defeat the underlying purpose of the Supreme Court's ruling?"

"Your Honor, my understanding of the Supreme Court's purpose is different. The way I read *Briscoe* is to protect witnesses from allegations which may or may not be true. Here we have proven allegations. It seems that these facts fairly cry out for an exception to the *Briscoe* rule."

"Counsel," Judge Boyle interrupted. "I would like to change the focus for a question or two. I am more concerned about the other aspect of this lawsuit: the claim arising from the search of the Landis home and the strip-search of the little girl. Can you tell us how this case differs from this court's opinion in *Meyers?*"

It was a softball question the judge asked to get Peter off a more difficult issue and on to an issue he had a better chance of winning.

"Yes, Your Honor. The central distinction between *Meyers* and this case is this: *Meyers* said that actions taken by social workers after they come into court and place themselves under the authority of the juvenile judge are completely protected under the doctrine of quasi-judicial immunity. The flip-side of that ruling is that when social workers take unconstitutional action prior to submitting themselves to judicial supervision, they are not entitled to any claim of quasi-judicial immunity."

"Good answer," Bartholomew whispered in Willet's ear. "You need to counter that in rebuttal." Willet nodded and scribbled.

"Is it settled law that searches in the child abuse context require a search warrant?" Judge Thorpe asked.

"Yes, Your Honor, that principle of law has been settled for two hundred years. All government officials need search warrants to conduct non-consensual investigations in a person's private home. Recent efforts to find an exception to the Constitution for social workers conducting child abuse investigations have generally not been successful."

"What about the *Wyman* case from the Supreme Court?" Thorpe shot back.

"Your Honor, that case was not about a child abuse investigation. That case merely held that when the government gives you its money, it has the power to come into your home to check on its investment. The court was careful to say that there was nothing in that home visit that was a search or equated with a search. In this case, it is beyond any doubt that what was done was a search for activity of alleged child abuse that resulted in charges being filed against my client. *Wyman* is simply inapplicable under this fact pattern."

The red light was glowing when Peter finished the last answer.

"My time is up. Thank you."

Willet walked briskly back to the lectern. Boyle was waiting.

"Counsel, I want to ask you one question before you begin. Under your reading of *Meyers*, aren't all actions by social workers immune from suit? Don't you turn social workers into full-time judges by your reasoning? Aren't they more like police officers than judges? We don't give police officers that kind of blanket immunity."

"That's several questions, Your Honor," Willet began. Noticing a flash of anger on Boyle's face, "But they are all clearly asking a single point. Your Honor's concern is well-placed. However, my argument is slightly different from the hypothetical one you have proposed. I am not arguing everything that a social worker does is immune from suit. Rather, we contend that whatever activity that a social worker conducts which is for the ultimate purpose of the judicial system, the rule of quasi-judicial immunity applies."

"Doesn't that mean that 100% of all social worker investigations are immune from suit, and doesn't that mean they can never be sued for not having a warrant, no matter how many times the courts rule that warrants are required?"

"Judges are immune from suit for 100% of their rulings, Your Honor. The rule of judicial immunity arises from the status of their position. Social workers should be treated like judges, nothing more, nothing less."

"Well, counsel, it looks like your time has expired," Boyle said, looking at his panel of lights.

"I would like to say to both counsel. This case has been briefed and argued at the highest level. We commend you all."

Peter gathered up his papers, stuffed them in his briefcase, and motioned for Gwen and her parents to follow him.

"Let's go back to the conference room," he whispered once they were out in the hall.

They walked silently down the corridor. Gordon Landis exited the courtroom unnoticed just as they slipped inside the conference room door.

"I thought you were great, Peter Barron," Gwen gushed.

"Yes, good job," Stan added. "What do you think?"

"It's impossible to know for sure. But if outward appearances mean anything, we've got Judge Boyle on our side. Judge Thorpe seems to clearly be on their side. She used to be a juvenile judge here in Seattle, and Willet appears to know her."

"Is that fair?" Gwen asked.

"It doesn't violate any court rules or anything. If they had been law partners or something, that would be different. But she is not disqualified just because Willet appeared in her court a number of times."

"What about the third judge?" Stan asked.

"Yes . . . Judge LaSalle. Didn't ask a single question. Didn't make a single comment. He's the swing vote. And unfortunately, he didn't give us a clue as to the way he was leaning. Perhaps he was genuinely undecided and simply wanted to hear the arguments."

"When will we get a decision?" Gwen asked.

"It won't be anything like Judge Stokes, I guarantee you. Sometime between one and six months from now. The Ninth Circuit is a little faster than most appeals courts, or so Joe, my associate, and his appellate buddy experts tell me."

"Well, we'll just have to wait," June said. "As long as Gwen has Casey, I guess that's all right. I think we should go back to the hotel and check out then we can go out for a nice lunch down overlooking the Sound before we drive back. How does that sound?"

"Great," Peter said.

When they exited the building, Gordon Landis appeared from nowhere.

"Here's the happy family," he said sarcastically. "Only one problem: they're forgetting the child's father."

"Gordon you—" Gwen said.

"Gwen, let me handle this," Stan interrupted, putting his hand on her arm. "Gordon, you have been a nuisance to my daughter once too many times. We have always had a cordial relationship until now, despite the divorce, but you are starting to go over a line that is going to destroy all that."

"Well, it is *his* fault," Gordon said pointing at Peter. "He's wormed his way into Gwen's life. He's more than a lawyer. They're all scumbags. But he's worse. He's taking advantage of my family and making moves on my wife."

Peter's face turned bright red.

"Peter, don't do anything rash," Stan said. "Why don't you go on back to the hotel separately. I think I can work this out with Gordon. June and Gwen, you wait inside the door of the courthouse here. Let me talk with Gordon, and let me see if I can get some ground rules worked out that will avoid these confrontations."

Gordon liked the fact that Peter was being sent away. But he couldn't resist one more taunt as Peter walked away. "Go away, scumbag. This is just a family affair, scumbag."

"Shut up," Stan growled in a low voice.

After twenty minutes of shuttle diplomacy, Stan thought he had the matter worked out between Gwen and Gordon. Gordon would pick Casey up for visits at their house from now on. And he agreed to call the Mansfields first if he had any questions or concerns. Stan always had a special ability to deal with his former son-in-law.

As they were walking away, Gordon stopped. "One more thing. I want an understanding with you, Gwen, that Mr. Lawyer dude won't be spending the night in the home with my daughter."

"You better watch—" Stan said.

"Dad, let me answer this one," Gwen interjected. "Gordon, Peter and I have no romantic relationship at this point. We may or may not ever have one. But that is none of your business. In any event, I can guarantee you that if we have such a relationship, we will follow the highest moral standards. You will never have to worry that Peter Barron will ever spend the night at my house. And if you ever suggest anything like that again, I will never speak to you about anything—ever."

Gordon started to speak. Stan put his hand on Gordon's shoulder. "That's enough, Gordon. I've been very patient with you, but that's enough. I think you should go."

June Mansfield could stand it no more. "I, for one, would love to have Peter Barron as a son-in-law. He would be a prince compared to you."

"That's *enough*, June," Stan said.

Gordon walked away. June Mansfield's words burned in his ears. He got in his car, paid the parking lot attendant, and entered the on ramp to Interstate 5 which was only two blocks away. A mile later, he took the exit for Interstate 90 headed east back toward Spokane.

"Peter Barron as a son-in-law. Peter Barron as a son-in-law." June's words continued to ring in his head. As he crossed the floating bridge over Lake Washington, he turned the radio on to try to drown the words out of his mind. June's voice seemed louder and louder. He tried to scream them away, but the words "Peter Barron as a son-in-law" kept on torturing his mind.

As he got to the last area of development before heading over Snoqualmie Pass, he decided that the only way to get the words out of his head was to drown them. He exited the freeway at Issaquah and found a tavern that was just opening.

He sat down at a booth and ordered a pitcher of beer. In just a few minutes, he started to feel better, but the words were still there. Two more pitchers and forty-five minutes later, he felt fine. He got up, staggered to the door.

The bartender looked the other way. He didn't want any trouble with someone that intent on getting drunk before lunch.

Gordon weaved slightly as he made his way back onto the freeway heading east. The majestic Cascade mountains loomed directly in front of him. But Interstate 90 was a four-lane superhighway and he felt invincible as he worked his way up the early ascents of Snoqualmie Pass.

The effects of the alcohol were becoming more pronounced by the minute. He swerved slightly as he passed the first of the three ski areas at Snoqualmie Summit. His head began to spin as he passed the second. The road was slightly wet, but only from occasional drizzle dropping from the grey October clouds. It would be at least a month before any snow would fall at this elevation.

As he began the first two miles of the gentle descent, he rolled down his window to try to clear his head. For a moment or two it helped, but his head began to swim even more rapidly. He suddenly saw a semi proceeding slowly in his lane—the right lane—about two hundred yards in front of him. The trucker was apparently gearing down for the steeper part of the descent just ahead. Gordon was gaining ground on him much too quickly.

Gordon turned the steering wheel sharply to go around the truck. He crossed completely over the left lane, his left tires veering slightly off the pavement. Gordon tried to brake, but his foot could not find the pedal. He swung sharply, much too sharply, back to the right just as the road took a gentle left-hand curve. Gordon's 1987 Toyota went off the right-hand side of the road, rolled over once on the embankment, and plunged into the chilly October waters of Lake Snoqualmie. He passed out as his car rolled and never regained consciousness.

23

⁓

The foursome didn't leave Seattle until nearly three o'clock. It was a six hour drive back to Spokane, and they would need to stop for dinner somewhere along the way.

They passed over Snoqualmie Pass just before four o'clock. All signs of Gordon's wreck had been removed ninety minutes earlier. They made good time over the mountains past the old mining town of Cle Elum, on to Ellensburg, and around seven o'clock pulled into Moses Lake for dinner.

Gwen called Lynn Roberts from a pay phone in the lobby of the Kentucky Fried Chicken franchise. Lynn convinced Gwen to leave Casey with her for the night, since she couldn't possibly pick Casey up and get her home before ten-thirty or eleven.

After dinner, Stan and June both napped in the darkness as Peter's Explorer rolled eastward on I-90 past Ritzville.

"Peter, I think my parents are asleep," Gwen said. "Can we talk about us for a minute? It's only three days 'til the end of October."

"Yes, I know," Peter said reluctantly. Dropping his voice almost to a whisper, he said, "Gwen, can I talk to you alone when we get to your house? I don't want to take any chance that what I have to say will be overheard. I just want to tell you—no one else, OK?"

"I guess," Gwen answered. "I'll just be glad when the uncertainty is over."

"I think you'll have an answer real soon," Peter said forcing himself to smile.

Gwen leaned over and flipped on the radio. In fifteen minutes, she was dozing herself.

Peter pulled up in front of the Mansfield's house a few minutes after ten. He and Gwen drove in silence toward her house just seven or eight minutes away. Peter thought he would be sick to his stomach. He realized that this might be the last time he ever spent alone with Gwen—at least outside his office. Gwen could tell that he was upset.

They turned off 29th Avenue and headed down Janelle Court. Peter thought he saw something down the street near Gwen's house. He flipped his lights on bright.

"Gwen, there's a police car in front of your house."

"Oh no. What now? You don't think something is wrong with Casey, do you?"

"I doubt it. Aaron and Lynn know my car phone number, and we have been in range for an hour-and-a-half."

Peter pulled up behind the police car. "Let me talk with him," Peter said.

"Fine with me," Gwen said nervously.

Peter got out of the car, walked to the driver's side of the car and tapped on the officer's window.

"Yeah?" the officer said.

"Officer, I'm Peter Barron. I'm an attorney for Gwen Landis who lives here. We are just coming back from a federal court hearing in Seattle today. Can I ask why you are here?"

"We're here to notify Mrs. Landis about a traffic fatality."

"What?" Peter said incredulously. "Who?"

"I'm supposed to tell her," the officer replied.

"It's not her daughter, is it? She's spending the night at a friend's out in the valley."

"It's not her daughter. Why don't you just bring Mrs. Landis inside and I'll tell the two of you together."

Peter walked back to the car, with a shocked look on his face.

"Gwen, you'd better come inside. Someone's had an accident. He won't tell me who it is, but it's not Casey."

Gwen jumped out of her seat, grabbed Peter's arm, and headed for the front door.

"Please, come in," Peter said to the officer.

Peter and Gwen sat together on the couch. She was still clutching Peter's arm.

The officer sat on the closest chair.

"Ma'am, it is my sad duty to inform you that your husband has been killed in a car accident," the officer said.

"My husband? I'm not married."

"Oh no, I hope I haven't got the wrong address. Is your name Gwen Landis?"

"Yes."

"Who is Gordon Landis?" the officer asked.

The tears began to flow down Gwen's cheeks. "Gordon? Dead?"

"Gordon is her ex-husband, Officer," Peter said softly. "They've been divorced for a couple of years."

"Oh, I'm sorry," the officer said. "His car was still registered to this address."

"That's quite all right," Peter said in a calm voice. "She needed to know. They have a child, a little girl. She'll need to know about her father."

"Oh, I see," the officer said.

"Do you know what happened?" Peter asked. Gwen had buried her head in Peter's shoulder and was sobbing softly.

"His car left the highway on Snoqualmie Pass around noon. It rolled over and went into the lake. He was underwater for way too long before anyone could get to him."

"What happened? Do you know why he went off the highway in the first place?"

"The State Police are investigating. But they don't know for sure."

"Any clues at all? Was there any sign of drunk driving?"

"Well, there were no beer cans or anything like that in the car. He was underwater long enough that we are going to have to do an autopsy before we will know anything about alcohol. But there was one strange thing. There were no signs of braking at all. The investigators suspect brake failure. He didn't leave a single mark trying to stop before plunging off the road."

"Peter, stop," Gwen pleaded. "I don't want to hear anymore."

"I'm sorry, Gwen," Peter said putting his arm around her.

"Well, again, I'm very sorry, ma'am. Please let the Department know if we can do anything."

"Thank you, officer," Peter said as Gwen continued to cry quietly in his embrace.

The officer got up, let himself out the door, and closed it softly behind him. After about five or six minutes of silence, Gwen said, "We've got to call my parents. And his mother."

"I'll call your parents," Peter replied. "Who should contact his mother?"

"I think my mom would be best," she answered. "They always got along."

"OK," Peter replied. "Why don't you lean back on the couch while I go call."

Five minutes later, Peter held Gwen tightly as they walked back to his car. It was decided that she would spend the night at her parents' house. They would tell Casey in the morning.

Stan smiled weakly at Peter as he opened the door wide enough to let his daughter and Peter in together.

June appeared and immediately embraced her daughter. They were both crying quietly. Despite all that happened, Gordon was still Casey's father.

"I think we can handle it from here, Peter," Stan said softly. "Thanks again."

～

An hour later, Gwen laid down on the bed that had been hers as a child. She had cried enough, but was still in shock. Her mind was swirling. *How would Casey react? What should she say?* And with increasing frequency, the thought raced into her mind, *What does this mean for me and Peter?* The thought gave her hope for their relationship, but as soon as she went down that mental path, she felt guilty. As if Gordon had died because she wanted to be free from the dilemma arising from her divorce.

As she rolled the scenario with Peter over in her head one more time, a new, foreign thought suddenly entered her mind. *Peter should feel guilty, too,"* the thought said. *After all, it was his dilemma. He wanted to solve it more than you.*

Gwen suddenly remembered the time that Peter had told her that "I have even found myself wishing that Gordon would die from a mysterious ailment or something." "Or something! Gordon would die—or something!"

Her mind swirled in the shock and confusion. Another memory jumped into her thoughts. "Hey, he made it personal tonight," Peter said the night of their physical confrontation. "It's for me as well at this point," she remembered Peter saying. And later the same night, she had asked Peter how she was going to solve her problem with Gordon. "I don't know for sure. But this guy is really asking for it," had been Peter's reply.

The thoughts seemed to gang up on her. And the seeds being successfully planted, her mind raced on searching for other things that seemed to fit in.

Peter left them all alone for thirty minutes or so after the hearing that morning. Gordon had called him a scumbag repeatedly. They had seen his car go into the parking garage. Peter would know where it was.

And then tonight on the way home, Peter wouldn't talk to her about the situation even when her parents were asleep. He wanted to be alone. "I think you'll have an answer real soon," Peter had said. And he had smiled. Not a reassuring smile as if he had been released by God to marry her. A sick sort of smile. A smile she couldn't quite understand.

And then there were all of the questions Peter asked the police officer about the details of Gordon's death. No brakes. *No brakes.* No brakes. Why was he so interested in the details? Why was he so upset in the latter course of the evening?

Over and over and over she went through it all. Again and again she rejected the conclusion the path of thought led her to. Her thoughts swirled. The seeds were sown. Confusion, then doubt, then despair. Peter was somehow responsible for Gordon's accident. He had done something to his car which caused him to crash. Maybe the brakes. Maybe something else.

The thoughts shocked her even more than Gordon's death. But try as she might, she couldn't shake them. Finally, around two-thirty, she passed out from pure exhaustion.

Peter called the Mansfields around noon the next day. He especially wanted to hear how Casey was doing. She was crying and clearly upset, but also she seemed to accept the news. Death was not quite real to her.

After work, Peter bought a flower arrangement. He intended to deliver it in person and check on Gwen in the process. He arrived around five-thirty. She had only been home for about thirty minutes. She and Casey were going to spend the night with her parents. Gwen had come home just to gather a few things and then return.

She answered the door. The color drained from her face when she saw that it was Peter.

"Peter? What are you doing here?"

"I just thought I would bring you some flowers. I know that this is a very sad day for you. I know you are mourning and I am praying for all of you."

"Yeah, right," Gwen said bitterly.

"Excuse me?"

"Oh, never mind," Gwen said more confused than angry.

"Gwen, is something else bothering you? Did I offend you by bringing flowers? I'm really sorry if I've done something wrong."

"I don't know. I don't think I want to talk about it. Especially not with you."

"Gwen, you've got to help me. I know Gordon's death has taken you by surprise. It has taken me by surprise. I feel very sad. He was a human being who is now lost for eternity. I know I don't feel what you feel, but I am upset—for your sake, and especially Casey's sake as well. Can you please tell me what's going on?"

"You are going to think I'm crazy or something. But I keep thinking—oh, never mind. Just go away. Please!"

"I'll go if you really want me to. But frankly, you've got me scared. It sounds like something has really gone wrong. Gwen, I want to know."

"Oh," she said sucking in her breath. "OK." She couldn't look him in the eye. She finally looked at the floor and began, "Peter, last night I remembered a whole lot of things you have said. You said you wished Gordon would die. You said that it was personal between the two of you. You said that he was asking for it. You said that I would have an answer soon. And you said a lot of other things."

"But Gwen, I couldn't wish Gordon dead. It doesn't work that way."

"I guess not. But yesterday, after he called you names, you were gone for a long time while we talked with Gordon. You saw him parking his car. And suddenly, suddenly, his car was in the lake and he had no brakes. It wasn't just a wish."

"Gwen, you are right about one thing: You are crazy! But, hey, don't worry about it. Grief can play tricks on us all. Please, Gwen, please take my word, I didn't do anything. Nothing. I was planning to tell you last night that I was going to set you free. I never got clearance from God to change my view and I was going to let you go—I was upset about that. But I didn't think I had a choice."

"A choice. That's an interesting word. Which choice is worse? Marrying a divorced woman? Or murder?"

"*Murder?!* Murder? You can't be serious."

"I can't prove it. And I am not going to say anything to anyone else. At least until we find out from the police some more details. But I can feel it inside of me that you were responsible. I don't know how. But I just know that you are somehow responsible."

"Gwen. Gwen!" Peter said burying his face in his hands. "Gwen? I can't believe this. It's not true. It's just not true."

"I'm sorry, Peter. But I have tried and tried to shake the thoughts but it makes so much sense to me. And the idea of you doing something like this absolutely astounds me. But my mind won't let me come to any other conclusion."

"Gwen, please be reasonable."

"Peter. I'm sorry. Please leave. Now."

∿

It was Peter's turn to spend a sleepless night. He stood on his deck and watched the moon rise over the lake. He played their conversation over in his head time after time. What could he have said differently? At times, tears would well up and stop. Other times they overflowed for a short season. But the sickness in his heart and soul was unrelenting.

He had to admit that she had remembered his words correctly. And oh, how careless his words had been. The passage in Matthew where Jesus warns believers that they will give an account for every idle word convicted Peter that his sin of careless speech had far greater consequences than he ever imagined. He blamed himself over and over for discussing a relationship with Gwen when his leading from the Lord told him he shouldn't. The phrase "if only I hadn't . . . " rolled over in his mind countless times.

He prayed and confessed. And later on he would pray and confess. And pray and plead. And pray and cry.

A thin, strange voice tried to tell his mind that he should be concerned about criminal charges. But he knew better. He had done absolutely nothing more than utter careless words, and no prosecutor would ever file anything against him.

The moon passed overhead. He began to shiver as he sat, statue-still on his deck, trying to solve the unsolvable problem. Gwen, his beloved Gwen. He couldn't believe that she was gone.

As the night wore on, his sorrow for his own carelessness was replaced with a growing sense of bitterness. How could she believe such a pack of nonsensical lies? After all that he had done for her? She just couldn't be serious. But he remembered her voice.

So cold. So final. "Peter. I'm sorry. Please! Leave! Now!"

What would he do with her case? Whatever happened at the Ninth Circuit, the case would not be over. Either they would be sent back for a trial, or else one side or the other should, and normally would, appeal the case to the United States Supreme Court. Maybe he could find a constitutional law specialist to take over the appeal while he stayed on the case in name only. That would allow him to save face but avoid any significant contact between Gwen and himself.

"The ungrateful little . . ." He choked back the thought. He still loved her. Loved completely. Loved her forever. But as the bitterness would sweep over him again, thoughts of being unable to trust her became more than he could bear. Even if this all gets straightened out, I don't know. If she thinks the worst of me under these circumstances, what would happen if I really made a mistake during married life?

Around two-thirty, he went inside and tried to force himself to sleep. But sleep never came.

The sun rose, but the depression that had settled in his heart was intractable. There was no joy in the morning for a heart that had failed to rest.

Peter could not face going to work. Nor could he face the idea of telling Sally that he wasn't coming in. Her radar was too good. She would sense that something was wrong.

He called the answering service before Sally arrived. They would tell her at eight-thirty that Peter was emotionally exhausted from the case in Seattle and was going to spend the day by himself away from his home.

He threw a change of clothes in the back of his Explorer and headed east on Interstate 90. Liberty Lake was the last exit in Washington and he quickly passed into Idaho. Seventy-two miles later, he crossed the Montana Border and quickly began to ascend Lookout Pass.

It was a beautiful, dry fall day, and the cool air was crisp and clean. Peter rolled down his window just an inch or two and drove on to St. Regis. There he left the interstate and worked his way up a two-lane highway to the Clark Fork River—a beautiful, raging, whitewater stream.

He came upon a roadside park abutting the river. He stopped the Explorer, got out, walked to the rocky river edge, and then sat down. He occasionally picked up a handful of small rocks and threw them into the white swirling water that passed before him. For over two hours he did nothing but sit and watch, and nurse the bitter wound in his heart.

It was after one when it first occurred to him that he might be hungry. He drove five miles further up the road and found a country cafe which was packed with loggers and other people who worked hard with their hands and bodies to make a living. Peter was not dressed that differently from the crowd in the cafe. He had on blue jeans and a light wool jacket over a plaid shirt. He wore tennis shoes, not boots. But regardless of his clothes, he was still a stranger. The social rule of the Montana countryside is to quickly greet a single stranger and then leave him to himself. It suited Peter fine.

After lunch, his emotional state had improved to the point that he thought he could fake his way through a call to Sally. But nothing much more taxing than that.

"Sally, Peter."

"Where are you, Peter?"

"I went for a drive this morning to relax and I just kinda ended up in Montana. I've been working a lot of extra hours lately and I feel I need to relax a little more. I'm going to skip tomorrow too. I'll see you on Monday, OK?"

"I guess, Peter. You're the boss. Did you hear about Gordon Landis?"

"Yeah, I heard. Sad, isn't it?"

"Sure is, how's Gwen?"

Peter knew he had to get out of this conversation fast. "I think she's OK, but she's understandably upset. Anything else?"

"Stan Mansfield called to tell you that the funeral will be on Saturday in Davenport. That's where Gordon's mother lives. At 10:00. The Methodist Church."

"Uh . . . OK. Thanks."

Peter drove on north to Flathead Lake. He walked for a couple of hours, aimlessly circling the massive lake's shore, staring at the imposing Rocky Mountains of Glacier National Park. After dark, he found a roadside diner with big servings of bad food. A small motel offered cable TV. He lay down, having removed only his shoes and settled on an old movie. He was fast asleep before the on-screen romance began.

~

Gwen was awakened by a ringing telephone at 9:30 Friday morning. She still had trouble sleeping. It was the Washington State Patrol from Issaquah.

"Mrs. Landis, where should the autopsy report be sent? I understand that you were divorced," the officer said.

"I guess you should send it to his mother in Davenport. I can go get the address for you. Can I ask what you found?"

"Sure, I guess so. The official cause of death was drowning. But we also found a blood alcohol rating of .23."

"What does that mean?"

"That means that he was more than twice the legal limit for drunk driving. We have ruled it an alcohol-related fatality."

"What about the brakes—I thought they were faulty or something?"

"No, there was a question about that initially. But everything on the car seemed mechanically OK. It was an old car, not in the greatest condition, but the brakes should have worked. He may have simply passed out from the alcohol and ran off the road."

Tears of shame and sorrow flowed down Gwen's cheeks as she gave the officer the address of Gordon's mother over the phone.

In about fifteen minutes, she gained her composure enough to call Peter's office.

"I'm sorry, Gwen. He's gone. I think he's someplace in Montana. Said he was exhausted from the appeal."

"Can I reach his car phone there?"

"I doubt it. You would have to know the specific roaming code for the cellular system in Montana, and I have no idea what part of the state he's in. In any event, most of Montana is probably not in range of any cell sites."

"Do you think he'll call in?"

"I don't know. You want to leave a message?"

"Yes, please. Tell him, it's urgent that I talk with him. Night or day, he is to call me."

"Oh my, is something wrong?"

"Sally, it's just too hard to explain. Just tell him to call, OK?"

"Sure, Gwen. And Gwen . . . "

"Yes?"

"I'm really sorry about Gordon."

"Me too. Thanks."

On Friday morning, Peter found a place to rent a canoe and went for a two hour glide across a small corner of Flathead Lake. As he paddled across the pristine lake, he decided that he had managed to live for thirty-one years without Gwen Landis, and that he had been prepared to give her up just two days ago. He should simply get on with his life.

He spent the night at a motel on Lookout Pass. A movie on TV helped him pass the time from dinner to sleep. He woke at six, drove the eighty-five miles back to Liberty Lake, ran into his house at eight, showered, put on a dark suit, grabbed some sunglasses, and headed west toward Davenport. He slipped into the last pew in the church just as the service began.

Gwen was sitting in the front row next to Gordon's mother. Casey was next to her. Peter could hear her crying softly. He had steeled his heart toward Gwen, but he desperately wanted to go and hold Casey and comfort her. Stan and June were on the other side of Casey.

There were only about fifty people in a church which would seat three hundred. It was a sad, hopeless funeral. When it was over, Gwen was occupied comforting Gordon's mother as Stan and June led Casey down the middle aisle.

Stan saw Peter, and waved very discreetly. "Gwen has been trying to find you," he whispered.

"I've been out of town. Needed to relax. Tell her I'm sorry I can't stay. I need to get back."

"But she really wants to see you," Stan countered.

"This is all hard for me, too. Tell her I'll be in my office on Monday. I really wish I could stay, but I've got to go."

～

Gwen was crushed when her father told her that Peter had come and gone. But on later reflection, it gave her some hope. At least he came. Her heart banked on that fact as Peter continued to roam and walk and do his best to use the majestic scenery of the Pacific Northwest to erase her from his heart.

24

Peter returned home on Sunday night after eleven. His answering machine was blinking incessantly. He walked over and hit the play button.

"Hi, Peter. It's Gwen. I need to talk with you right away." Five such messages. On the last two, she had added, "Peter, I'm really sorry." He had anticipated the messages, and had prepared himself to ignore them.

He walked into his living room and fell on the couch exhausted. The books Pastor Lind had given him about divorce were still on the coffee table. Peter laughed, a loud sarcastic laugh, and wished that the books were his so he could throw them against the wall. He swept them off the coffee table with his foot. He liked the feeling.

He practiced the phone call he anticipated in the morning once more in his head. He was ready.

Peter rode the elevator to his office at 8:35 Monday morning. Sally would be there with coffee ready. He would get back to practicing law with other worthy, fee-generating cases that he had neglected at least to some degree for several weeks.

"Good morning, Sally," Peter said with greater enthusiasm than normal. "Coffee smells great."

"Glad to see you back. Are you all rested?"

"You bet! Ready to get back to practicing law. That Landis case won't be bothering me for a few weeks at least. The Ninth Circuit's got it on their shoulders for a while."

Sally made panicky motions, pointing toward Peter's office. "She's waiting for you in there," Sally said in a whisper.

Peter's face turned bright red. "Gwen?" he whispered in reply.

Sally nodded.

Peter rolled his eyes, paused for an instant, steeled his resolve and walked in.

"Good morning, Peter," Gwen said a little too sweetly. She had obviously heard his comment. It was the only dig she would make in return.

"Hi, Gwen," Peter said, closing the door. "You're here bright and early. I didn't know you had an appointment this morning."

"Peter, please don't play games with me."

"Play games with you? All right, Miss Client, how can your lawyer be of assistance to you this morning?"

"I don't want to talk with my lawyer. I want to talk with Peter. Just Peter."

"I'm not sure that just Peter's in."

Gwen closed her eyes and shook her head. "I didn't think you would make it this hard. Please, Peter. I'm trying to apologize to you. Please let me talk."

"All right. Talk."

"Peter, I was completely wrong. I listened to thoughts I should never have believed. The autopsy came in. Gordon died from drowning, yes. But it also showed he was drunk. Very drunk. Point-two-three or something. You probably know what that means. There was nothing wrong with his brakes. Peter, I accused you unfairly. In light of the way you have treated me, I behaved wrongly beyond explanation. Peter, more than anything in the world, I want you to forgive me."

He was silent for a long time. "Drunk, huh? One might have thought that explanation of events might have occurred to you a little earlier. Which story makes more sense? Peter murders

Gordon? Or, Gordon gets drunk and crashes?" He waited. His voice was intensely bitter.

"You're right, Peter. You are absolutely right. I should have thought of that. I don't know what came over me. I'm asking you to forgive me."

"Well, I am glad to be cleared of the charges. I thank you for that." He sat silently and glared at her.

"Peter, are you going to forgive me?" she asked looking him squarely in the eye.

"I guess it is my duty to forgive you. But, my trust in you is shot. If you are so quick to condemn me for something I didn't do, what would you do if I ever really did something wrong when we were . . ."

"Married," Gwen said finishing the sentence he was unwilling to complete. "I understand, Peter. I understand that this was not a minor accusation. I accused you of murder. You have a right to be bitter. But I wish you would forgive me anyway."

"I said I forgave you."

"I know. But I wish you would really forgive me."

She suddenly stood up. She felt herself losing her composure. "Peter, I have to leave, good-bye."

His bitterness had triumphed. But the victory left him sick to his stomach.

Gwen could not bear to tell her parents what happened. She spent extra time each day reading the Bible—especially the Book of Psalms. Time and again she cried out to the Lord, "Please God, help me know what to do." She felt comforted whenever she spent time in Scripture, but plans of action simply evaded her.

On Wednesday evening at work, Gwen felt as if she could no longer bear the load alone. She called Lynn Roberts during her dinner break. Lynn agreed to meet with her on Thursday morning. It was an interruption to Lynn's home schooling schedule, but she could tell from Gwen's voice that it was important.

Gwen told her parents that she needed to spend some time talking with Lynn about dealing with the "recent events". She would
leave Casey at their home at ten, visit with Lynn, and go straight to
work at three.

Lynn's older children were busy at work in the school room
when Gwen arrived. The younger children were playing in the adjacent family room with Legos, blocks, and cars. Lynn asked her
oldest son to watch the younger ones.

The two women settled in the dining room of the Roberts' home.

Settled with their coffee mugs, Lynn simply looked at Gwen
while she waited for a sign that she was ready to really talk.

"I guess I called this meeting," Gwen said with an embarrassed
smile.

"Right," Lynn laughed. "You seem upset. You wanna talk about it?"

"My life has turned upside down in the last week. Gordon's
death. And now Peter. . . . " She was determined she would not cry.
She stopped talking to try to regain her composure.

"Peter?" Lynn asked. "What's going on with Peter?"

"Hasn't he told Aaron?"

"I don't think they've seen each other in more than a week. Last
Friday Peter took off on some trip. We didn't see him Sunday. And
tomorrow, Aaron is in Portland."

Gwen tapped her fingers against the side of the mug. "I've made
a real mess for myself. I think I've ruined everything with Peter.
He's furious with me. I've asked him to forgive me. He says he did,
but he hasn't really."

"I'm afraid I'm totally lost. You are going to have to start at the
beginning and put some of this in context," Lynn said.

"Oh," she said, exhaling audibly. "Where do I begin? Well, I guess
I should start by telling you Peter and I are—or I probably should
say were—in love with each other."

Lynn looked surprised, but said nothing.

"Peter blurted out his feelings to me a few weeks ago."

"But I thought he had a conviction about divorce," Lynn said.

"Oh, he did. Or does. Or something. Anyway, he told me that he
loved me, but that he didn't feel right about it because of the

divorce. He then said he would try to search out an answer from God and let me know one way or the other by the end of October."

"That was kind of a nasty thing to do. He should have kept his mouth shut if he felt God didn't want him involved with you."

Gwen brightened inside. "Yeah. Tell me about it." Gwen took a slow drink of coffee. "Well, I have been very fond of Peter for a long time, but I tried to wait for him to give me some kind of signal that he thought things were OK before I really plunged in. And I didn't say anything about the way I felt—at least not anything clear to him for a long time.

"But Gordon started hassling me," Gwen continued, "and one night about two weeks ago, he arrived at my house after eleven and started making trouble. I couldn't get my dad on the phone, so I called Peter, who was still at the office working on my case. He came right over and masterfully forced Gordon to leave. He was really great," Gwen said smiling at the memory.

"No fight?" Lynn asked.

"No," Gwen said shaking her head. "Just a little shoving on Gordon's part. Anyhow, I was really scared when this was going on and still pretty shaken up by what had happened. When Peter got ready to leave, I didn't want him to go. I told him that I loved him and wanted him to always protect me or something silly like that."

Lynn gave her an understanding smile. "It doesn't sound all that silly to me."

"Well, a week ago Wednesday, Gordon was killed in a crash. Drunk—as I guess you read in the paper."

"Yes," Lynn replied nodding.

"I was up almost all night, really upset. And I started having these bizarre thoughts that Peter was somehow responsible for Gordon's death. At first I thought that he wished him dead or something. But then, I dreamed up this crazy scenario where I thought Peter had done something to Gordon's car to cause it to crash."

"Gwen? You thought that?"

"It's awful, isn't it?"

"Had Peter ever done anything that was legitimately suspicious?"

"No, of course not. But he had said some things. Like one time he said that he wished Gordon would die, but afterwards he said it was an evil thought and he would pray for Gordon. Anyhow, I pieced together a string of isolated comments, added two-and-two together, and got forty-seven."

"Did you tell Peter all this?"

"Sort of. And that's the real problem. I told him these crazy thoughts. I told him I couldn't really believe them, but somehow it just seemed unbearable to go into a relationship with someone who had ever wished Gordon was dead, especially when Gordon *did* die. Things like that. I was talking craziness."

"Well, Peter should have understood that you were just upset by Gordon's death."

"That's what I thought. But he avoided me for several days, and he was very cold with me when I went and asked for forgiveness. And he has completely ignored me since then."

"That just doesn't sound like Peter."

"I really can't blame him. It was a pretty lousy thing to accuse him of."

"Well," Lynn said. "Let me make some observations. First of all, Peter bears primary responsibility for all of this. He had no business falling in love with you and especially telling you under these circumstances. He is a mature Christian and knows better. You are a young believer, and while you did some unwise things, it doesn't seem all that bad under the circumstances. And I hate to say this, because I love Peter like a brother, but he is being a real creep right now. There is no explanation for his decision to hold onto the hurt after you asked for forgiveness. He's just plain wrong. Men!"

"Are you just saying that to make me feel better?"

"No, Gwen. That's what I really feel. I can't believe Peter! What has gotten into him? I'm going to have Aaron straighten him out as soon as he gets home."

"Please Lynn. Don't do that. I just feel uncomfortable about that. In fact, I almost didn't come to you because I thought you might want to do that. But I simply didn't have anyone else to talk to. If Peter comes back, I want him to come back on his own."

"I guess I can understand that," Lynn said. "I'll let it go for a while. I may come back to you later and ask for permission to intervene. But I'll ask you first."

"OK, that's fair."

Lynn prayed for Gwen out loud. After a long hug, Gwen left for work with a lighter heart than she had known in days.

∼

As Gwen drove to work, she thought over the events of the last several days once more. As she contemplated Peter's exodus to Montana, a thought came into her mind. A vacation. An escape.

She had taken several days off since May because of all the legal proceedings. But she hadn't had a real vacation. It would be difficult to arrange quickly, but she suddenly became fixated on trying to get out of Spokane. The only place she could afford to go that was truly "away" would be to her sister Pam's in Walnut Creek, California.

She got to the hospital about fifteen minutes before her shift started and called her parents.

"Hi, Mom. How's Casey?"

"She seems fine today. Are you at work?"

"Yeah, I had a great talk with Lynn. It really helped. Listen, the reason I'm calling is because I have a really crazy idea."

"I'm listening," her mother said.

"How would you and dad like to go with Casey and me to visit Pam?"

"That's not a crazy idea. When?"

"Tomorrow."

"Now *that* is a crazy idea."

"Mom, I'm serious. With everything that has happened, especially now because of Gordon's death, everything has tumbled in on me, and I need to get out of here for a while. I don't want to do anything elaborate, just go to Pam's and sit on her patio. Go to the park. Walk around the mall. Maybe go into San Francisco one day. Just take it easy. I think it would be good for Casey, too."

"How would we ever get ready in time to leave tomorrow?"

"Mom, it doesn't take that long to pack a week's worth of clothing and fill a car with gas."

"You've got your mind set on this, haven't you?"

"Yes, but I haven't asked anybody here at work. I didn't want to ask unless you and Dad would go with me."

"Well, I'll ask him."

"You two talk it over for a while. I'll call you in an hour."

～

Gwen's supervisor and father both understood the circumstances surrounding Gordon's death. The emergency vacation was approved. The nine-hundred-mile drive would begin in the morning.

During her dinner break, Gwen called Lynn Roberts. She told Lynn about her vacation plans and gave her Pam's address and phone number. Gwen secured a promise from Lynn that she would tell Peter she had a way to contact Gwen if there were an emergency regarding the lawsuit, but only for that purpose. Lynn promised she would deliver the message on Sunday.

～

On Friday night at 9:30, Donna Corliss and Mr. and Mrs. Conner Stockton waited patiently on the B Concourse of the Spokane International Airport for the last United Airlines flight from Denver. Stephen had caught a late afternoon flight from Washington Dulles to enable him to connect in Denver.

On October 13, Stephen had received his formal notice that he had passed the Washington State Bar Examination. The letter from the Bar Association said, "For you it was a piece of cake." It was a form letter sent to all the successful applicants.

In order to be a full-fledged lawyer, he had to take the final step of standing before a judge of record in Washington State, raising his right hand, and swearing to conduct himself according to the rules of ethics and to uphold the Constitution of the United States and the State of Washington. The certificate would hang on his wall throughout his career and proclaim that his official date of admission to practice law was on Monday, November 7, 1994.

It would be a fast trip. Arrive in Spokane Friday night. Swearing in Monday at nine. Flight at noon. Arrive Dulles 11:30 P.M. At work in the nation's capital Tuesday at 9:00.

He and Donna had agreed they would spend Friday night at his parent's house—together. On Saturday, they would spend the day with his family, but they would go out alone on Saturday night and return to the apartment they shared together.

He was first off the plane. Not many people fly first-class from Denver to Spokane. He quickly kissed his mom, gave his dad a clumsy man-hug, and then lifted Donna off her feet and swung her around before kissing her fervently. She was thrilled at the reception.

They cuddled in the back seat of his dad's Mercedes as they drove down the Interstate, up the South Hill, past the modest houses south of Comstock Park where Gwen lived, and on to the modern imposing homes of rock and glass that hung on the edge of the cliff that abruptly defined that part of Spokane.

The weekend was definitely off on a hopeful note for Donna's plan to secure an escape from Spokane.

~

Gwen, Casey, Stan, and June were packed, loaded, fed, and watered by 9:15 on Saturday morning. They hoped to get to Bend, Oregon, that day and complete their journey on Sunday.

Gwen sat in the back seat with Casey and read books to her for the first hour or so until they left the Interstate at Ritzville, turning south for the Tri-Cities on U.S. 395.

Casey settled in to play with her dolls for a while, which allowed Gwen the luxury to just stare out the window. The gentle hills of eastern Washington were patterned in varying shades of brown. The wheat farms that comprised practically all of the next seventy-five miles of highway were half exposed brown dirt and half light brown wheat stubble. The harvest had been over since late August. The stubble would remain unplowed until the next spring. It was the perfect scenery for someone who wanted to look at nothing of interest and think nothing of importance.

At 11:30, the Mansfield's Oldsmobile crossed over the Columbia River on the bridge that spans the communities of Pasco and Kennewick, Washington. Both towns were initially bedroom communities for the Hanford Nuclear Project built at the end of World War II. It was there that the internal-radioactive components had been manufactured for the bomb that was dropped on Nagasaki to end the war with Japan.

Gwen's family wasn't interested in nuclear energy that Saturday morning. They only wanted lunch, which they found at a Wendy's just off the highway in Kennewick. It was the last opportunity for food for over a hundred miles.

As they left Kennewick, heading up the much higher Horse Heaven hills—peaks that would be called mountains east of the Mississippi—Casey quickly fell asleep. Noticing her granddaughter's slumber, June turned in her seat and said to Gwen, "I don't mean to pry, but I've been curious about something for a long time."

Gwen guessed what was coming.

"What's the deal with you and Peter? I can't figure him out. In some ways he seems like he has devoted all of his time to you, but I don't hear about dates, or romance, or . . . or anything. I don't get it."

"That's what I thought you were going to ask. Mom, it's a really complicated story, and I don't want to hide anything from you, but the honest truth is, I don't know how to answer you."

"Does he like you? And you know what I mean by that."

"A few days ago, I could have answered that question easily. I would have said, yes, he likes me. And I like him—a lot. But now it's more complicated. And maybe it's over."

"Over?"

"Yes, we had a big misunderstanding right after Gordon died. I really don't want to explain the details. It was mostly my fault. Peter got really upset and took off for a couple of days. I went to see him on Monday and asked him to forgive me. He said he did, but he's still very angry."

"Have you talked since?"

"No."

"Does he know we're going to California?"

"No, and I'm not sure he cares."

"He cares," her father interjected.

"He used to care," Gwen replied.

"No, he still cares," Stan countered. "You were fighting before the funeral, right?"

"Right."

"Well, I saw the way he looked at you in church. He may have run right out to avoid you, but his eyes told me a great deal. He still cares."

"Dad, I just don't know."

"Gwen, listen to your Father. Peter wouldn't give up on you," June said. "I think he's the greatest. He's got to come around."

"Maybe," Gwen replied.

After another minute or two of silence, her dad said, "This vacation is about Peter, isn't it?"

Gwen stared out the window for a long time before answering. "Mostly," she finally said.

"Hmm," her father replied. "Sounds to me like you care, too. A whole lot."

With that, the inquisition ended. Gwen looked out the window as they made their way down the magnificent Columbia River gorge which defines the border between Washington and Oregon. It was the perfect scenery for dreaming big dreams.

～

Conner Stockton had insisted that Stephen take Donna to the Manito Country Club for dinner. Dad's treat.

They dressed in their very best. Donna's dress had been a gift from Stephen's parents at Christmas. It was Stephen's favorite.

After their cocktails had been served, Donna said, "I'll bet you eat at a lot of fancy places in D.C."

"Not very often. I don't make that much money, yet. But a couple times my boss and his wife have taken me out to dinner."

"Just the three of you?"

"Yes," he lied.

"Well, how would you like to make it a foursome the next time he asks you out?"

"You?"

"Yes, me. You still interested?"

"I think so. What do you have in mind?"

"Well, you are making this pretty awkward for me. Generally a girl gets asked these things."

"Marriage? You're ready?"

"That's not the most romantic proposal I've ever heard. It is a proposal, isn't it? You've asked so many times. Do you still want to marry me?"

Stockton had enjoyed himself a great deal since returning to be with her. He had dated a half-dozen girls or so. And he certainly found them entertaining. He hated to give all that up so soon. But this is the life that he would be returning to in two years, and his parents accepted her, and....

"Yes, Donna, I still want to marry you. Here, let me say it right. Donna, my sweet, will you marry me?"

"Yes, of course."

"Do you have the date planned, the dress bought, the license ready?"

"No, Stephen. I'm not that brazen. But how does Christmas strike you?"

"Wow. That's quick. I'm not sure. Can you do a wedding right in that length of time? My parents will want a really big shindig."

"Well, I guess you're right. How about Valentine's Day, assuming it's on a weekend?"

"I couldn't take a long honeymoon then. Three or four days are the most I could get off. No real vacation for me until summer."

"I don't care if we have an official honeymoon right away. Just being with you would be enough."

"OK, I guess that sounds like as good a time as any. Let's do it!"

As he kissed her across the table, he wondered if he should cancel his date for next Friday night. Probably not, he concluded. After all, he wasn't engaged when he made it. It was his first loophole, and he still wasn't officially a lawyer until Monday.

᛫᛬᛫

Pastor Lind's sermon wasn't on forgiveness, nor bitterness, nor anger. But those were the topics in the Lord's sermon for Peter that Sunday. When the congregation sang a praise chorus, extolling the majesty of God, the Holy Spirit reminded Peter that God was also a God who forgave sin. When the offering was taken, and the Elder reminded the congregation for the five hundredth time, that God loves a cheerful giver, Peter's inner thoughts were invaded from on high with the truth that bitterness and cheerfulness couldn't exist in the same heart. After forty-five minutes of being pounded by the conviction of the Holy Spirit, the pastor could have read a phone book for his message, and Peter would have still responded to the invitation to raise his hand and get his heart right with God.

Lynn Roberts was peeking when every head was supposed to be bowed and every eye was supposed to be closed. She was tickled to death to see Peter's hand go in the air. She wished that she hadn't promised Gwen that she wouldn't tell Peter her whereabouts.

After the service was over, Peter found his way over to the Roberts after scanning the congregation several more times to make sure Gwen hadn't slipped in the back.

"Looking for someone, Peter?" Lynn asked coyly.

"Have you seen Gwen and Casey?"

"I don't think they are here today," she answered.

"Do you know where they are?"

"Not exactly," Lynn said truthfully enough—knowing they were still driving to California.

"Ly-y-nnn," Peter said. "I'm a lawyer. I will cross-examine you until you tell me exactly what you know."

"Peter," Lynn said lowering her voice. "I promised Gwen I would-n't tell you where she was. She's on a vacation. She told me to tell you that I have her address and phone number—although she isn't there yet—in case an emergency came up in her case. But I am not supposed to give it to you for any other reason."

"How long is she going to be gone?"

"I guess I can tell you that. A week. She'll be back a week from tonight."

Peter paused and looked around. The crowd was thinning out. Aaron gleaned the essence of the conversation and began herding the kids toward the car. "Has she told you what's been going on?"

Lynn nodded.

"I've been a little creepy to her."

"Oh, I wouldn't say that, Peter," Lynn interjected.

Peter's countenance brightened for a moment.

Lynn looked him in the eye with a wry grin.

"I would say you've been a colossal jerk."

～

The week passed slowly for Peter. But the Lord continued to work on his heart.

On Thursday morning, he rose before dawn to run. As he ran, along the damp roads, he saw the first ray of sun shoot over the mountain and cast its light across the lake with a glistening bril-liance. A new day. A new day. There was some truth for him in that. As he ran he tried to listen with his spiritual ears.

He thought of what is must have been like to be in the Garden, at the beginning of the new day on Resurrection Morning. The great-est new day of all. *If it hadn't been for His death on the cross, there would never have been that new day*. The thought swept through his spirit into his conscious mind.

Peter suddenly saw the truth God had for him. He had built a relationship with Gwen upon a false foundation. That relationship had to be torn down, destroyed—it had to die, at least for a season.

It was wrong for Peter to have pursued Gwen in his heart. It was wrong for Peter to have enticed her into loving him. God would never have been honored if he would have smoothly transitioned from a wrong relationship into marriage.

He had to stop running. He bent half over, hands on his knees. "God I know I have confessed this in various ways, but I want to try to get it right this time," Peter said, praying out loud in the stillness. "You tell me that I am supposed to give thanks in everything. I haven't been willing to do that about all this. I should have had a thankful spirit out of simple obedience, but I have tried to cling to a relationship you didn't want me to have. Thank You God, for tearing it down. Thank You for letting it die. And God . . . God if You will allow me a second chance, I want Your blessing to build a new relationship on a foundation that honors You. Jesus, I love you. Amen."

He looked up and saw a neighbor he knew driving slowly past him, staring. The full, complete peace that swept through Peter's soul was worth any price—a little embarrassment with a neighbor was well worth it.

～

Peter began calling Gwen's home Sunday afternoon at three o'clock. He called once an hour, hour after hour. At ten o'clock he called and at the fifth ring, was about to hang up.

"Hello," Gwen said.

"Gwen, you're home."

"Peter? Yes, we're home. I just got in and put Casey in bed."

"Gwen, I need to talk with you. I was—well in the words of our dear mutual friend, Lynn Roberts—I was a colossal jerk."

Gwen giggled. "She said that? How much did she tell you?"

"Not much. She steadfastly refused to tell me where you were. Where were you?"

"We went to my sister Pam's in California. We had a great time."

"Gwen, I really want to talk with you—at length, and as soon as possible."

"I'm not sure that I give appointments to colossal jerks."

The phone line was silent.

"Peter, I'm teasing you. I'll talk with you. When?"

"How about right now?"

"No, I am way too tired. And if you think we have to talk a long time, I have a lot I want to discuss as well. We're going to need at least two or three hours."

"Are you working tomorrow?"

"Yes, I'll be working all week, three to eleven. How about one morning this week?" Gwen asked.

"Ugh. I have hearings on Monday and Wednesday. And I have a deposition on Tuesday which I can't change. It was already rescheduled once before because of our hearing in Seattle."

"So Thursday?"

"I guess, unless you want to talk after you get off work at eleven or early some morning."

"I want to have a clear head when we talk. What I have to say is very serious."

"Is it good serious or bad serious?" Peter asked.

"It all depends on your perspective," Gwen replied.

"Don't leave me—"

"Peter," she interrupted, "let's just wait."

"OK, Thursday. Nine at my office?"

"Make it nine-thirty; I've got to get Casey over to my parents. And if we meet at your office, you just can't sit behind your desk."

25

~

At fifteen minutes after nine on Thursday, Sally buzzed Peter on the intercom. "Morgan Howard on line two."

"Good morning, Morgan."

"Good morning, Mr. Barron; have you seen a copy of the Court of Appeals decision?"

"What decision? There has been a decision!"

"Associated Press is carrying a story on the wires that the Court released a decision this morning. According to the story, it was affirmed in part and reversed in part."

"That could be good or bad," Peter said.

"Let me read to the bottom of this. It looks like you lost. I'm sorry, to be the one to tell you. Any comment?"

Peter's ears burned and he could feel his heart pounding. "I'm sorry, Morgan. I'm going to have to get a copy of the decision. I'll do that right now and call you back as soon as I can."

Peter sat at his desk shaking his head. "We lost. We lost. I can't believe we lost. They sure didn't waste anytime on it either. Three weeks! Turkeys!"

Peter buzzed Sally. "Please get Joe and come in here right away."

Less than a minute later, a concerned-looking duo burst into Peter's office. With one look at Peter's face, they just sat down and waited.

"Morgan Howard from the *Spokesman-Review* just called to tell me that the Ninth Circuit issued their opinion in *Landis*. We lost."

"Oh, no!" Sally gasped.

"Any chance he made a mistake? Did he have a copy of the opinion?" Joe asked.

"He was just reading me bits of a story off the AP wire. I'm not a hundred-percent sure that the AP got it right."

"I wouldn't get my hopes up on the possibility that they made a mistake," Joe said, shaking his head.

"How can we get an opinion right away?" Peter asked. "The clerk will just stick it in the mail to us today. We may not get it until Monday."

"I know a guy in the U.S. Attorney's Office in Seattle," Joe replied. "I'll get him to fax it to us."

"Great. Call him from here."

Joe walked over to Peter's phone. His friend was in and was happy to do Joe a favor.

"I can't believe it!" Peter said again, this time slamming his fist on his desk. "What are we going to do now?"

"In everything give thanks, for this is the will of God in Christ Jesus concerning you," Joe said.

"You just learn a memory verse?" Peter said—but he was clearly teasing. "You're right, Joe. But would you mind praying? I'm still too upset."

"Sure, Peter," Joe replied. Joe was not a practitioner of lengthy prayers. "Lord, we are saddened by this decision. Give us wisdom on what to do next. Help us especially to know if we should take this case to the Supreme Court. And thank You that, despite this decision, You have allowed Casey to be returned to her mother, and You have allowed Gwen to become a Christian. In the name of Your Son, Amen."

"What decision?" It was a female voice from behind Joe and Sally. Gwen stuck her head inside Peter's door. "I heard your prayer. What's going on?"

"Gwen," Peter said standing, "it looks like the Ninth Circuit has ruled against us. We lost."

"When did you find out?"

"Just a few minutes ago. A reporter called. We haven't actually seen the decision. Joe has a friend who's going to fax us a copy right away."

"What does this mean?" Gwen asked.

"Well, we have to read the decision to be sure. Apparently it means the entire lawsuit has been thrown out. We're finished."

"And that's it?"

"That's it unless we take the case to the Supreme Court and they accept the case and then they reverse the decision."

"Can't we do that?"

"We can. It's fairly expensive. But the real problem is that for every one-hundred cases that are filed in the Supreme Court, they accept only one case."

"Won't that *Heart of America* outfit help us with the expenses?" Gwen asked.

"I certainly hope so," interjected Sally, who paid the office bills.

"We are going to need to read the case and then make a decision. And we also are probably going to have to ask some constitutional law expert if he thinks we have a decent chance."

"I think I hear the fax machine ringing," Sally said.

"Bring it to us as each page comes in," Peter said.

Peter and Joe stood together at Peter's desk and read page after page as it came over the fax machine. There had been no mistake. They indeed had lost their case. The majority ruled that social workers who are in the process of investigating cases which end up in child abuse litigation are immune from suit for everything they do in preparation for or during such a lawsuit. It took them nineteen pages to reverse that part of Judge Stokes's opinion. It only took a page and a half to dismiss Peter's suit on the perjury and document tampering. The Supreme Court had ruled on the point. They would countenance no exception.

The only bright spot in the opinion was a fifteen-page angry dissent written by Judge Boyle. He had voted to give Peter and Gwen victory on both counts.

"Boyle's opinion will definitely help you get the attention of the Supreme Court," Joe said.

"Are you sure?" Peter asked.

"Yeah, I'm pretty sure of it."

"You know any constitutional experts we can call?"

"Well, there's always Charles French at University of Michigan Law School."

"A professor?"

"Yeah."

"You know him?"

"I just met him once at a seminar he taught on constitutional issues for federal prosecutors. He's probably argued thirty cases in the Supreme Court."

"Can you get hold of him?"

"I can try. "I'll call right now," Joe said, leaving for his own office.

Sally remained at her desk reading the opinion.

"Peter, I am still proud of you," Gwen said. "You worked hard. And I thought you were great in court that day."

"If I was great, it was the last time in three weeks that I was great," Peter replied. "I guess it's time that we discuss the important stuff. Lawsuits—pfffft."

Gwen just smiled.

"Well, I probably need to go first," Peter said.

"Only if you get out from behind that desk and come over here and sit beside me. I want to talk with just Peter, not Peter the lawyer."

"I was a real creep that day, wasn't I?" Peter said, moving slowly, but delibertly to Gwen's side of the office.

"I think the correct term is 'colossal jerk.' Lynn really has a way with words."

"Guilty as charged," Peter said, smiling. Looking suddenly serious, he said, "Gwen, you were kind and gracious when we last talked here. I was rude and bitter and angry. I've got a lot of things to ask your forgiveness for, but let me start with that. I ask you to forgive me for acting selfishly and foolishly that day. It was a time that you needed to be understood and forgiven. I did neither. By the way, I do really forgive you for what you said about me and Gordon's accident. But as I am about to confess, I think I'm responsible for that one, too."

"Peter, thank you for saying all that. Yes, I do forgive you. It did hurt me a lot to be rejected right then, but I do know why you did it. I was surprised, but I do understand."

"I appreciate your forgiveness and understanding."

"Sure."

"Well, there's something more fundamental I need to address. I was wrong to let my emotions run away with me. I was wrong to lead you on. I was wrong to entice you to respond to me with your emotions. I had no business being anything but your lawyer. I was wrong. Not only did I sin, but I led you down the wrong path as well. Gwen, please forgive me."

A single tear trickled out of each eye. "Yes, Peter, I forgive you."

"I've got something else I want to talk with you about, but I want to save it until we discuss what you wanted to bring up."

"To tell the truth, the things you said are what I was going to confront you about. Basically, I was going to say, 'Peter Barron, you done me wrong by leadin' me on.' Sounds like a country western song, doesn't it?"

"Yeah, it kinda does."

"That's all I really had to say. It kind of shortens the time we needed when you plead guilty and ask the court for mercy," Gwen said, smiling.

"You're starting to catch on," Peter replied with his eyes twinkling.

"Oh, there is one other thing," Gwen said.

"Yes?"

"Where do we go from here?"

"That was the other subject I wanted to discuss with you."

"Good. You go first."

"About a week ago, I was out running and the Lord was really working on me. Basically, what I concluded was the way we had started was really a wrong foundation. I had a conviction that I shouldn't have violated. But I did. If we had gone forward from that wrong foundation, right into . . . into . . . a relationship right after Gordon's death, we would have been building on the wrong foundation. As much as these fights and separation and anger and bitterness have hurt us, I'm convinced that our relationship had to go through a kind of death." Peter paused looking for words.

Gwen's heart rose in her throat. "Is that it? Our relationship has to die?"

"Our old relationship had to die."

"What do you mean by that?"

"Well, I've asked God to give me a second chance to have the right kind of relationship with you. And now I'm asking you to give me a second chance also. I want a new relationship with you. A new life with you."

"New *life*?"

"Yes, life. That's how long marriages are supposed to last, aren't they?"

Gwen was trembling as Peter took both of her hands and gently stood her up.

"Gwen, will you marry me? I want to build a new life with you and with your precious Casey doll, too. Will you?"

Gwen lowered her eyes and said, "I guess it all depends."

"Depends on what?"

"It depends on if you mean running off to Idaho this afternoon and visiting a justice of the peace or if you intend to have a proper wedding at our church." She was smiling broadly. "Yes, Peter, I'll marry you. I love you so much."

He hesitated for a moment. Peter looked deep in her eyes once again. And then he kissed the lips that he had longed for and dreamed about. There was no hesitation. There was no guilt. There was only passion—pure passion.

"By the way," Peter said, still holding Gwen tightly in his arms, "there'll be no Idaho Justice of the Peace. I want the biggest church wedding in Spokane, so that everyone can see the luckiest guy in the world marry his dream girl."

After a few minutes, Peter said, "I really do need to ask your father. What do you think he'll say?"

"What he'll say to me is, 'I told you so.'"

"Is that anything like 'yes'?"

"It's exactly like yes," Gwen replied.

∼

About fifteen minutes later, Peter and Gwen emerged arm-in-arm from Peter's office, their faces beaming brightly. Joe was standing next to Sally's desk giving her some changes for the last draft of a new complaint in another case.

"Uh . . . I'd say you two are taking this loss in the Ninth Circuit surprisingly well," Joe said.

"Oh, that," Peter said. "You win some, you lose some. Sally, I'm going to be out for the rest of the day. We need to run up to Gwen's parents house for a little talk, and then I am taking my fiancé to lunch."

"Fiancé?" Sally said with mouth gaping. "Fiancé?"

"Yes, this surely sets the record for the best showing of appreciation I have ever had from a client on the day I lost their case," Peter said smiling.

Gwen laughed softly and cuddled closer to Peter's side.

"I knew it! I knew it! I just knew it!" Sally declared. "It was inevitable with you two. I just wonder what took you so long."

"I can assure you that you don't want to hear the whole story," Peter replied.

"Congratulations to both of you!" Joe said, beaming. "If you had to choose between winning the case or winning the girl, I think you chose the right one."

"There's no doubt about that," Peter said. "But we are still going to win this case. Supreme Court, here we come!"

26

~

"School of Law," the female voice said over the speakerphone.

Peter quickly picked up the handset. "Professor Charles French, please. This is Peter Barron; he is expecting my call."

"Just a moment, please."

A few seconds later, a deep, elegant voice came on the line. "Good day. This is Charles French."

"Professor French, this is Peter Barron. I believe we have a phone appointment to talk about my *Landis* case."

"Oh, yes, Mr. Barron. Happy to talk with you and happy to help out. My old friend Joe Lambert speaks so highly of you."

"He has to. We've got to work together every day," Peter said playfully.

"Well, in any event, you are lucky enough to have one great case," the professor said.

"And that's only half the story. Just last week, I was fortunate enough to get engaged to Gwen Landis."

"Well, congratulations. But I don't think I would mention that fact to the Supreme Court."

"Do you think it's a problem that I'm marrying her?"

"No, no, no. You just shouldn't mention it in passing or anything."

"Thanks for the advice."

"Hopefully, I will be able to give you a little more relevant legal advice as well."

"You are very gracious to make yourself available. I appreciate it more than you can know."

"Well, let me start from the beginning. I'm sure you know most of the basics about the Supreme Court, but—"

"Professor," Peter interrupted, "you should assume that I know nothing."

"Oh, OK. Well, the first thing is that you have to get your case accepted for review. That is the very hardest step. Less than one case in a hundred gets accepted. You have great facts and a very interesting case; I think your chances are about one-in-thirty that it will be accepted. But let's see what we can do to improve those chances."

"Yes, those are still very long odds."

"The way the Supreme Court reviews cases is very important for you to know. All of the cases are reviewed by each of the justices individually. Each judge has two or three law clerks. The law clerks are supposed to read each cert petition or appeal thoroughly. And then they write a summary of each case for their own justice. Each justice will carefully read that summary and then will at least look at the cert petition or appeal itself. The degree of their own interest and the amount of attention they pay to the papers you file will be heavily weighted by the summary that their law clerk prepares."

"It sounds like the most important step in the most important court of the country is controlled by a bunch of twenty-four year olds."

"Mr. Barron, you learn quickly. Are you sure you didn't go to school here at Michigan?"

"Thanks," Peter laughed.

"So as you are preparing your papers—by the way, I suppose you know that your case should be a petition for a writ of certiorari, not an appeal—"

"Yes, that's what Joe said, too. What's the difference?"

"Pragmatically, almost none, except for the format of the papers. Historically, appeals were taken in certain categories of cases where there was more of a presumption that the Court was going to review the case. But in modern practice, it really doesn't make a difference. You have to convince the Court that your case is vitally important to the whole country, not just to your client, no matter if you call it an appeal or a cert petition."

"This sounds like more of an uphill challenge all the time."

"Challenge is a good word. Your first challenge is to get one justice of the Supreme Court interested enough in your case that he or she wants to bring it up for discussion in a meeting of the justices. The way the Court does it is this: there are several dozen cases listed on their agenda each time the justices meet. They have a standing rule that they don't discuss all of these cases. So if even one justice on the Court doesn't bring your case up for discussion, then your cert petition is going to be denied automatically and the justices will never have said one word about it to each other. So goal number one, again, is to find one justice interested enough in your case to bring it up for discussion."

"OK, I'm writing that down."

"And in order to do this, you have got to try to get inside the minds of one or two key justices and get a good grasp of their legal philosophy in this area of law. Then you write your cert petition almost as if it were a personal appeal to those one or two justices. But, you have to be careful about that, because in order to get past step two, you have to have four justices vote to grant review of your cert petition."

"Step one, get one justice to bring it up. Step two, get four justices to vote in favor of granting the petition," Peter repeated.

"Very good."

"Do you have any suggestions for which justices I should target for this cert petition?"

"Let's do this by a process of elimination. Winston and Kraus are obviously out. They are both big-time conservatives in the wrong sort of way. They are law and order kind of guys who believe that the cops are always right. You'll never get their votes, period.

"Geisler is more of a liberal but he hates everything that is traditional. I think he's one of those liberals who hates parents and believes the government should raise all the children and so on. If you were representing a burglar or a rapist, Geisler would be on your side for sure. But a parent? Probably not."

"I'm getting this down," Peter said.

"Warden, Gilbert, and Swindon are the moderates. I don't think they really have a judicial philosophy except to be moderate about everything. They may go with you, they may not. But I don't think that any of them should be your targets at this stage."

"OK, got it," Peter said.

"That leaves you with three. Stauffer, Dowling, and Rose. Stauffer and Dowling are liberals—but liberals of a civil libertarian bent. They may love big government, but when big government tramples on an individual's civil liberties, they usually side with the individual. Rose is the only conservative civil libertarian on the Court. He hates big government. He distrusts any agency that invades spheres of private property, or family, or religion, or gun owners, etc. His philosophy is so clear that I think Rose should be your number one target. But I would be pitching hard to Stauffer and Dowling as well. And in the end, the three of them have to get one of the moderates to come with them to accept the case, plus an additional one of the moderates to vote with them in order for you to win."

"This is amazing," Peter said. "How do you know all this?"

"I learned it the old-fashioned way, bashing my head against the marble walls of the Supreme Court. You just have to do this kind of work for a long time to find out what works and who believes in what."

"Well, I really appreciate this more than you can ever know."

"I am very glad to help out. Now let me really play the professor and give you an assignment. I want a five-page outline of your cert petition in one week. Then I want your draft of the petition itself three weeks after that. I'll give you my input, and then you can make whatever changes you like from my suggestions. That Ninth Circuit decision is awful. I've got some grandkids who live in California, and I don't want their families invaded like this. I don't want the courts out there to simply turn their backs on the parents and bless everything social workers do. I'll fax my home phone number and address."

"You are a fantastic encouragement."

"Thanks. And congratulations again."

"I haven't won yet."

"Gwen Landis. You won her, right?"

"Yes. And thanks."

Peter, Gwen, Stan, and June agreed on Saturday, May 20, for the wedding. Even though Gwen had been divorced for nearly three years, they decided that it would be more appropriate to have the wedding a bit more removed from Gordon's death. And although Casey was already very fond of Peter, it would give her a little more time to heal. Pastor Lind gave his hearty blessing. Lynn and Aaron agreed to be the matron of honor and best man.

⁓

David G. Humphrey was delighted to hear that Peter was on the phone. "Yes, put him right through, Cindy."

"Good morning, Peter. How's the case going?"

As Peter explained the loss in the Ninth Circuit and the need to appeal to the Supreme Court, Humphrey clenched his fist, pulled his bent arm toward himself, in the familiar signal of victory and silently mouthed the word "Yes!"

"That's just terrible, Peter. I'm so sorry to hear of this loss. This is why *Heart of America* is so critical. We have to keep fighting. If the Supreme Court takes the case, then you will have a greater precedent when you win."

"That's an encouraging way to look at it," Peter replied.

"How much money will it take to pay for the appeal to the Supreme Court?" Humphrey asked.

"I think that our out-of-pocket costs will be about fifteen thousand dollars, assuming the court takes the case. It would be nice to get some money for our attorney's fees. So far the money you have been so gracious to send us has only covered out-of-pocket costs—we have not been able to pay any of our attorney's fees," Peter said.

"Well, we'll do our best for you. You can count on that. But I think for sure we can cover the fifteen grand."

"That's great, that really does help," Peter said.

The marketing mavens of the direct mail agency agreed with Humphrey's assessment. Taking this case to the Supreme Court would put donors into high gear. They couldn't help eclipsing the over $300,000 they raised on the first go-round.

Peter worked as much as he could on his cert petition to the Supreme Court during the daytime. But every evening from five until seven, he would get in two hours of concentrated research and preparation. One evening, Peter discovered a case from the United States Court of Appeals for the Second Circuit which gave him great hope. It also embarrassed him a little that he had not found it earlier. It was called *Hill v. City of New York,* and had been decided in 1993.

In that case the court held that while judicial immunity for social workers certainly applies to everything that happens during a trial; social workers were not immune from filing the initial papers if they contained information that they knew to be false at the time of filing.

Peter was so excited about finding the case, he called Professor French at home to tell him about it.

"Ah, yes," French said. "I was wondering when you were going to find that case. I was going to tell you about it in a week or so, but I'm glad you found it. You know how important this case is, don't you?"

"Sure," Peter replied. "It gives us a high-level case which announces a rule of law which is a lot more favorable to us."

"That's true," the professor said. "But it's a lot more important than that. One of the best ways to get the Supreme Court to agree to take your case is to argue that your case will solve what they call 'a split between the circuits.' Here you've got the Ninth Circuit saying that in California, Washington, Oregon, and the rest of the far west, social workers are to be provided legal protection from the very beginning to the very end. And the Second Circuit rules that in Connecticut and New York, social-workers are immune from suit only during the trial itself. That is a dramatic difference between the circuits, and you need to try to convince the Supreme Court that they should settle this difference and make one rule for the whole nation. After all, the Constitution should mean the same thing in all the federal courts of this country."

"Wow. Why didn't they teach us this stuff in law school?" Peter asked.

"They probably did. But most wannabe lawyers never pay that much attention because it is well known that there is not much money in constitutional law."

"They were sure right about that."

"Peter, there's one other argument that I think you have been missing in this whole case."

"Yikes. What's that?"

"Let's see if you can figure it out. I'll ask you some questions, OK?"

"Sure, I'm game. I never claimed to be a constitutional lawyer."

"At what point in the process did they falsify the computer records?"

Peter thought for a moment. "Uh . . . It was after the state case was all over. It was after we had filed the federal civil rights suit."

"Do you get my—"

"Oh, my goodness! I am an idiot!"

"I take it you understand my point," the professor said.

"Yeah, they have immunity for perjury done during the state trial. When the state trial is over, the immunity is over. We should be able to clean their clocks for document tampering they did during the federal trial."

"You got it."

"Well, at least I learned it now. We just tell that to the Supreme Court and that will take care of it, right?"

"Not exactly. You've got a little problem."

"What kind of problem?"

"You can only bring up issues in the Supreme Court if you previously raised those same issues in the district court at the trial level, and in the circuit court at the appellate level."

"Does that mean I can't make this argument at all because I didn't see it until now?"

"Again, let me say, not exactly. The Supreme Court recognizes that there is a difference between issues and arguments. You have raised the issue of whether you can sue the social workers for the document tampering. You need to simply say, 'We've raised this issue all along. But here is one more argument to support our position.'"

"Will that work?"

"Probably. But again, it will depend to some degree on how it strikes a twenty-four year-old law clerk. If they think you should have seen that earlier, they may advise their justice not to take the case because it could have easily been resolved if the plaintiffs' lawyer would have made the right argument earlier."

"I feel really bad. Have I committed malpractice?"

"No way. And besides, I don't think your fiancé is likely to sue you for it anyway."

"I think you're right. OK. I'll work it in carefully and see what the justices and their clerks think."

"When do you think you'll have your draft of the cert petition done?"

"Next Tuesday. That's three days before the deadline you gave me."

"Excellent. That means I can take a couple weeks and you will still have plenty of time to get the petition filed within sixty days of the Ninth Circuit decision."

∼

Donna Corliss was happy to hear from Stephen on a Friday night at six—Spokane time. It meant she wasn't the only one at home alone on a weekend party night.

After a few minutes of pleasantries, Stockton got to his point.

"Donna, have you had the wedding invitations printed yet?"

"No. They've been designed, but the order is being placed next week. Your mom has just been delightful in working with me on all these details."

"I'm glad to hear that you and mom are getting along so well, and I don't want you to take what I'm about to tell you in the wrong way."

Corliss sat down, frozen in dread.

"Yeah. . ." she said.

"I'm afraid we're going to have to postpone the wedding."

"Postpone? Postpone? Stephen, what do you mean? Do you really mean postpone—or cancel?"

"I said postpone and I mean postpone," he said angrily.

"Til when?"

"Until July or August."

"July or August! Why?"

"Because I heard today from my dad that your federal case is going to be appealed to the Supreme Court. It hasn't been filed yet, I checked. But it's going to be filed at any time."

"So?"

"So! So! It's not appropriate for me to be married to a woman whose case is coming before the Supreme Court. In fact, we need to officially call off the engagement until later as well."

"Stephen, something is wrong. You're just backing out."

"Donna, I am not. I'm trying to help you and protect you."

"Right." The sarcasm was thick.

"Just listen to me. If my boss knew that I was engaged to a woman who's cert petition was before the court and I didn't tell him, he'd make my life miserable. He'd probably even fire me."

"He would do that?"

"Justice Jesse D. Rose *would* most definitely do that. But if we are not engaged or married when the case is filed, there is a very good chance that I would get assigned the case to screen it for him."

"Yeah? Why is that a big deal?"

"It's a big deal because I would write a summary telling him what the case is all about and make a tentative recommendation about accepting the case or not. I'd have at least a little input on whether or not the Court will take your case. But if we are engaged, I'll have none."

Corliss cursed Peter Barron viciously. "Can't he leave me alone?" she added.

"So, you see my point?"

"Yeah, I do. I can't say I'm happy about it. But I understand. I want this case behind me more than you do."

"And if the Court doesn't take the case, maybe we can get married in April or May."

"All right. I guess you really are just looking out for me. Thanks." Corliss began to cry. "I'd better go. It's OK. I just have to cry for a while."

"All right. I'll call you later this weekend. And I'll see you in just a few days. Christmas is just around the corner."

"OK. I love you, Stephen."

"I love you, too."

As he hung up the phone, his doorbell rang.

"Carol! Hi! Geez, you look like a million bucks. I'll grab my jacket, let's go."

~

Casey bolted out the front door the minute she saw Peter's Explorer at their front curb. Gwen was not far behind, hurrying to lock the door and get downtown before the real crowds hit. By nine-thirty, the stores in downtown Spokane would be jammed on this, the last weekend before Christmas. Next Saturday would be Christmas Eve.

Peter quickly tucked Casey into the back seat, giving her a warm hug. He opened Gwen's door with a flourish, reaching out ostensibly to help her step up to the high seat of his vehicle. Instead he grabbed her around the waist, swung her in a complete circle, and then kissed her before she could say a word.

"Yeeee," Casey squealed

"Well, good morning to you too, Mr. Barron," Gwen said, smiling, her eyes glistening brightly in the morning sun.

"I hope you're ready for the best Christmas shopping trip ever."

"Absolutely," Gwen replied.

They had a delightful day walking and shopping, holding hands, stealing kisses, and staring at each other with extended gazes. As they strolled hand-in-hand down the mall, Peter leaned over and whispered to Gwen, "It's just how I dreamed it would be."

"Me too," Gwen said, squeezing his hand. *"How could this be more perfect?"* she thought to herself.

They headed to Gwen's home around five, with the back of Peter's rig loaded with goodies. They had managed to buy Casey a number of presents by one of them taking a walk with her for a few minutes now and then.

Peter insisted on paying for everything despite the fact that 1994 was looking like a down year financially.

After Casey was in bed, Peter and Gwen sat on the couch and snuggled in each others' arms.

"Next Christmas, we can sit in front of *our* fireplace out at the lake and watch the fire."

"That'll be great, Peter. I really can't wait," Gwen said, snuggling just a bit closer.

27

Donna and Stephen spent Christmas Eve together at her parents' house in Connell. Shortly after eleven, Stephen left her there and drove an hour-and-forty-five minutes through the frozen wheat fields back to his parents home so he could be with them on Christmas morning.

He was doing his best to use his week at home to convince Donna that everything was fine between them despite the postponement. He wished he could convince himself as well. Among the throngs of Washington Capitol Hill staffers who were accustomed to seeing and working for one of the five-hundred-thirty-five Senators and Congressmen, his job as a law clerk for just one of nine justices of the Supreme Court gave him near celebrity status. He liked the attention, and he liked the females who were attentive.

At 7:00 on Christmas Eve, Peter, Gwen, Casey, and the Mansfields attended the Christmas Eve service at Valley Fourth Memorial. Casey was in the angel choir with her fellow five-year-olds. It was hard to tell which of the four adults who brought her was beaming the most.

Peter convinced them all to spend the balance of their time to together at his house on Christmas Eve. As Gwen helped him decorate earlier in the day, ideas of what she could do to improve Peter's spartan-like furnishings and decorations began to capture her imagination.

The Mansfield tradition was to open presents on Christmas morning. Peter had been raised in a Christmas Eve present-opening family. They compromised by deciding to open a single "small" present on Christmas Eve at Peter's house.

Casey opened a Cinderella doll that Peter and Gwen had picked out for her. She squealed with delight and ran to show it to her grandmother. Gwen would have been next. But Peter insisted that she be last because he had "a special present, although it *was* small." Gwen felt her joy surge in anticipation. She had not yet received an engagement ring from Peter and was confident she was interpreting his hint correctly.

June received a pair of leather gloves that matched the new coat she would receive from her husband on Christmas morning. Gwen had collaborated with the two men in her life to coordinate the purchases.

Stan got a variable-speed drill set that Peter had picked out solo. "Finally, I've got another man to shop for me! Hooray!" he exclaimed.

Gwen gave Peter a sweater which she hoped would bring out the blue in his eyes.

"It's great, babe. I love it."

Peter then produced his present for Gwen from behind the couch. Her heart sank when she saw the dress-box sized present. *Peter is the type who would disguise a ring,* she told herself. But the box did have the weight and feel of a dress. She opened the box and to her great disappointment there was no ring. She found not a dress, but a classy silk Anne Klein suit, in beige.

"Oh, Peter. It's absolutely stunning. I've never had anything so gorgeous."

"Well, you're just going to have to get used to it." Peter said with a smile. "It's your Supreme Court suit. I want you to wear it when we go to argue our case."

"Thank you so much. It's beautiful. You have terrific taste." She quickly checked the size on the tag. "It is the right size, I sure hope it fits."

No matter how wonderful the suit was it couldn't compete with a ring. Gwen had managed to mask her true feelings from Peter and Stan, but her mother was not fooled.

"Why don't you go try it on?" June said.

"Absolutely," Peter added beaming. "You can use the guest bedroom."

"Oh, OK," Gwen said. *Maybe he'll give it to me tomorrow*, she hoped.

A few minutes later she appeared in stocking feet. "I think it fits," she said.

"*Think* it fits?" Peter exclaimed. "It's perfect, and you look stunning. We'll get two votes on the Court just when they look at you."

"It is very, very nice, honey. Just gorgeous," her mother said.

"Yeah, it's great," Stan added. "And practical, too. It's even got pockets."

"Oh, yeah, pockets," Gwen said, thrusting her hands in absentmindedly. Her right hand struck something small and round. She pulled it out, held it up to examine it, and then burst into tears. It was a full-carat diamond solitaire in the classic four-prong setting.

Peter stood and took her in his arms, "Well, I guess I should apologize. It's too small isn't it? " he said feigning disappointment.

"Oh, you stop," Gwen said, hitting him on the chest and laughing through her tears. "You tricked me. I patted the pockets from the outside looking for a little box. It didn't occur to me that you would put the ring in the pocket by itself. It's so beautiful, Peter, and the suit is just gorgeous. Thank you so much."

Then looking deep into his eyes, she continued, "I'm going to wear this ring with pride, Mr. Barron." And with that, she kissed him with a lingering, passionate embrace which was returned with full abandon.

Stan cleared his throat and said, "C'mon June, let's go make coffee."

～

On, Wednesday, January 11, Peter finished his final edits of his forty-eight page cert petition. Professor French's edits had proven to be invaluable. He even volunteered to review the final version overnight before Peter sent it to the printers. He made several more changes that Peter quickly agreed made the presentation clearer and stronger.

"I cannot tell you how much your help has meant to me on this brief. I wish I could pay you."

"Well, if you ever recover attorney's fees, we'll report the hours to the court and ask to be included. Otherwise, forget it. It's an important case."

"Won't I have to put your name on the pleadings or something to allow you to get attorney's fees?" Peter asked.

"You're probably right," French said. "It would be the first time in a long time that my name will be on a cert petition except as lead counsel."

"Oh, I'd be happy to list you as lead counsel," Peter countered.

"No, no, no. You've done the work. I've just coached. Put my name down in the second position."

"Terrific. I was hoping I could con you into that. Joe tells me that your name on the brief will dramatically increase the chances the Court will look seriously at my petition."

"Oh, a little maybe. But Peter, you need to have your expectations in order. And I am very serious when I tell you this. Your case has risen well above the average for a great number of reasons. It is interesting factually—there is a split in the circuits—you have a strong dissenting opinion from a respected judge—"

"And I have your name on the petition," Peter interjected.

"OK, OK. Even with all of that, your chances are no better than one in 15 that the Court will take your case. You've risen way above the one-out-of-a-hundred odds, but this is still a long-shot. If one justice, who likes your case and wants you to win, believes that it is impossible for him to get five votes in the final analysis, he may actually see to it that your cert petition is defeated. He'll wait until a similar case comes up in a few years when there is some switch somewhere on the Court. You are trying a single lawsuit. They are playing a complicated game of constitutional chess."

~

Peter overnighted a hard-copy and a computer disk version of the brief to RAM Printers in Hyattsville, Maryland, just as the professor had instructed. Located in a small, non-descript building in a lower-middle class business district, this print shop was known among the well-informed as the shop which prints the official original decisions of the Supreme Court. The printers would guarantee that the brief was properly filed the day it was printed. Peter enclosed a check for the filing fee in the package. He also had to get them a $4,500 check to pay for the printing costs before the brief would be filed. He promised the printers they would have the money by next Wednesday when the print job was scheduled to be completed. Had it not been for Professor French's association, they would never have extended credit to an unknown lawyer from Spokane, Washington.

Peter had been too busy with the cert petition to hound David G. Humphrey about his latest fund-raising efforts. But now that his work was done on the cert petition, it was time for a call to Kansas City.

"*Heart of America*," a sweet voice sounded.

"Hi, this is Peter Barron, the lawyer handling—"

"I know you, Mr. Barron," Cindy Walters said. "Your case is very important to us."

"Well, I'm glad to hear that. Is Mr. Humphrey in? I need to ask him if he can send me a check for $4,500 for the printing fees for our Supreme Court petitions."

"Well, he's not in right now. But there probably won't be a problem. He whooped and hollered with delight every time I gave him a copy of the daily results from the mail shop."

"How much have you raised?"

"I really don't know the total number myself, but quite a lot. I guess that depends on your definition of what quite a lot means. I'll have him call you. And I'll make sure you get a check today or tomorrow."

"I'm really in a pinch—I will need it sent overnight."

"No problem, Mr. Barron. I will be my pleasure."

Humphrey never returned his call that day. But before noon the following day, a check for $4,500 arrived from *Heart of America*. Humphrey preferred to simply mail a check for the needed amount rather than answer a lawyer's follow-up questions about money. Peter was curious about all this, but he couldn't argue with the results.

~

Willet was served with her copy of the cert petition by mail the following Friday. The Supreme Court rules gave her the option of replying or not. After lengthy discussions with Matt Bartholomew and the Attorney General, it was decided that they would send in a short letter saying that they believed that the decision below had been correct and they saw no need to respond. Willet liked the approach. Short, haughty, and confident.

Upon receipt of that letter on January 20th, the Clerk notified the Chief Justice that the case was ready for inclusion on the justices' docket for discussion. *Corliss* v. *Landis* was set for discussion on Friday morning, February 3.

~

Stephen Stockton had been watching the docket like a hawk. He had commandeered a copy of the cert petition as soon as it was filed in the clerk's office. His plan was to offer to trade the case for another one with Justice Rose's other clerk. The case, being from his home town, would naturally hold a special interest for him, he would argue.

The story and excuses proved to be unnecessary. Justice Rose assigned him the case as a part of the regular rotation of assignments between his two clerks.

Stockton had to work doubly hard on his presentation. It would be very bad for him personally if the judge looked into the case and found his analysis to be deliberately misleading. He had to be very accurate, but he had to spin the facts and the legal theories in such a way that would diminish Justice Rose's natural interest in this kind of case.

He summarized Peter's arguments in seven tightly written pages. But he had been a clerk long enough to understand that it was the opening summary that was the most critical in setting the tone for the Justice's review of the case.

This case poses very unusual facts, but quite routine issues, of constitutional law. There are two basic "questions presented:"

(1) Whether a social worker is immune from a civil rights suit for making a warrantless search that is an integral part of a child abuse case?

(2) Whether a social worker is immune from a civil rights case for alleged perjury and falsification of documents?

This Court has well-developed doctrines of judicial immunity covering both issues. Social workers are officers of the court, not police investigators and as such their immunity for home visits seems well-premised on Wyman v. James. *Even if a Court were to reach a contrary conclusion on the legality of this particular entry, no reasonable social worker could be expected to distinguish this case from the circumstances in* Wyman. *Since the law is not "clearly established" to the contrary, immunity must be granted.*

The second question presents nothing more than a frontal attack on this Court's ruling in LaHue v. Briscoe. *As intriguing as that question is in the abstract, it is a settled doctrine of this Court. An interesting factual point is raised that a part of the alleged falsification apparently took place after the underlying state child abuse case was over.*

However, this was not discussed by either of the lower courts and not found in any of the briefs of counsel below. Even interesting issues cannot be raised in this Court for the first time.

Proposed recommendation: Vote to deny cert if the matter is raised for discussion.

〜

Justice Rose had forty-five cert petitions to review with his clerks in preparation for the February 3rd meeting of the justices. They would discuss less than a dozen. They would probably grant review to only one or two.

As he glanced through the stack, Stockton didn't even have to look. He had the pile memorized. *Landis* was next.

"Hmm. Interesting facts. I always like cases with interesting facts. But, we can't go around pleasing ourselves, can we? We've got a Supreme Court to run here. Doctrines to pronounce. Decisions to make. Protests to engender. Creating the fodder for the next election. Important stuff here. I can't just grant cert because the facts amuse me."

Stockton was smiling. He knew the judge was carrying on for his benefit.

"Huh? Eastern District of Washington. Isn't that where you're from, Stephen?"

"Yes, Your Honor. It is."

"You know any of these lawyers?"

"No, Your Honor. This case made news last summer while I was studying for the bar, but I have only seen the lawyers on TV. Don't know them personally." Stockton instantly realized it was a mistake to have mentioned TV. Now the case was interesting enough to have been on TV, and he remembered watching it.

"Is that so? Well, I hate to sound like I am making fun of your hometown, but just because a case makes news in Spokane, doesn't mean it meets the criteria for Supreme Court review."

Stockton was relieved. "My feeling exactly, Justice Rose. I've recommended against granting cert."

"I see you have. Sounds open and shut to me, too. Let's move on."

～

Later that evening, Jesse Rose entered the study of his home and pulled a stack of reading from his briefcase. The *Landis* cert petition was one of nine he had left to personally review from the materials Stockton had delivered to him earlier in the day.

Rose walked across the room and turned on a small stereo and dialed in the "Smooth Jazz" station, his habit when reading briefs and petitions.

After an hour of unusually boring cases, he picked up the petition in the *Landis* matter. "Ah, yes. Interesting facts. TV news in Spokane. I remember this one," the justice muttered to himself. "It's about time there was something interesting in one of these cases."

He had read about warrantless entries before. And he had seen lots of strip searches of children in papers filed before the Court. As much as he detested them, it wasn't that different.

"I'm going to have to teach that Stockton kid the meaning of interesting," he said out loud, starting to skim rather than read.

And then his eyes struck the paragraph describing a sitting federal judge going into a state office building with a computer expert and personally discovering tampered documents. "Now that *is* interesting," Rose said aloud.

He switched back to reading half-way through, then flipped back to the front cover and discovered, for the first time, his old acquaintance, Charley French's name on the cover. "He's not in the lead! I wonder if he's getting ready to retire?" he thought.

Five pages from the end, he simply stopped reading. He took out his list of cases he used in the conference of the justices. Next to the case name *Landis v. Corliss, et. al*, he wrote, "push for grant of cert," and went on to the next case.

～

On February 3, Chief Justice Winston, one of the law-and-order conservatives, called the meeting of the justices to order, precisely at the scheduled time of 9:30. Winston was very popular with the other justices—at least as it pertained to his administrative and organizational skills. The meetings were run skillfully and without undue delay.

A quick report around the table disclosed there were fourteen cases that one or more of the justices wanted to discuss.

"That is quite a lot," the Chief Justice reminded them. "We'll have to keep up the pace."

Justice Rose was fourth in seniority on the Court. Discussion of cases went in order of the seniority of the justice interested in bringing the case up for discussion.

About 10:45, it was finally his turn. "I have only one case to discuss at this point," he began. "All my others were brought up previously. I'd like to have us consider the case of *Landis v. Corliss.* It's number 27 on your list for today."

There was some scrambling among each of the justices piles of paper. No clerks were allowed in the room. Each justice had to keep track of it alone.

"Didn't we just decide all this in *LaHue v. Briscoe?*" Justice Kraus began.

"Three of us weren't on the Court then," Justice Dowling replied. "I'm not sure that the outcome would be the same today."

"Surely that is not a reason for granting cert, is it Justice Dowling?" the Chief said, looking over his reading glasses with raised eyebrows.

"No, Chief, you're right, I guess."

"Well, if I can make the pitch for my case, here we've got a federal judge who personally discovers document tampering by state government social workers with some ingenuous computer technology. And if you aren't intrigued by interesting facts, how about a split in the circuits on an important constitutional issue?

"The Ninth Circuit has granted absolute immunity to social workers from the beginning of their investigation all the way until the case is over. The Second Circuit much more sensibly has limited absolute immunity to conduct that occurs after the case is initially filed in court. Do any of you believe that social workers should be absolutely immune, no matter what they do, as long as they eventually file the case in Court?"

Everyone knew that Chief Justice and Kraus probably did, but he didn't press the point.

"OK, is that it?" the Chief Justice asked looking round the table. "Anyone else want to speak to this case?"

"All right, all in favor, raise your hand."

Justices Rose, Dowling, and Stauffer immediately shot their hands up.

"I count three, one short. Cert will be denied. Can we move on?" Winston asked.

"If I could, Your Honor," Justice Swindon said, "could we hold it there for just a minute. I wasn't quite ready to vote on that last case. In fact, I'd like to ask that we table the *Landis* matter to next week. I can announce at the beginning of our meeting whether I am going to vote for cert or not. I won't take up any more discussion time."

"Fine, fine. The matter is tabled." Next to the case name the Chief Justice wrote, "tabled 2/10." And then after that, "Work on Swindon to vote no."

~

Justice Swindon, typical for a swing voter, suddenly became very popular. Rose, Stauffer, Dowling, Krauss, and the Chief Justice each called and made appointments with his secretary for visits in the next three working days.

He listened politely, even intently, to their arguments, but was non-committal at the end of each conversation.

~

Stephen Stockton carried out his own reconnaissance mission with Justice Swindon's law clerks. The clerks were free to discuss the cases among themselves, but the views of their own justices were considered to be confidential. But a carefully worded, "How do you see the case *personally*—you, not the justice?" would sometimes loosen lips and give at least a window of insight. But Stockton struck out completely.

～

The following Friday, Justice Winston called the meeting to order. "All right, I believe the first matter of the day is *Landis v. Corliss*. Justice Swindon asked that the matter be tabled until today so he could consider his vote."

"Yes," Swindon began. "I appreciate all of the helpful advice I got this week, and I sure don't want to offend anyone, but I am afraid that I am going to vote 'no.'"

"OK. Cert denied will be the order," the Chief Justice said, smiling.

"Chief?" said Justice Gilbert, one of the two women justices. "I heard about all the meetings you all were having with Justice Swindon, and I got intrigued with what all the fuss was about. So I went back and studied the case with interest. I'm going to vote yes. So I guess that means 'Cert granted?'"

"Yes, it does, Justice Gilbert," he said with a scowl. "Now let's move on."

～

Stephen Stockton learned about the decision as soon as Justice Rose returned to his chambers after the meeting. He wanted to call Donna immediately, but the news was embargoed until Monday at 10:00 A.M. Any breach of security, if discovered, would cost him his job and brand him for life. He wanted to help, but Corliss wasn't worth the risk. And he had an interesting evening planned with the redhead from the Senate. She could learn about it all on Monday. He would call her right at ten. She would still know before anyone else.

～

Professor French called the Court Clerk at 10:00 A.M. sharp on Monday. It had been on the calendar on Friday, it could be announced that Monday.

"Case number please?" the assistant clerk intoned.

"94-6877."

French could hear her tapping the numbers in on the keyboard. "Cert granted."

"Yes!" French yelled into the receiver. "Thank you very much!" he said hanging up to look up Peter's number.

"Rookie," the clerk cursed as she rubbed her traumatized ear.

It was 7:10 A.M. in Spokane, "Not too early to learn good news like this." the professor reasoned. But he only had Peter's office number. He dialed it anyway. It rang and rang. As he was about to hang up the answering service finally picked up the line.

"Peter Barron's office."

"This is an answering service, right?"

"Yes, sir. The office opens at 8:30. Would you like to leave a message?"

"No ma'am, I need to speak to Mr. Barron immediately."

"Is this an emergency?"

"No," he said with exasperation. "But this is extremely important."

"I'm sorry. I can only attempt to reach him at this hour for an emergency."

"OK. OK. Have it your way. Tell him it's Professor French. And it's an emergency. A Supreme Court of the United States emergency."

"Just a moment, sir," the operator said, rolling her eyes.

"Professor?" came Peter's voice in about a minute. "Supreme Court emergency?"

"Yes! Yes! My boy. A good emergency. No, it's a great emergency! Cert was granted. You did it, Peter!"

French heard the phone drop followed by whooping, hollering, and stamping on the other line.

"Sorry, I dropped the phone," Peter said in a moment. "This is incredible! I can't believe it."

"Peter, you did a great job. But the hard part comes now. You have got to convince the highest court in America to reverse or modify some two-hundred-year-old trends in the law. Can you do it?"

"With your help and God's blessing, I'm beginning to think we can really do it."

28

Gwen was awake, lying in bed, planning her wedding for the umpteenth time, when she heard an incessant pounding on her front door. She glanced at the clock. "7:40 A.M. This is weird."

She glanced about the room looking for something to protect herself if necessary. She quickly threw on a bath robe, grabbed an old golf club out of her closet, and headed for the front door.

"Who is it?" she cried in her most threatening voice.

"Gwen, it's Peter. And open this door at once! You won't believe it."

"I already don't believe it," she said fumbling with the deadbolt. As the door swung wide, "OK, now please—"

Peter didn't wait. He bent over, grabbed her in his arms and held her tight and spun her around the living room yelling, "Yessssss!" at the top of his lungs. "Gwen, we did it! The Supreme Court took our case! I just found out! We did it! We did it!"

"We won the whole thing? I thought we were just waiting for the initial ruling or something."

"Don't get technical on me now! Yes, it's just the preliminary ruling. But it's the hardest part. Only one in a hundred cases get this far. Yes, yes!"

He spun her again. His foot hit the leg of a chair that toppled into the table lamp, sending it to the floor, with a crash. And they fared no better, tumbling to the floor in laughter.

"Well, as long as we're down on the floor why don't we pause for a word of prayer?"

"Very funny," Gwen said. And with that, Peter jumped to his feet and pulled Gwen to hers.

"Of course I was joking, but I really would like to thank God for this. It is so awesome. To think that we are going to present our case to The Supreme Court of the United States of America. Doesn't that blow you away?"

"I feel sorry for the other side already," Gwen said, smiling. "God has been with us every step of the way."

Casey wandered out of her room to see what all the noise was about. Peter and Gwen were on their knees beside the couch, praying, then laughing and hugging. Casey, huddled in the hall with her special blanket, silently watched and smiled.

Willet was not pleased with the news. She had been happy to do battle with Peter Barron in any forum where she had more experience. But only one of two thousand lawyers ever argues a case in the Supreme Court, and she was not one of them. And now Peter had hooked up with Professor French. "Surely, Peter will offer him the case," she thought. The idea of facing the formidable French in oral argument scared her even more.

She called Corliss immediately.

"I already heard," the social worker said.

"You have? How?" Willet asked suspiciously.

Corliss had never told Willet about her relationship with Stephen Stockton. Now was not the time to reveal that fact. "Oh, I just have a personal friend who is a lawyer and he found out somehow."

"My, news travels fast. The Supreme Court just announced it two hours ago. Does Rita Coballo know?"

"Yeah, I called her in Sacramento before I came to work."

"Well, at least we'll all get a state-paid trip to Washington out of this."

Corliss smiled at the thought of being paid to visit Stephen. "When do you think that might be?"

"It all depends. It depends if anyone gets any extensions of time for filing their briefs or if they do it on time. If every brief is filed right on time, there is a small chance the Court will still hear the case this term. They don't hear oral arguments much after the first of April."

"What happens if the briefs are filed later?"

"Then the case wouldn't be heard until next October. The Court is essentially closed from July 1 until October 1."

"When would the Court make its decision if it heard the case in October?"

"Probably in January or February 1996."

"You have got to do everything you can to get this case heard this year."

"Why?" Willet asked. "I might need more time to do a good job for you."

"I didn't want to tell you this, but I am waiting until this case is over before I get married. I want it over ASAP!"

"Sure, but why—oh, never mind. That's your business."

"Thanks, Gail, I appreciate that."

～

Peter worked hard on his brief. He counted the days and realized that if he dawdled with his opening brief, taking the full time allotted by the court rules, plus the time Corliss would have for her reply, including one extension of time which is routinely granted, then his reply brief would fall due on the third day of his honeymoon.

Nothing was going to interrupt his wedding. Not even the Supreme Court. Nothing.

Professor French was pleased to see Peter working so hard and so early on the brief. But it was less work than Peter imagined because so much of the work had been required in the course of preparing the cert petition.

After four weeks of research, writing, and faxes to and from the University of Michigan Law School, Peter was ready again to send his brief to RAM printers.

Printing costs loomed in his mind once again. He picked up the phone and dialed.

"Miss Walters, this is Peter Barron again. Is Mr. Humphrey in?"

"Oh, hi, Mr. Barron. Let me check if I can get him."

She got Humphrey on the intercom. He was searching through his stack of news clippings, looking for his next worthy cause.

"Yeah."

"Mr. Humphrey, it's Peter Barron on the phone."

"Uh . . . I'm busy right now."

"What if he wants something for the Supreme Court? We've raised over $350,000. At least that's what I typed in the report to the board last week. Can't we send him some more?"

"That number is the gross. And don't you ever tell that to anybody. I can't talk right now. Just tell him I'm busy, and say I want to know what he absolutely needs right now. We're doing the best we can."

"Mr. Humhrey, please?"

"I'll send him a check, Cindy. I promise. Just get me an amount."

～

Stockton confirmed the analysis of timing that Willet had given to Corliss. If they hurried, they did have a chance of getting the case heard on the last week of oral arguments. Cases might be heard as late as the week of April 3.

Corliss became obsessed with the idea that this case had to be argued and decided in April so she could get married. Stockton winced every time she brought it up.

Willet succumbed to Corliss's pressure and submitted her brief in just three weeks. Peter called her to request an extension of time for his final brief. He normally had just ten days to file.

"Mr. Barron, under normal circumstances I would cooperate, but my client has specifically instructed me to push this case hard. She wants it heard this term."

"Why?" Peter asked. "What's her rush?"

"She told me it was personal. That is where I ended my inquiry and I suggest you do the same," Willet said curtly, hanging up the phone.

"I do beg your pardon," Peter said looking at the phone handset. *What a happy bunch. Gwen was right. They are witches.*

The Saturday morning idea of visiting travel agents to plan their honeymoon would have to be postponed. He would now be working all day.

"How often will this happen when we are married?" Gwen asked just a bit testily when Peter informed her of the news.

"Before Gwen Landis, my Saturdays were pretty laid back. I worked only if I wanted to. You have been the cause of all this involuntary overtime," Peter said with good nature. "You and the Supreme Court. Nobody else could make me change."

～

Stockton looked at the court schedule with dismay. Oral arguments would be held Thursday, April 6. Corliss's persistence had paid off—at least with the calendar of the Supreme Court. Donna would be pressing hard for marriage after the court date.

～

David G. Humphrey was on the phone, Sally announced. Peter couldn't believe his ears.

"Mr. Humphrey, this is a surprise. I thought you were avoiding me."

"Nonsense, Peter, and please call me David. I've just been busy."

"So I hear. How's our fund-raising going? Can I get some kind of report or something?"

"Yes, of course. In fact, how would you like me to deliver them in person?"

"In Spokane?"

"No. In the other Washington. Washington, D.C."

"What do you have in mind?"

"I have in mind a big appreciation banquet. We could hold it the night before your Supreme Court argument and give you a big check for attorney's fees."

"That sounds good except for one thing: I can't possibly do it the night before I argue the case. I'll need to keep cramming, and in any event, I would be far too nervous."

"How about the evening of April 6? After the argument?"

"That would be much better."

"Great, we'll be there with a large check."

"I'm afraid I need to ask you if there is some way we can get a small check ahead of time."

"What's that about? More printing costs?"

"No. Airline tickets and hotel rooms. I need three tickets and three rooms."

"OK, you need one, who are the others?"

"I need one for Gwen, she's my fiancé now."

"Really? Congratulations."

"And I need one for Professor Charles French from the University of Michigan. He has argued over thirty cases in the Supreme Court and has been helping me with this one for free. I really need him for my final preparations. And he's going to sit with me in oral argument and kick me under the table if I do anything wrong."

"OK. Another ticket from Michigan."

"So will that be two rooms or three?"

"What?"

"I thought that the two of you, now that you are engaged—"

"Mr. Humphrey, maybe you don't remember, but I told you in our first conversation that I am a born-again Christian. It will be three rooms, thank you very much."

"Be that way," Humphrey said under his breath after he hung up. "Your check just got cut in half."

Humphrey hit the intercom button.

"Cindy, can you come in?"

"Yes, Mr. Humphrey, I'll be right there."

It was pink today. She looked great in pink.

"Cindy, sit down please. I need you to take some notes. We are going to have a major event in Washington, D.C. I need you to help me with the planning. And, to show my appreciation, you are going to go and participate in the festivities as well."

"That sounds exciting. What do I need to do?"

"We are going to have a Supreme Court Victory Banquet. It'll be a fund raiser. First call three hotels and get catering menus and prices faxed here for dinners ranging from three hundred to five hundred. Try the Hyatt Regency on Capitol Hill, the Stouffer at L'Enfant Plaza, and the Ritz Carlton in McLean. I hear that their food is outstanding, but it's a ways from the Supreme Court."

"Got it."

"And then I'd like you to draft the announcement flyer for the banquet to put in a letter we'll send out to our list. Those who can give $100 or more will be invited to attend. We'll have special tables for those who give $500 and a private reception for those who give $1000 or more. Let's make it lunch with our lawyer immediately after his argument in the Supreme Court for those who give a thousand or more."

"Anything else?" she asked sweetly.

"There will be lots of other things. But just one more for right now. Whichever hotel you book for the banquet, I want you to book four rooms for the day of the argument and the prior two days as well. That would make it April 4, 5, and 6."

"OK, got it. Four rooms. And I need you to book five airplane tickets."

"Peter Barron and Gwen Landis will be flying out of Spokane. A law professor by the name of French—his name is on our copy of the brief—is coming from Lansing, Michigan. And then you and me."

"That's five tickets and four rooms? Who stays together?"

"We do, Cindy. You and me. It'll be fun."

As the words of protest were forming on her lips, Humphrey interrupted. "And it's a great way to ensure those large bonuses as well as guarantee your job security, if you get my drift."

She looked at him, expressionless, and said nothing.

～

Peter and Gwen finally made it to the travel agency. They wanted someplace warm by the ocean. They considered the Caribbean and Cancun, but settled on the more traditional Hawaii. They wanted to avoid the tourist trap, Waikiki, and were leaning toward Maui. But the middle-aged travel agent, who had been to Hawaii more than a dozen times, warned them that Maui was becoming trendy in its own right. It was not the place to go if they were looking for isolation, she told them.

They were considering Kauai until the agent warned them of heavy rainfall. The Big Island of Hawaii? Too many bugs. Black sand beaches.

Finally, she carefully recommended something she had been steering them toward all along.

"There is one hotel on the North Shore of Oahu—that's the island Honolulu is on. It's called the Turtle Bay Hilton. It's a beautiful resort, right on the beach. And the North Shore of Oahu has the biggest waves in the world. It's my favorite place in Hawaii."

"You wanted us to choose it all along, didn't you?"

"Yes. I love it. But I wanted to make sure that your tastes are right for it. It's all by itself. No developments for miles. A little town called Kahuku is up the road a bit—five or six miles. But, if you get lonely for the bright lights and big city, Honolulu is about forty-minutes away."

"It'll be perfect. Can you give us prices for airline tickets, a jeep rental and two weeks at Turtle Bay?" Peter asked, turning to Gwen for her agreement.

"Two-week honeymoon at the Turtle Bay Hilton? Ooh, how about dumping her and marrying me?" the agent teased.

"Not on your life, sweetheart," Gwen shot back with a smile.

29

~

On Tuesday, April 4, David Humphrey arranged for his wife to drop him off at the airport. He needed to get there early—lots of phone calls he told her. He would take no chance that she would see Cindy Walters meeting him at the terminal for their 10:00 A.M. flight.

She would have missed seeing Cindy in any case. Cindy was late.

At 8:00 A.M. Cindy was at the office, although everything for the trip had already been packed and given to Humphrey to bring in his larger brief case. And she was dressed in jeans and a loose lavender T-shirt. Humphrey would have been very disappointed.

She went to the files and withdrew all financial records concerning the Landis case. She carefully copied them, taking great care to see that everything was in the correct order. Once she was finished, she dropped the copies into an oversized envelope.

Cindy then went to her own desk and began to take out all of her personal items and load them into a cardboard box.

She picked up the telephone and called Humphrey's extension, knowing full well he would not answer. When the voice mail picked up, she uttered six words and hung up the receiver.

Finally, she took out a printed form, carefully filled in the blanks and attached it with a prepared adhesive pouch securely to the envelope.

It was ten minutes before the other employees were due to arrive. She locked the front door and slid her office key through the crack.

She walked downstairs and left to spend the rest of the day with her boyfriend, who was waiting in the parking garage.

⌒

Peter was full of nervous excitement as he and Gwen were thrust back in their seats as their jet powered down the runway in Spokane. Aaron cashed in some of his frequent flyer miles and got them upgraded to First Class round-trip. "An early wedding present," he said.

They would meet the professor at the airport and rent a car to travel to the Hyatt Regency on Capitol Hill together.

When they landed, the professor was waiting for them at the gate. His flight had arrived twenty-five minutes earlier.

"Well, Peter, glad to finally meet you," the professor said. He was sixty, about five foot six, white haired, with a healthy glow radiating in his face, and piercing steel-blue eyes.

"Professor French, the pleasure is all mine."

"And I can see from looking at your bride-to-be that the most important part of this case has already been favorably resolved. I am absolutely delighted to meet you, Miss Landis," he said with a slight bow.

"Thank you so much. Now I can see why you have won so many cases in the Supreme Court. You certainly have a wonderful way with words."

"Oh-h-h," he laughed. "I have just had the fortune of good cases and weak opponents. And, unfortunately, you have only a great case. Your opponents are far from weak. They know what they are doing."

"Well, I guess we should go get our luggage and analyze the case at the hotel. I'll drive and you navigate if you like, Professor."

"That's fine, on one condition. You call me Charlie."

"Fair enough," Peter said.

They worked their way through the maze of baggage claims and rent-a-car counters. After a short bus ride to the rent-a-car location, they were underway. Shortly after entering the George Washington Parkway, Gwen called out excitedly, "Look, Peter, there's the Capitol! Oh, pardon me, Dr. French. This is my first trip to D.C."

"Don't give it a second thought. We should never let age and false dignity rob us of the excitement of seeing things for the first time. It is a pleasure to share such a moment with you," the professor kindly offered. "OK, you will want to take the next exit right onto 395 north."

After they made the exit, they were immediately on the Fourteenth Street Bridge, and the Jefferson Memorial loomed directly in front and just to the left of their lane of travel. The Washington Monument was clearly visible just a little further off to the right. The tidal basin around the Jefferson Memorial was illuminated, showing off the hundreds of Japanese Cherry Blossoms which were near the end of their spectacular blooming cycle.

"The road splits just at the end of the bridge. Bear right. In a mile or so you will see an exit which says U.S. Capitol. Take it."

"You give as good directions about driving as you do about writing Supreme Court briefs," Peter said.

"Thanks. It's helpful when you've been here a few times. I'm about to take you on a round-about way to the hotel. We could get there a little faster through a tunnel, but I have a feeling you'd both like a close look at the Capitol Building and especially the Supreme Court."

"Oh, yes!" Gwen said enthusiastically.

"OK, now bear left here on this exit and take the lane that says 'U.S. House of Representatives.'"

Peter went up the ramp, rounded a curve and came to a red stop light.

"That massive squarish building in front of you is the Rayburn Building. It is one of the three buildings which house the members of the House and their staffs. Turn left at the light, Peter, and bear immediately right. Turn right at the next right, and you are on Independence Avenue," Charlie said.

As they turned the corner, the Capitol Building loomed dramatically off to their left. Peter slowly went up the Hill.

"At the second light, you need to turn left on First Street . . . And now on your right is the Library of Congress. I think it is the ugliest of the main tourist buildings on the outside, but the most beautiful of all on the inside. Kind of like some precious people I know.

"And now on your right," Charlie said with a flourish, "is the Supreme Court of the United States."

"Oh my, goodness," Peter said. "It is absolutely beautiful. And scary."

"Scary?" the professor said.

"Yes. It seems too important, too awesome for someone like me. I don't feel I belong in a place like this."

"Peter?" Gwen asked. "Can we stop and get out for a minute?"

"Sure," Peter said. "Charlie, where should we park?"

"Turn right at the light at the far edge of the Court's boundary. You can park there at night at least for a few minutes. This area is reserved during the day."

They got out of the car, walked up four steps to the main sidewalk, and then up a second small flight of stairs to the main plaza area in front of the Supreme Court. A fountain bubbled to their immediate left. A police guard took note of the trio and kept on strolling.

"Peter," Gwen said, "I'd like us to pray, and ask God to bless you and guide you when you appear here on Thursday. I think there is something important about us doing that right here on the property. Would that be OK, professor?"

"To show you that I am a professor, I must confess I am not sure I know precisely what you mean by your question, so let me give you three answers: a constitutional answer, a spiritual answer, and a practical answer. Constitutionally, we can pray in any of these buildings. We are not the government. We are free to pray. Spiritually, I would love to join you in prayer. My wife and I attend a conservative Episcopalian church that believes the Bible is the unchangeable word of God, not a negotiable instrument you pick and choose from. But, practically, the Court gets some protesters who come here to supposedly pray, but really just make trouble. If we go sit on those benches over there on your right, we can pray there for as long as we care to and no one will say a word."

Peter appreciated the professor's prayer very much indeed. But it was the prayer of his bride-to-be that really touched his heart. Last May, she was crying, spiritually lost and forlorn in the back parking lot on the Spokane County Courthouse. And now, eleven months later, she was upholding him in prayer sitting in front of the Supreme Court of the United States. God was indeed a mighty God.

～

David Humphrey had been in the hotel alone for several hours—at his wits' end. He had called the office countless times—although he had not yet checked his own voice mail. No one knew where Cindy Walters was. The only thing that was unusual was that an office key had been found under the door when they arrived that morning. Other than that, they had no clue.

One employee suggested calling Mrs. Humphrey to see if she had left a message there. "She'd never call there," was his curt reply.

Finally, at 7:30, he called the office one last time after leaving his seventh or eighth message on her home answering machine. Humphrey didn't know whether to be furious or concerned for her well-being. He decided to check his own voice mail to see if he had any other messages. Yes, there was one message: "I quit. And I'll get even."

～

Peter, Gwen, and Charlie French went to dinner at the hotel. As they worked their way across the massive lobby of the Hyatt Regency, overhung by a twelve-story angled glass wall, Gwen realized that they were not going to the pleasant but rather ordinary coffee shop that occupied the back half of the lobby floor.

They rode an elevator to the top floor and entered the Capitol View Club, an elegant restaurant with the absolutely best view of the Capitol of any restaurant in Washington.

At first, the professor was reluctant to discuss the case in great detail at the risk of being rude to Gwen. But she promptly reminded him that she was the client, and not only was she interested, but she wanted nothing more than the most efficient use of their time so they could be at their best on Thursday.

As Peter walked Gwen back to her room, which was a floor below his, Gwen held on to his arm and sighed loudly. "Peter, this is all so spectacular for me. And maybe what I'm about to say is nothing more than a tourist's runaway imagination. But somehow, I keep thinking that you belong here. Maybe not right away. But someday."

"It's probably just the french onion soup. You'll get over it."

"Maybe. Maybe not."

Arriving at her door, Gwen kissed him lightly on the lips. She slipped quickly inside. Just before it was completely shut, she opened it again, "Good night, my love," she whispered.

～

Gwen caught a tour bus in front of the hotel the next morning at 8:45. Peter and Charlie French took the fifteen minute walk up the hill to the Supreme Court. Charlie knew every inch of the building, and most of the people. Just before ten, they went through a screening line reserved for lawyers who were going to watch the Supreme Court in action. Four cases were scheduled that morning. Professor French believed that watching the Court in action for the two morning cases was the best and fastest education Peter could obtain.

Peter's awe at the marble and velvet quickly faded when the cry, "Oyez, Oyez, Oyez" rang out and nine older people dressed in long black robes assembled themselves and stood behind nine black leather chairs—identical except that each chair was custom-built to end exactly at the top of the justice's head. It would not do to have a diminutive Supreme Court Justice look like he was sitting in his father's oversized chair.

Peter pulled out a pad to take notes. "Put it away," the professor whispered. "Just watch and listen closely. Especially watch their eyes."

Peter was fascinated with the give and take and the extraordinary sharpness of the lawyers and at least most of the justices. By watching the eyes of the justices, Peter could see when lawyers scored points, made errors, and especially, when they were boring.

When the Court broke for lunch, Charlie gave Peter his own analysis as the two of them sped across town to the conference room of a large firm. One of Charlie's former students, who had clerked for the Court under now-retired Justice Carroll, assembled a moot court for Peter for that afternoon. Professor French told the assembled seven men this was Peter's first argument in the Court and they should all treat him accordingly.

"I think he is quite well-prepared on the substance of the case. Now let's get him ready for the Court itself."

These were not random lawyers. Among the seven, they had argued seventy-nine cases in the Supreme Court. Some had been in the Solicitor General's Office and had accumulated a great number of appearances. Peter soon realized how impossible it would have been without the professor's tutelage. Peter was, in every way, the least experienced person in the room, but he knew the case best, and he was willing to listen and learn. After three hours, the professor called a halt, wanting Peter to reserve some stamina for the next day.

When they returned to the hotel at 4:30, Peter's message light was blinking in his room. "You have a package at the front desk," the receptionist said.

He crossed the lobby just as Gwen was arriving back from a day of touring. They met, embraced, and walked together to the front desk. "I'm supposed to have a package," Peter said.

A few minutes later, the clerk returned with a thick Federal Express Package.

"Who is that from?" Gwen asked.

"I have no idea . . . Oh it's from Cindy Walters."

"And who is Cindy Walters?" Gwen said with mock jealousy.

"She's the secretary for *Heart of America*. I've only talked to her on the phone. She seems real nice."

"What's in the package?"

"I have no idea, but there is a message down here on the memo line. 'Don't open until after you argue. You must open before the banquet.' What's that supposed to mean?"

"I don't know for sure, but my guess is that it would be best to follow her directions."

"Well, I better give this to you to keep in your room. It would drive me crazy until I peeked."

"OK, I'll take it." And she resolved that she would take a quick peek when she got it to her room, just to make sure there would be no unpleasant surprises.

Twenty minutes later, Gwen glanced in the package, thumbed through a couple dozen pages without removing them from the package. "Just a bunch of financial reports. She's right. Peter can read these later."

ᨆ

The trio had a quiet, simple dinner at the American Cafe in Union Station, a short walk away. Their conversation was light and barely touched on the case—again at the professor's subtle direction.

Peter tried to go to sleep at 10:00. The last time he remembered looking at the clock, it was 1:36 A.M.. In eight-and-a-half hours, he would stand before the Supreme Court of the United States.

30

~

At 8:30 A.M., Charles French loaded all of the briefcases into a cab and headed up the hill to the Supreme Court. Peter wanted to take the fifteen minute walk to help him relax, and Gwen insisted on walking with him. 9:00 was the required check-in time.

Peter looked at Gwen and said, "You look like a 9-to-nothing ruling in that suit. I'm so glad you're here with me."

As they crossed Constitution Avenue at First Street, the line for those wishing to watch the morning's arguments was already forming on the plaza in front of the Supreme Court. About seventy-five people were in line, There would be four or five times that number by the beginning of Court at 10:00.

Peter led Gwen to the east side of the Court building to the regular business entrance of the Court. They sent Gwen's purse through the x-ray machine, and walked through the airport-like metal detector.

A huge bronze statute of John Marshall, in a sitting position, loomed in front of them down the marble hallway. The statute depicted him with only a copy of the Constitution and a quill pen in his hands. "That's misleading," Peter said as he paused to look at the statue.

"What are you referring to?" asked Gwen.

"Well, from that statue you get the idea that the Constitution was the most important thing in Marshall's life, but that's not true. The Bible was the most important thing in Marshall's life. He believed it was the foundation of the Constitution, without which we couldn't govern this country."

They passed in front of the statute, turned right at the next hall, and caught an elevator up two floors to the clerk's office where Peter would meet Professor French and check in. When the elevator arrived, the doors opened, revealing Charles French, waiting for them.

"You made it," he said smiling. "In plenty of time."

"Yeah," Peter said, taking a deep breath.

"Relax," said French. "You're going to do very well."

They walked a few steps around the corner, said a few words to the clerk, and were ready to go. It was 8:50.

The professor suggested that they go up to a lawyer's lounge in the library area. They chatted, Peter asked a few questions, and then began pacing nervously back and forth in front of the window which looked out on the Capitol Building.

Peter looked at his watch. 9:10. More pacing. A couple questions. A trip to the drinking fountain. Pacing. The watch. 9:17.

Finally, at 9:25, the Professor led the trio in a brief, earnest prayer for Peter. His mounting nervousness began to concern the professor.

They went down the elevator two floors to the Courtroom of the Supreme Court of the United States. It seemed bigger to Peter than it had the day earlier. The marble columns rose forty feet from floor to ceiling. Red velvet hung between the columns in an elegant pattern across the back and the sides of the courtroom.

As the professor led them inside the bar and up to the front counsel table, Peter realized that the bench was not straight, but had two wings angling into a small straight section. The two justices sitting on the far ends of each wing were actually closest to the counsel tables. The Chief Justice, and one justice on each side would occupy the center section.

A stream of lawyers began to come through the bar and sit in their seating area just around and behind the four sets of tables for counsel. One by one, friends and colleagues of Professor French began to come up and ask him about "his" case. The professor was quick to introduce Peter and tell each lawyer that it was "Peter's case," but Peter quickly excused himself, far too nervous to engage in chit-chat.

At 9:40, Gail Willet, flanked by Matt Bartholomew and Allen Radcliff, the Attorney General of Washington State, entered and sat at the front counsel table on the right-hand side of the courtroom. Bartholomew and Radcliff came over immediately and shook hands with Peter. Willet reluctantly followed suit.

~

Peter was surprised that seeing someone familiar, even Gail Willet, made him a little less nervous. "*She's as much on edge as I am,*" Peter thought as he shook her hand and smiled.

Peter gave a quick, discreet smile to Gwen who was seated in the first row for spectators, right behind the lawyer's section. Another deep breath. *There's Donna Corliss,* he noticed, two rows back on the opposite side of the courtroom.

~

Corliss was looking at Stephen Stockton who was seated along the right edge of the courtroom in a section reserved for court personnel. He could feel her stare, but looked down at the legal pad on his lap. David G. Humphrey arrived at 9:50 and barely got a seat in the last row. The seating clerk had not been impressed that Humphrey had funded the first case of the day. His requests for better seating were met with a blank stare.

9:55. A last glance at his notes. A ten-second prayer. The last hour had been the longest of Peter's life.

The Marshall suddenly appeared in his formal cutaway coat, striped trousers, and stiff collar.

"Here we go," the professor said. Peter, the professor, and all the lawyers prepared to stand with the first syllable.

"Oyez! Oyez! Oyez!" came the Marshall's cry.

The justices started to quickly file in from behind the velvet curtains. "The Supreme Court of the United States is now in session. All ye having business for this honorable Court please draw near! God save the United States and this honorable Court."

Skipping only a half-a-second, Chief Justice Winston said, "Case No. 94-6877, Gwen Landis and others versus Donna Corliss and others." Peter nervously scrambled to his feet and headed immediately to the lectern which seemed to be just ten feet away from the center of the bench. "Mr. Barron, welcome to the Court. You may begin."

"Mr. Chief Justice and may it please the Court. There are three basic issues before the Court today. First, do social workers have to follow the Fourth Amendment to the Constitution, or may they search homes under standards that would clearly be unconstitutional in any other context? Second, are social workers absolutely immune from suits for violations of constitutional rights for all actions taken from beginning of an investigation through the conclusion of child-abuse litigation? And third, should a social worker be immune from suit for deliberate fraud committed at any stage of a trial? In this case, we have demonstrated fraud by government officials before, during, and after the trial had been completed."

The words had been carefully scripted with the professor's help and memorized. Peter had delivered them flawlessly. The professor had warned him that he would never get through it all without a question being thrown at him. Both men were pleasantly surprised.

Justice Kraus leaned forward in his chair. "Why should we be concerned with your first issue? Isn't this just a suit for damages?"

"We have sue1 for damages, Your Honor, but you can see that our complaint also seeks a declaratory judgment asking for a ruling that it is unconstitutional to enter a home for a child abuse investigation when the only cause for the visit is an anonymous tip on a hotline. We are just as interested in setting the right legal precedent for every family in America as we are in obtaining proper relief for Gwen and Casey Landis."

The professor beamed. Peter was doing well.

"There is a two-hundred-year-old provision of the Constitution that requires that any time a government agent wants to enter a home, that agent must have a warrant or else proof of exigent circumstances. The respondents have conceded—once fraudulent documents were unmasked—that they have no claim to the exigent circumstances doctrine. The State of Washington stands before this Court today and asks that they be authorized to invade any home at any time if someone, anyone, breathes an anonymous tip into a child abuse hotline"

Justice Geisler held his pencil in both hands. "Counsel, with the epidemic of child abuse that is obviously going on in this nation, doesn't the rule of the Ninth Circuit make common sense if our goal is to protect children?"

"Your Honor, I have two replies. First, the Constitution is applicable at all times and in all circumstances. We have always had child-abuse in this country—"

"At this level?" Geisler interjected.

"No, Your Honor, we are a much larger country and our moral condition has indeed declined. But the incidence of child-abuse that is presumed to be an epidemic is grossly over-inflated by the inclusion of demonstrably false cases into the record. Accordingly to a well-known child's rights organization, over 60% of the claimed two million cases of claimed child-abuse are unfounded. Casey Landis has been statistically included as an abused child. The only abuse this four-year old suffered was at the hands of the two state-employed CPS investigators who took her into her bedroom without her mother, closed the door, and strip-searched her. Every child who is traumatized in this way has been unnecessarily abused. The fastest way this Court could dramatically protect children from unnecessary abuse is to rule that the strip search of Casey Landis was unconstitutional. Hundreds of thousands of children would be protected in the first year if this Court would simply say to the nation's social workers, 'Get some proper evidence and go have a five minute visit with a judge before you barge into a home in a non-emergency situation.'"

Professor French could barely contain his smile.

"I suppose that information you just recited is in the record, counsel?" Geisler shot back, hoping to catch the rookie off-guard.

"Yes, it is Your Honor. It is on page 43 of the Joint Appendix."

Charlie French saw Justice Rose smiling slyly as he made notes.

Rose saw Peter's time slipping quickly by and decided to prompt him to move on to the second issue. "Counsel, let's assume we agree with you and rule this search to be unconstitutional. Does that mean you can sue these social workers now? Doesn't the law have to be clearly established?"

"That is correct under the traditional rules. The Ninth Circuit abandoned these rules and gave full unconditional immunity to social workers from beginning to end. We obviously think that this blanket immunity is unwarranted by this Court's ruling and is clearly contrary to two-hundred-years of American constitutional jurisprudence."

Peter breathed quickly, heard no questions, and kept on going. "Under the traditional rule, we can sue the social workers if their entry into a home without a warrant violated the clearly established law. We think the law was clearly established for three reasons. First, this Court's decision in *Wyman v. James* makes it clear that investigatory searches by social workers must adhere to traditional Fourth Amendment standards."

"Didn't we rule that social workers have the right to enter homes without a warrant in *Wyman*?" The Chief Justice asked with eyebrows raised.

"Not exactly, Your Honor. The precise ruling was that New York could cut off the welfare funds for a mother who refused the social worker's request for entry. Mrs. Wyman had a choice: Government funds or her privacy. Gwen Landis had no choice. An armed police officer was there to force the government's entry into her home."

Peter saw his yellow "five-minute warning light" come on. "In the brief time I have left, let me say just a word about our third issue. Would it not shock the vast majority of Americans to learn that social workers can deliberately lie when they file charges and never be sued by the person who had been wronged? Or that social workers can tell lies on the witness stand and never have to make any restitution for their actions? Or that social workers can fraudulently change documents after a case has already been concluded and still walk away scot-free without ever facing a suit for damages they have deliberately caused by their own fraud?

"A constitutional interpretation that protects those who do evil and denies relief to innocent people strikes at the heart of our social covenant. Surely the founders never dreamed that such a rule would protect the kind of deliberate wrong-doing that is not merely alleged but proven in this case.

"We do not advance an abandonment of the traditional rule, but a refinement that simply says, fraud committed to start a child-abuse case or fraud committed after a case has been concluded can be readily redressed. And if there is clear and convincing evidence of fraud which exists without the need for initial discovery, then in such cases, fraud committed during a trial can also be the subject of a federal civil rights lawsuit."

"Wouldn't Congress have to change the rule that you seek to change?" Chief Justice Winston asked.

"It is our position, Your Honor, that this Court invented the rule which protects the fraudulent; therefore, it is certainly within the Court's jurisdiction, and some might say responsibility, to change this rule to more broadly protect the innocent."

Peter saw the red light and started to walk back to his table. He suddenly remembered his instruction on the final ritual. "I ask this Court to reverse the decision of the Ninth Circuit Court of Appeals."

There was a brief titter among the lawyers section for his rookie error at the very end. But every knowledgeable person in the courtroom was deeply impressed with all other aspects of the maiden voyage of Peter Barron, Esq., before the Supreme Court bar.

"Masterful," Charlie French whispered as Peter sat down and grabbed up his pen to take notes for his two-minute rebuttal.

Gail Willet's performance was technically perfect. She was smooth. Her answers demonstrated thought, preparation, and knowledge of the relevant precedents.

But Justice Rose went after her in a relentless fashion that frightened Stephen Stockton to his core. It was obvious that his boss was going to be writing the opinion which attacked the constitutionality of his girlfriend's actions. The only question was whether his opinion would be the majority or the dissent.

Willet closed strongly. "The Ninth Circuit protected children all over the West. No one dies of a strip search, as distasteful as that term may seem. No one has broken arms or cigarette burns or scalds from a warrantless search. Children are dying. Children are being bruised, broken, and battered. People who are in the business of protecting these children are not perfect, but the criminal courts can sort out the truly bad apples. If we make child-abuse workers the target of every fee-hungry lawyer in America, we will have timid child-abuse workers and more of the battered and broken and lifeless bodies that are the real statistics of child abuse."

"Be careful in your rebuttal," French whispered. "She was pure emotion. It will gain her a little, but the law wins votes."

"Mr. Barron, you have just ninety seconds remaining. And I'd like to ask you a question." The Chief Justice knew how to take the wind out the sails of a planned rebuttal. "Today you argue that you should be allowed to sue for the document tampering because it occurred after the state child-abuse suit had been completely concluded. Why didn't you raise that issue in the lower courts?"

Professor French glanced at the face of the Chief Justice. If Peter tried to bluff the court or excuse his behavior, it could cost him a vote—maybe two.

"Two quick parts of an answer. First, we alleged the facts including the timing of the tampering. We advanced a theory that Gwen Landis should be allowed to sue for that act of fraud. It is our position that we raised the issue. The other side certainly had notice of the issue. But did we raise the argument as precisely as we did in this Court? No, Your Honor *I* did not. And the only reason I didn't is that I simply didn't recognize the argument until someone with more experience pointed it out to me. I guess that's why I practice law—I practice because I am far from perfect." And with that it was over.

Peter's spirit was rejoicing in his honest answer. But his lawyer's mind told him that he had just admitted his incompetence and it would cost him the case.

"Hurry!" Professor French said. "Pack your things and let's go out the side. The Chief will call the next case in seconds and will get mad if we dawdle."

Peter's heart sank. The professor was disappointed. He could tell.

Gwen saw them leaving. She quickly left her bench and walked down the aisle toward the back of the courtroom.

The professor led Peter down the side hall, and around the corner to the spot where Gwen could see them. French motioned for her to come their way and join them. They were still within earshot of the open doors and alcoves to the courtroom, and the professor was determined to get away as soon as possible.

He quickly paced down the hall and ducked into the cloak room at its end. "Yes! Peter," he said putting his arm around the shaken barrister. "That was the best answer you could have possibly given. This Court sees so many pompous jerks who think that the name of the game is being the Supreme Lawyer; they hate it. Humility and knowledge. Humility and knowledge. That is the way to do it. You were fabulous." Turning to Gwen, "He was fabulous! Don't you think?"

Gwen's head was spinning, but she nodded enthusiastically anyway.

"I thought you were mad or disappointed in me," Peter said.

"No, not at all! I was so afraid I was going to explode with joy if I said anything. I knew I had to keep my mouth shut completely or I would receive a letter from the Marshall's office warning me about the decorum of the Court or some such thing."

"Let's get the car and head out of town for a de-briefing lunch. I think I know just the spot," the professor suggested. "It's a fabulous French place called *L'Auberge Chez Francois*. I discovered it when I was the Deputy Solicitor General of the United States, living in Virginia."

Upon hearing the name Gwen smiled to herself, "I guess I'm not in Spokane anymore."

The drive to the restaurant was somewhat quiet. Peter sat and watched the passing scenery in deep reflection. The moment would last forever in his mind, but it had been the quickest hour of his life.

～

On their way back to Washington, Gwen suddenly remembered the package from Cindy Walters. "Peter, don't let me forget to give you that envelope from the *Heart of America* lady when we get back."

"Oh. I wonder what that stuff is?"

"I peeked," Gwen admittedly weakly. "It's just a bunch of financial records."

"That could be interesting," Peter said. "I've wondered about all the money they've raised. I guess they have decided to just give me the raw numbers or something."

"Do you think they'll give you any money for attorney's fees?" Gwen asked.

"Humphrey promised me a big check at the dinner tonight. Charlie, I should give it to you. I would have crashed and burned long ago if it wasn't for your guiding hand."

"Nonsense, Peter. I'll let the State of Washington pay me after you win nine-to-nothing."

"Well, there's no way it's going to be unanimous in my favor."

"It doesn't have to be, does it?" Gwen asked.

"No, just five votes. You should start praying for five votes," the professor said. "It's going to be close."

～

Peter and Gwen dropped the professor off at National Airport. Responsibilities at the law school the next morning prevented him from attending the banquet. They were soon back at the hotel, preparing for the banquet.

～

Donna Corliss spent a restless afternoon in Stockton's apartment. Although she had spent the night with him, he made her come in separately. He did not want to be seen with her, lest anyone make the connection.

She had planned to go sightseeing, but being shunned by Stockton while she was at the Supreme Court was more than she could bear. Something was different about him here in Washington.

She laid down on the couch and turned on the TV with the remote control. She mindlessly watched a third talk show and fumbled with her left earring which proceeded to come loose and fall into the crack between the cushions on the couch. The more she reached, the further it fell, until she gave up and lifted the cushion out of the way.

"Gross!" she exclaimed, upon seeing the variety of food particles under the cushion. But then her eyes saw something sticking out below the other cushion. It was a hair clip, decorated with a green ribbon. Three long red hairs dangled from the clip. Corliss's spirit welled up with fear and anger.

～

Peter and Gwen held hands as they descended the escalator from the Hyatt lobby down to the banquet rooms in the basement. Humphrey had left Peter a message asking him to be there at 6:45 so he could go over a few details before the banquet began at seven. Peter carried the envelope of financial records under his left arm.

They saw two middle aged women off to the right at a table festooned with a placard declaring "*Heart of America*—Supreme Court Victory Banquet."

"I hope no one gets in trouble for false advertising," Peter said.

"We're gonna win," Gwen said confidently.

"Blind loyalty always scores points with me," he replied.

They walked up to the table.

"Hi, I'm Peter Barron—"

"Barron, Barron, let's see if I have your tickets here," the woman Humphrey hired from the temporary employment agency said. "No, no, I don't see it. Did you send in your check?"

"Uh . . . I think I'm supposed to be a speaker or something."

"Indeed he is!" Humphrey's voice boomed suddenly. "Good to see you, Peter. And this must be Gwen. You are lovely, my dear. Peter was really lucky—I mean blessed, to have found you."

"Thank you so much," Gwen said with a courteous but distant air. She instantly distrusted him. "But I think I am blessed far more."

"Well," Humphrey began. "Let me give you a few logistics. I want the two of you at the head table just to the right of the podium. You'll be seated beside the chairman of my board, former Congressman Stan McElliot and his wife. I'd like you, Peter, to speak for about fifteen minutes—just tell us about the case and especially the events of today. It would be very nice if you could mention the importance of the funding you received from *Heart of America*. But the first thing after I introduce you is the presentation of a large check—to you. OK?"

"Sure, that's very nice," Peter said.

"Let me take you in and introduce you to Congressman McElliot."

Peter and the Congressman chatted throughout dinner. He seemed like a very sincere and sensible man. After fourteen years in Congress, he retired. "If you can't accomplish something in that amount of time, you never will," was how he put it. McElliot had a reputation as a true conservative, with a warm personality that made it difficult for even the most liberal person to dislike him.

The dinner was chicken. Peter and Gwen thought it was delicious. The Congressman and his wife thought if they saw another chicken on a plate they would die, no matter what sauces or decorations had been dribbled on it.

The two-hundred-and-fifty people in the room shifted their chairs as the program began with a patriotic song. Suddenly Humphrey was at the podium to introduce Peter. Peter's nerves were nearly as jangled as they had been this morning.

"Ladies and gentlemen. This morning our speaker argued *Heart of America*'s first case in the United States Supreme Court.

"As you know, *Heart of America* is a conservative, non-sectarian organization dedicated to advancing the family. Our aim is to protect all families in America. Although we are not a religious organization, we recognize that the families of this nation are well-served by the three great religions of our land—Judaism, Christianity, and Islam."

Gwen gave Peter a surprised look as the word "Islam" was invoked.

"We are committed to families. We are committed to freedom. And we are committed to faith—whatever faith one chooses.

"Peter Barron is an attorney from Spokane, Washington who took, for free, a case for this lovely lady seated to his left. Little did he know when he began the case that he would end up in the Supreme Court of the United States, nor did he imagine that he would end up with the client as his fiancé. They will be married later next month."

The audience responded with polite applause.

"But this morning, our man, Peter Barron, gave the performance of his life before the Supreme Court. I know many of you saw him. Others will hear him tonight for the first time."

Bending down, Humphrey pulled a large cardboard check out from underneath the table.

"Before Peter begins, I'd like to give him this check for $7,500 as *Heart of America*'s final donation on this case. Peter, here you go and congratulations."

Peter took the check, smiled, and awkwardly laid it back on his chair. A more traditionally-sized check had been taped to the back of the cardboard presentation.

"Thank you very much for that very generous introduction, and your repeated generosity."

Peter launched into a ten-minute explanation of the issues in the case and gave a quick description of the oral argument that had just occurred.

"And now I would like to thank the very generous donors who have given to *Heart of America* with such an open heart to this case. Thanks to your generosity, *Heart of America* has raised over $600,000 to support this case."

Humphrey turned white as his own hair. "How does he know the amount?" he thought.

"With this generous check I received tonight," Peter continued, "nearly $30,000 of the amount raised has been received by my office to pay for the expenses of this case. I am sure that Mr. Humphrey will tell all of you all the wonderful things he has been able to accomplish for the *Heart of America* with the balance of the money. Again, I want to thank you, the donors, for your belief in freedom and your desire to see families protected in the Supreme Court."

Humphrey's skin went from white to red, but he still managed to get to the podium and announce, "Before we go on, it's time for another song."

Humphrey walked across the podium to Peter. "What are you doing? You ingrate! You don't know what you are talking about!" he whispered with forcible anger.

"It's all in this package I got from your girl, Cindy Walters. She sent it to me here at the hotel."

"That little bleached-blond bimbo!" Humphrey exclaimed. "What am I going to say now?"

"Try the truth," Peter said. "But suit yourself. Gwen and I are leaving."

As they were leaving, the Congressman whispered in Peter's ear. "The board will look into this at our next meeting in June. I've wondered about this Humphrey. Can you leave me your package?"

Peter nodded and handed it over.

"Thanks for doing this," McElliot whispered. "It's a little embarrassing, but well-done."

Humphrey was beginning to extol the many fine programs that *Heart of America* envisioned for the future, as Peter and Gwen ascended the escalator and walked out the front door of the hotel.

"What a day," Peter said with an exhausted sigh.

"No kidding," Gwen agreed. Let's not have a banquet immediately following our next Supreme Court Case, OK?" she joked.

"Hey, look!" Peter shouted pointing to the horse-drawn carriage just outside the glass doors of the hotel. "C'mon, let's go."

～

At that hour, arguments were well underway at the apartment of Stephen Stockton.

"Yes, there was a redhead," he finally admitted. "And a blonde, and a brunette." He yelled, too angry to care.

"What are your intentions with me, lover boy?" Corliss snarled. She was hoping for an abject apology, a little groveling, and then a plea for mercy. She needed him back.

"Well, Donna . . . I guess my intention is to drive you to the airport in the morning."

"What do you mean by that?" she hissed.

"You can't trust me with other women. I guess I've proven that. And I cannot trust your fundamental honesty after what you did in this case. Donna, it's over."

"Honesty!" she screamed. "You're the one who is a liar. You've been stringing me along while sleeping around like an alley cat. You pig, you filthy, ungrateful pig!"

31

⌒

Peter and Aaron opened the side door of the church to get their cues. The entire front of the sanctuary was tastefully graced with green garlands and cream-colored roses. The arrangements were on alternating pews and windows to the back of the church.

Peter could see the crowd of just over two-hundred settling in place. Everyone seemed to be there.

Pastor Lind gave the signal. Peter and Aaron, in their simple black tuxedos with cream-colored ties and cummerbunds, walked from the side door to their places at the front of the sanctuary.

"He is sooo handsome," June Mansfield whispered in her daughter Pam's ear. Gwen's sister nodded and smiled.

The pianist paused from the light, airy classical music she had been playing, and began playing a more dramatic, yet lilting piece by Mozart.

Casey in a pink frilly satin dress, with hair in ringlets and ribbons, began to walk down the aisle. "Slowly, slowly," she said to herself, hearing her mother's words in her mind from the practice session the day before. She scattered a mixture of pink and cream-colored rose petals in the aisle as she made her way to the front of the church.

Lynn followed about ten paces behind. Her long, dark hair was pulled back and hung gracefully to her shoulders. As she walked down the aisle, she smiled, remembering what Aaron had said, "You're more beautiful than the day I married you. Thanks for being my wife." Her tea-length pink dress was simple, yet elegant.

The music changed again. Gwen and Stan appeared in the back. Peter breathed hard in anxious, yet happy anticipation.

As the march began, everyone stood to get a look at the prize of Peter Barron's heart. Her ivory-colored satin dress shimmered in the filtered afternoon sun and candlelight. Her hair was pulled back and kept in place with a golden hairband, studded with pearls. Peter had never seen anyone so beautiful in all his life.

The service was simple. The pastor was eloquent. And the vows were recited from memory without flaw. Peter eagerly kissed his bride until June thought she was going to swoon just from watching them. Then Peter departed from the script, bent down, scooped Casey up in his arms, and gave her a warm, fatherly hug.

～

On the fourth night of their Hawaiian honeymoon, the phone rang in the dead of night startling Peter and Gwen out of their sleep. Peter untangled Gwen where she had been sleeping in his arms and glanced at the clock. It was 4:30 A.M.

"Something's wrong," Gwen said nervously.

On the third ring, Peter finally found the phone.

"Hello?"

"Peter!" Sally cried. "I got through."

"Sally? What's wrong?"

"Nothing, nothing, nothing!" she said with machine-gun rapidity. "I'm sorry to wake you. But Professor French tracked me down at home through the answering service. The Supreme Court has ruled on your case. But he won't tell me the result. Didn't even give a hint. He insists that he tell you first."

Peter's mind did a quick calculation and realized that it was 9:30 A.M. in Washington, D.C. "It's Sally," Peter said to Gwen. "The Supreme Court has ruled."

"Did we win?"

"I don't know. Professor French wouldn't tell her."

He flipped on the light, wrote down the number, and, nervously hugged his wife. "This is it," he said dialing the phone.

"Professor?" Peter said when he had answered.

"Peter? I'm sorry to call so early while you are in Hawaii. But I thought you'd want to know."

"We're dying. What happened?"

"Five to four. The vote was five to four."

"Which way? Did we win?"

"Peter, most lawyers never get to even argue a case in the Supreme Court; you should be proud of what you have already done."

"We lost, didn't we?" Peter asked, his heart falling to the floor.

"No, you impatient whippersnapper," he said with a jovial laugh. "You won. I was just trying to give you some perspective on how important this really is."

"We won!" Peter screamed. "We won!"

The professor heard the phone hit the bedside table and fall to the floor. laughing and shouting blared through the phone. The professor waited patiently and smiled.

Fifteen seconds later, Peter picked up the phone again. "Sorry, professor. We just got carried away. Have you seen the opinion?"

"Not yet, but one of the law clerks, who used to be one of my students gave me the basic details. You won basically everything. The search was unconstitutional. You can sue them for that. You can sue them for the false information used to file the case initially. And you can sue them for the document tampering. The only thing is that their false testimonies during the trial are still protected. I'd say it was a grand-slam home run."

"It's a miracle from God," Peter replied.

"And that it is," the professor said. "You go back to sleep. I'll fax the opinion to your hotel later in the day."

"Thanks again for everything," Peter said.

"I wonder if it is on the news?" Gwen suddenly said. She scrambled to find the remote control and clicked the channels to find CNN.

They didn't have to wait long. The second story began with a graphic of the Supreme Court building. Their case was the lead decision of the day. The reporter on the scene gave a quick report of the vote and its meaning.

"And for a comment from one of the participants, we go to our live camera in Kansas City."

A beaming David Humphrey suddenly appeared on their screen.

"What?" they cried out in unison.

"We here at *Heart of America* are very grateful for this landmark decision from the Supreme Court. Our organization was the sponsor of this important case, and we look forward to taking other cases to the high court to protect American families and American freedoms. If anyone would like to join *Heart of America*, our 800 number is—"

"Oh, pleeese!" Gwen yelped, throwing the remote control device at the image of David G. Humphrey. The TV clicked off when the control hit the floor.

"Good arm, babe. This is so fantastic. But you know I'd rather have you than any five-to-four victory in the Supreme Court."

Gwen looked contentedly into his eyes and smiled.

"Now, it might be different if the vote was eight-to-one or seven-to-two. But you are much better than any five-to-four vote."

Gwen hit him with a pillow as they laughed and tumbled back into each other's willing arms.

~

The End